Wolves Within

ii

This story is for my Amma

Table of Contents

The Divine Mother

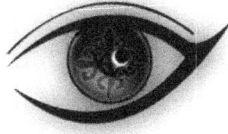

Hail O Bhudevi, Sridevi, the Mother Supreme
Who incarnates in many forms
Who created the Universe, moving and unmoving
She who has no end or beginning

Bless us O' Divine Mother of the Universe

Who gave birth to the entire universe through her cosmic womb
And battled with the fiercest of demons to their doom.

Whose love won the heart of an open lotus as a seat
And who roams on the back of a noble lion to enemies' defeat.

Who travels to the four corners of the earth to bless
And rushes to every direction to destroy enemies' prowess.

Whose benevolence sustains us against misery
And whose malevolence drives away evil through lethal energy.

Whose skin reflects the golden lustre of sunlight
Or the velvety darkness of the starlit sky at midnight.

Whose eyes can be gentle like the lotus bud when tender
Or blaze, sparkling fiercer than a raging fire in anger.

Whose hair is dark, bountiful and curly, like the clouds that
across the sky dance
Or dense with locks matted; smoke-hued by relentless penance.

Who is adorned by necklaces that like the lightning glow
Or wears garlands strung with skulls of demons destroyed by
her blow.

Who attires herself in the colours of the rainbow
Or is adorned with snakes as anklets and bracelets, hoods
raised to strike her foe.

Who is bathed in saffron, a fragrant flower
Or drenched with the blood of asuras seeking undeserved
power.

Who gives those who desire divine knowledge or earthly
possessions
Or grants ultimate moksha to those with no desires or
expectations.

Who dwells in the abode of the wicked as misfortune
And in the heart of the virtuous as good fortune.

Hail O' Divine mother of the Universe

The ultimate judge of justice
And yet the only forgiver of injustice.

Sudeshni Mirza

Behold, I send you forth as sheep in the midst of wolves: be ye therefore wise as serpents, and harmless as doves.

Matthew 10:16

Prologue

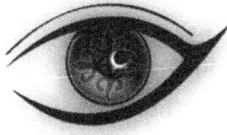

Dust did not have the chance to settle on the trapdoor before it crashed open; a wrinkled brown hand emerged from its murky depths, succeeded by a head wrapped in a dark shawl and a torso that bulged under the crone's clothing.

The woman strode towards one of the numerous shelves decorating the dark room and, moving aside many of the bottles in the front row, reached for a relatively small, oddly shaped flask right at the back. As her fingers closed around the narrow tube of glass, her excitement was almost palpable; her clothing rustled as if it had a life of its own, and wisps of grey hair escaped from underneath the shawl.

She regarded the bottle. The vial contained a viscous liquid the colour of old blood; the crone tilted the glass and the liquid crept sickeningly in the direction of the gravitational pull.

Holding the glass cylinder, she moved around the first few shelves, into a hidden clearing in the middle of which some bricks were arranged to form a square, with an empty space in the middle. The void was scorched black, and a foul smell emanated from it.

The old woman, mumbling incoherently to herself, lit a fire inside the brick altar and then crouched in front of it, head bowed. Her murmurs transformed into chanting, which gradually grew louder and louder. Finally, at what sounded like the climax of her chants, she threw her head back and cried out something in a foreign language.

She then reached into her voluminous clothing and brought out a small wooden box. She opened the box and retrieved a lock of black hair from within it. She picked up the hair with her old fingers and dropped it into the fire. The smell of burning hair paled in comparison to the stench when she emptied the phial of blood–red liquid over the flames.

Finally, the crone lifted her right hand and held out her index finger as if admiring it for the last time. She moved it progressively closer to the white-hot tongues of flame, stopping maybe a millimetre from the ribbons of heat before plunging her finger within.

Chapter One

Beginning of the End

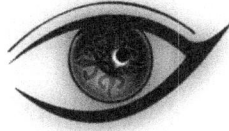

Sathi wrenched herself upright, the woman's cruel laughter still echoing in her ears. Her heart pounded like a steam engine and her clothes stuck to her, drenched with sweat. She was panting with the effort to breathe calmly when her alarm went off, deafening her with an annoyingly cheerful tune. Blind and disoriented, she reached out and groped for the clock, finally managing to turn off the well-meaning music.

She shook her head and tried to rub the nightmare out of her eyes along with the sleep. Urgh! It had been so horrible. Snatches of the same dream had been plaguing her for the last few days, but they had been nowhere near as vivid as this time.

Sathi pressed her palms to her eyes, compressing her eyeballs until they started to hurt. This was the first time she'd dreamt anything this clear or specific. She took in a deep breath, crossing her legs beneath herself on the bed. She couldn't shake off the feeling that what she had seen was important. She obsessively thought back over the dream, the hooded woman, the ritualistic fire, the ominous chanting... She frowned. She had to admit, the dream just creeped her out.

Giving up, she heaved herself up off the bed, and yawning, headed for the bathroom. She kept wondering about the woman, those innumerable bottles, the crone's nefarious chanting as she got ready for school. Who was she? What did her sinister actions mean? Why had Sathi been dreaming of her?

Sathi was so distracted that it was only as she was reaching for the shampoo bottle that she remembered that it was her birthday today. She blinked, freezing in shock. She was officially an adult. Wow!

The realisation was followed by a sudden rush of hope, a rush of sweet, elusive hope. As though someone had pressed the fast-forward button, she rushed through the rest of her morning business, all the time trying to quench the feeling of anticipation that rode on the inside of her throat and threatened to choke her.

He hasn't cared for eighteen years. Why would he start now? she asked herself viciously. Hot on the tail of Cynicism, Hope countered, *This is different. You don't become an adult every day. He'll be there.*

Sathi tried to ignore the quarrelling voices as much as she could, and flew down the stairs two at a time. She rushed headlong into the kitchen and paused just inside the doorway, slightly out of breath. The kitchen, with its wide, spacious proportions and bare walls, was exactly the same as it had been last night.

Exactly the same, that is, except for the plate and mug that had been left to drain near the sink.

Heart sinking, she abandoned the kitchen and walked towards the front door, flipping aside the curtain camouflaging the small window next to the door. She knew what she had expected to see and she was not disappointed. The driveway was empty, the gravel newly kicked up by tyre tracks. Obviously, her father had not deemed it necessary to stick around to wish his only daughter a happy birthday. She should have trusted her own scepticism.

Hope had turned into a sullen lump in her throat, making it difficult to swallow. Cynicism reclaimed its original space, smug.

Sathi left for school without breakfast, loath to return to the empty kitchen.

The first thing Sathi saw as she walked back into the silent kitchen was the note from her father, propped against the electric kettle. Deliberately, she dislodged the piece of paper by picking up the kettle and filling it with enough water for one cup. She then slammed it back onto the counter and flipped it on.

As the water boiled in the background, she opened the note. It contained familiar words: 'emergency – conference – unavoidable – money enclosed' etc. She crumpled the note in her fist and cursed herself for even entertaining a hope.

Will I never learn?

She dropped the crumpled paper on the floor and headed up to her bedroom. Mechanically, she changed into shorts and a comfortable T-shirt, and then returned to the kitchen, made a cup of tea and wandered into the living room.

Sitting down in front of the TV and sipping her tea, she flipped through the channels, neither seeing nor hearing any of inane reality shows that had annexed television.

As always on her birthday, her thoughts were on her mother.

And as usual, she had lots of unasked-for alone-time to ruminate on the subject. *Amma* had died giving birth to her back in India, breaking her father's heart and driving him to seek respite in a foreign country devoid of painful memories. Even after eighteen years, he still had not gotten over the death of his wife. Even now, there wasn't a single photo of her in the house, not a single article of clothing, not a single memento. Nothing, in short, that would remind him of her.

Except, of course, for his daughter.

When she had been younger, Sathi had pestered her father with questions about Amma. He had either skilfully evaded her enquiries or simply snapped at her. She had long since learnt not to ask.

Although Sathi had never known her mother, her absence was almost a physical pain that she carried within her every waking moment. The void was there in her every action and thought, trapped inside her without any outlet. Maybe if she at least knew something,

3

anything, about her mother, the pain wouldn't be so bad. Maybe if she knew what her mother had looked like, or what she had liked and what she had disliked, what books she had read, which movie characters she had made fun of, what she had liked doing for fun, whether she had been serious or silly, fun or sedate, emotional or practical, smiley or frowney...

But the truth was, Sathi didn't know squat about her mother.

Sitting there, brooding on stinging memories, she felt her familiar yearning for her mother turn into simmering anger. What right did her father have to lock away the memory of her mother in his own heart, blocking all access from Sathi? What right did he have to estrange Sathi from her?

With grim determination she stood up, deciding that if there was just one little memento of her mother somewhere in the house, she would find it today, on the eighteenth anniversary of her mother's death. Even if it meant turning the house upside down.

Sathi slumped against her father's ransacked desk, the last of the furious energy that had possessed her for the past hour ebbing away. She had turned out every drawer in the desk and rummaged through every crevice in his study. She had found nothing. Nada. Zilch. There wasn't a single damned thing there that related to her mother.

As she fought the despair that was lowering over her like a familiar umbrella, her eyes focused on the wooden panels that covered her father's desk, specifically on one particular panel. It looked different from the others. It had scuff marks on it, scuff marks which marred the otherwise smooth surface. Intrigued, Sathi leaned forward on her knees and fingered the much-abused wood, pulling and pushing to try and understand the anomaly.

Then she got the idea of pushing sideways, and suddenly the panel gave. A hidden compartment folded out with a muted thud. Hardly daring to believe her luck, Sathi lifted out the solitary object in the drawer: a rusted tin box.

It was locked, and however much she pulled at the padlock, it would not budge. Obviously the lock was not as old as the box seemed to be.

She reached up and drew open one of the drawers that she had already pawed through. She felt around inside and her fingers brushed against the bunch of keys she had seen there during her earlier search. She lifted them out and examined each one carefully; there were about six or seven keys on the single ring, but not one was small enough to fit the tiny lock of the box.

Resigned, she replaced them in the drawer and sat thinking for a while. Then she used the edge of the desk to propel herself to her feet and headed for the kitchen, rummaging around there for a few minutes before returning to sitting cross-legged on the floor of the study. In her hand was a hammer.

As she lifted the hammer in her hand and braced the padlock against the edge of the desk, the thought invaded her mind that she really shouldn't be doing what she was doing. It was one thing to go through her father's *open* desk in his *open* study. It was another thing altogether to break the lock of a box that he had hidden in a secret compartment and obviously didn't want anyone, i.e. her, to see.

Serves him right for shutting me out.

She allowed all the anger and pain and hurt her father had doled out to her over the years coalesce at the forefront of her mind, and firmly brought the hammer down.

Clank!

The mystery box flew open. Along with the broken remnants of the padlock, the secrets of the box lay bare before her; a ring, a golden necklace and a bunch of papers, yellowed with age and sticking to each other like a herd of frightened sheep.

Sathi recognised the chain as a *thali*, the ceremonial chain placed around the bride's neck by the groom during a Hindu wedding. The locket was leaf shaped, with an interesting symbol that looked like a 3 with a tail. She paused, tracing the sign with her finger. She was sure she'd seen it before somewhere, but try as she might, she couldn't remember where.

Dismissing the odd symbol, she lifted the thali out. She fingered the gold chain reverently, realising that it must have been her mother's. She reached out and felt the cool band of her mother's wedding ring, moisture building in her eyes.

As she used her hands to wipe away some fugitive droplets, something else in the small tin caught her attention. Taking the thali out had exposed a small pile of torn-up paper, pushed unceremoniously to the back corner of the box. Sathi carefully gathered the pieces; bright colours winked out at her.

Painstakingly, she tried to put the jigsaw together. The pieces were made of card and torn up into minute bits. Finally, she managed the task and leaned back slightly to observe the full effect. It was the picture of a majestic woman; she was dressed in a deep red sari, traditional Indian attire composed of six metres of cloth folded and tucked elegantly around her body. Hair the colour of a midnight sky flowed out from under a gold crown glistening with precious stones, and the rippling black waves lapped around her hips.

That was where her similarities to a woman ended. She had many hands, each holding various objects; a trident, a conch, a sword, a mace, a bolt of lightning, a *chakra*, a glowing globe of fire, a bow and arrow, a scroll and finally, a drooping pink lotus blossom. She stood inside yet another lotus flower, this time one that was fully open and resting on the water surface as if on air. Behind the woman was a *veena*, a traditional musical instrument played in accompaniment to Karnatic music, and a single peacock feather.

Sathi recognised the illustration.

When she had been younger, her father had not been able to leave her alone for so many days at a time as he did now, for fear of prosecution, and he had found an alternative in the form of an old Malayali friend of his whom he persuaded to double as a babysitter. It was through endless days spent in the musty house with the friend and his family that Sathi learnt the language and culture of Kerala, her parents' home state. The friend's wife was a devout Hindu and kept photos of Hindu deities in the house. One day, when left to her own devices, little Sathi had gravitated towards the brightly-coloured depictions in framed pictures and later asked her about them. There had been one photo in the collection much like this torn-up picture. Her "aunt", as she called herself, had explained to Sathi that the woman was Devi, the divine mother, who personified nature and was the supreme female deity in Hindu mythology.

Sathi wondered why the picture had been torn up. And why had the scraps not been thrown away, but kept safely in this box, which seemed to hold all of her father's most treasured belongings? She wished she had the answers – her father and his motivations remained a complete mystery to her even after eighteen years of living with him.

She refocused her attention on the jigsaw puzzle on the floor. There was something about the regal woman that made it difficult for Sathi to tear her eyes away from the picture.

Her father's secret box was niggling at her, however. Sathi could hardly breathe when she thought of the prospect of finding out something, anything, about her mother from the papers in that tin. So, promising herself that she would find some Sellotape and attach the pieces of the photo together later, she turned her attention back to the yellowed parchment.

It was a letter, written in an elegant cursive hand that she had never seen before. The ink was smudged and the paper was well-worn under her hands. There were blots where the ink had run, as might happen if someone had cried upon reading it.

Leaning back against the desk, Sathi started to read it.

Darling Nakul,

How are you? I am counting the days until you come back to me. I hate the thought of you being all the way in London, with no one to look after you – apart from Devi, of course. I ask her every day to pay special attention to you. And yes, I will be honest; I also want you to be right next to me, not halfway across the world! I never claimed to be unselfish. As annoying as you can be when you are worried, I miss you. I feel the loss of that sense of safety you give me dearly. But then, what excuse would I not give to make you hop on the next plane home?

Anyway, talking of separation, here is another reason why you should hurry back: I have a feeling that he-she is an impatient one and will come out sooner than expected, whether we are ready or not!

Joy suffused Sathi's mind as she realised that the letter was her mother's, and she eagerly flipped over the single page.

There is something else. I have been blaming you for my uneasiness, but that is not the real reason. They came for a visit last night. They... well, they started again with the persuasion. They should've known by now that I am not going to back down. If it had not been for this blasted hospital's policy, all this would have been over and done with by now. No matter. We have taken care of all the details and as long as our little he-she is well, I will be able to sort this out come March.

And as for them... well, maybe I am just being paranoid. When I asked them to leave, they were not the least bit ruffled. They just smiled – those cruel smiles I am becoming accustomed to – and walked out without a single sound of protest. The lack of reaction makes me think that they are up to something. And I am not in a position to find out what they are planning now, not when I am pushing eight months.

Just hurry back to me, my love, and these worries will be put into perspective in my mind. I will be able to ignore their doomed efforts and concentrate fully on the joy our child will give us.

Loving you always,

your Madhu

Sathi continued to frown at the letter long after she had read the last word.

Who were "they"? Why did her mother sound so dismissive of them despite the fact that their late night visit had obviously unsettled her? What were they trying to persuade her to back down from? What had the hospital delayed? What was she going to sort out in March?

And most of all, why did her mother's words fill Sathi with such foreboding, light-hearted though they were at times? The letter was full of contradictions, as if Amma herself had been confused about her own feelings.

She read the letter through again twice, but each time failed to come up with any answers. Finally, Sathi was forced to admit defeat and she turned her attention to the next paper in the small pile. She brushed off a thick layer of dust from it and gasped.

It was a photograph of her mother.

Despite her triumphant joy at finding this hidden cache of her father's precious possessions, Sathi had not really expected to find a photo. Now, her eyes feasted on her mother's face greedily, drinking in her features.

Amma was very beautiful. Unruly black curls briefly kissed her mocha-tinted skin as they bounced down around her face and well below her shoulders, disappearing off the edge of the photograph. A dimple danced joyfully in her cheek near her lips, which curved in a rose-coloured crescent. Her eyes looked directly into the camera, piercing in their intensity but comforting in the kindness that so obviously inhabited the soft brown rings.

Sathi didn't know how long she sat there, staring at her mother's photo, trying to fill up eighteen years' worth of need in just a few minutes. She could not get enough of Amma's smile, her eyes, her adorable dimple.

After a long time, she set it aside reluctantly, and picked up the last of the papers left in the pile. It contained a few sheets stapled together, but the papers were yellowed like the rest. They were plane tickets, showing the itinerary of a journey from India to London. Sathi was about to replace them with her mother's photo again, disappointed, when Amma's name jumped out from the lines of text on the ticket: Madhu Varma. Sathi clutched the papers close to her face, scanning the page.

It must be really old, from before Amma went back to India-. Sathi broke off mid-thought as she stared uncomprehendingly at the dates.

Passengers: Nakul Varma, Madhu Varma and Sathi Varma. Departure: 22nd Jan 96 from Cochin, Kerala. Arrival: 22nd Jan 96 at London Gatwick.

January 1996. Seven months after Sathi had been born. How could her mother have come back to the UK on the 22nd of January if she was supposed to have died in childbirth on the 15th of June? Sathi's head spun with trying to absorb this onslaught of information. What did it all mean?

She could tell she was on the point of losing it and tried to sort through everything methodically and find a logical explanation. She rechecked the dates. She counted the months from June to January. She read through the whole of the stapled bunch of papers, thinking that the ticket must have been from before her mother died and that there would be a cancellation on the next page.

There was indeed something on the next page. Not something that cleared up the confusion, however. Something that made it worse.

Passenger: Madhu Varma. Departure: 3rd Mar 96 from London Gatwick. Arrival: 4th Mar 96 at Cochin, Kerala.

So. Her mother had gone back to India barely two months after she had come to London. Alone. Nine months after she was supposed to have died. Frantically, Sathi gripped the letter and scanned it, trying to find that one line she had noticed earlier:

We have taken care of all the details and as long as our little he-she is well, I will be able to sort this out come March.

Sathi squeezed her eyes shut and applied two fingers from each hand to her forehead, attempting to massage out the throbbing headache that seemed to have taken up permanent residence there. She could only see one possibility. The tickets must have been booked well in advance, and the plane that was supposed to have left with her father, her mother and herself in January must been minus one passenger, due to unforeseen circumstances.

Circumstances like, say, a child murdering her mother as she came into the world.

An iron fist caught hold of her heart and began to twist and turn it in a familiar dance of torture.

Sathi tried to refocus on the answer to the mystery of the plane tickets. Yes, that must be what had happened. She could easily pick up the phone and call the airlines and confirm that her mother had not travelled on either the flight in January, or the one in March. However, she didn't move. She stared at her mother's letter, her attention drawn in particular to the line:

The lack of reaction makes me think that they are up to something.

What if her mother's intuition had been right? What if her visitors had given up on persuasion and resorted to something more effective?

Sathi swallowed hard, scared to continue. What if her mother had not died in childbirth?

Her head was shaking back and forth even before she had completed the thought. It must be just a coincidence. *Isn't Amma's death the reason why Dad settled in London, away from the memories of their happy life together in Kerala? Isn't that why he...*

Sathi stopped abruptly, and then finished the thought. *Isn't that why he's hardly spoken two words to me since I can remember? Because he blames me for his beloved Madhu's death?*

If that were not the case, what justification did he have for hating her? And what of her mother? Was she still alive in India? Had Sathi been separated from her Amma by a less final barrier than death? Or had she died, not at Sathi's tiny hands, but at those of the sinister people that Amma had talked of in her letter?

Sathi was truly sick of unanswered questions. Pushing the papers off her lap in disgust, she stormed upstairs to her bedroom and brought down a pack of playing cards. Clearing a space on the floor, she proceeded to lay them out for a game of solitaire.

Chapter Two

Is Ignorance Bliss?

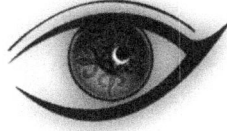

To the casual observer, playing a game of cards might not be the expected reaction from a young girl who has just found out that her mother may be alive after years of believing her to be dead. However, Sathi, quite isolated in the world, had got into the habit of turning to fate for answers to pertinent questions.

At the age when she realised how truly alone she was in this world, she had turned to the comforting advice of her cards. All the questions and worries a child normally confides in her parents she had poured out into her cards.

At twelve years old she had been told, quite frankly, by a popular boy at school that he wanted her to go out with him. She'd come home and fretted, trying to separate should dos from want to dos. She had wished that she could put the problem to her mother and have her sort it out and tell her what to do. Finally, Sathi had brought out her cards and played a game of Patience, asking for the answer to give the boy. She had become stuck in the game, unable to move forward. She had got her answer.

The next week she saw the boy in the cafeteria with his shiny trainers covered in the mashed potatoes of the nerdiest boy in their class, grinning as his friends laughed and egged him on. Ever since, Sathi had never chosen her conflicts without the cards.

Fate determined whether you won or lost at solitaire, nothing else. And Sathi figured that since there was no one else around to answer her questions, fate was the next best thing.

Today, she was in need of answers more than at any other time in her life.

Mechanically, she retrieved her cards from the wooden box where she kept them (the original cardboard sheath had disintegrated long ago) and began shuffling. She laid out the cards, alternating between hidden cards and open cards, positioning the seven rows in decreasing strength. She re-ordered the cards that were left over in her hands, fiddling with them until the edges were perfectly lined up. Then she set them down next to her seven rows, and closed her eyes.

Did Amma die in childbirth?

Keeping this crucial question first and foremost in her mind, she began to play, flipping cards over, re-arranging them, red, black, red, black, red, black...

Then, after she had been playing for a few minutes, she became stuck. She sifted through the cards, but there was no way for her to move further in this game.

Her breath encountering a sudden traffic block, and her hands shaking, she gathered the cards, reshuffled them and laid them out again, this time fervently thinking, *Is Amma alive?*

A black Jack, she needed a black Jack. Sathi went through the pile once, twice, three times. Desperately, she moved the King around, trying to uncover a black Jack.

Finally, she admitted defeat, flinging the useless cards down and burying her head in her fists. Great heaving sobs broke out from her chest. They were not the tears of a young girl. They were the laments of a heartbroken woman whose last hope had been quenched.

Once her sobs had subsided into infrequent hiccups and she had regained some control over herself, Sathi lifted her head. She caught sight of the picture of the Hindu goddess, still lying on the floor where she had left it.

A very strange thing happened. For the briefest moment, the deity's lips seemed to lift just a little more at the corners and her eyes became warm and encouraging. Then, just as abruptly as it had come, it was gone, and the face of the goddess was set again in rather stern lines.

Sathi edged closer to the picture and scrutinised it for a few moments. It was as if this incredible goddess had told her, *Go on. Finish what you started.*

As if she knew Sathi had one more question to ask.

Deciding that the picture was not going to give up its mystery any time soon, Sathi resolved to follow the advice given to her, imagined or not. She closed her eyes and took a deep breath, clearing her mind. She was determined not to be weak as she asked this crucial question. She opened her eyes and said clearly, 'Was my mother murdered?'

Just six syllables. Six syllables that in isolation were quite innocuous.

Sathi, looking down at the cards, realised that she had not laid them out for a new game. Huffing in annoyance at herself, she first gathered the small pile of cards that she had thrown down earlier.

She froze when one of those cards caught her eye. Disbelieving, she pulled it out.

It was the Jack of Spades.

The card had definitely not been there in that pile the last time she rifled through it. She had painstakingly gone through each and every card, searching for an answer that meant that her mother was alive. That one day she would be able to melt into Amma's arms and rest her head against her soft cheek.

And here it was. The very answer she had dreaded the most. Although she still had a long way to go before she would win this game, she knew instinctively that she would get there.

She played the rest of the game as a robot might, and by the end she had four neatly-stacked piles of cards in front of her. Sathi was glad that at least the cards were orderly, because her mind seemed to have become incredibly cluttered. It was as if her brain was purposefully creating chaos so that she would not be able to process what her victory meant. Even as her body responded, turning the normally warm blood to ice, her mind refused to deal with this new certainty. It happily puttered about, thinking of the most trivial things it could, protecting Sathi from utter destruction.

Suddenly her head was far too heavy to hold up, the effort it took to keep her body upright too much for her. She curled up on her side on the bare carpet, rested her head on her arm and drifted off to dreamless sleep.

When Sathi awoke, it was fully dark and her muscles were screaming at her to stretch out from the foetal position she was curled up in. She obliged them and rolled so that she was lying on her back facing the ceiling. She noticed a few cobwebs decorating the far right corner. *Hmmm... I should probably do a bit of dusting. It's been ages.*

Feeling full of energy after her nap, Sathi spring-cleaned the house from top to bottom. Dusting, vacuuming, washing, the whole lot. Having collapsed back on the sofa after her efforts, she surveyed the room with satisfaction. Perfect.

Using the armrest of the sofa as a pillow, she slept like a top until the morning.

Sathi only woke up when the harsh rays of the Saturday mid-morning sun made the back of her eyelids burn like fire. The heat bore deeply into her skull, splintering her sleep. Keeping her eyes firmly shut against the invasive light, she purposefully rolled off the sofa and onto the floor, opening her eyes only when she had them protected from the glare.

Drawn as irresistibly as if to a train wreck, her eyes fell on the still-assembled pieces of the jigsaw that made up the picture of the Hindu deity. Remembering the promise she had made to herself, Sathi taped the scraps of paper together and then sat gazing at the fractured image of the goddess, finally allowing memories of the previous night to play through her mind like a surreal movie.

The letter. Those plane tickets. That cursed game of solitaire. Could the cards have been telling her the truth? Or was fate playing a cruel trick on her?

The place where she guessed her heart ought to be felt like it had the approximate density of lead, thumping dully as if in response to the zombie state she found herself in. Sathi wanted to shout and scream at someone, demanding answers. What use were dumb rectangles of card anyway? Who in their right mind would play solitaire to get the answer to the question "Was my mother murdered"? Cards don't have brains, they can't see into the past!

And yet...

Sathi knew that she was on the verge of hysteria again, or maybe she was already in a fully-fledged panic attack. She could hardly think straight and knew that her panic was feeding her irrationality. She took a deep breath, pulling the air right into herself and imagining that those life-giving molecules were washing through her body, purifying it.

It was true that consulting playing cards for advice was an unusual thing to do. But did that mean they were unreliable? No. The cards had never let her down or given her misleading advice. Every time she chose the course of action shown to her by the cards, it had turned out to be the right thing to do. She had never regretted her choice.

Which meant that she would have to accept that what they were telling her now was the truth. Which meant that she had to face the glaring inevitability the truth presented. The one that revealed that her mother had been murdered.

That word seemed to bounce around in her head, echoing off the edges of her consciousness. It was one thing to accept that her Amma had died and was inaccessible to Sathi. It was another matter altogether to think that she had been taken from the world by someone else...

Sathi's inner voice trailed away as another, more startling thought broke through her shock. Her mother had not died in childbirth. Even if she had not been murdered, the plane tickets confirmed that Amma had safely returned to London a few months after Sathi had been born.

Ever since she had learned the cause of her mother's death, Sathi had blamed herself bitterly for having been born. Because surely, if she had not been born, her Amma would still be alive, even if Sathi would not have existed to know her. Every night she had tried to bargain with whatever unseen forces were out there and begged them to replace her life with her mother's. No one had ever bothered to answer.

Now tears began to track thickly down her cheeks as Sathi realised that her birth had nothing to do with her mother's death. After all these years of believing herself to be responsible for the death of her own mother, her newly-freed conscience seemed a stranger to her. She had nothing to feel guilty about, she had done nothing wrong! She was not to blame for taking the most precious person away from her father.

For the second time in as many minutes, her thought process skidded to a halt, her slow mind realising that her father had lied to her for her entire life. He had infested her with guilt, feeding it with his constant withdrawal. Her blood began to pound violently as she processed her father's deceit.

How dare he hide the truth and let her blame herself again and again for Amma's death? How could he have let her think that she was responsible for her own mother's death?

She wiped her tears away vehemently, her sudden rage making her oblivious to the fact that more salty water replaced what she absently rubbed off.

The white hot fury she felt was bewildering, especially after her brief relief, but there was no room for further speculation. Her only thought was revenge. All this time her anger had been directed at herself. Now, knowing that her mother had not died at her hands, the time had come for her to act.

She would find Amma's murderer and rip them from limb to limb. Then she would dump the miserable piece of garbage at her father's feet.

The anger had cleared her mind, burning through her confusion and doubt and leaving her filled with confidence. She knew exactly what she had to do.

Sathi cleared her throat loudly.

Her father, long since returned from his "emergency" trip and at present sitting in front of his work laptop, did not bother to glance up.

Sathi decided that there was no point in mincing words. After more than a week's worth of silence and careful planning, it was time to break the news. She might as well jump straight in.

'I want to take a gap year.'

At that, her father looked up in surprise. Sathi had never expressed any interest in the idea of taking a year out in the middle of her education. In fact, she had already been offered a place at university to read Architecture and was all set to begin college in September.

After a moment, though, her father shrugged and returned to his work. Sathi gritted her teeth. Why did she still feel hurt at his obvious dismissal? Suddenly she wanted to hurt him just as much as he had hurt her, she wanted to force him to care. So, although she had technically got the permission she wanted, she carried on speaking.

'I'm going to Kerala.'

Finally, she got the response she was looking for. He turned around so quickly that the black leather swivel chair tilted up on just one wheel and was on the point of tipping him over before it landed safely back on the carpet. His violent reaction was the final confirmation she needed that the cards had been telling her the truth.

Sathi felt as though she had turned into a statue as she watched her father's expression freeze in a mask of incredulity. She noted absently that his black eyebrows had become an almost cartoonish zigzag and realised that he had neglected to shave that morning. Then her gaze shifted to his eyes; where before she had only seen indifference in those hollow orbs, now the wildness in them nearly undid her; they were the eyes of a haunted man.

'What?' he shouted, leaping out of the chair and inevitably over-balancing it in the process. He did not seem to register the crash as he stood staring at her with accusatory eyes.

Sathi moved her shoulders. 'Why not? It's my homeland. What was the point of learning all that Malayalam if I'm not going to put it to any use?'

Why didn't her eyes burn now, when she was getting ultimate proof that her Amma had left her forever? Why else would her father react so vehemently to Sathi's decision to visit the place of her mother's death?

'No. No way.' As if to emphasise the point he shook his dark head back and forth. 'You are not going out to India alone and especially not to that place...' He broke off suddenly as he realised what he had nearly said.

'What?' she demanded. 'Why especially not to Kerala? It was your birthplace, and mine. Why are you so averse to it?' Sathi continued to goad him, hoping that he would tell her the truth, hoping that for once he would take her into his confidence. She knew she would lose her vindictive desire to hurt him if only he would open up and admit that he had been lying to her. Admit that he had pushed her away, although for *why*?

She saw the flip in expression that occurred as her father's anguish turned into what Sathi recognised as hate, mixed with another expression she couldn't quite identify.

'Don't you dare talk back to me!' he thundered. 'You are my daughter and you will listen to me. You are not taking a gap year and you are not going to Kerala. Clear?'

It was funny, Sathi mused, how things could have changed so drastically. In the past, when she angered her father, his shouts would penetrate right through her like gamma radiation and she would crumble inside. Now, watching the muscle jump in his left jaw, the only emotion she felt was a strange scientific intrigue about how the muscle could move in isolation like that. The reinforced-concrete wall that had recently been constructed around her heart left her unaffected by her father's anger. It meant nothing to her now.

'Yes, that's crystal clear, apart from one minor point,' she replied. 'You just said I'm your daughter and that's why I have to obey you. Well, I may still be your daughter, much to your chagrin, I'm sure, but let me notify you that I am now a legal adult. So what I do is my business, and my business alone.'

Sathi started to turn away, but then remembered a point of courtesy. 'By the way, I will be leaving early tomorrow morning. I have a flight to catch'.

With that, she strode off to her bedroom, ignoring the insistent mental voice that warned her that she would have to live a thousand lifetimes to pay penance for the new expression on her father's face.

Chapter Three

God's Own Country

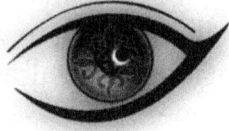

Unsurprisingly, Sathi couldn't sleep on the seven-hour flight that lay before her. Thoughts buzzed like a hive of bees in her brain, and the fact that she had been up since 3 am did not seem to make much difference. Giving up on sleep altogether, she turned to stare out of the window, watching the twinkle of the plane's wing lights against the background of a coal black sky.

After she had found out that Amma had been murdered, her father had come back home late on the Sunday night and had left for work before she woke on the Monday. By the time he had returned that evening, she had already set things in motion. Her visa had been approved within the week, the flight ticket paid for with money out of her personal account, and she had a solid destination in mind.

To convince herself that she wasn't going mad, she had telephoned the airline her parents had booked their tickets from in order to confirm that her mother had indeed travelled to India in March, many months after Sathi's birth. However, the airline did not keep records from so many years ago, and Sathi had been in a bind about how to proceed. Using her father's prolonged absence, she had once again searched her father's study.

It hadn't been until she took out the hidden compartment in his desk again and poked around in there for the second time that she found the small cards wedged at the back. They were boarding passes for Sri Lankan Airways, belonging to the three passengers who had travelled to the UK on the 22nd January 1996. It was true that she didn't have evidence that her mother had travelled to India in March, but this at least proved that Amma had been alive and well in January. Sathi had held her mother's card in her hands for a long time, trying to convince herself:

She hadn't killed her mother. She was doing the right thing.

Before leaving, she had done some research on Kerala, the odd wobbly-edged crescent that inhabited the south-west corner of India. Unfortunately, that "corner" had turned out to be a pretty big place. It consisted of fourteen districts, and had it not been for some letters she had found that had been sent to her father from his old friends in Kerala, she would have been reduced to roaming around the place like a vagrant.

As it was, she had found out that her parents had been living in Palakkad, the seventh district, before her father relocated to London. Their house had been in a small hill-station area called Nelliampathi. Excitement filled her at the thought of seeing the house her parents had lived in, but, reconsidering, she thought it was unlikely that the building would have been left to stand unoccupied. Sathi assumed that her father had sold the house and cleared out all their belongings. There would probably be little point in tracking it down for clues.

At some point in the middle of her manic planning, Sathi at last gave into exhaustion, waking only when the air stewardess shook her shoulder and made her put the seatbelt on for landing. Bleary-eyed, she walked through the Dubai airport and somehow managed to find her way to the right gate in the psychedelic, maze-like airport.

The change in atmosphere at the waiting area was startling, as she had her first encounter with a group of mostly Malayali people. The worst part of it was the staring. It was unbelievable how people thought it was acceptable to doggedly shadow someone's movements like watching a football match; you couldn't breathe without drawing an interested gaze.

One of the passengers – sitting with his legs blocking the way for everyone else – decided to play music out loud on his phone, and sat there enjoying the video on his smart screen. Sathi looked at him in disbelief, but he was completely oblivious to the fact that no one else wanted to listen to his song. Disgusted, she slumped lower in her seat and tried to ignore the insistent music.

When the pre-boarding announcement sounded, everyone immediately rose to their feet and started loudly picking up their suitcases and duty free bags and lugging them over to the gate. They then stood there, milling around the small space, until each of their respective zones were called. When her zone was called, Sathi was forced to push and shove in order to reach the gate, trying to avoid stepping on toes and tripping over widespread belongings.

Even inside the plane, people seemed to treat it as a social setting. They lounged in the narrow aisle and chatted obliviously as they fiddled with their luggage, blocking the way and exasperating the stewardesses.

Tired and irritable, she gratefully collapsed into her seat at last. Sathi set the touch screen to show the flight details and tried to tune out the steady stream of Malayalam that was emanating from the other passengers.

She watched the numbers on the display change to 3:00 to 2:00 to 1:00, and finally to 10 minutes. Sathi turned to look out of the window again, this time eager to get her first glimpse of her homeland.

It took a while, but gradually the thick white clouds parted to reveal a blanket of velvety green. Sathi caught her breath, not quite able to take in the utter beauty of the scene that had unfolded before her eyes. The green hats of millions of trees were edged by the glistening indigo waves of the Indian Ocean, which lay like unbroken glass, complementing the green. She glimpsed endless paddy fields, with small roads winding their way around them as though man had made way for nature, rather than the other way round.

Sathi couldn't believe just how much she had been missing out on.

Immigration was long. It also involved a lot of stamping. And re-stamping. You couldn't accuse the staff of not being diligent in their work; the officer scrutinised her face for at least five minutes, making sure that she was indeed Sathi Varma, as her passport claimed. In fact, he took so long that she herself began to doubt whether she had got hold of someone else's passport by mistake.

Finally, he gave her a curt nod and a grimace that she guessed was meant to be a professional smile and handed the documents back to her. Resisting the urge to check the name on her passport, Sathi strode quickly towards the exit after collecting her bag. She declined the aid of a helpful porter with a smile and stepped out of the air-conditioned airport.

Whoosh! A blast of hot air hit her straight in the face, causing the small hairs on her arms to prickle. It distracted her for a moment from the masses of people whose eyes were focused directly on her. Glancing up, she realised her mistake and looked back down at the floor again straightaway, avoiding the intense stares of dark-skinned men, women and children alike. Speed-walking now, she ducked into the first auto-rickshaw she could find.

'Angamaly KSRTC bus stand, please.'

Obsessively, she recited her itinerary to herself under her breath. *Cochin to Angamaly, Angamaly to Thrissur, Thrissur to Nemmara, Nemmara to Nelliampathi.* She had gone over it so many times that she knew it off by heart, despite the strange names.

However, soon the rushing city drew her attention away from her worry that she would get lost. It was so diverse, so full of life, so busy that she didn't know where to start. The driving itself was terrifying; the auto driver squeezed and coaxed his rickshaw through the narrowest of spaces possible. He didn't have any issues overtaking from both sides, he didn't believe in checking blind spots and his mirrors appeared to be there for decorative purposes only. All rules seemed to have gone straight out of the window, and after observing for half an hour (all the while clinging on for life with blanched knuckles), Sathi concluded that driving in India was about getting from Point A to Point B as fast as possible without hitting anything, or allowing anything to hit you.

The landscape itself was a huge disappointment. After the vision from the plane, she had expected to be immersed in that lushness as soon as she stepped out of the airport. Now, feeling the hot wind whip through her hair and the dust particles blow into her eyes from the open window of the rusty Kerala State Road Transport Corporation bus, she felt deflated.

Yes, there was greenery - countless coconut trees lined the busy streets. Yes, there was water. But there were also grey monstrosities that had taken over the city, big blocks of stone and concrete that looked grossly out of place in such a supposedly romantic setting. Her irritability and tiredness were not helping her to feel more generous towards her homeland.

Her disgruntled mood began to become less so as she changed to a different bus, which would take her from Thrissur district to Nemmara, the closest town to the hill station where Amma had lived almost all her life. As they travelled past the city centre into more remote areas of Kerala, the landscape changed accordingly, getting closer to Sathi's idealised version. Soon, as night began to fall, she saw only the jade green of the ancient tree-tops, the runes of dark brown etched on the trunks and thick, lush shrubs lining the roadside. Domestic animals metamorphosed into wild elephants, deer and even the gleam of the eyes of some kind of large cat, reflecting the glare of the bus's headlights. As the day disappeared beneath the horizon, forest land took over and transformed Kerala into a mythical utopia, blotting out the distasteful memory of the city centre.

This was more like it!

Sathi lifted the plastic sheet that prevented water from entering the bus and leaned out of the open window, breathing in lungfuls of the sweet night air. The smells were amazing; it was so much more than could be described. The aroma that tantalised her senses was that of moist earth and jasmine, spices and rain. It was the monsoon season in India, and the rain pounded against the top of bus and against the windows with a strength and power that awed her.

Her reverie was broken somewhat when the conductor said something along the lines of how if she didn't want to become an insectivore she should put her head back inside the bus. She ignored him.

Unfortunately, she had to take his advice when they began the long climb up the ghat road, the likes of which was unavoidable if you wanted to reach a hill-station like Nelliampathi. At first she did not mind the twists and turns brought on by the steep hairpin curves and riotous, bumpy road. Soon, though, her stomach began to feel like a volcano about to erupt. Fervently grateful for the window seat, Sathi tightened her arms around herself and discovered that closing her eyes and leaning back helped a lot with the nausea. Even so, she was relieved when they finally came to the end of the narrow mountain pass.

The bus drew into the small village just as dawn was breaking, the sun's incandescence temporarily muted by the soft colours of sunrise. So it was bathed in the red and orange shades of the gently rousing star that Sathi first set eyes on her mother's home town.

The village had the feel of timeless existence, as though time had passed by without disturbing this little community: it was untouched and untouchable. There were small shops dotted around the place, although most had metal shutters in front of them due to the early hour.

There was however a tea shop open; it was no more than thatch over stone, but there was a man standing behind the stall, the music of frothing milk presenting the irresistible notion of the addition of caffeine to the system, especially to one that had been travelling non-stop for close to twenty hours. Trying in vain to control the sheer volume of saliva accumulating in her mouth, Sathi struggled over with her heavy bag, thankfully collapsing onto the wooden bench outside.

The elderly man looked over at her and smiled; his eyes showed kindness as well as a twinkle of amusement at her inelegant sprawl across the bench. Sathi grinned back, slightly sheepish. Soon she was sipping a cup of strong, sweet, milky tea and listening to the casual small-talk of the tea-maker, who chattered away to her. Within minutes he had given her an abridged version of his whole life in Nelliampathi.

Thanks to the snail-like pace at which Sathi's brain cells were working, it took her a few minutes of blissful tea-slurping to realise that she had, by pure dumb luck, stumbled on the one person who would be perfect for gathering precious information. Hiding the sudden excitement her blinding insight had brought on, she began, the Malayalam flowing through her lips more easily than she had expected it to.

'Manish uncle', she began, using the term to pay respect to his age, 'do you know someone who used to live here in Nelliampathi called Madhu Varma?'

He pursed his lips, wrinkles criss-crossing his dark forehead, scratched his head and slowly said 'Hmm... Madhu Varma...'

The only thing required to complete the scene would be for him to stroke his non-existent beard. Before she could snort with laughter at the mental image – that she was sleep-deprived was obvious – Manish replied, killing her mirth.

'I don't know if it's the same Madhu you're looking for but there was a girl who used to live further up into those hills. I think she married and left a while ago.'

As he spoke, he pointed off to the distance, gesturing to the hill of hundreds of rows of tea plants whose leaves gleamed brightly in the sunlight and even further off, small white specks that she supposed were buildings. He continued as Sathi narrowed her eyes, attempting to bring the white into better focus. 'I think her name was Madhubhala. Yes, Madhubhala Kumar,' he said decisively.

28

At those words, Sathi's head whipped around, betraying her earlier casual air. Madhubhala? That had been Amma's full name? A wave of shame washed over her. How could she not have known her own mother's name?

Then bitter rage took over as she remembered the reason for her ignorance. It was not as if she had been given a choice. She focused on the other part of the mystery, trying to distract herself from the sudden desire to punch something. The last name, Kumar. After puzzling over it for a few moments, she got it: Kumar must have been Amma's dad's name. Sathi's grandfather. Sathi interrupted Manish, who had long since moved on the conversation, urgently gesturing in the direction of the houses in the distance.

'Is there anyone still living there? Madhubhala's parents?' she asked.

'Oh no, God bless them, they both died in an accident when their little girl was only three or so years old,' Manish said, shaking his head at the tragedy.

Sathi's heart sank; death everywhere. Then Manish's next words caused new hope to blossom in her chest like a dove unfurling its wings, sweeping away her initial despair. 'Kumar's sister and her husband still live there though, with their children and grandchildren. They took in Madhubhala when Kumar and his wife died, you know.'

She could hardly bring herself to accept the truth behind his words, even though this is was exactly what she had been hoping for. She had a family!

Eagerly, she started asking Manish for the exact address; she felt that she could not wait a moment to see her new relatives. Adrenaline rushed through her body, and the earlier fatigue was gone in a flash. She was ready to climb that hill then and there, even with her heavy bag.

She thrust a pen and a scrap of paper into Manish's old, callused hands, all but shaking the poor guy in her excitement. He accepted the paper and started scribbling on it, using the lid on the pan of hot water as a writing surface, saying, 'Sure, I'll give you the address. But they're not here at the moment. Their youngest son is getting married and they went to Kollam a couple of weeks ago to attend the wedding.'

That night, Manish was woken up by the sound of his cellphone ringing. It played the upbeat tune of "Thoma's style", the super-hit Malayalam song inspired by "Gangnam style", as he slowly got up. His limbs creaking in protest at being disturbed, he reached for the light switch on the wall somewhere to his right. As he picked his phone up from the bed-side table, he glanced at the display; the number was unfamiliar. He accepted the call and held the handset to the ear that was slightly less deaf when compared to the other.

'Hello?' Manish squinted at the needles on his clock face; it was well past midnight. Who would be calling him at this hour? Then his eyes widened as he recognised the voice on the other end of the phone.

'You?' he croaked, incredulous. It was like getting a phone call from a ghost.

'Listen carefully to what I say,' the voice ordered.

Chapter Four

Extravagance of Absence

T he dark room had grown dust and debris at an exponential rate, but the glowing embers of flame within the womb of black ashes still lived. Despite the lack of human assistance, a fiery tongue of orange periodically spat out sparks of fading oxygen, which fizzled and died when confronted with the grey stone of the floor.

As though an invisible camera was zooming in, the fireplace grew, claiming and keeping captive the spotlight. Through the murky mask of fire, glimpses of black and dark red could be seen, as something within shifted and stretched. Safe in the nourishment of the flame, seven pairs of rusty irises gleamed.

Sathi shot up from her bed, the damp clothes sticking even more due to the stuffiness within the motel room. She barely noticed. Those grotesque eyes were still sneering at her from her mind; she had to get out of there.

Taking what had to be the quickest shower in history, Sathi threw on some clothes and slung her backpack over her shoulder. Then she got outdoors by the fastest route available, save the fire exit. She wasn't that desperate. Yet.

The fresh mountain air washed like a caress across her face, blowing her long hair back and reminding her how to breathe normally again. Sathi stood still in the sunshine, closing her eyes and tilting her face to the sun like a starving flower. The light was warm on her skin, darkening the tan that was already there.

Despite the early hour and her temporary solitude, she could hear people starting to make a move, and neighbouring windows and doors were opening. Not in the mood to deal with inquisitive stares, Sathi reluctantly left the sunshine and wandered into one of the virtually empty coffee shops that lined the street.

Once armed with a steaming cup of coffee, she tried to sort out her plan of action. After employing a few choice swear-words at the spectacular timing of her uncle's wedding, Sathi tried to work out the feasibility of travelling to Kollam and taking things from there.

This idea turned out to be a non-starter - leaving aside the fact that attempting to find her great-aunt and great-uncle in a huge district like Kollam would be like searching for an anonymous quote within the thousands of books that occupied the British library (God knows she'd tried that often enough), there was also the small glitch that Kollam was all the way down in south Kerala.

To top it all, she was low on money; she had used up most of what she had for her plane ticket and barely had enough now to pay for food and a room. She would have to get a job soon, and couldn't waste money by travelling cross-country. Or cross-state. Or whatever.

So her best option – her only option really – was to wait and pray that the wedding celebrations spanned over days as opposed to months. Sathi clenched her fists in frustration. Right now, waiting seemed like the worst thing in the world. Impatience was a tiresome companion; the more you tried to subdue it, the harder it was to bear, sitting atop your chest and thumping its fists.

There was one way to appease it, however; her yearning to meet her long-lost relatives was rivalled only by the desire to see the house in which her Amma had grown up. There was nothing stopping her from following the directions given to her and taking herself up there.

Mollified at having finally reached a decision, Sathi paid for her coffee and left, heading in the direction of the tea estate entrance, which she had discovered was the only way to reach the top of the small hill. As the gawking gatekeeper swung the heavy iron gates open for her, her eyes wandered to the mesmerising sight of the shiny cuticles of millions of tea leaves reflecting sparkling green light in the early morning sun.

She stepped inside the gates and braved the unending staring of the boy-man who had let her in to make sure she knew which direction to set off in. Then she began navigating the narrow path, allowing the delicious aroma of fresh tea to flood her senses. Sathi could not decide what she most loved about India; the sights, smells, sounds and tastes were of such potency that they should have been distracting, yet instead they fitted together like sectors of a circle, balancing each other out perfectly.

The climb had an almost meditative quality. She got a sense of peace from the delicious monotony of the walk that she had not felt whilst asleep in a comfortable bed; the raised carpet of emerald green was drenched with dew drops, the sun-kissed leaves trailing the gently rolling slopes. Waves of mist floated across the indigo sky, the puffs of white appearing to lean down and embrace the hills of Nelliampathi like an old friend.

Sathi reached the top long before she had taken her fill of the amazing scenery. After waving the piece of paper with the address at a passer-by and an ensuing conversation involving a lot of invented Malayalam words on her part, Sathi set off towards her mother's ancestral home, a spring of excitement lightening her steps.

She had to slow down as she approached low-hanging vines and tree limbs, though she barely felt them brush against her, her attention completely consumed by the white house that now loomed before her.

Although she knew that the inhabitants were not at home, Sathi was still startled by the air of abandonment that clung to it after only a few weeks of standing empty. Slowly she circled it, trying to connect to it in some way, at least on an aesthetic level. However, the architecture was very basic and commercial, as opposed to the many unique structures she had noticed already since arriving in India.

Seeing the house where her mother had grown up did little to bring her emotionally closer to Amma. In fact, the impersonal feel of the building and the shuttered windows repelled her.

She walked the perimeter of the house once more, just in case, but she was finally forced to admit to herself that there was no point in staying here. She turned back the way she had come, and saw Devi.

At least, she assumed that the stone statue that peeked out at her from behind the sparse branches of a mango tree was a depiction of the Hindu deity, the same goddess her mother had apparently believed in.

Drawn like Icarus to the sun, Sathi's limbs gravitated towards the temple of their own accord and like a slave, her body followed suit. Despite being medium height, she had to bow her head as she stepped under the cracked archway. The small temple was a complete ruin; there were great big fissures in the mud-browned walls and ceiling, and the floor was strewn with dead branches and twigs that had been abandoned by leaves long ago - the building as a whole seemed to have collapsed in on itself. The pedestals were cracked and the idols of the gods were blanketed in layers of dirt and grime, their immortal eyes barely visible. Sathi was shocked that a temple had suffered so much neglect. There was a Ganapathy temple opposite Manish's teashop that was lit with hanging lamps at all times of the day and bells pealed out every morning and evening, lightening the air with their music. That was how this shrine should have been.

There was something else wrong with the temple, aside from the obvious, that Sathi couldn't quite put her finger on. She stood at the centre of the ruined building, her eyebrows furrowed in thought and her gaze locked absently on the crow perched precariously on a tree branch outside. It was while she was watching it peck at the minuscule particles of its preferred food source that Sathi suddenly realised what was bothering her: there were no sounds of life inside the temple.

Since she had stepped out of the airport, there had been no shortage of background noise. As she travelled from Cochin to the more secluded hill station, the busy clamour of traffic had simply transformed to the hullabaloo of wildlife, be it the trumpeting of wild elephants or the chirping of crickets.

Walking into the temple had had the same effect as entering a vacuum, where not even air molecules existed to transmit the hum of life. Birds did not indulge in idle gossip and the wind that gently swayed the bushes outside seemed strangely mute.

In fact, looking around, Sathi realised that there were no ants or even house lizards to be seen within the temple, despite the fact that these two gregarious species seemed to hold an open invitation to all buildings and houses and were not usually shy in accepting the hospitality of their unwitting hosts.

Sathi thought of the cliché of the deafening silence, and realised how apt it was. The silence was a physical ringing in her ears, an unpleasant echo that reflected and magnified loneliness.

Then a male voice cut through the hush like a newly-freed cork through air.

'It doesn't really look like a place fit for the gods, does it?'

Sathi spun around. The white-haired man leaning against the crumbled arch continued speaking.

'Of course, it's a paradox. You do something the gods don't like and they leave and go about their business elsewhere. Without them, what's the point in having a fancy house? So the temple falls to pieces. Then you can't carry on doing whatever it is that you were doing to annoy them in the first place.'

He paused, seeming to reconsider. 'No, that's not strictly true. They can carry on. In fact, they *do* carry on. Although for how long? Yes, that's the point, isn't it?'

Having run out of steam – and breath, probably - the man looked expectantly at her. She took advantage of the pause in his distracting rambling to examine him; his bushy beard was the same shocking white colour as his hair, which stood out in tufts away from his head, almost as if they had a will of their own.

Yet he did not look old. He was middle-aged, appearing even more youthful because of the shrewd twinkle in his blue-green eyes. Sathi blinked in surprise. She had never seen a variation from the typical dark brown eyes since coming to India.

Sathi felt her cheeks grow warm as she realised that she had been standing there gawking at the man while he regarded her (and her lack of manners) with amusement. She focused on his words in order to regain some dignity.

'What do you mean, that the gods just left? How can they leave if they're supposed to reside in the temple?'

The man appeared delighted with her curiosity. 'I don't know that they're supposed to do anything. However,' he continued as Sathi opened her mouth to protest, 'they do usually come to visit the temples when they are most needed, especially when the hearts that pray to them are pure. See, the gods are all different. Like humans, some are impatient, some are wrathful, some are lethargic and so on. The tempers of some flare up like a forest fire, wreak utter havoc and burn out soon after. Others have endless patience; they forgive every atrocity imaginable until things go beyond a point of no return. Then and only then will the tolerant gods take action. Once they make that decision, stopping them is like trying to turn the force of the tide.'

He gestured around at the temple, positioning himself more comfortably against the fragile wall. 'This is a temple for Devi. Respect has been given to the other gods, hence the many pedestals, but it was predominantly built with the intention of worshipping Devi. Now, she is the most patient goddess of all. Do you know why?'

Sathi mutely shook her head, enraptured by his mention of Amma's goddess.

'Simply because before she was the ruler of the world, she was a mother. Of course, the act of giving birth does not define motherhood, but true mothers have unconditional love towards their children. That's a blessing and a curse. It's easy to love a good child, but it is the unlucky mother who must juggle her irrational love and her despair of children who are also murderers, rapists and thieves. She gives her children every opportunity to right their wrongs.'

He paused and gazed intensely at her, those blue eyes vaguely disconcerting. 'You don't appear convinced,' he noted.

Sathi shook her head again, this time with more force. 'I'm not. What's the point in being that patient? I understand that being a mother makes it more difficult, but surely you have to be able to cut your losses and accept that some people are never going to change? It seems to me that the idea of punishment is twisted if those doing evil are forgiven while the good people are suffering. How can the gods show favouritism like that?'

Sathi didn't know why she was standing here arguing with the man. He obviously had a few screws loose and the sensible thing to do would have been to nod politely and then make a quick escape. She wasn't even religious and here she was contradicting a pious Hindu.

She couldn't help herself though. It seemed to her that there was little justice in the way the world worked; her mother, and her parents - Sathi's grandparents - were dead, but she would bet all she had that Amma's murderer was still walking around with nothing in the world to worry them. Was there any justice in being tolerant to people like that? This apparent patience seemed too much like delaying tactics, a procrastinator's way of dealing with problems: by ignoring them and hoping that they would vanish on their own.

The gentle tone of his voice made her eyes smart as he replied. 'Sathi, you need to understand that the gods have their reasons, reasons that we, as humans, cannot even understand before it's too late. Half the time we don't even realise how many potential disasters they resolve for us. They are bound by the forces of fate, by the movements of the planets, by timing, just like we are. Do you know the story of Devi Kanyakumari?'

Sathi had heard of Kanyakumari; the southernmost tip of India, bordering Kerala and Tamil Nadu, was famous. It was a popular tourist spot where the Indian Ocean, Bay of Bengal and Arabian Sea met in a swirling display of nature's immense power. She even vaguely remembered that there was some religious significance to the place. But she had never heard of this Devi Kanyakumari. The white-bearded man continued before she could say so.

'An avatar of Devi, she was a human goddess born to defeat a ruthless *asura*. The asura had gained a boon of the gods that he could only be killed by a maiden. However, as a goddess who had taken a human form on Earth, Kanyakumari Devi fell in love with, and agreed to marry, Lord Shiva without knowing her fate.

'Maybe if she had already killed the asura before she met Shiva, things would have turned out differently and she might have been able to marry him and live happily. As it was, the timing wasn't right and the gods couldn't let the marriage happen: the demon was destroying countless innocent lives. They slyly detained Shiva, who returned unmarried on his wedding day.

'Betrayed and heartbroken, Devi Kanyakumari flung her wedding flowers and grains of rice on the ground, where they still adorn the beaches of Kanyakumari as glittering gemstones: a testament to her wrath. Later, still a maiden, she destroyed the demon and fulfilled her *dharma* of that birth, ridding the Earth of an evil that she had been born to destroy. Her happiness had to be sacrificed. Being a god is not as easy as you might think.'

Sathi would have piped up that she had never thought being a god was easy, but her mind was spinning with the story she had just heard, of the maiden goddess and her tragedy. If anything, hearing about the goddess Kanyakumari had just confirmed her theory: the best people had the worst luck.

Those unusual eyes targeted her again, even more penetrating than before. 'No, no, no. You're missing the point, Sathi.'

She could only stare in astonishment. Could he read her mind?

'You still don't understand. Maybe a different source will do the trick. Come with me.' With this command, the man walked backwards out of the temple, beckoning her to follow. Sathi obliged, even if only to move back into the sunshine, away from the dark, damp dwelling which, according to the man who could give Santa Claus a run for his money, was without inhabitants.

Only later would she realise that she had never told the man her name.

'You have got to be kidding me!' Sathi's gaze was not on the accused, but focused in disbelief on a simple white sign with a green border; it announced that the office that White-beard had led her to belonged to a Mr Srinivasan Panickar, an astrologer by profession.

Conscious of silence from the physical space that White-beard should have occupied, which was somewhere to her right, Sathi glanced over her shoulder and nearly had a fit. She whirled around, but there was no sign of him. He had vanished into thin air. Either that or he had escaped into the one of the numerous houses they had passed whilst walking uphill to this lone office, using the cover of the conveniently viscous vegetation while she had been glaring at the address board like an idiot.

Sathi slowly swivelled to face the board again. Her incredulous expression transformed to one of consideration as she realised that visiting this Srinivasan might well be a good thing; after all, she was stuck for a few days until Amma's family returned to Nelliampathi. Maybe this guy had been here long enough to be a good source of information. Besides, she had never come across an astrologer before, someone who could supposedly ascertain information about a person's life by studying the planets. She had no idea what to expect, but felt a curiosity that she couldn't let go.

Resolutely, Sathi marched forwards and knocked on the office door. There was no answer. She considered for a second, and then reached for the knob. The door swung open, showing a plain, small waiting room that contrasted wildly with Sathi's imaginings, and beyond that, a closed wooden door.

Before she could change her mind, she strode over and rapped her knuckles on the much-abused wood, barely waiting for vocalised permission before entering. The man sitting at the desk pushed the gold-rimmed spectacles further up his long nose, an expression of surprise stamped on his face at her abrupt appearance.

The astrologer quickly pulled on his suit of professionalism, and offered her a seat, which she took, feeling awkward and a bit foolish as she sat there. He asked for her name, her dwelling, the star of her birth (her birthday according to the Malayalam calendar – he had to spend ages looking it up when she told him she had no idea). Then, when he finally had all the information he required, he began to chant something in a language that was not wholly Malayalam, barely audible over the rattling of the tiny sea-shells that he rolled against the desk with the palm of his hand. The combined effect of the soothing sound and the mesmerising movement was almost hypnotic, and Sathi was startled when at last he stopped spinning the shells, closed his hand over them and started to divide them into groups of three.

There was just one shell that remained after he had divided the others in threes, and Sathi realised with a jolt of surprise that this guy was working on the principle she used when consulting her cards; fate determined how many of those shells came into his hands, and which number would come out when they had all been divided up.

Sathi was also impressed by how much mathematics was involved; the astrologer consulted many different charts and tables and compared data before he even started rolling the shells. She looked around idly, and noticed a framed certificate that said he had an MSc in Astronomy and Astrophysics. Her eyes widened as she contemplated the amount of work and study that must have gone into his career.

The astrologer cleared his throat, and she immediately returned her attention to him. 'I'm seeing a lot of adversity in your life,' he said. He pointed to a chart drawn in chalk on his desk, and put his finger on the single shell that had come out. 'You have been faced with a dilemma lately, and there is a purpose to your actions right now, a very specific purpose.'

Sathi leaned forward, captivated by what he was saying. It was all true!

'There is a great enemy whom you have to defeat. The enemy is strong, very strong, and it will be a long, difficult battle. You will have to succeed in order to achieve peace.'

He frowned, his eyebrows drawing together. 'But,' he continued, 'you will not succeed alone. There is someone else... without their alliance you will not be able to do what you need to do.'

Sathi opened her mouth, but the astrologer had not finished speaking. 'You will fail in your purpose if you attempt it alone. There is another who has as much right to justice as you do.'

When his gaze fell on her, it was unfocused. Then gradually it became lucid enough to observe her pissed-off expression.

'Are you finished?' she asked politely.

He blinked twice in succession. 'Well, yes, but...' he trailed off as Sathi reached into her pocket and drew out some money, which she placed on his desk.

'I do not need anyone else's help to avenge the death of my own mother. Goodbye.' She slammed out of the office, leaving him to stare after her in silence.

He closed his eyes in concentration and slowly, his confusion faded. Realisation dawned, as well as pity for the girl who had just left. His eyes opened. *Poor child. She will have to learn the hard way.*

As he shook his head sadly, his eyes moved to the framed image on his desk. They rested on a revered depiction of the serene Vishnu. *She doesn't understand yet*, he thought pensively.

Chapter Five

Cannibals & Card tricks

Sathi was hungry. She had been walking blindly after storming out of the astrologer's office, past the abandoned temple, past her mother's house and down the long descent to the centre of the small village. Now she paused and changed direction, heading towards the closest place where she could scavenge some food: a resort balanced precariously on the edge of the forest that enveloped most of Nelliampathi like a massive green blanket.

She forced her limbs to move, but her mind was still back in that astrologer's office. A mixture of anger and fierce hope burned in her. The anger, at least, she could understand. What other way was she supposed to react when told that someone else had to hold her hand if she wanted to avenge her mother's death? Besides, who could that person be other than her father? Who else had as much of a right to revenge as she did?

The thought of her needing her father's help to defeat her mother's killer fuelled her anger even more; what had he done in the eighteen years he'd known that his wife had been murdered? Nothing! He'd had no intention of tracking down her killer.

So why then did hope swell in her heart at the thought of her father coming to help her?

Sathi forced her attention away from the thought before it could drive her mad, and focused instead on the resort she was walking through. Even as she made a bee-line for the restaurant, she couldn't help but notice and admire the beautiful cottages that were scattered around the place, built almost inside the forest itself. They had been constructed mostly from wood, with gorgeous sloping roofs that fitted the square structures like little caps. There were ample windows and a majestic wooden door devoted to each cottage, as well as a small veranda edged by a wide interrupted parapet two feet off the ground.

Sathi sighed happily, forgetting her earlier turmoil as she got caught up in the beautiful architecture, and wished she had enough money to live in one of these cottages instead of her own cramped motel room. Then as soon as she had completed the thought she wanted to kick herself. She wasn't here on some tourist trip, to live in a picturesque cottage and go sightseeing. What did it matter where she slept?

After that she kept her gaze on the outdoor restaurant building, which was built in a similar style to match the rest of the resort. She at last reached the entrance, slipping inside unnoticed. The reason her arrival was overlooked was the commotion taking place at the centre of the otherwise empty room; a tourist was attempting to order a meal, whilst the native waiter tried in vain to understand his American drawl.

'French fries... French FRIES,' the red-faced man was enunciating, using both hands to make rectangles in mid-air in an attempt to bring to life the precise dimensions of the complex object that he was describing. The waiter's wide, dark brow was furrowed, lines criss-crossing as though the connection of the correct ridges of thought would allow him to understand something he had obviously never heard of. The ridges deepened further as the American repeated 'French fries' yet again, this time in a wistful murmur. Ironically enough, this seemed to have more of an effect on the waiter than the aforementioned sophisticated hand gestures, and comprehension dawned on his face.

'French? No, this no French. This India!' A proud smile lit his face as he said the last words, and his right hand rose to cover his heart. One could almost hear the Indian national anthem ringing out in the air around them.

The American was, unsurprisingly, baffled. 'What? No, I'm talking about French *fries*.' At the waiter's mumbles of 'fries... frying pan *veno?*' the tourist seemed to have reached the pinnacle of his resourcefulness; then he bounced back with laudable persistence, exclaiming, 'Finger chips!'

One pale hand twitched towards his collar, as if to lift it in tribute to his own intelligence. Then the American realised that his server was backing slowly away from him, his expression the personification of horror and his lips mouthing the word 'finger' over and over again.

Sathi, attempting to smother her giggles, decided to intervene before the waiter called the police to arrest the American for cannibalism. She consoled the despairing tourist, making rash promises, before turning to the waiter and explaining in Malayalam, 'He's talking about fried potato.' The guy looked at her blankly, confused at her sudden appearance. She sighed and asked him to point her towards the kitchen.

'She was absolutely amazing, madam, she handled that *gora* so smoothly, even though he looked like he was close to crying. He should have told me he just wanted a bit of deep-fried potato, he didn't need to bring the French into it. You should've seen her, she rolled the potato strips in masala and then fried them until they looked like bars of pure gold. I had a taste when she wasn't looking, it was incredible, and when she served it to that *ulukka patta* out there I thought he'd start singing. Said he's never tasted whatever-he-calls-it this good before and he'll want it every day, sent up to his cottage.'

Ravi – that was the waiter's name – paused in his rapid Malayalam/Hindi to take a breath. His boss seized the opportunity to speak, knowing that this might be her only chance, considering Ravi's extraordinarily large lung capacity.

'Did you say your name is Sathi?' the lady asked Sathi in slightly accented English, her eyes fixed on Sathi's face. She was a tall woman, maybe in her late twenties, and her dark shoulder-length hair provided a nice contrast to the business-like *churidar* she wore.

As Sathi nervously nodded, she saw Ravi beam and open his mouth again out of the corner of her eye. The woman hastily resumed speaking. 'Have you got any previous experience working in a restaurant?' she asked.

She hesitated and then said, 'I've waitressed before.' The steady job was the main reason her bank account had been large enough to buy a ticket to India: the idea of asking her father for money repulsed her.

'Well, since I have a customer who wants your food every day, I do not have any choice but to hire you, do I?' was the woman's reply.

Her mouth flopped open. There was a smile threatening to emerge on her prematurely lined face as the woman – her new boss! – continued.

'You will act as assistant cook, and you will help out with serving as well when we are busy. It would also help greatly if you could take orders when Ravi is the only waiter because,' she paused to throw Ravi an amused look, 'as you know, he does not know English and is inclined to blame that on our customers. You get Sunday and a weekday off, depending on the schedule of the chief cook, and you can have a room in staff accommodations. Meals, of course, you can have from here.'

Before Sathi could even begin to process this amazing news, delivered with such deft efficiency, something happened that caused her to wish that she had the ability to turn invisible at will; her empty stomach, well and truly exasperated with her, gave a deafening rumble, echoing like far-off thunder.

There was a moment of infinite silence, in which Sathi tried not to see Ravi grinning at her, and then the boss-woman was firing at Ravi. 'You are responsible for Sathi until she becomes used to the job, and right now I want you to show her to her room and give her the keys. Sathi, I want you here tomorrow at 10 o'clock sharp, ready to prepare lunch, all right?'

Sathi, her face feeling far too hot for comfort, nodded again and murmured her heartfelt thanks, refusing to look at Ravi as he gestured for her to leave first. Just as she passed the doorway, she heard her new boss's carefully controlled voice ring out.

'And Ravi? Make sure to get some food for Sathi first, won't you?'

Once she had sufficiently satisfied her stomach, in the company of a deeply amused Ravi, Sathi enlisted his help in bringing up her things from the motel and transferring them to her new room. What her boss had casually described as "staff accommodations" made her gasp aloud when she saw it. It consisted of a long line of the cottages that Sathi had coveted earlier placed back to back, with an inner corridor joining them as well as a veranda punctuated by several wide teak pillars.

As soon as they had dumped Sathi's things in her room - a small rectangle with a bed in one corner and a tiny attached bathroom - Ravi showed her the common staff kitchen at one end of the row of cottages. They made tea (nowhere near as good as Manish's) and sat out on the veranda drinking it. It was raining again, and Sathi, leaning against one of the pillars comfortably, tilted her face so that the spray of droplets washed against her skin, cool and fresh. Much as she liked Ravi, she wished he would just sit quietly and enjoy the gorgeous scenery with her. From where she was sitting she could see the far-off mountains covered in green, and the mist that hung over them like a smoky screen, drenching them with an other-worldly beauty. Nelliampathi, she decided, was absolutely perfect.

As Ravi's incessant chattering continued in the background, Sathi found herself thinking unexpectedly gratefully of her father, who, by asking his friend to babysit her, had exposed her to a spice-filled kitchen and a patient teacher, allowing her to get this job. Even as she reminisced, however, the thought crossed her mind that she would not have needed an external source for either had her mother been alive. It would have been Amma who would have told her to lean back as she added chilli powder and wiped her stinging eyes when the pungent odour of onions permeated them.

Ravi, noticing how his new friend's face had become hard and her eyes steely, bade her goodbye, thinking she needed some privacy and rest. Sathi remained there on the veranda for the rest of the evening with only the rain and her black thoughts for company.

Sathi's life in Nelliampathi fell into a pleasant routine; every day she woke to smell the clear mountain air and the exotic scents offered to her by the forest which surrounded her on all sides. They varied from day to day, yet remained unwaveringly intoxicating.

On the days when she didn't have to work in the morning, she strolled down the winding lane through the tea estate to Manish's tea shop and started the day with his amazing potion. The sweet old tea-maker refused to let her pay for her tea and she tried to repay the debt by buying small gifts and leaving them discreetly on his stall. Money was not so tight any more now that she did not have to pay for food *or* accommodation and she felt brave enough to buy some essentials for herself as well.

When she had to work long hours, she found Ravi to be a comforting companion; his loose tongue meant that she was rarely forced to come up with topics for conversation and it provided a pleasant change from her own internal monologues.

Ravi was only half Malayali, although he had married a native Keralite and settled in Nelliampathi (his wife was pregnant with their first child and Ravi had already made Sathi promise to visit them on her day off). His mother was from North India and this was the reason for the Hindi words interspersed within his Malayalam. Sathi was actually beginning to pick up some of Ravi's odder phrases, although her favourite was still ulukka patta, meaning "idiot".

Delighted to hear her use the slang in relation to a ruffian boy who had one day come flying into the kitchen, knocked over a tureen of spicy vegetable soup, skidded on the slippery floor, crashed into the pots and pans that had been meticulously stacked against one wall and after all that tried to make off with some *roti*, Ravi had made a deal with her; he would teach her Hindi and in return Sathi would teach him English. Ravi's broken attempts at English became the new standing joke between the staff, among whom was the chief cook, a grizzled old woman whose bark was definitely worse than her bite. Sathi grew to like the kind heart that lurked beneath the rough tongue, and harmony existed in the kitchen with the elder woman in charge of making the more traditional Indian dishes, whilst Sathi experimented with European dishes and the amazing effects of green chilli, usually with a willing Ravi as her guinea pig.

Despite joining in with equal measure in the hard work and hilarity of her new job, Sathi fell asleep each night with the image of her mother imprinted on the back of her eyelids.

Yet that image was underscored by a sense of failure.

Sathi supposed that to everyone else she appeared to be a normal girl come to experience India on her gap year, spending her days divided between work and sight-seeing. Did they have any idea that she had actually come to avenge her mother's murder? Could she blame them for seeing only a tourist when they looked at her? What exactly had she accomplished, after nearly a month in Nelliampathi? Once she had found that Amma's family were not in town, she had lost her purpose. The need to see her relatives, after all, was something secondary, driven by the desire to know more about her mother. Sathi had come to find the one who had ended her mother's life.

But how can I find out about Amma's death if I don't know anything about her life?

Apart from teasing a few more details out of Manish and gently interrogating the other staff and the native guests living in the cottages, she was no further on in her ridiculously amateurish investigation than when she had first arrived. She needed to talk to Amma's family. Sure, some of the others living near the resort knew *of* Amma but they only had the basics; her parents had died in a tragic car crash, she was adopted by her father's sister, she got married, left for the UK twenty odd years ago and died due to childbirth. As far as they knew, she had no enemies, no one she had a fight with, not even any close friends. No one even knew she had returned to Nelliampathi after Sathi had been born.

She just couldn't understand it. How was it that no one, *no one*, knew the truth about her mother's death? How could they all be completely oblivious to the fact that she had been murdered?

Unless...

Sathi bit her lip. Had she been too quick to jump to conclusions? No, she told herself firmly. Remember the boarding pass? That little piece of paper was proof that Amma had returned to the UK, safe and well, several months after Sathi had been born.

So why doesn't anyone in Nelliampathi know the truth?

In desperation, she decided to try to use the cards to ascertain whether her mother's murderer was still in Nelliampathi. She got out her battered old pack and sat cross-legged on the floor of her room. She set them out as normal, but instead of the question she had meant to ask, the only thought in her mind as she picked up each rectangle of plastic was: is Amma alive?

She lost the game, of course, as she knew she would. She couldn't help hoping, even though she knew it was stupid. Everyone who had known her mother also knew that Amma was now sojourning in the after-world.

Sathi glared down at the ordered chaos of the cards. She gathered the offending items and shuffled them rapidly, not caring that she was damaging them even more in her haste, not caring that she was taking her anger and frustration out on brainless objects.

She slapped them down again, thinking, *Is the bastard who did this to Amma still in Nelliampathi?* She played on impatiently, stacking the cards up, Spade, Diamond, Club, Heart, thinking of the punishment she would inflict on her mother's killer, of how she would set up a whole torture chamber just for him as she exacted her sweet revenge.

Then suddenly, the four Kings were looking imperiously up at her as she reached for the next card. She looked absently at the Joker and then back at the stacks. With a sense of detachment, she realised she had won the game. Which meant her mother's murderer *was* still here!

Excitement growing in her like a fire amid dry, cracked leaves, she picked up the piles and reshuffled them thoroughly, wondering which question to ask out of the hundreds that had sprung up like a fountain from that one victory. *Will I find him? Will I find out the truth about Amma's death?*

No. She would eliminate those kinds of questions. She knew from experience that they were pointless; they were about the future, and "the future is too dependent on human choice for the cards to give a definite answer", as a snotty website had admonished her when Sathi looked up Tarot cards, the closest anyone had come to what she did with ordinary playing cards.

After some more thought, she decided on her question. Again, she laid the cards out. This time she became stuck within five minutes. Frowning, she rephrased the question, and tried to carry on with the game with the layout she already had. At first it seemed to work, and she felt triumphant. Then unexpectedly she lost again. The cards were saying that she had neither met nor seen Amma's killer in Nelliampathi. She supposed that was understandable, but the cards were acting weird; usually if the answer was no, she would lose the game immediately. The cards had built up her expectations and then brought them crashing down again just as quickly.

Irritated with them, Sathi roughly put them back inside the wooden box where they lived and resolved to get an early night. She threw the windows wide open so she would hear it the instant the rain returned, switched the lights off, and got into bed.

Instead of falling asleep as soon as her eyes closed as she wanted, her mind wandered, thinking of the hopelessness of finding her Amma's killer, of how little she knew about her own mother, about how her father had done virtually nothing to stop her coming to Kerala. She thought of the furious energy she had felt that night in her father's house when she realised that she had not been the one to bring about her mother's death, the certainty she'd felt.

She scoffed and turned onto her side. She was no closer to finding Amma's murderer than she had been on the day she vowed vengeance. That energy had covertly returned to wherever it had come from. She couldn't help but remember the astrologer's discouraging words, warning her that she would fail without an ally.

As she lingered on the threshold between the world of sleep and that of wakefulness that night, the image of the Hindu goddess inexplicably rose to take centre stage in her mind. Before she drifted away into darkness, she found herself fervently begging the serene deity, *Please don't let me be alone any more.*

Chapter Six

A Muddy Stranger

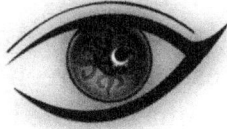

Mr Zakiy, you *must* visit your parents more often.'

And you must *learn to keep your beaky nose out of other people's business*, Zakiy thought irritably. He looked away from the gatekeeper before he could do something he wouldn't regret later, and his eyes focused on the single pearl of light that burned with a fierce intensity in the middle of the enormous hallway. A pang of nostalgia flared in his chest as he remembered how that small oil lamp used to be the centre of his home, the heart of the household, back before...

With a mental shake of his head, Zakiy left the thought incomplete. His searching eyes found the lamp and its flickering light once more. Now it was little more than a showpiece, an empty, meaningless object, just like this house.

'Mr Zakiy! Why are you not replying?' demanded Abdullah. 'You must think of your parents.'

Zakiy turned his attention back to the busy body gatekeeper and gave him a cheery grin. 'Hey, you know what they say about too much of a good thing,' he said conspiratorially. 'My mere presence has such a powerful impact that I wouldn't want to tire them out with too many visits.'

Abdullah's expression changed in no way, and he continued to give his usual impression of having something stuck way too far up his butt. 'They are suffering so much, and they need their son there with them at this time. You must think of them,' he repeated, sounding like a broken record.

Zakiy controlled his urge to shout that he would have spent his every waking moment with them if they let him. Instead, he kept the smile on his face and did what he always did when Abdullah grated too thinly on his nerves. 'Dattu said he saw someone trying to jump over the wall yesterday. He's out there now, fitting nails and broken glass to the top with a new layer of concrete.'

Sure enough, the gatekeeper's expression filled with outrage at the thought of someone interfering with the way he ran the house. 'What! Why didn't he come to me first?' he fumed.

Zakiy shrugged haplessly. 'Well, he wanted you to supervise him with such an important task, but I told him to carry on. I know how busy you are...' he trailed off, letting the bait sit there.

He didn't have long to wait. With a self-important huff, Abdullah turned and strode off, finally leaving Zakiy in peace.

'Beef-witted ratsbane,' he muttered under his breath. He stretched, pushing his arms up over his head as far as they would go and then letting them fall back to his side.

Zakiy glanced bleakly around the hall, purposefully avoiding the oil lamp. For the sake of something to do, he began to trudge up the stairs, his bare feet slapping against the granite floor. His footsteps echoed off in the silence of the empty house.

He rubbed his eyes as he climbed, only just realising how tired he was. And yet the thought of sleeping in this house, every corner of which was haunted by memories he'd rather not recall, repelled him.

By the time he reached the top of the ornate staircase, he had made up his mind. Moving purposefully now, Zakiy padded across to his old bedroom and picked up the bag he had dumped on the bed just a couple of hours ago. Rifling through it, he made sure he had everything he needed. Then he walked back out of the room, down the stairs and let himself out quietly through the back door.

Whatever else he did tonight, Zakiy refused to keep company with memories.

Half an hour later, Zakiy had set up camp in the clearing in the forest behind his parents' house. He went through his usual routine of gathering sticks from the forest floor for a campfire, but his heart wasn't into it.

No matter how much he usually tried to ignore Abdullah, his words nevertheless bugged him. He would have loved to go home for a few days, but his father had as usual laid down the law and forbid him to come.

Zakiy supposed that he could have ignored his father. He certainly didn't mind getting into a fight with his dad, but then his mother and Zoya would have gotten caught in the middle – and who knew how Aman would react? Zakiy would never forgive himself if he was the cause of upsetting Aman.

The fire crackled and embers detached itself from the flames to disappear into the night. The air was quiet, with the odd chirp of a cricket, but that didn't help soothe his restlessness.

Zakiy stood up and brushed off his shorts, deciding that he would go for a walk. Maybe he could tire himself out physically, and then his mind would finally shut off and he would be able to sleep.

He was only a few minutes into his walk when the skies opened, and the monsoon returned with a vengeance. Zakiy was soaked to the skin within seconds. He cursed himself for thinking that walk was a good idea.

'Oomph!'

Thud!

Zakiy hit something solid and stumbled back, blinking through the heavy rain to see what he'd crashed into. He could make out a shape on the ground, a shape that was moaning as it lay on the forest floor.

54

'Hello? Are you okay?' Zakiy asked. He held out his hand towards the stranger. He could just make out long hair, so it must either be a girl or a guy who must get mistaken for a girl pretty often.

'I'm fine,' a voice mumbled. Definitely a girl. She spat out hair from her mouth and glanced up at him through the rain.

Zakiy held out his hand again, and this time she accepted it, letting him pull her to her feet. For a moment they both stood with the rain pouring down on them.

'I'm Zakiy, by the way,' he said, flashing her a grin.

'I'm Sathi,' she said, smiling back reluctantly.

'Nice to meet you.' He paused. 'Although, I wish it were under better circumstances.'

She raised her eyebrows, and he indicated the rain that had slowed down to a drizzle now. 'Drier circumstances,' he clarified.

'Right. Well, I'll let you go now,' she hinted, taking half a step back.

Zakiy glanced around. 'Wait, where were you heading? There's nothing out here in the forest. Let me at least walk you back.'

He couldn't be sure, but he thought she was blushing as she shook her head emphatically. 'No, thanks. I'm fine.'

Zakiy stared at her, wondering what her problem was. 'I won't bite. I'd feel better if I walk you to wherever you're going.'

The girl's head snapped up and her spine straightened. 'I don't really care about making you feel better. Just leave me alone.'

Taken aback, he could only stare. 'Ookay. Sorry for bothering you.' With those words he turned and strolled back to the campsite, whistling.

It took several minutes for Sathi's cheeks to cool down.

She couldn't believe what a fool she'd made of herself with that guy. She'd been wandering around in the dark for more than thirty minutes, trying to find the beautiful clearing she'd once stumbled across.

Sathi had woken up in the middle of the night and hadn't been able to fall back asleep. Lying there, she'd had the fantasy of camping out in the clearing. She'd packed up her sleeping bag and torch and set out, full of determination to find the clearing, only for the torch to die after about ten minutes and for the heavens to belch out rain on her not long after.

On top of everything, she'd bumped into that guy and gotten herself thoroughly muddy from being on the wet forest floor. So, she hadn't exactly been in the mood to deal with his chivalry and questions about where she was going.

Maybe it was stupid, but she wanted to keep the clearing to herself. If she told him what she was looking for, he might decide to camp out with her. Anyway, how was she supposed to trust him?

Sathi trudged on, desperately hoping that she was close to finding the clearing. If not, she was basically lost out here in the forest and would have to walk for at least another half an hour to get back to the resort.

She shivered and wrapped her arms around herself. Maybe she should go back. The thought of failure was distasteful, though, and the memory of the clearing taunted her.

Five more minutes, she told herself. She would keep looking for another five minutes, and if she still couldn't find the clearing, she would admit defeat and return to the resort.

After several minutes, she thought she saw a glimmer of light through the trees. Excited, her stride lengthened, and she got a glimpse of the stream that marked the border of the clearing.

She rushed forwards, and for the second time that night, bumped into someone and went crashing to the floor.

A muttered oath made her glance up, and she stared at the guy sprawled on the ground, the armful of twigs he'd been carrying strewn on the floor around him.

He looked up and his brown eyes met hers, widening in recognition. 'You?'

Groaning internally, Sathi got up and held out a hand to him. 'Hello again.'

56

With a sigh, the guy took her hand and pulled himself up. 'I thought you wanted to be left alone,' he said pointedly, raising an eyebrow.

She crossed her arms. 'I do. That's why I came to this clearing, so I could camp out here...' She trailed off as she took in the tent set up on the ground, next to the wet remnants of a campfire. 'Seriously?' she exclaimed. 'You couldn't find anywhere else to set up your stupid camp?'

He coolly started picking up the dry twigs. How had he kept them dry? 'Well, I wasn't aware that this clearing belonged to you. You should've put up a board.'

Sathi's hands were trembling with anger. 'I don't need a board,' she shot back. 'This property belongs to my parents,' she lied wildly, crossing her fingers behind her back.

He straightened and fixed her with an intense gaze. 'Really?'

She kept eye contact. 'Yeah. So, you're technically trespassing on private property.'

He blinked at her for a few moments. 'Huh. Well, I'm sorry about that. I've been coming here since I was a kid, you see, and I always felt attached to it. Almost like it was calling to me.'

Stunned, she waited for him to continue, but he seemed lost in thought. Feeling ashamed of herself for her lie, she hesitantly blurted, 'Well, you can stay here if you like. I mean, you already have your tent set up.'

He looked up in surprise, and then grinned. 'Are you sure?'

She nodded mutely, already regretting her offer.

'Thank you, m'lady,' he said quietly.

'Why don't you take my tent?' Zakiy offered, glancing down at the sleeping bag she'd brought. She'd spread tarpaulin underneath, but it still wouldn't be very comfortable with the ground as wet as it was. At least the rain had stopped.

The fire he'd somehow managed to build was still burning away merrily, and he'd lent her a pair of shorts and a t-shirt to change into.

She wouldn't admit it to him, but if felt wonderful to be dry and clean again.

'No, I can't take your tent,' she told him, even though she had ducked in there earlier to change, and experienced how warm and cosy it was.

'Please. It's the least I can do, since you're letting me camp out on your property,' he said, eyes wide with sincerity.

Right. What could she say to that? Sathi reluctantly agreed and said goodnight, retreating into his tent and flopping down on his sleeping bag.

Despite being able to appreciate how much softer it was than her own thin mattress, Sathi couldn't get comfortable. Her conscience was pricking her, keeping her from the welcome embrace of sleep.

She couldn't get over her stupid lie. Why had she blurted out that she owned the land? More importantly, what on earth made him believe her?

She sat up as a sudden thought struck her. What if he was a rapist or murderer? What if he was just waiting for her to fall asleep so he could attack her?

Sathi crept over to the tent entrance and peeked out. He was lying across the tent, about ten feet away. His chest was rising and falling evenly, and if she concentrated, she could hear a soft snore.

She debated silently about her chances of getting away without waking him (assuming that he wasn't faking). Sathi decided her fight of flight response was far too strong to be able to get any sleep. Escape it was.

Sathi slipped through the tent and then cursed as she realised she'd dropped her bag when she fell for the second time and had forgotten to pick it up again. There was no way she could leave it behind, not when it contained her most precious possession – the picture of her mother.

On the other hand, there was barely any light to see by. How was she supposed to find her bag? She glanced at the guy and saw a dark shape nearby that could be her bag. She crept over and lifted the bag onto her shoulder, barely breathing.

Sathi was just about to make a run for it when a flashlight clicked on, blinding her.

'What the hell do you think you're doing?'

Maybe she was a kleptomaniac, Zakiy hypothesised, as he saw the girl hoisting his bag onto her shoulder. He stood and approached her, holding the flashlight high.

She held out her arms. 'Look, just let me go. I don't want any trouble.'

Was she for real? Did she expect him to let her steal his stuff? 'You know, you can get treated for what you have nowadays,' Zakiy said calmly, trying to think back to the police shows he'd watched. 'Then you won't get in trouble anymore.'

The girl had stilled and was staring at him, eyes wide.

'It's nothing to be ashamed of,' he continued, stepping slightly closer. 'It's a disease, really. It's not your fault. But you can choose not to let it control you.'

'What are you talking about?' she asked flatly.

He was almost close enough now. 'Your kleptomania.'

'You think... why would you think I have kleptomania?' she demanded, crossing her arms.

'Because you're stealing my bag.' With those words, he lunged forward and yanked the bag strap off her shoulder. It got caught on her arms, and the zipper opened, spilling half the bag's contents on the floor.

'What the hell are you –' Her outrage fizzled out as she stared at the bag. 'That's not my bag.'

'I know,' Zakiy said. 'It's mine.'

'I thought it was mine.'

'Do you do that with all the stuff you steal?'

Her glare returned. 'I'm not a thief, or a kleptomaniac or whatever you think about me. I thought this was my bag.'

'Right.' Maybe he should check her into KA – Kleptomaniacs Anonymous. Was that even a thing?

The girl pinched the bridge of her nose. 'Look. I know it looks bad. But I was looking for my bag, and I thought yours was mine. I'm really not a thief. If you could just lend me your torch, I will find my bag and be on my way.'

Zakiy raised his eyebrows.

Her eyes widened in disbelief. 'You really think I'm going to steal your torch now?'

He didn't reply, and she threw up her hands in exasperation. 'Fine! Just do me a favour and shine the torch around the floor so I can find my bag.'

Zakiy sighed and pointed his torch at the floor. The first thing he noticed was his stuff, spilled out on the forest ground. He knelt to pick them up, and suddenly the girl caught hold of his wrist. 'Is that yours?' she asked urgently.

He looked up at her in exasperation. 'Of course, it's mine. I just told you that.'

She shook her head, eye alight with a strange excitement. 'No, I meant *that*.' She was pointing at his box of Tarot cards.

Zakiy picked it and brushed off a few leaves. 'Yes. It's mine. Just like all the other things that I keep in *my* bag.'

She ignored his sarcasm and yanked his torch out of his hand. 'Hey!'

He prepared to chase after her, but she was back before he could react. She had a bag in her hands and was digging around inside. She thrust the torch back into his hands and pulled out a pack of plain playing cards. She waved them at him, grinning.

'You want to play rummy?'

She took a deep breath. 'I play solitaire. I ask a question as I play. If I win, it's a yes, if I lose, it's a no. Sometimes it's the only way I can get answers.'

Sathi said all this in a rush, managing to look both vulnerable and expectant at the same time. Zakiy was dumbstruck, looking from the cards in her hands to her face and back again. She played cards to get answers?

It was only when Sathi's expression began to turn uncertain at his lack of reaction that Zakiy pulled himself together. 'It sounds like you use those playing cards in the same way as Tarot is used.'

She nodded eagerly. 'How did you find out about the cards?'

He hesitated; how much to tell her? He didn't feel like going into the full explanation, and anyway he'd only just met her. Granted, he didn't get that inner guard going up as he usually did when he was talking to an outsider, but she was still practically a stranger.

Then he remembered her explanation about playing solitaire, and his rationality dried up: it had to be a sign. *Ok, Allah. I'm trusting you to trust her.*

'When I was in school, I had a friend who was really into things like this. You know, numerology, weird talismans, zodiac signs and then this, Tarot cards. We all used to tease him mercilessly because he went around trying to make money out of the other students, selling these amulets and things, fortune-telling and doing Tarot readings for them. I didn't believe in the rest of the stuff but there was something about the cards that always intrigued me.'

He lifted his hand, showing her his cards again. 'Then I saw these in a shop window. The woman's face on the box just sort of jumped out at me.' He shook his head, thinking of the way those eyes had nailed him where he stood, and gave a short laugh in remembrance.

'Her expression seemed so peaceful and so... wise. It's amazing isn't, how a small thing can make such a difference to your whole life? I went in and bought the cards on an impulse and haven't been parted from them since.'

An unwelcome voice sliced through his mind, and Zakiy just barely stopped himself from shuddering as it reminded him of how it had been before he found the cards.

Quickly, he let his eyelids close so that the only light his eyes received was that which had already been filtered by the innocuously small blood capillaries that reigned over those protective folds of skin.

With the red glow as his backdrop, Zakiy thought of Allah, letting borrowed serenity displace the turbulence that had struck him so suddenly.

He opened his eyes and glanced at Sathi. He couldn't help smiling at the avid way she was listening. Her eyes were narrowed in concern, though, and he realised that she had noticed his brief slip in composure. He hurried on with his explanation without giving her a chance to ask questions. 'That picture at the front is the image on one of the cards: the last card in the Major Arcana, The Universe. In a traditional pack, it's called The World. The Psychic Tarot is so much better than the traditional sort though.'

Zakiy opened the box and let the cards spill onto the floor in front of them, light from the fire hitting their laminated surface and becoming scattered, making it look as if specks of gold were dancing across the cards.

'Look how expressive the pictures are. You can just study them and get a real feel for what they mean, without ever even opening the book.' He indicated the small guide that came with the box, which explained what each card meant. He thought about the last time he'd used the cards, about what they had shown him... *No, no. Focus!* he told himself sternly.

Sathi had bent over the display of brightly coloured cards fanned out on the ground, her eyes wide and her fingers hesitantly tracing the bright artwork they depicted. Zakiy watched her reaction with a mixture of amusement and incredulity. What were the odds that he would bump into someone who had almost exactly the same habit as he did? Allah must have a hand in it. Zakiy had no idea what He was up to, and wished as always that his God wasn't so damn mysterious.

Zakiy was distracted from the familiar frustration when he felt something tickle his leg. Glancing down, he realised that one of the Tarot cards had fluttered down onto his lap when he shook the box over the floor.

He flipped the violet-backed card over; it showed two hands, one male and one female, gripping each other just above the wrist, as if they were helping each other up over a cleverly concealed cliff, with coloured flags fluttering in an invisible wind behind them. The card was edged by a deep purple background, and a number three sat snugly at the top, with the words "Partnerships and Alliances" mirroring it at the foot of the amethyst border.

Wordlessly, Zakiy held the card up for Sathi to see. She gazed at it for a moment, a cleft forming at the centre of her forehead. Then a smile flicked her lips upwards as she looked at him, her own brown eyes filled with wonder. He knew there was no need to say anything. It was a clear message, and it banished all remaining doubts from his mind.

Thank you, Allah.

After that, neither of them could stop talking. Zakiy made the most delicious cocoa she had ever tasted, and they sat around the campfire until it had burned itself out almost entirely.

They talked on and on about the cards until Sathi nearly fell asleep in mid-sentence, at which point Zakiy insisted that they sleep. She had reached the tent entrance before he remembered the question he had wanted to ask her.

'Sathi,' he called, watching her turn around and brush her hair out of her face. 'Why were you trying to run away with my bag earlier?

He saw the fire return to her eyes and suppressed a grin. She chose not to rise to the bait, instead calmly saying, 'I was scared that you were dangerous, and wanted to get away before you killed me.'

Suddenly Zakiy had to work much harder than usual to maintain his casual smile; he could feel his jaw clenching slightly and his hands curled involuntarily. 'What made you change your mind?'

She smiled at him. 'I think you know the answer as well as I do.'

Chapter Seven

Flag of Truce

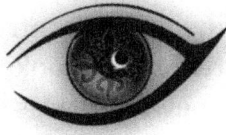

Sathi awoke to the sound of church bells in the distance. Despite being part of a country where more than eighty per cent of people were Hindus, Kerala had a remarkable reputation for religious diversity and tolerance. About a fifth of Malayalis were Christian, and nearly a quarter practised Islam. In Kerala, you could find temples, mosques, and churches, all within walking distance of each other. At dawn and dusk, the bells in the temple would clamour joyously, on Fridays and during the month of Ramadan, the "Adhan", or Muslims' call to prayer, would greet everyone exuberantly five times a day, and on Sundays, like today, church bells would chime happily, signalling morning mass.

Sathi felt remarkably well rested, despite having gone to sleep only towards 4 am. She smiled to herself and shook her head in wonder. Making the decision to trust Zakiy had been so simple after discovering that amazing commonality between them. It was as if someone was laying people and things in her path, all of them adding up to give her exactly what she needed, at exactly the right time.

Inevitably, the idea of who that someone might be slipped into her thoughts; she remembered how she had been thinking of her mother's goddess, Amma's Devi, before she fell asleep at the resort. Was the goddess real? Had she been listening to Sathi? Had Zakiy been the answer to her plea for company?

She had been thinking of her father when she formed that impromptu prayer. She admitted that now. He had never been far from her mind since the astrologer's irritating warning. Actually, thoughts of her father had been plaguing her ever since she came to India. She had known that her father hated her but surely he was not so cold that he didn't care that she was still alive?

Sathi remembered when her father had first told her that she didn't have a mother. Her initial reaction had been a sort of puzzled surprise. So what that basically meant was, she would have one big person dressing her and putting her to bed instead of two. She didn't mind that, not as long as she was read *The Jungle Book* before she fell asleep. That was okay.

Then she started school. She remembered the weird little twinge she would feel as she watched the other mothers. She would stare for a bit too long than was polite and her eyes would sting rather painfully. But then her father would arrive, and he would lift her onto the front seat of the car, a bit gruff perhaps, but he would always give her seatbelt a little tug to make sure it had fastened securely before he drove off.

Of course, all that changed when her babysitter became her surrogate father. Her father's old friend from Kerala would meet her at the school gate, engulfing her in a warm, but foreign, hug and tell her that she could call him Uncle Sunil. He would take her to his house and let his wife, "Aunty" Lekha, take her under her wing. Sathi learned to follow her around the kitchen to ease her boredom as the schooldays at their house extended into weekends.

That was when she first began to feel the loss of her mother. Her guilt-filled yearning for an absent woman had become a festering wound that kept growing in direct proportion to the time she spent at her fake uncle and aunt's house. As far as she knew, her father never thought to check in at any of those times to make sure that she was safe, well-cared for, that she was happy. Why would he bother now?

A hopeful voice piped up - *but he knew Sunil and knew you would be safe there. After all, you don't know for sure that he didn't check in with them.*

Immediately, Sathi put a stop to that line of thinking. It was filling her with a confusing, noxious cloud of emotion that was part frustration and part longing, something she honestly didn't have the energy to deal with. *Coming to Kerala isn't like popping over to Sunil's house. Did he even try to stop you when you left?*

Unbidden, the memory of him forbidding her to take a gap year flashed into her mind. Sathi viciously silenced the optimism that reared its head at the thought. *He just wanted to be in control! You leaving didn't suit his convenience, so he decided to pull the "I'm your father" card.*

Well, he was a bit too late.

She forcibly changed the direction of her thoughts, instead thinking of Zakiy's initial shock last night over the Tarot cards. Sathi's grin sobered as she remembered how she had peeked through the tent opening at him as he shifted his weight, trying to find a more comfortable position on the ground. She had given up trying to convince him that she should be the one sleeping outside; the guy had some old-fashioned ideals about being a gentleman.

Resignedly, she had picked up the thickest wool blanket and softest pillow and gone outside. As she dumped them on his mattress, she had said casually, 'I suppose this paradise is big enough for two people. You can stay here on the one condition that you take your tent back from tomorrow onwards.'

Sathi sighed and stretched. She peeked outside to see that Zakiy was already awake and bustling around the campsite. He had folded up her sleeping bag and bedding, and she carried it into his tent for the time being.

Zakiy had to leave for his college classes, and they made plans to meet up afterwards at the resort. Sathi ducked into her room so she could change into slightly more professional clothes for her shift.

Before leaving her room, she dug out her Bageera piggybank (the disgruntled old panther had always been her favourite). It held her hard-earned savings and was hidden at the bottom of her large suitcase.

She wasn't sure how much a tent would cost, but she was determined to buy one today, no matter what.

Chapter Eight

Broken Barriers

The day was chillier than normal; a biting edge had crept, uninvited, into the wind and the bright sunshine did nothing to dispel it, tolerant of the discomfort. Sathi pulled the thick shawl more tightly around her shoulders, keeping pace with Zakiy as they headed back to the resort. She had worked the morning and afternoon shifts and had then decided to go and meet him at the Government Engineering College, where he was in his final year of study.

She was still embarrassed at how she had been caught out in her lie. Yesterday they'd gone to Zakiy's house and met his caretaker. The guy had blurted out that the campsite actually belonged to his parents.

She couldn't believe Zakiy owned "her" clearing and hadn't said anything to contradict her when she had been lying her head off. No wonder he'd thought she was stealing his bag.

She had to admit that he was being really good about it though. Apart from some mild teasing and the occasional reference to her as "her ladyship" the day before, after his employee had let the cat out of the bag, Zakiy hadn't mentioned it and was acting normal.

He had needed to print something after college, so she had agreed to detour to an internet café; while he scratched his head at some of the more obscure diagrams he had just printed off, she had checked her email, and read a message Chloe had sent her in the middle of her holiday in Canada. Chloe had written, *You lucky thing! It's freezing cold here and to think of you in India – it must be so lovely and warm. All the tan I built up in London before the holidays has vanished, and now I look like a snow man! No, hang on, that should be snow-woman...*

Sathi had snorted at the thought of the stick-thin Chloe ever resembling a snow man/woman, but conceded her point about the tan; weirdly enough, many of her friends back at school had been jealous of Sathi's naturally dark skin, whereas in India, everyone seemed to be obsessed with being fair-skinned. The TV commercials here were full of skin creams that would supposedly make your skin paler in fourteen days: Sathi couldn't see how that was possible, unless the moisturisers contained bleach, or something even worse. At the same time, over in England people were literally spray-painting their skin orange. Sathi had once accidentally bought a bottle of tanning cream without reading the label properly, and after a day of using it even her dark skin had begun to glow an unnatural orange. She had immediately thrown the almost full bottle in the bin.

Sathi constructed an appropriate reply to Chloe's email, a wry smile twisting her lips, and struggled through the week-long mixture of junk mail and Facebook messages. Once she reached the end of her unread mail, she refreshed her inbox and double-checked the electronic bin, just to be sure, and quenching a pang of disappointment, she Googled the day's flights from UK to Kerala.

Zakiy, having finished pulling his hair out over the diagrams, had found Sathi sitting staring at a long list on the screen, a webpage she quickly shut down as soon as he announced his presence. Now she was telling him about her day at the restaurant as they walked along the opposite edge of the tea estate, back towards the resort, and Sathi trailed her hand along the top of the wet, nature-polished leaves as she related how Ravi had received a phone call from his pregnant wife that afternoon, immediately sending him into a panic attack.

'He hyperventilated so much that I had to take the phone from him and ask someone to get him a paper bag, which took a while to explain, I can tell you,' she said.

They rounded a corner, and Zakiy stopped smiling abruptly as he noticed a few schoolboys, not much younger than Sathi, who had formed a loose semi-circle enclosing someone Zakiy couldn't see. The boys were laughing and pointing, their faces pinched and ugly.

Sathi, whose line of vision was blocked by the bend in the road and the bus-stand full of people gaping at the free show, hadn't noticed what was happening and carried on speaking as Zakiy used his superior height to crane his neck, trying to see beyond the boys.

'*Bhabhi* was thoroughly exasperated with him - she blamed herself for marrying a highly-strung North-Indie. She'd just called to remind Ravi to bring home mutton *varval* because she has a craving for it. Or maybe I should say, her baby has a craving for it!' Sathi looked down at the glossy green leaves, smiling.

Finally, one of the boys shifted, giving Zakiy an unobstructed view; there was a woman huddled against the rock-wall, her unkempt black hair hanging around her face in disarray, her mud-coloured sari torn and tattered. She didn't seem to care about the cold; she had wrapped a thick blanket around a small bundle, which she kept clutched to her chest. Her head was bowed, and she moved her lips as if reassuring the wrapped object, although her words were drowned out by the boys' laughter.

Now they began to throw rubbish at the woman, leaning down and picking up old paper and wrappers off the floor. She didn't respond, except to turn away so as to shield her bundle with her own body, holding her arms tightly over it. Before Zakiy could react, one of the boys darted forward and took hold of the wad of cloth in her hands, violently wrenching it from her grasp.

'Anyway, when he heard her voice Ravi must have thought: wife – baby – arghh!'

Sathi looked around at him, puzzled at the lack of reaction, just as Zakiy strode over to the boy holding the bundle, drew back his fist and punched him in the face. The resounding crunch of the nose breaking masked the small cry of surprise that escaped from Sathi's lips as the sea of natives parted at last, and she saw the keening woman for the first time.

Zakiy's blood was pounding behind his ears, angry as lava, and he regarded the boy with disdain as he bent over in pain. Zakiy was thirsty for him to recover and fight back. The nasty piece of work didn't have enough courage for that though; shoving the bundle into Zakiy's arms, he took off down the road, his friends following after throwing furtive looks at Zakiy. Caught off guard, and alarmed at the lack of sound emanating from the roll of fabric, he looked down at the heavy weight in his arms.

It was a stone wrapped in layers and layers of cloth.

He had to make himself try and swallow around the sudden lump in his throat. Slowly, he approached the woman. She had made herself as small as possible, as if that would still her pain, and was hunched on the ground, moaning softly.

Zakiy gently lowered the stone into her arms, standing still as she eagerly reached for it and hugged it close, crooning as she tenderly rocked it. He stood looking down at her, fighting down the mysterious thunderstorm occurring within his chest cavity.

He sensed rather than saw Sathi at his shoulder; she stepped forward, and pulling the shawl from around herself, gently wrapped it around the woman and her child.

They sat across the table from each other, neither uttering a word. The bustle of the crowded restaurant lent them a rare bubble of privacy, one that they had not yet had the heart to take advantage of.

Zakiy saw Sathi's eyes flick over to him, and she asked, 'I thought you never lost your cool?' He closed his eyes, scrunching them tightly shut so he didn't have to see the woman rocking a stone in her arms, her features schooled into an adoring smile. His fist was throbbing, but the physical pain was a welcome distraction in his mind.

'Sometimes cool is there to be lost,' he replied, not opening his eyes. Ignoring his inane retort, Sathi reached across the table-top and encased his hand in her own small warm one.

At that small symbol of trust and comfort, Zakiy finally met her eyes, and he knew he could tell her. No - he *had* to tell her. He didn't know why, and Allah knew he didn't want to live that nightmare again, but it was too late. The journey had already begun and the choice was between crawling the length of it alone and walking it with someone he trusted. He started to talk.

'My parents left all our ancestral property in Nelliampathi and shifted to Bangalore with my brother and me when I was seven years old,' he said in a voice that was croakier than he liked. He cleared his throat and forced himself to continue. 'It didn't make much sense to me at the time, I had grown up among these hills, and I loved it here. I wasn't old enough to realise that my parents were faced with a much bigger dilemma than leaving behind their homeland.' Zakiy didn't let himself feel. He commanded his vocal chords to vibrate, and made his lips move accordingly, forcing words out through his mouth.

'My brother had just turned ten when he first started behaving... oddly. It started with him not being able to sleep at night; I remember hearing him roam around his room, sometimes up until 2 am. It got worse and worse, and he ended up pacing restlessly well into the early hours of dawn. I could hear him talk to himself as well. Most of it was utter nonsense, something about the army being out to get him or some such military rubbish, but whatever was going through his mind was obviously scaring him senseless. When he still couldn't sleep at night, he started getting paranoid. He accused my family of sabotaging his food, he said that's why he couldn't sleep.' Once he had forced Zakiy to taste his food first, to make sure there nothing in it that was causing his insomnia.

His lack of sleep and paranoia had been a dangerous combination that inevitably reached a climax in violence. 'When that didn't make any difference, he put a knife to our mother's throat.' He ignored Sathi's sharp intake of breath, and continued to glare at the table as if all the answers to the questions of the universe were written there. He heard Aman's familiar voice, twisted into something awful beyond belief, something so alien to his familiar boyish tone: *You put something in my coffee, didn't you? DIDN'T YOU?*

'That's when my parents packed up their life here in Nelliampathi and set out in search of the best psychiatric care they could find for him. We relocated to Bangalore; my parents sought medical advice from NIMHANS hospital. It's supposed to be one of the best mental health hospitals in India. We stayed there for about two years, but not even continuous treatment for that long had any effect on Aman.

'My parents roamed around the country, trying to find that one miraculous hospital that would revert Aman to his old self again. That definitely didn't happen, and all the so-called professionals had to offer was that he was suffering from schizophrenia and that it was unusual in a ten-year-old. As if that was useful, for all the effect the medicines had on him. Eventually my father became weary to the point of illness with the physical and mental exhaustion. We settled in Mysore and I began to work for my SSC.'

Seeing Sathi's querying look, he reluctantly explained, 'SSC is Secondary School Certificate - they're equivalent to GCSE's.' He paused. 'Those were the worst days.'

Why couldn't he stop talking? Zakiy shuddered as his brain, against his strict orders, allowed snippets of that year to splay through his conscious mind, sadistic tendrils that had begun to spread as soon as he saw the boys and their torture and had slowly, covertly, slipped around the edges, infiltrating and finally dominating his thoughts, violating them. Visions of those days that had been living nightmares; a deep gash across his mother's face, Aman with his eyes burning as if on fire, another group of boys, drunk, secretly afraid, the stones that had broken the front windows, Aman's retribution...

A gentle pressure on his tightly fisted hands loosened them, at the same time slackening the hold those dark tendrils had on him. Zakiy seized on the brief ray of light that had filtered through, and pushed the memories out, far away and yet never far enough. He had to keep talking. It was his only salvation, otherwise he would drown in that web of misery and fear. He had to swim, no matter how long it took to reach the shore, no matter that he'd never managed to reach it in all the years he'd been swimming. He owed it to his brother.

'My parents made a safe haven for me to study in. They used black card to block out light from my bedroom window so Aman wouldn't come and shout at me when he couldn't sleep. My mother especially had to deal with him a lot, and she used all her energy to make sure I got some peace. Somehow, we got through, and I got good results.' How he had got those results, only Allah knew.

Still looking down at the plastic table-top, Zakiy continued, 'That really was the worst year. In the two years after that things changed. Aman wasn't back to normal by any means but instead of the horrible, unpredictable violence, he became afraid.'

He wished he knew how to describe it properly. You had to live with him to understand; it was like he had become scared of life itself. Zakiy remembered how Aman would spend endless hours huddled next to his father, not saying a word, not going anywhere, just sitting staring around him with his eyes wide and filled with a chilling fear.

When Zakiy asked his father what Aman was looking at that made him so afraid, his father had sighed heavily and replied, 'Unspeakable horrors'. Ones that only Aman could see.

'He started to sleep again, but only when his head was cushioned on our father's lap. That's how it is still. He hasn't changed since I left to come here.'

It was as if Aman's illness had stolen his childhood, and now he was back to being a child again, after all these years. But children grew up, whereas Aman...? Zakiy couldn't finish the thought, and had to gently disengage a hand from Sathi's to wipe away the pearly drops of moisture that had leaked from beneath his closed lids.

Sitting across from Zakiy, Sathi felt her heart break for him. Clamping down on the tears that threatened to overflow from her own eyes, she cleared her throat rather noisily and asked him, 'Why did you come back here to study? There must have been engineering colleges in Mysore, right?'

Zakiy glanced up at her. Even though he hated talking about this, the way she reacted made it more bearable. She didn't try to offer meaningless assurances or act uselessly horrified, unlike the few adults he had been forced to confide in on those days when he had arrived at school in a state of near hysteria. It was only later that he learned to hide his emotions, to think of school as a blissful escape where he forgot the existence of the bloodthirsty creature that had begun to look out through his brother's eyes. Sathi sat almost as still as stone, and the only evidence for the effect of his story was the emotion in her eyes and the lines on her forehead as she unconsciously frowned. She was *real*.

'Yeah, there were,' he replied. 'But my father refused to let me go to college there. He'd had enough after that horrible year when I was studying for the SSC exam. He wanted me to go as far away from home as possible and escape that cramped lifestyle.'

His father had been adamant and they had argued back and forth, neither backing down. Zakiy had not seen his father so animated since Aman became ill, but any relief he'd felt had been eclipsed by disgust that his father expected Zakiy to just abandon his family. The fact that Aman seemed to be better was inconsequential - his father still had to stay with him twenty-four seven to keep him calm, leaving Zakiy's mother to look after everything else, including the newest addition to the family - a little sister Zakiy had not witnessed grow to a toddler. His parents had no life. How could he just leave them?

'We had a lot of ugly quarrels over it. Then we realised the constant arguing was making Aman agitated and irritable.'

Stopping as suddenly in the middle of their shouting match as if someone had pressed the mute button, Zakiy and his father had looked first at the plate of food lying smashed on the floor and then at each other in horror, transported instantly to that time when Aman's mood would change as quickly as the flip of a switch; to those dark days when he had the strength of ten men and the violent rage of a bucking bull.

'That's when I agreed to compromise. I told my father I'd spend four years away from home and earn a degree. Then I'd go back to Mysore to get a job.' He would not abandon his family. His father eventually agreed; he knew how stubborn Zakiy could be. He probably thought he could attempt more persuasion once those four years were over. Or maybe he thought Zakiy would be too high on the intoxication of freedom by then to fulfil his promise to return.

'Then it was a matter of choosing the place. That wasn't much of a choice for me because ever since we had to leave Nelliampathi I've wanted to come back.'

He frowned even as he remembered his guilty joy at returning to his homeland, recalling his father's reticence when Zakiy proposed the college in Nelliampathi. If he didn't know better, he would have said that his father was afraid, though of what, he couldn't even begin to guess. His father had loved Nelliampathi just as much as he had, and it had broken his heart to make that non-existent choice between his son and his home.

His father, eyes wild, had frantically suggested a million different colleges, all far away, but Zakiy had remained unmovable. His father, relieved that his son had at least agreed to leave Mysore, had resignedly given in as the unusual exertion took its toll on his already weary body.

And so, Zakiy had returned to Nelliampathi, to the home that had ceased to be a home.

Chapter Nine

Partnerships & Alliances

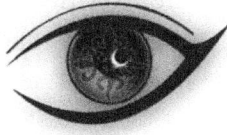

S ilence, subdued, held court.

Zakiy took a sip of the warm *jeera* water that had been placed in front of them by the waiter, wanting to hide how shaken he was, how vulnerable he felt talking about this after so long. He hadn't meant to share this much detail.

Of course, he had always been able to talk nonsense effortlessly and endlessly; *what's that idiom, talk the tail off a monkey? No, that's not it. I'm sure it's not a monkey – tail off a donkey? That doesn't sound quite right either...* As Zakiy kept his mind busy trying to think of the exact words of the saying, he surreptitiously banished those tendrils, feeling that they had been allowed freedom for far too long.

'Hind leg off a donkey!' Zakiy exclaimed in triumph, finally remembering. He looked up to see Sathi staring at him as if he had lost every last square nanometre of his mind.

'You know, that saying,' he offered, grinning at her, trying to lighten the tension that clotted the air around them. He wished he hadn't opened up so much to her. Now she would always look at him with pity lacing her eyes. He didn't want it. He wanted the easy familiarity they'd had before that homeless woman had broken a dam inside him.

'I was trying to say to myself that I could talk the hind leg off a donkey, only I couldn't remember the exact words – talk the tail off a monkey doesn't have quite the same ring to it, does it?'

Sathi's answer was accompanied by a reluctant upward tug of the lips that failed to crease the skin around her eyes, but she nevertheless mimicked his attempt at light-heartedness. 'No, I guess not. Although I think that in your case, all organisms belonging to the animal kingdom would run for their lives to save their hind legs and/or tails from the fate of amputation.'

Sathi hesitated. She felt in awe of just how much pain Zakiy had suffered in his short life. How was he still functioning as a human being? How had he survived?

But had he really survived? She was starting to think that his goofy humour was a mask he pulled over himself to avoid a never-ending pain. Much as she hated to see his sorrow, hiding behind the defence of wit couldn't be good for him.

He had to try to find a way to move past it, either by doing something to help his brother or by accepting that he couldn't be helped. Surely he could only do that if he talked his plan of action through with someone? Unfortunately, it looked as if that someone was going to be her.

'Zakiy,' she interrupted, stopping what she was sure was more typical Zakiy-drivel. She paused. How does one go about this? She wished she had time to go read a psychology textbook. No, actually she wished she could find a qualified professional for Zakiy to talk to and then run in the opposite direction, away from something that was way out of her comfort zone.

Yet, like it or not, Zakiy had chosen to confide in her. She had to honour that trust.

Glancing up, she realised that she had his full attention. Pushing aside the question of whether that was a good thing or not and swallowing a sigh before it could escape the confines of her throat, Sathi decided to barrel her way through.

'What are you going to do?'

There. That was the crucial question. She needed to know whether he had a defeatist attitude or if he wanted to actively do something to help his brother.

'Well,' he replied, looking around the restaurant, 'I think I'm going to try and catch the eye of that waiter. They're doing a special today – have you ever tried *karimeen pollichathu*? You're missing out if you haven't. It's amazing! I don't know about you, but I'm famished.'

Jeez-Louise, he was maddening! Well, if he thought acting stupid would get her off his case, he was sadly mistaken. She had always had a reputation for stubbornness, and now it was going to be put to good use. Resolutely, she fixed a glare on her face. 'Zakiy, you know that's not what I'm talking about.'

He was looking back at her with a half-smile playing around his lips, but one look at his guarded eyes confirmed what she already knew.

'You're not hungry? Seriously, if you don't want fish, there's lots of other stuff you can try. Kerala food is...'

She never found out what Kerala food was, because at that moment he yelped. She'd kicked him under the table. Not too hard, but enough to get his attention.

'What are you going to do about Aman?'

'I don't know. I'm just a college student. Let the politicians handle it.'

Huh?

Zakiy must have taken pity on her, because he helped her out. 'What do you expect me to do about *aman* - world peace? Not even the idiots who call themselves politicians have managed to do more than make pretty speeches, and while I find your confidence in me flattering, I really don't think there's much I can do about it.'

How could the same person who made her laugh more in a few days than she'd laughed in her entire life also have the ability to make her want to scream in frustration? Her patience wasn't just waning, it was gone, the last drops dripping away with increasing rapidity. Pulling all her self-control to a concentrated point inside herself, Sathi strove for a reasonably calm tone.

'Zakiy, what are you planning to do about your brother Aman once you finish your degree?' she gritted out. That should cover all the loopholes.

Or not.

'Well, I guess saying hello to him would be a good start. What do you think?'

Plop. There went her last drop. 'Would you stop acting like you're stupid?' she hissed. 'I have *never* met a more irritating person in my life. What is *wrong* with you? I'm trying to help, and all you're doing is fielding everything I'm asking like some insane tennis player!'

Zakiy, unfazed by her outburst, cocked an eyebrow. 'Who said I wanted your help? What makes you think you can help anyway?'

Sathi felt like she'd been slapped in the face. She started to shout back at him, demand why he'd told her everything if he hadn't wanted her help. Then she closed her open mouth as the last part of his reply echoed in her mind. *What makes you think you can help?*

That was the problem, she realised. He'd gone through life keeping his sorrow close to his heart, using his humour as a shield and acting like a child, never letting anyone know the pain that the man beneath suffered. For some reason, he had opened up to her, and he was embarrassed by the fact. He'd also convinced himself that no one could really understand, nor could they help. So he was trying to push her away, not wanting her to be a constant reminder of a past he was continuously striving to forget.

Well, it was true that she probably could never understand the true extent of what he was going through. But she'd had her own encounter with loss and pain, although she was beginning to think that there were far worse things than physical death. Aman's awful life was proof of that. That's what made her, albeit unconsciously, think she could help Zakiy (even though at the moment she wished that wringing his neck came under the category of "help").

The problem was, *he* didn't know that. He wasn't the only one guilty of keeping secrets.

Damn.

'I'm not really in Kerala for a gap year. Well, I am, but, well, not for normal reasons, you know, not, well, not as a tourist,' Sathi babbled. Why was it so hard to be articulate now? Typical timing.

She started to direct her gaze at the table, then realising that she was repeating exactly what Zakiy had done earlier, she forced herself to lift her chin and meet his eyes. The lack of reaction on his poker-face first made her falter, and then inexplicably spurred her on.

'I came to Nelliampathi because I recently found out that my mother was murdered. She returned here alone a few months after I was born and never came back home.' Sathi continued to hold Zakiy's gaze as the mask finally cracked, first shock and then compassion leaving their marks. She looked away. Now she knew why he hadn't wanted sympathy.

Come on, Sathi.

'So, I'm not asking you this because I have some kind of perverse curiosity,' she explained to the floor. 'When I found out that my mother hadn't died in childbirth as I was tol- as I thought, and that she'd been murdered, I was faced with a dilemma. I could either mourn her death and spend the rest of my life not knowing who had taken her life, or I could come out here to a country I've never been to before, alone, and try to find a needle in a haystack.

'Then I realised that having at least that choice was better than having no options at all. And that's what made my decision. I really do want to help, and at the moment the only thing I can think of that will help is finding out whether you have a similar decision in mind.'

The lunchtime rush had ebbed somewhat, and the noise had fallen to a level that did not make your eardrums vibrate painfully. The waiter on duty would not let them get away without ordering for much longer; in fact the guy, having taken a well-earned break, was making his way towards the other customers enjoying a late lunch and loitering at various tables.

Sathi didn't know whether to feel relieved or exposed now she had finally told someone the true reason for her hastily-planned gap year. All those thorned memories she had been trying to keep at bay were now swirling around her mind, in a cloud so dense that she was surprised she'd managed to speak through it.

'Sathi.' The familiar voice, thick with sincerity, drew her attention back to her companion. Zakiy's eyes met hers. 'I'm sorry.' She nodded. Her throat was too tight to allow speech.

Now that they had been allowed access, those unwanted memories entrapped her in a haze of emotion. Her first day at school; watching the mothers greet their children with kisses and exclamations over how tired they looked while the dads scooped them up and tossed them in the air, laughingly catching them in waiting arms. Looking through the windows of her babysitter's house, waiting for the precise moment when her father's white sedan would finally pull into the small driveway. Hurling herself into arms that stiffened at the unwanted contact. Gradually learning that she shouldn't give affection where it was not desired. The confused, guilt-wracked ball of anger and frustration that had been her sole companion on her birthdays, or as she grew to think of them, her mother's death-days.

No! She didn't die because of me. It wasn't my fault.

Her mother had gifted her with an escape route eighteen years after its formation – an escape through truth. Sathi had been freed from guilt, but had an equally dangerous jailer taken its place?

'Sathi? Sathi!' Zakiy's worried voice pierced the fog, and she realised that he had been trying to get her attention for a while. Sathi shook her head, as though she could physically remove those unwelcome thoughts. She didn't need this. Not now. Her aim here was to help Zakiy, not to indulge in a therapy session for herself. He had, with his amazing personality, managed to budge that heavy cape of grief from her shoulders. He deserved at least the same from her.

She smiled reassuringly at him. She must not have been very convincing, though, because his concern did not fade.

'Are you okay?' he demanded.

'Yes. Yes, I'm fine, honestly. I felt disoriented for a second, that's all,' she hedged.

'It's 'cos you haven't had anything to eat, isn't it?' Zakiy frantically looked around for the waiter without waiting for her reply, whilst at the same time keeping an eagle eye on her.

'No, it doesn't have anything to do with eating,' she said, grabbing his arm when he ignored her. 'Zakiy, seriously. I'll just drink some water and I'll be fine.' On good faith, Sathi reached for her untouched glass of jeera water and took a long drink.

'I still think you should eat something,' Zakiy said stubbornly, although he felt less anxious now that she was looking more like herself. The expression she'd had on her face had been that of a stranger. A stranger who, to be truthful, had scared him.

'About Aman,' Sathi began, but he interrupted her.

'No. Not until you've had something to eat.' He ignored her look of exasperation and finally caught the eye of the waiter, who was already heading their way with a determination that would put the Indian army to shame.

They didn't speak again until their meal had been served (including *karimeen pollichathu*, a dish consisting of fresh flatfish cooked inside a plantain leaf and fried to piping hot perfection). He watched Sathi with narrowed eyes until she had filled her plate and swallowed her first few mouthfuls.

Then he bought several more minutes by helping himself to the various dishes, even though he felt as though he had left his appetite somewhere back in the middle of the Antarctic. Immediately, Zakiy found himself side-tracked by the thought.

Can you leave your appetite in the Antarctic if you've never been there? *I suppose if the appetite is metaphorical, then it stands to reason that you can metaphorically leave it behind wherever you want to. Although, would you actually ever want to leave your appetite anywhere...? No! Stop it.*

Zakiy took in a deep breath and blew it out again. 'The only concrete plan I have at the moment is to finish this degree and go back to Mysore. I should be able to get a decent job there.'

He paused, bracing for those tendrils to raise their ugly heads. 'As for Aman, I'm not sure exactly what I'll do, but I'm sure as hell going to do everything I can that might help him get better.' Sure enough, old memories were threatening to break the surface, ones that he thought he had buried long ago.

Sathi, with a forkful of rice suspended in mid-air, frowned thoughtfully. 'Have you thought about taking him to a psychiatrist again? I know your dad tried everything, but that was years ago. There've been advances in medicine since then, haven't there?'

He nodded, not surprised that she'd got to the crux straightaway. Something weird was happening with those memories though. They were there but there was something different, something that made them fainter, the tendrils were behaving oddly... With great effort of will, he refocused on the conversation.

'Exactly. My father won't be keen on the idea - he's lost his trust in the medical profession, I reckon. I haven't, and I'm going to make sure I've exhausted all of the care that modern medicine can provide for Aman.'

His words had been filled with confidence, but within he felt an awful fear; what if there was no hope for his brother? What if all the king's horses and all the king's men weren't enough to put his Humpty Dumpty back together again?

Those tendrils, which had inexplicably begun to recede, rushed to the fore with renewed vigour, feeding off Zakiy's doubt and anguish. He was drowning again, the shore within reach, but his fingertips were slipping. '*We're* going to make sure of that.' Sathi's voice suddenly gave his fingers an unexpected hold, and the tendrils disappeared. They didn't just slink to the edges; they had gone altogether, a feat his defensive humour had never managed.

Zakiy stared at her, shocked beyond words at what she had said.

84

Sathi understood Zakiy's reaction; after all, she felt exactly the same way about the words that had just come out of her own mouth.

Okay, Sathi, what the hell are you playing at? Acting like an amateur psychologist is all well and good, but have you forgotten that you're here to find out who killed Amma? You can sympathise with Zakiy, but you can't randomly decide to trek over to Mysore, Karnataka! Besides, this is something he has to do on his own. His brother's illness is none of your business-

Her self-chastisement broke off abruptly when Zakiy leaned forward across the table and asked in deadly earnest, 'Sathi, will you come with me to Mysore?'

She panicked. 'What? No. No, look, I'm sorry. I didn't mean... I can't...' she trailed off awkwardly, filled with guilt and a strange, joyful desire to say yes. What was *wrong* with her?

She tried again. 'Zakiy, I'm really sorry – I don't know where that came from. It's not that I don't want to go with you. I would love to, if that's what you really want, but I can't leave Nelliampathi until I find out who murdered my mother.'

Sathi was astounded when she looked up to see Zakiy wearing his typical cheek-stretching grin. 'Ah, but you won't have to! We'll track down that beslubbering milk-livered pignut of a person together and deal with him and then we'll get the first train to Mysore!' he exclaimed with the air of someone explaining that one plus one equalled two.

Despite the gravity of what he was saying, she had to ask: 'Beslub what?' Was he even speaking a known language?

Zakiy's smile nearly split his face in half. 'Why, m'lady, don't tell me you haven't heard of the infamous Shakespearian formula for swear words?'

Still beaming, he reached into his pocket and pulled out a flattened old phone. He clicked through it for a few seconds and before Sathi could enquire whether he routinely sat on his phone to make it so flat, he handed it to her.

The screen showed three columns of the most bizarre collection of words she had ever seen. As far as instructions went, there was one line simply saying "Combine one word from each of the three columns below, prefaced with 'Thou'". The words "beslubbering", "milk-livered" and "pignut" were in the first, second and third columns respectively, nestled among other equally ridiculous archaic terms including yeasty, gorbellied, pribbling, boil-brained, fen-sucked, canker-blossom, jugger-mugger and interestingly, mumble-news.

Speechless, Sathi looked from the phone to its owner. She stared at him. Then she stared at him some more. Then, as her mind remained stubbornly blank, she decided that a bit more staring was in order. Finally the hilarity of the situation apparently became too much for Zakiy's self-control, and he started laughing in loud guffaws. At the carefree sound of it, Sathi's own restraint snapped and she joined in with her own only slightly hysterical laughter.

They eventually regained their composure, although half the restaurant was staring at them by that point, and sat there holding their sides.

'You. Are. Utterly. Insane!' Sathi managed to gasp out at last, although she had to admit that whoever had thought this up was a genius.

'Sathi, *darling*, we've gone over this before,' he responded, affecting a posh British accent. 'Don't keep telling me things I already know. It really makes me want to test the durability of your brain.' She couldn't think of a comeback that was biting enough, so she just kicked him again. Much harder.

As she waited for his melodramatic wails of pain to subside, her own indulgent smile faded. She had just remembered his proposition. Sathi mentally prepared herself, thinking of the right words, the ones that would convince him.

'Zakiy, it's very generous of you to offer to help me find the...' her smile was short-lived as she used his phrase, 'beslubbering milk-livered pignut that killed my mother. But I can't let you do that. You have to understand that this is something I have to do alone.'

'Firstly let's shorten him to the BMLP – the problem with these insults is that they're a bit of a mouthful. Secondly,' he continued, his expression becoming calculating, 'is there some rule that says you have to do this alone? Wouldn't it be nice to have someone who knows the people here better than you do and is also conveniently a brave knight sworn to protect you?'

Sathi was about to argue that the brave knight had better things to do with his time than babysit her when another voice, a remembered voice, rang through her mind: *You will fail in your purpose if you attempt it alone.*

Her eyes snapped to Zakiy's as she realised that the astrologer might not have been referring to her father after all. She remembered how she had met Zakiy at a point when she was feeling utterly hopeless about ever finding Amma's killer.

What if he'd been talking about Zakiy?

As though he had sensed victory, Zakiy slowly held out his arm over the table. An offer. Without another backward thought, Sathi reached out and, ignoring his outstretched fingers, grasped his forearm. His eyes widened as he realised what she was doing; as his long fingers closed around her own wrist, the pair sealed their alliance in an ancient gesture immortalised by the exquisite artwork defining a certain Tarot card.

Chapter Ten

Snatches of a Spirit

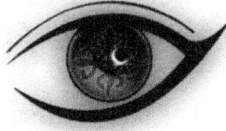

No. No. No. No.

The single syllable had become a mantra in Sathi's mind as she methodically went through the pile of old newspapers stacked in front of her, skimming the text of each article, one by one. To one side of her sat another, much smaller pile. Every time she saw it out of her peripheral vision, an odd shiver went through her.

In the background, she could hear Zakiy wittering on about how he was starving and fantasising about the pastries that would be available in the bakery next door to the library. His rambling should have been distracting; instead, it was the opposite. There was something about it that was soothing, like background music that you can tune in to when you feel like singing along, but ignore otherwise. If he did want to tell her something important, only the tone of his voice would change; when that happened, he would have her full attention.

No. No. No. She scanned the bold print of the article headings on the front page of the paper she was currently holding. "Eight-year-old rape victim responds well to treatment". *Like there's any kind of treatment in the world that can help a* child *survive something like that?* "The personal assistant of the Prime Minister has resigned." *Gee, thanks. Now I can sleep soundly at night.* Her tired crankiness combined with the reminder of the sheer amount of violence in the world was manifesting in sarcasm. How could they put something as trivial as news of a resignation on the same page as a child rape victim?

Wearily, she turned the page, bracing for more of the same. "Indians among those kidnapped". *Good Lord, the hypocrisy is endless! People are people; it's as simple as that.* Territory dispute over a footpath. More party politics. The current value of gold; ha! Casualties of a terrorist blast. Winner of a photograph competition (huh?) Then, of course, sports news, comic strips and the crossword.

Wishing she could do the Sudoku puzzle instead, Sathi set the newspaper in the discard pile on the vacant chair beside her and yawning, reached for another one. Her heart gave a strange lurch as the word "death" jumped out at her. But no. It was the obituary of some old politician who had apparently been beloved of the ruling party at the time.

Whatever. Choosing to ignore the bittersweet mixture of disappointment and relief swirling within her, she sneaked a sideways peek at Zakiy.

Despite the constant stream of nonsense emanating from him, Zakiy was making steady progress through his own heap of Malayalam papers (although his OCD tendency resulted in a stack that was far neater than hers).

It had been his idea to look through old newspapers for some clue about Amma. Just as they had first visited the local library three days ago at his suggestion; not that Sathi expected her mother to be in the news headlines but surely there must at least be an obituary, *some* record of the person who had given Sathi life? Of course, they had first checked the papers in the year 1996, when Amma had returned to India, but there had been nothing there of interest.

Unfortunately, Sathi didn't know exactly when her mother had been born, so there were a lot of years to cover. Multiply that by the average number of articles on a page, the number of pages in a newspaper and the number of different newspapers available, and you get such an obscenely large answer that you desperately try to divide it by an infinite number of tens in a fruitless attempt to diminish it to a more manageable value. Of course, having two people poring over the papers instead of one halved that mountain.

Even so, they had been feverishly reading for the past three days, with one or both of them always haunting this private corner, and had come up empty-handed.

No, that's not entirely true, Sathi corrected herself. She cut a glance at the mound of papers that had been put aside. They hadn't found anything useful that would help to solve the mystery of Amma's death, but they had recovered a treasure chest of a different type.

Every time she became tempted to give up with the tedious task they had undertaken, a glimpse of the articles set aside strengthened her resolve.

But first things first, she thought regretfully as she returned to the job at hand. For the next half-hour or so, there was only the sound of pages turning and paper crackling its pleasure at being handled with care. Even Zakiy had fallen silent after the librarian, in her cruelly starched sari, made her rounds and glared pointedly at him through thick convex lenses.

Then Zakiy gave an exclamation which Sathi guessed would bring the librarian on them in about five seconds flat. She lifted her head to hush him, afraid they would get thrown out. There were still so many papers to peruse.

The admonishment vaporised en route to her throat when she saw his triumphant expression. Her voice was a dumbstruck whisper, hindered somewhat by an emergency meeting of her blood vessels in the conference room of her heart. 'You found something?'

'Well, m'lady, why don't you decide that for yourself?' Zakiy replied mysteriously. 'Cast your eyes upon this picture and see if you recognise the small person grinning away at the camera.' With a flourish, he laid the newspaper clutched in his hand on the table in front of her and stepped back, allowing her an unobstructed view.

It was the third page of *The Hindu* newspaper, printed on the 5th April of the year 1982. The page was, as always, dense with a mass of text, but Sathi's gaze was drawn towards the photo above the short article at the bottom right corner.

She barely read the bold text, "13-year-olds win first prize in Junior Art Competition". Her eyes zeroed in on the girl who laughingly held up a big trophy, with her other hand clutching the wrist of a second girl with swinging pigtails and a studious face. They both stood to one side of a large glass exhibit showing an image of a life-sized woman carrying a woven basket; despite its intent as the focus of the photograph, Sathi only saw the display of the appliqué-work as extra details in an afterthought as she stared at her mother's adolescent self.

There was no doubt that the teenager was Madhubhala Kumar herself, because those young features - barring the curled unruliness of her black hair and the wide unreservedness of her smile - had been copied exactly onto her daughter; Amma's young, smooth coffee skin, rounded cheeks and dark almond-shaped eyes with their tangled lashes lived on in Sathi.

Those eyes were rapidly becoming oceans of water, and her throat was throbbing as it did before she came down with a cold, except that the sensation was a thousand times more intense. Sathi tried to blink the tears back quickly. She didn't want Zakiy to see her bawling like a baby. Control was beyond her, however; her chest tumultuous, her eyes stinging, she felt as if she was trying to hold a hurricane back with feeble arms.

Through it all she somehow heard someone clearing their throat, and she glanced up reflexively. He was looking at her, and when he spoke his tone was brusque but his eyes were unbearably gentle.

'I reckon I've earned the right to a delicious meal, including as many unhealthy delicacies that bakery can yield up as possible. Furthermore,' Zakiy continued pompously, 'it is my duty as a good citizen to introduce you to the amazing talent of Indians to make sweets and pastries - I'll even make a gallant effort to smuggle some in under the nose of the Stick-insect.'

Despite herself, Sathi snorted out a laugh, although it sounded deceptively like a sob once it had escaped the constraints of her throat.

The hawk-eyed, starched librarian did resemble a stick insect remarkably well. She managed a weak nod, and without further ado Zakiy gathered his wallet and walked noisily past her, laying his hand, warm and heavy, on her shoulder just for a moment as he passed.

Her eyes closed at the contact, and the flood started in earnest, pouring down her cheeks and blurring her vision until she could barely make out Amma's face on the soaked newspaper. She traced her free curls with her finger, the lines of her cheeks, her smiling lips, and leaned down and kissed the salty photo.

Her sweet Amma was not totally lost to her after all.

When Zakiy returned, she was waiting for him, dry-eyed and clutching a piece of paper that was decorated with her own handwriting. Before Sathi could say anything, he complained in a whisper, 'The Stick-insect caught me at it. She said I could either bin the goods or take them back to the shop. I just count myself lucky that she didn't tell me to raise my arms above my head and read me my Miranda rights.' He shook his head in mock disbelief before continuing, 'Anyway, I left them in the Jeep so we can go have a break now and come back after we've filled our stomachs to aching.'

Despite the casual tone of voice, Sathi knew he was watching her closely. She rose, gathering up a pile of printed sheets as well as the newspaper with Amma's photo on it.

'The idea of filling our stomachs sounds wonderful, but there's no need to come back here,' she replied, matching his nonchalant air as she took Zakiy's arm and started to lead him back towards the door of the library. He gave her a quizzical look, but she shook her head slightly and flicked her eyes across to the front desk, signalling that she'd fill him in later. She could feel the librarian's glare on their backs as they walked out into the rain.

The sweet droplets that hailed the monsoon fell like snowflakes, forming a seamless dome on every surface they touched. They soothed her itchy red eyes and ran like her miniature rivers down her arms, the short hairs forming convenient bridges.

92

Sathi shielded the papers under her T-shirt as they made a dash for the cover of Zakiy's Jeep, propelling themselves inside and banging the doors shut the instant before the rain intensified to violently slap against the roof and windscreen of the car like an angry god throwing a tantrum; she knew from experience that the water would feel like stones thundering against her body if she had had the misfortune to still be outside.

'Phew, that was close.' She looked over to see Zakiy sitting with his back against the door, grinning at her around the huge plastic bag set between the passenger and driver seat. The big red letters "Shanta Bakery" printed across the white plastic drew her eye.

She turned back to him. 'No wonder you couldn't smuggle that in. Did you buy out the whole store?'

'Of course I didn't!' Zakiy replied indignantly. 'Well, okay, maybe. I offered the owner a good price, obviously, but I think he's too attached to his shop. So naturally the next step was to buy everything and put him out of business until he's ready to yield.' He added, pointing at his own head, 'I've got *kishney,* you know.'

Sathi didn't even bother to respond to the first part of what he'd said, but she didn't recognise that last word he's used; 'What does kishney mean?' Maybe it was Hindi for brain tumour or something. That would certainly explain his idiocy.

Zakiy gave her a reproachful look. 'Come on, m'lady, you have to keep up with simple anatomy if you're to survive in this science-dominant society.' He indicated his head again before continuing, 'Kishney... kidney'.

She shook her head, wondering why she kept being surprised at the rubbish this moron came up with so diligently. 'You think your kidneys are in your head, and you say I need to have a better understanding of anatomy? Really?' Before he could say anything else equally hare-brained, she reached for the bakery bag and grabbed the first cardboard box her fingers touched. 'Here,' she said, opening it and taking out a bar of some sort of Indian sweet and stuffing it whole in Zakiy's mouth, 'maybe this will keep you busy for a while.'

Thankfully, it worked and whilst he chewed furiously she took a square of the sweet for herself, looking down at the scrap of paper that she still held in her hand as she bit into the pastry.

'Whazzat?' Zakiy asked, now licking his fingers. She flashed him a look of disgust and passed him a bottle of water to wash his hands.

'It's the address of the high school where Amma studied,' Sathi told him. 'The name was in the article about the exhibition and I asked the librarian whether she knew where it was.'

'Excellent! Let's see.' He reached for the paper, and as she juggled the sheets to hand it to him, the newspaper in her lap slipped down to the floor of the Jeep. Zakiy bent and retrieved it. 'How come you have the original of this but photocopies of the rest? Stick-insect didn't seem like the type to let you keep it out of sentimentality.'

Sathi shifted uncomfortably. 'Er, she said I had to pay a fine for it. It was in too bad a condition.' She didn't mention that it had been wrinkled and crusted with the salt of her tears once she was finished with it, but she was pretty sure that he guessed that part when he handed it back without further comment, extracting the address deftly from her quiet fingers as he did so.

He studied it silently for a minute. Then he started the engine, saying, 'It's in Nemmara. That's not far from here, so we can go right now.' He glanced at his watch. 'It's only a half-hour drive. There's enough time before school ends for the day.' He looked at her for confirmation and she nodded gratefully, thinking how lucky she was that she didn't even have to ask. He took initiative as if it were his own mother's school they were visiting.

She put the seatbelt on and settled into the seat as Zakiy pulled out onto the road. She thought about how selfless he was being; here he was, wasting his own time between a busy schedule at college to help her with this insane wild goose chase. In comparison, Sathi felt incredibly self-centred. Had she thought once about his brother since that day in the restaurant? Had she once asked after him?

She cleared her throat. 'How's Aman?' She saw raw pain flash across his face, and felt even more wretched. *Congratulations, Sathi.*

He replied before she could attempt to take back her words. 'He's okay. He came to the phone the other night when I was talking to my mum. He hasn't done that in ages.' He fell quiet, staring out of the rain-speckled windscreen, and then added, 'It felt good to hear his voice after so long.'

'I'm sorry,' she mumbled, hating herself for re-opening a fresh wound. Again.

He spared her a glance before turning back to the road. 'Don't be. I'm taking it as a good omen.'

'Omen?'

'Yep. I reckon it's a sign that Allah – my preferred version of God – approves of the idea of us working together.'

'About that,' she began, bracing herself to say the words, much as she didn't want to. It was time to stop being selfish, though. 'You really don't have to do this.'

'Do what?' Zakiy sounded genuinely puzzled.

Sathi gritted her teeth. 'This,' she repeated, gesturing around at the Jeep in general. 'You don't have to act like my chauffeur and pore over musty old newspapers and buy me food like you don't have a hundred and one better things to do!' She was breathing hard by the time she finished, and she felt on verge of tears again. She wished her chest wouldn't ache so much.

Zakiy pulled the Jeep over abruptly onto the bumpy sand of the roadside, eliciting a cacophony of honking from the other occupants of the road. He ignored their mouthed insults as they manoeuvred past him, and pulling up the handbrake, he twisted around in his seat so that he was facing her as before, his back propped against the driver door, only there was no trace of a grin on his face now.

'I'm not acting as your chauffeur,' he told her sternly. 'This is the job description of a good friend, and I'm all for doing a job well and enjoying myself in the doing. You would do the same for me, so don't ever blame yourself for wasting my time.'

When she didn't reply, he sighed and started looking for a space to get back onto the road amidst the heavy traffic. He continued,

'Anyway, I waste my own time far too much for you to claim any responsibility for the fact, so you can just wait your turn.' He glanced at her to see her staring disbelievingly at the saloon car ahead.

'Fine,' he said after a few minutes of silence on the road, 'You can think of the time I'm giving you now as a loan. You can pay me back with your own Sathi-time once we're in Mysore. Deal?' Zakiy flashed her the eye-crinkling grin she loved, making her smile back automatically. 'Oh and by the way, I don't have a hundred and one things to do.' Once again he shot her a grin, only this one was decidedly cockier. 'The last time I checked, it was only ninety-nine point nine.'

'Oww!' was the last thing he had to say regarding that particular topic of conversation. He did seem to have some difficulty in controlling the Jeep for a moment, though, and this may have been the reason for his abrupt, but necessary, renewed focus on the road ahead.

Chapter Eleven

Birds & Brooms

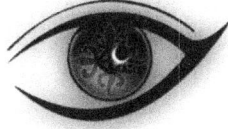

The sun shone forth feebly to illuminate the low, sloping roofs of the outdoor classrooms, the thatched shell held up by concrete pillars and the rooms aerated by the presence of low ledges that substituted for walls. A wide painted archway rose imperiously above the long building that encased the more sheltered classrooms and staff-rooms, and tall white letters proclaimed "*Kendriya Vidyalaya*", smug at their successful capture of the drops of rain that were even now proudly displayed on their surface.

The Jeep hovered in front of the intimidatingly tall front gate, complete with iron bars twisting to form the beautiful likeness of an enormous sunflower. Some part of Sathi's mind appreciated the symbolism: a place of education where children (supposedly) reached for knowledge just as flowers reached for the sun.

However, the hidden meaning that may or may not have been deliberate was a non-issue to most of her brain as Sathi had her first glimpse of Amma's school; the place where her mother had returned, morning after morning, to study, to talk and laugh with her friends, to play pranks. Had she played sports? Had she acted onstage? Had she had a favourite teacher, like Sathi did? This was the place where her mother had grown from a care-free girl to a young woman on the brink of college-life, ready for the fresh adventures that awaited her.

Including death.

Sathi was startled by the cynical malevolence of the thought, which had slipped through as if freshly escaped from an aerial flute. How could she have thought such a thing?

Guiltily, she peeked at Zakiy, as though he could somehow read the awful direction her thoughts had taken, and breathed a silent sigh of relief upon observing that he was pre-occupied in trying to park his Jeep into the empty space beneath a cherry blossom, which spread its bountiful branches in a wide circumference and formed a natural umbrella casting a cool shade over most of the parking area.

'Bird cherry, they call it,' he remarked as they hopped down from the Jeep, indicating the tree's low-hanging limbs.

Sathi glanced up, pushing to the back of her mind the guilt that her morose thought had brought on, and noticed that the fruit was smaller and more berry-like than the deep red cherries available in UK. The mostly lime-coloured berries hung from the copious boughs like a thousand globular earrings that had been fastened to the tree to beautify it.

She saw a cherry blushing enticingly at her among its green-skinned kin. She reached up and, plucking the berry from its fragile stem, popped it into her mouth. Wow! Her eyes closed of their own accord as the sweet juiciness of the cherry exploded against her tongue and the roof of her mouth. Even the skin had a crispy sweetness to it.

She looked up eagerly to see if she could spy any more of the gorgeous fruit... and her gaze lighted on Zakiy, who was regarding her with an expression somewhere between humour and incredulity. 'Hmmm.'

'What?' she demanded, feeling weirdly defensive.

'I was going to say, they call it bird cherry because only the birds seem to like it – people grow it for shade, not for the fruit.' He paused to raise an eyebrow at her. 'Now I know why you're so different; you're not a human at all, you're a bird masquerading in the skin of a girl, aren't you? Aren't you?'

Her irritation melted like ice when confronted with salt, and she rolled her eyes at him, replying on auto-pilot as she attempted to grab another ripe cherry that dangled just out of her reach. 'You've found me out. I was trying so hard to mask my true identity from you, but this cherry was just too much for my self-control.'

A longer arm pushed down the branch so that the red berry was within range of her extended hand. She took it and offered it to the owner of the arm. 'Why don't you try it before you slam it?' With a shrug, he accepted the fruit and swallowed after a couple of chews.

'Well?'

'It's nice,' he admitted. 'But,' he continued sternly, 'this does not mean I'm a bird.'

'Did you two come here to eat cherries, or did you have a different reason to visit the school?' The unfamiliar voice had them both jumping guiltily and turning around to face its source.

A middle-aged woman stood just beyond the generous breadth of the tree, wearing a shabby brown chiffon sari and a sheen of sweat on her dark brow. She held something that substituted for a broom in India. It was a bunch of what looked like thin long sticks tied together with a piece of string to discriminate handle from brush; the flexible twigs were held in a tight cylindrical structure nearer the string tie, providing a firm grip, whilst the longer section of the broom was allowed more freedom to sweep hard surfaces with amazing efficiency.

As she waited for an answer, the woman began to roughly knock the handle part of the broom onto the opened palm of her left hand. Although Sathi knew from experience of tidying her room at the resort that it was just a way to level the sticks so they did not slip out of the knot that kept them together and was something that had to be done frequently in the process of clearing a floor, she could not help but find the gesture vaguely threatening. The woman's grim expression did nothing to detract from Sathi's apprehension.

'Erm… we were just…um…' she floundered as she tried to think of a plausible reason for stealing cherries from the grounds of a high school. She glanced at Zakiy, the master of improvisation. After all, he was her self-appointed knight in armour. It was his job to get her out of such scrapes. He seemed to remember his responsibility, because he shook off his surprise. Then he opened his mouth and said, 'We were testing the cherries to make sure they're suitably delectable for the consumption of the students here.'

What? I am going to kill *him!*

Sathi, aghast, looked from the master of idiocy to the woman, furiously wracking her brains to find some way of damage control, and was stunned when she saw the woman's stern air relax into a smile, a thousand lines regenerating on her face in response to her good humour. Her onyx eyes sparkled. 'Is that so? Then I thank you profusely for your kindness,' she paused and her grin intensified. 'Now that you have performed your good deed you can be on your way.' She glanced pointedly at Zakiy's Jeep.

Cue my interference. 'Actually, we're here to, um…' No, "find out about my dead mother's school life" won't do. No way. 'To find some information about an old friend of mine, who used go to this school.' It wasn't a complete lie. If Amma was alive she would have been Sathi's friend, she was sure of it. She held her breath, wondering if the woman would accept her story.

To her relief, she stopped brandishing the makeshift broom like a weapon and seemed to be weighing her words. 'And how do you plan on accomplishing that?'

Good question. Then Sathi reined in her errant thoughts to focus. *Stick to the truth.* 'We were hoping to talk to the head teacher here.' She could see Zakiy staring at her, but her attention was fixed solely on the woman in front of her.

'I see,' she replied. She seemed to withdraw slightly and then a sudden gleam appeared in her eyes, which contrasted with her dishevelled appearance. She appraised Sathi, from her rain-peppered

T-shirt all the way down to simple white Hawaii slippers, next directing her scrutiny back up to inspect Sathi's bare neck.

Sathi tucked her hair behind her ear self-consciously as the woman, appearing disheartened, switched her sharp gaze to Zakiy, giving his trendy green button-up shirt and dark grey slacks a more appreciative look. She shot another glance at the Jeep, although it was more calculating now than humorous. Finally her eyes returned to meet Sathi's impatient – not to mention irritated – gaze.

'Well, one of you should be able to get something out of her.'

'What?'

'Her?'

Sathi and Zakiy looked at each other, and then back at the source of the cryptic remark. An amused smirk greeted them, and the woman seemed to be choosing her words carefully as she spoke. 'I think you will find that our Headmistress will require some – how do I put it – motivation to give you the information you want.'

Sathi stared back into those bottomless black eyes, trying to discern the innuendo the woman was obviously putting on her words.

'What do you mean?' Zakiy's tone was a reflection of the same confusion and frustration she was feeling.

The woman shrugged and replied, 'What I said. I can't make it any clearer.'

Sathi had had enough of this cat and mouse game. 'In that case, why don't you do something useful and take us to the Headmistress's office,' she snapped. 'It's her we need to talk to.' She didn't add 'Not you', but the sentiment nevertheless reverberated in the vacuum that followed her words.

Far from becoming offended, the woman's patronising smile widened to resemble that of the Cheshire Cat. She turned abruptly, looking over her shoulder at them and commanding, 'Come with me', before heading in the vague direction of the oblong building that housed the indoor classrooms, and hopefully, the Head's office. Sathi exchanged a look of mutual understanding with Zakiy before hurrying to do Her Majesty's bidding.

Issues. The woman has issues.

They were led through the expansive front grounds of the school, which mostly consisted of bushy emerald trees and a multi-coloured array of shrubs that had been tamed into submission in order to form the basis of a gorgeous garden. On either side of the narrow stone-lined driveway that snaked through the middle of the floral display, the trees seemed to enclose them from above as their sprawling branches rose to form a hood of deep mossy green. They filtered the rapidly fading sunlight, a natural sieve separating different wavelengths of light; only the unwanted jade permeated the flesh of the leaves, with their veins jutting out like the endoskeleton of a vertebrate.

As they passed the thatched outdoor classrooms, Sathi's eyes were drawn towards the numerous long wooden benches and matching desks that filled each room, all occupied by students eagerly awaiting the end of the school day. Many turned to stare as they walked past, and though Sathi's gaze swept each in turn, in her mind every single one was a replica of her adolescent mother.

She was filled with wistful questions: *Did Amma sit at that bench? Did she lean her arms on that desk when she was bored with a lesson? Did she sit with her feet up at break, chatting with a friend while her dark hair swung to frame her face?* An image of the other girl in the newspaper photo, the one with the pigtails, filled in the place of her mother's companion in Sathi's imagination. *I wonder how close they were. Was she Amma's best friend?*

The sight of the school's elaborate stage, decorated with grand gold curtains and glowing trinkets and an ornate lamp waiting to be lit for some sort of celebration in the near future, caused all thoughts of the other girl to become superseded by new questions: had Amma liked acting? Had she performed before an audience full of people? Had she danced? Had she liked to sing?

Sathi glanced at the woman walking in front of them and impatiently wished she would accelerate to a velocity that was faster than 0.2 mph. She was distracted from boring a hole into the back of the woman's head with her eyes when Zakiy sidled closer to her, and after a furtive glance at the woman's retreating form, leaned down to speak in a low voice. 'Do we really have to talk to the headmistress?'

She looked up at him in surprise, and whispered, 'Yeah, of course we do. She's our best shot at finding out about my Amma.'

He didn't reply, and walked on at her side in silence with a weird expression on his face. Sathi frowned down at the floor, thinking. She remembered the way he had stared at her when she first expressed the wish to talk to the Head. What had he expected? It was true that she hadn't spelt out her intention beforehand, but she had thought it was the obvious thing to do once they reached the school.

She bumped him from the side. 'What's up?' she asked.

He shook his head stiffly. 'Oh, come on, what?' He snuck a look at her, and shook his head again more forcefully. 'You'll make fun of me,' he muttered in an undertone.

He was afraid of being made fun of? He was such a nutty character. 'I give you my solemn oath that I won't make fun of you,' Sathi murmured, her curiosity winning the war it had been waging with her amusement.

'I'm...I've...' he shot the woman another cautious glance before continuing. 'I've got a phobia of head teachers,' he admitted in a muttered breath.

'Huh?' said Sathi succinctly. She was prevented from saying much more (not that she had any idea what to say) because the woman had finally stopped in front of a set of closed mahogany doors after leading them up a few steps onto the west-facing edge of the large building, which was shaped like an inverted E with the middle wedge broken off, leaving a large open space in front that seemed to be used as a playground.

Sathi barely had time to read the plaque above the expansive doors, "Dhayalakshmi Nair, Headmistress", before the woman they had been following knocked sharply on the wood. The echoing raps faded away as one door creaked open.

A feminine laugh floated through the doorway like fragrant perfume, and a soft voice trilled, 'Oh, I'm so sorry, Minister. What with looking after six hundred students, I never know a moment's peace!'

Sathi could faintly hear a deep male voice rumble something in reply, and the shiny rear of an intricately coiled mane of hair became visible for a moment before the owner of the voice turned away from her visitor at last.

The Headmistress stepped out onto the shallow veranda that decorated her office wing, the royal blue silk of her sari giving way temporarily to expose the golden straps of the high heels that encased dark, petite feet with toenails painted the exact shade of sapphire as her dress. As she cleared the doorway she pulled the door closed with a soft thud and turned to direct her gaze at the woman who had led them; the lack of grey in her plaited bun of black hair belied the age suggested by the thick make-up, which attempted, unsuccessfully, to disguise her wrinkles.

Her heavily-lined eyes became cold and hard as she snapped, 'Sheila, where's the tea for the minister? Can't you do anything you're told?'

Sathi was shocked at the vitriol that spiked the Headmistress's previously melodic voice. She glanced at Sheila, aka Her Majesty, who appeared positively scruffy when compared with this perfectly groomed woman; she was flushed and there was no trace of the sneer that had infuriated Sathi earlier as she replied demurely, 'I'll bring it now, madam.' She paused.

The Headmistress made an impatient noise at the back of her throat. 'What is it?'

Sheila looked at Sathi and Zakiy. The Head seemed to notice them for the first time, and gave them a cursory glance before returning her heavy gaze to her servant. 'Who are they?'

'They asked to see you, madam,' Sheila said.

The Headmistress regarded them again, and finally spoke. 'I am entertaining someone at present,' she told them, twitching her gaze between her and Zakiy. 'If you want to talk to me you will have to wait. Or you will have to return at some other time.'

Zakiy moved forward slightly and said hurriedly, 'We'll wait.' Sathi nodded her acquiescence after shooting him a questioning look.

'All right. You can sit there,' she responded shortly, pointing at the small row of plastic chairs that had been laid out to one side of her office doorway. 'Sheila, bring that tea immediately. I must not keep the Minister waiting any longer.'

The words cracked the air in a premonition of the crash of the door against its frame as Headmistress Dhayalakshmi Nair disappeared back into her office in a swirl of blue silk.

Sheila headed back down the steps without another glance at either of them.

Chapter Twelve

Homo Sapiens *In Situ*

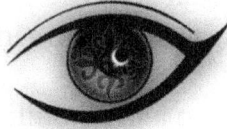

Zakiy sighed in relief and moved to one of the chairs, plopping himself down inelegantly and glancing up at her expectantly. After a moment, Sathi followed suit.

'That was unexpected,' she huffed out as she sank into a chair. Now that she had been forced to think about it, she realised that she had been picturing someone warm and welcoming as her mother's old Headmistress; this aloof, impeccably attired woman was jarring to that image.

'I know, right?' he retorted. 'It went much better than I thought it would.'

'What?' she hissed.

He looked back at her in surprise. 'I fully expected her to pounce on us like a lioness.'

She couldn't believe it. 'Er, she did pounce on us. And what about Sheila?' The Headmistress had treated her like a slave, humiliated her in front of strangers. No one had the right to behave like that, not a headmistress, not even a queen.

'Sathi, this is the standard,' he replied after a moment, speaking quietly. 'At least she didn't say flat out that she can't see us – she gave us the option to wait.'

Hold on. He called that command an option? She was getting angry now - how could he defend that woman?

'Why are you so eager to suck up to her, anyway?'

Zakiy ignored that. 'Don't you think you're overreacting just a little bit? She didn't actually say anything except that we'll have to wait because she's busy. And we both got irritated at Sheila, remember?'

Instead of glaring and stalking away like she wanted to, she thought about what he was saying. Mulling over their conversation, she had to admit to herself reluctantly that Zakiy was right. That *was* all she'd said. And as for Sheila... well, to be honest the Headmistress hadn't even been as rude as Sathi had been to Sheila in the parking lot.

She frowned. If that was the case, then why had she reacted to the Headmistress with such dislike? Was it simply because she hadn't met Sathi's expectations?

Sathi compared her to Mr Sonsrac, who was now the Assistant Head at her old school: a fact that she had constantly kept forgetting because he never changed his behaviour depending on who he was talking to or put on airs like this woman did. It had been the Headmistress's body language that spoke louder than her words.

'Sathi.' She looked up, her eyes filled with frustration. Zakiy continued, 'I know you must be used to a more approachable person as HM, but this is the norm for most Indian schools. They tend to value respect more than amiability.'

She was sick to death of talking about head teachers. 'Look, let's just agree to disagree,' she replied tersely. She glanced around for a source of inspiration to change the subject, and saw another cherry blossom, a younger one, standing sentry to one side of the steps that led up to the Headmistress's office.

She turned back to Zakiy with a stern expression that was not too difficult to fake. 'I have a bone to pick with you, Mr Brave-Knight-in-

Shivon Mirza Sudesh

Shining-Armour. I'm thinking of reducing your monthly salary due to shoddy work.'

He was instantaneously indignant. 'What shoddy work?'

'What did you say to Sheila - that we were checking the taste of the cherries? Was that really the best you could come up with?'

He was quick to defend himself. 'Hey, it worked, didn't it?'

'Yes,' she conceded. She smiled sweetly at him. 'That's why I'm not making you redundant.'

Before he could retaliate, Sheila returned with a glass filled with creamy tea and left again just as quickly after silently passing it through the doorway of the Headmistress's office. Sathi stared after her, the mock spat with Zakiy forgotten as she bit down hard on her lower lip.

'So, what's my name?'

The question startled her; she gaped at Zakiy. 'Do you have amnesia or something?' she enquired tentatively.

'No, no, I meant my official name,' he replied, seeming impatient that she hadn't understood straightaway. 'You can't keep calling me Mr Brave-Knight-in-Shining-Armour. It's way too long. Although I must say I like the sound of it.' He went off into dreamy state for a few moments before returning to earth and continuing, 'Anyway, knights must have a name starting with "Sir", you know.'

Sathi nodded seriously. 'How about Sir Stupid?' she suggested. 'It even alliterates.'

'Hmmm... I see the merit in it,' he responded, stroking his clean-shaven chin thoughtfully. 'But no,' he said decisively. 'It has to simply ring with glamour.'

'Sir Idiot? Sir Moron? Sir Obtuse? Sir Nut?' She kept up a steady stream of ideas, enjoying herself immensely.

'I've got it!' Zakiy exclaimed triumphantly after a few minutes. 'Sir Galliant!'

She snorted unattractively. 'Gallant? You?' she teased.

'It's Gall*iant*, not gallant. *I* like it.' Now he looked like a petulant little boy, with his lips pouting. Impossible to refuse.

'Fine. You can be Sir Galliant.' She sighed dramatically. 'But I had my heart set on Sir Obtuse.'

'Pah!'

An attendant in khaki brown work clothes took hold of the large bronze circle that was tied to the metal bar on the ceiling in front of the Head's office doorway, and lifted an object that resembled a hammer, except that it had a rounded head like a pendulum instead of jagged teeth.

Clang! Clang! Clang! The resonance was damped only lightly due to air resistance, and the bell rang unhindered throughout the saturated school grounds. Within five minutes a small group of about ten students, both boys and girls alike, of ages ranging from twelve to eighteen, had congregated in the middle of the long corridor that adjoined the Head's wing to the east-facing block of the main building. Their rain-dampened clothes rustled as they fell into formation, displaying the efficiency of a well-aerated combustion reaction, with the older, taller students arranging themselves stoically behind the excitable younger children.

The attendant directed an uncertain glance at the closed doors embellishing the HM's office before raising his mallet again. Clang! The manual bell tolled once more to signal the stilling of the bored fidgeting of the choir of uniformed pupils and the rise of the students and teachers alike to their feet in the outdoor classrooms.

Zakiy realised what was happening, and had just enough time to stand up, pulling on Sathi's arm to force her to do the same, and whisper in her ear, 'They're going to sing the national anthem.' The recital began, the high soprano of the younger ones mingling fluidly with the deeper, melodious tone of the near-adults.

'Jana-gana-mana adhinayaka jaya hé
Bharata bhagya vidhata...'

Zakiy added his own bass to the mix as he joined in whole-heartedly with the school's token of respect to its home country, remembering with fierce pleasure his own schooldays of singing to the gorgeous tune and reliving the joyful pride he used to feel each time. Echoed by every human being occupying the various buildings of the school, the words rang out unique and distinct, their intonation as flawless as their meaning.

Thou art the ruler of the minds of all people,
Dispenser of India's destiny.
Thy name rouses the hearts of Punjab, Sindh,
Gujarat and Maratha,
Of the Dravida and Odisha and Bengal;
It echoes in the hills of the Vindhyas and Himalayas,
Mingles in the music of Yamuna and Ganga and is
Chanted by the waves of the Indian Ocean.
They pray for thy blessings and sing thy praise.
The saving of all people waits in thy hand,
Thou dispenser of India's destiny.
Victory, victory, victory to thee.

'Jaya hé, jaya hé, jaya hé
Jaya, jaya, jaya... jaya hé!'

The last tremulous note lingered in the air like a half-forgotten dream, and soon became lost in a flurry of activity as the newly-freed children made a rush for the sunflower-adorning school gate, a sea swirling with midnight blue and white swept along on its own enthusiasm.

He glanced across at Sathi, curious to see her reaction to the anthem; she was standing with her eyes tightly shut, her lips lifted softly at the corners and the wavy black hair framing her rapturous expression like a curtain that has been drawn back to glimpse the early-morning sunrise. Her eyes opened as Zakiy watched, and they met his in wonder.

'Wow.'

'Yep,' he agreed. 'Wow.' There was nothing more to be said.

The Headmistress's door, which had remained firmly closed throughout the singing of the national anthem, finally cracked open. The HM stepped outside with the current Education Minister of Kerala in tow, a tall, portly man wearing a white shirt and *mundu*, his dark hair artistically greyed to display his age to his full advantage. They remained in deep conversation, even as the Headmistress led the Minister down the steps and towards the ambassador car that awaited, complete with driver.

'Thank you so much for coming, Minister,' she said at last, her voice a pleasing carol. 'I look forward to you inaugurating our new indoor auditorium tomorrow. We can discuss the last few details about your generous donation then.'

'Of course, Mrs Nair, of course,' came the ponderous reply, and the Minister placed his thick palms together in a gesture that the Headmistress mirrored with her own well-manicured hands, and got into his car, installing himself atop white seat-covers depicting the saffron and green hues of the Indian flag. The HM stood watching the car drive off, the whining siren cutting a smooth path through the school children who were still pouring out of the gate.

'Zakiy!' The frantic whisper drew his attention back to Sathi. 'I'll talk to her alone.'

He stared at her. 'What? Why?' Didn't she want him there?

'Because, you know,' she faltered. 'Because of your phobia.'

'Oh.' The breath he hadn't realised he'd been holding burst out of him in a relieved chuckle. 'It's no big deal. I was just kind of kidding around with you earlier.' He continued brazenly, 'Remember, it's my duty as Sir Galliant to never stray from your side, however big or scary the dragon.'

'Are you sure?' she persisted, her wide brown eyes intensely seeking reassurance.

'A hundred percent,' he asserted, berating himself silently for letting his silly schoolboy fear of the head-teacher figure get the better of him, however momentarily.

'Okay.' Only now did she allow her expression to display her need for company; he knew then that he had done the right thing. He grinned confidently at her and turned to watch the HM make her way back towards them, the blue strip of sari that hung over her left shoulder flaring out behind her. When she drew level with them, she gazed at both of them in turn with that heavy stare of hers.

'Come in,' she said imperiously once she had completed her scrutiny, leading the way inside her office. As hinted at by the extravagant double doors that opened out into it, the room was spacious and painted a light cream to match the exterior of the school building. A large Godrej steel desk occupied most of the square area, with chairs on one side of it not unlike the ones they had vacated not long before. On the walls hung framed proof of the various awards that the school had received over the years and a glass showcase hugging one wall served its purpose well by displaying numerous trophies won for sports and arts.

The HM gestured them onto the plastic chairs after taking her seat on the decidedly more comfortable, not to mention expensive, swivel chair on the side of the desk opposite them.

'Now,' she said, 'you are too old to seek admission for yourselves and too young to seek it for your children. So why did you want to see me?'

'Ms Nair, we...' Sathi began, but she was interrupted immediately.

'You will address me either as Headmistress or as madam.'

Sathi gave Zakiy a quick sideways look. 'Erm, right, madam, we've come to ask about...' She cleared her throat. 'About a student who used to study at this school. She would have been here during the years 1980 to 1987.' Sathi must have done the calculations earlier because there was no hesitation as she rattled off the dates. 'Her name was Madhubhala Kumar.'

The HM fingered the golden nameplate in front of her in silence, tracing the embossed alphabets that declared that she was Dhayalakshmi Nair, B.Ed.

I just hope she really is a dhaya *Lakshmi, as her name claims*, Zakiy thought wryly. Finally she spoke. 'I was not working at this school during those years. Even if I was, I could not possibly give out details about a student, present or former.'

He could see that the news had hit Sathi hard; she'd probably wanted to speak to the headmistress who had been at the school when her mother had been studying here, someone who had actually known her personally. Although Sathi was telling herself that she was only trying to find out about her mother's life in order to get clues about her killer, Zakiy knew she craved knowledge about her Amma as a man wandering the dry sand of the desert craved water. Sathi's mirage had just been shattered.

'Do you have the address of the person who was head teacher at that time?' he asked, giving Sathi the opportunity to compose herself. He heard the stiffness of his own voice, and knew it was an externalisation of the inner distrust he felt of the Headmistress.

The HM's finely plucked eyebrows rose. 'I thought you wanted information about a former student, not a former headmistress.' Zakiy was silent. He remembered this typical sarcastic tongue of old.

'We want both.' Sathi's voice had the unmistakable tone of defiance in it, and he saw that she was regarding the Headmistress with a look that bordered on a glare.

'Well, I'm sorry,' the HM replied. 'I cannot help you with either.' She paused meaningfully. 'Unless, of course, you can help me in turn.'

With a white hot streak of anger, Zakiy realised what she was getting at; before he could let his temper get the better of him, he took a deep breath, reminding himself that they were here for a very important reason, and that it would not be constructive to give the over-dressed old woman in front of them a resounding slap. He pushed aside his indignation and thought quickly. He remembered the last letter he had received from his parents and gave himself a mental nod. Yes, he should be able to arrange for...

'But how can we help you?' Sathi's frustrated voice interrupted his thoughts. 'Please, madam,' she pleaded, 'at least try to find out the college where Madhubhala went to after she left here.' She hesitated as though she had to force herself to say her next words: 'She... she was my mother. Please.'

The Headmistress acted as if she hadn't heard the raw grief in her broken voice, and pulled a pile of papers towards her, untying the string that bound it. 'Please see yourselves out. I have a lot of work to complete.'

Sathi stood up, a dangerous calm in her posture. She placed both of her palms on the desk, and leaned forward until her face was level with that of the Headmistress's. The clear, young eyes bored into the old, kohl-lined ones. 'Go to hell.'

Without another word, she turned and marched out of the room, the doors banging behind her as though a hurricane had just passed through.

Zakiy remained looking at the older woman, who continued to ignore him steadily. The proposition he had meant to put forward rose to his tongue, but he couldn't bring himself to say it; he suddenly found the synthetically perfect face in front of him unbearably repulsive. He got to his feet.

'You should be ashamed to call yourself the headmistress of a school,' he told her, and followed Sathi's path through the double doors of the empty shell of an office.

Chapter Thirteen

Turkey 007

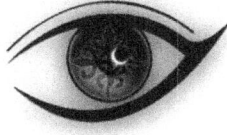

Zakiy found Sathi glaring up at the elaborately decorated stage in the encroaching darkness with her fists tightly clenched and arms crossed as though they would never straighten again.

'Forty-five minutes,' she muttered when he drew level with her.

'What?' he blurted, startled.

'Forty-five minutes!' Sathi repeated, almost shrieking in her rage as she whirled to face him, her flashing eyes livid. 'That's how long she kept us waiting while she simpered to that minister. God knows how long she'd been crawling to him before we *interrupted*.' She put a sarcastic twist on the word as she emitted it with distaste.

All for money. 'She wanted a bribe, you know,' Zakiy told her. She looked at him, the brown of her irises inseparable from her black pupils under the shadow of the approaching night.

'Of course,' she replied. 'That was the "help" she wanted from us. I should have guessed.' She stopped to shake her head in disbelief. 'Is this what it means to be a headmistress?'

'Not all of them are like this.' His resolve wavered, and he continued, 'Sathi, I've got some money in the bank here. We can take it out tomorrow morning and then come back here.' His parents had sent the cash to pay last month's instalment of his college fees, but he could explain things to them and pay it back later. Sathi's need was greater than his.

She gazed at him with a slightly glazed expression, as though she didn't quite understand what he was saying. Then something truly spectacular happened. She exploded.

'No way in hell will we pay that *thing* a penny!' Sathi stormed at the top of her voice, not giving a damn about anyone who might be listening. 'Who does she think she is? Does she think she can sit on her cushy little chair and manipulate anyone under her nose for money? Is that where cash for the school goes, into her silk saris and Chanel make-up? This is what happens when small-minded people are given power, it goes and scrambles their tiny little brains and they start to think they're God! Why should you give her money? To look something up on a computer? Even if I have to go back to that library and stay there for a month reading old newspapers, I won't let you pay that -'

'Madhu?'

The fight taken out of her as though she was a balloon pricked by a pleasantly sharp needle, Sathi spun to confront the owner of the enquiring voice that had so casually uttered her mother's name. Zakiy moved to her side in an unconscious, but swift, gesture and together they gazed upon the strange apparition that had detached itself from the shade of the stage; he was medium height, bespectacled, with a greying moustache and decorative goatee, and appeared for all the world to be a trendy, but harmless, old grandpa. However, one distinguishing feature destroyed this optical illusion at second glance. There shone behind his spectacles a certain protruding glimmer that assured those beholding it that the person they had in their company, in that poor, rattling brain of theirs, had a multitude of spare parts and screws loose.

'Is that you, my dear girl?' He squinted through his fogged lenses at the mute Sathi, and took a step forward to get a better look. The smoking cigarette in which he had obviously been indulging under the cover of the dwindling daylight dropped unheeded to the floor.

The man seemed to give himself a little shake after a few moments of the stunned silence that greeted him. 'No, of course you're not. She'd be all grown up now. Yes. I am sorry, child, I'm finding that age and confusion are too friendly with each other and too afraid of separation to grow at different rates. Yes.'

He couldn't seem to help continuing to stare at her, despite his contrite words. 'It's uncanny how familiar you look, though,' he added. 'I must be getting muddled in my old age. Yes. And yet,' he hesitated. 'Yet, the way you were speaking just now, you sounded just like Madhu, this girl I used to teach, when she was having one of her rants. Yes. That same expression, that same ferocity.' He smiled, his wistful fondness for the young girl he had known evident in every ridge and line of his face.

Sathi at last found the diffident voice that had been so obliging when she was employing it at full volume less than five minutes previously. 'No,' she said, her tone a brittle instrument. 'I'm not her, though I wish I was.'

'You know her, do you?' the old man asked eagerly.

Zakiy's heart tore at the melancholy in the voice that answered. 'No. I never knew her.' She seemed unable to continue. He glanced back at the man, who, bewildered, seemed to be about to question Sathi further, and deterred the attempt by asking, 'Is there somewhere we can talk in private? It's Madhu we've come to ask about.'

The man ripped his eyes away from Sathi. 'Yes, of course. We can go to my office. Yes. That's what we can do. Follow me.' With an agility that was at odds with his silver-grey hair, he made an about-turn and started heading back towards the long E-shaped building. When they made no move to tail him, he looked back at them quizzically, and said with a sudden mischievous smile that left no doubt that he had guessed the subject of Sathi's outburst, 'It's okay. We'll take a long cut around the opposite wing of the Head's office.'

Zakiy shrugged at her and began to follow, but Sathi tugged him to a stop, allowing the old man to pull ahead. 'Zakiy, I really did try to be more open-minded towards that woman after what you said, but she... she's a...' she trailed off, rendered helpless by her disgust.

He helpfully supplied, 'She's a spleeny earth-vexing giglet. I couldn't agree more.'

A reluctant laugh burst out of her, and she caught him unawares with a sudden hug, murmuring as she squeezed, 'Thank you for offering to bribe her.' She paused, and shook head at how that sounded. 'You know what I mean. I didn't mean to erupt like that when you suggested it. I really am grateful.'

He made a croaking noise that made it sound as though his throat was being vacuum-cleaned, and rasped, 'Can't... breathe...' Sathi let go of him after giving a death crush in revenge for his theatrics, and he told her, miraculously recovered, 'I quite like you when you erupt – as long the eruption isn't directed at me, that is. So please, keep it up.'

Then offering his elbow, Sir Galliant escorted his giggling Lady to the mad prof's office. It turned out to be an empty classroom; it was a cleaner's ultimate nightmare, with papers strewn all over the desk, pens rolling on their cylindrical axes and threatening to fall either this moment or the next, a blackboard smudged with chalk-drawn numbers and equations, and an avalanche of to-be-marked notebooks cascading down from the desk onto the chair. The mad prof, as Zakiy had impulsively christened him, swept up a couple of books that had decided that the short distance from desk to chair was not enough to constitute a real adventure, and had braved the perilous journey all the way to the black oxide floor. He straightening up, and deposited them on top of the already disintegrated heap on the desk. An outdated old computer monitor sat precariously in a corner as though it was a fat guppy placed most unceremoniously in a mug of coffee instead of its familiar old water bowl.

The prof neglected the chair full of books and perched on the edge of his desk, encouraging them to do the same on the various long desks that lined the room.

'So, you want to ask about Madhu, do you?' he said. 'Yes. Yes, a splendid girl, no doubt about it. Yes. How do you know her?'

Zakiy glanced at Sathi, who answered his silent question by replying, 'She's my aunt, but I've never met her because I've been raised in the UK. We're trying to find her since she's my only relative in India.'

Only he witnessed the way her middle finger was raised slightly above her index one, the subtlest crossing of fingers. Zakiy saw plainly why she had chosen a harmless lie instead of the painful truth. He would have done the same himself faced with a man who had a grandfather's doting adoration for her mother.

'I see. Yes, I can see the family resemblance. Yes. Well, my dear, I would be glad to help all I can, but I'm afraid we lost contact with each other a long time ago.' He added, 'Yes', a syllable he seemed especially partial to.

Of course they knew that already. 'That's all right, sir,' Zakiy interjected. 'If you could just tell us which college she went to, that would be most helpful.'

A dreamy expression crossed his heavily crinkled face. 'Ah yes. It took her a long time, you know, to choose which subjects she wanted to carry on with. Yes. Too good at everything, she was, and yet her main hobby was playing the fool.' He smiled, and his tone had that indulgent depth which makes all criticisms weigh less than a hummingbird's feather.

'An ace mathematician, of course, yes, brain like a computer,' he continued. 'Bright as an infinity-watt bulb. Yes. She should have made Maths her main subject, but she chose Chemistry, along with Physics added on. Yes.' He sniffed, as though the memory of his pet student's betrayal still rankled after twenty odd years. Sathi, unfamiliar with how college worked in India, shot Zakiy a puzzled look. He signalled to her that he would explain later, and prompted the mad maths prof (newly re-christened), 'Do you remember where she studied?'

'Yes, now, that's a more difficult matter. Yes,' he said decisively. The old prof thought for a while, clicking his tongue in an unconscious habit. 'Now, which one was it?' he asked his blackboard, as though the formulae written on it would rearrange itself to form the name of the college. 'Yes. It was... it was in Trivandrum... I know! It was Mar Gregorios! Yes!'

'Sir,' Zakiy began hesitantly, unwilling to dash cold water on the triumphant expression of the prof or the excited one of Sathi's, 'Isn't that a law college?'

'Oh. Oh dear. Yes. I believe you are quite right. Yes.'

Abashed, the maths teacher chewed his lip, his brow lined with thought. Presently, his face lit up with realisation. 'Yes, I remember now. It was Lourdes Matha Institute.'

Zakiy sighed. 'That's for hotel management.'

'Oh no, I was sure that was it. Yes. Wait, no, it was PMS.'

'What?' Sathi looked at the prof in disbelief.

Zakiy shook his head at her. 'Dental college.'

'St Stephens?' Mad prof looked at Zakiy pleadingly.

He frowned. 'Isn't that in Delhi?'

'What about Anugraha Matha?'

It was Zakiy's turn to give the prof an incredulous look. 'That's a nursery school!' he exclaimed.

Mad prof looked crushed. 'Yes,' he agreed miserably.

By this point, Sathi seemed quite prepared to strangle the poor old prof. Then his abysmal memory struck a match just long enough for him to save himself.

'She sent me a letter! Yes, yes, yes! Madhu sent me a letter a few weeks after she joined college, telling me all about it. When all this new technology started to make letters obsolete, I made my son scan it and email it to me. I can find it in a jiffy! Yes,' saying which, he lunged for his dilapidated old computer and began to coax it to life. Five minutes later, the trio were staring at a rather pixelated version of the Hotmail login page.

The mad maths prof rapped his knuckles against the desk and clicked away maddeningly with his tongue. 'Now, what was my password?'

'Mmmphh!'

Startled at the noise, Zakiy glanced over at Sathi to see her standing with her body angled away from them, trying to hide the fact that one of her fisted hands was stuffed into her mouth to muffle her scream of frustration.

'Are you all right, dear? I have some cough syrup, if you want it.' Full of blundering goodwill, the old prof gazed at Sathi in concern.

Guessing that attention drawn towards her would be the most dangerous thing possible at the moment, Zakiy distracted him, assuring, 'She's fine. The password, think of the password, sir.' Struck with sudden inspiration, he suggested, 'Is it your wife's name, or something like that?'

The prof looked back at him rather blankly out of his thick-rimmed glasses. 'Maybe. Yes,' he answered. He paused, and asked Zakiy in a mildly curious tone, 'What's my wife's name?'

Zakiy recoiled and shot a horrified glance towards Sathi, from whom explosive sounds were now emanating. 'Er, I don't know, sir,' he muttered, feeling utterly out of his element with this man. He recalled a Facebook post he had once guffawed over: "Some people aren't just missing the odd screw. The whole freakin' toolbox is gone!" The mad prof seemed to be the finest specimen of one such distinguished individual. Zakiy admitted to himself that he was fighting a losing battle, and tried to discern which of his college friends would be best accomplished in the fine arts of hacking.

'Turkey 007!' the prof suddenly exclaimed, and began to feverishly peck at the old keyboard. Even though he knew it was pointless, Zakiy couldn't give up the opportunity: 'Your wife's name is Turkey?'

'Yes. What? No, no, it's my favourite bird. Yes. Why would it be my wife's name?' Shaking his head at the lack of sense of today's generation, the old maths prof ogled at the computer screen, which now showed a long list of emails.

'Ooh, Arun's commented on my Wall! Now, he's a crazy old man if I ever saw one.' Chuckling to himself, he started to click onto the highlighted email. Then he started guiltily and turned back around to them.

'What did you two want, again?'

There's no telling what number of misfortunes would have befallen the wacky old school-teacher had a distraction not arrived in the merciful (for the prof) form of Sheila, who entered the classroom bearing a glass of tea, identical to the one she had silently passed through the door of the Headmistress's office earlier. The indulgent smile that had been adorning her lips froze and then faded as her gaze came into contact with Sathi instead of the maths teacher. Sathi seemed just as speechless as her eyes locked with Sheila's.

Before the silence could become even more awkward, the prof started to literally jump up and down on his chair, causing the wood to creak its protest. 'I've got it!' he yelled, tapping excitedly on the monitor. 'Yes. I knew it was Mar something – it was Mar Ivanios College!'

Sathi seemed to be relieved for an excuse to tear her eyes away from Sheila. She moved to stand behind the prof so she could look over his shoulder at the computer screen. 'Are you sure?' she asked, her tone wary as she hungrily read the scanned letter there in her mother's neat hand.

'Yes, yes, yes,' he insisted. 'See, it's written right there. Yes,' he concluded triumphantly. Zakiy read the truth in her glowing expression as Sathi turned to meet his eyes.

'It's in Trivan... Trivandrum,' she confirmed, tripping over the strange name of the capital of Kerala.

Yes! he exulted, before getting back to business. Okay, so, from Nelliampathi it's about 350 kilometres to Trivandrum. So that was about six hours, Zakiy calculated. Maybe seven. It would take at least a couple of days to get there and back. Most probably three. If they set out tomorrow before dawn they should get there by early evening. They could stay the night and visit the college the next morning before heading back.

There was only one glitch; he had a presentation tomorrow of a project he had been working on for the last couple of months, which was essential for him to pass his final year.

Damn the timing! he fumed. Zakiy wondered whether he would be able to talk to his assessor and postpone his presentation to Tuesday. Monday was a holiday anyway. The assessor was a nice guy, he would listen to him. Yes, that's what he would do. Zakiy resolved to go and talk to him as soon as he dropped Sathi off at the resort where she worked.

Immensely pleased with himself, he tuned back into the conversation that had been flowing around him just in time to hear Sathi say, 'Vidhya Raman. Do you remember her?' She stuck the newspaper that had led them to this school under the maths prof's nose and pointed at the other girl in the photograph, the one wearing pigtails and standing next to her Amma. Not surprisingly, the prof was shaking his head back and forth dubiously, his glasses held to the bridge of his nose with one finger.

Obviously he only remembered details that made a deep impression on him, such as the fact that his favourite student had not chosen his subject to carry on with at college.

Sathi seemed resolved to squeeze out every last sliver of information she could out of him, however. 'What about the old head-teacher? The one who was here when my Am...' she caught herself just in time, and coughed to cover up her mistake. 'When my aunt was studying here? Do you have their contact details?'

The prof looked quite surprised to hear that there *had* been a head teacher before the current one; Zakiy was preparing to drag Sathi away before she fried what remained of the old guy's memory cells when a quiet, composed voice broke in.

'She died a few years ago. She was quite old when she retired.' All the eyes in the room flew to her, but Sheila directed her words to Sathi alone as she handed the tea to the prof. 'The current headmistress is the second one after Mrs Prathap left.'

Sathi seemed to have difficulty in meeting Sheila's unruffled gaze. 'Oh. Right.' She looked at Zakiy. 'Then I guess we should be heading back?'

He nodded, relieved at the thought of escaping the sticky tension in the room. He watched as Sathi went to the prof and asked him if she could use his computer to forward the letter to her own email. He agreed after giving his Facebook messages a wistful look. Then, thanking him, Sathi started back towards Zakiy, striding past Sheila with her eyes fixed straight ahead.

Then just as she got past her, Sathi made an abrupt about-turn and caught hold of the older woman's arm. Staring earnestly into her eyes, Sathi squeezed the calloused hand affectionately. 'Thank you.'

The radiant smile that caught hold of Sheila's expression and conquered her glistening black eyes was worth more than a million silk saris put together.

Chapter Fourteen

Storm in a Teacup

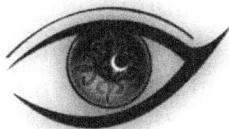

S athi awoke to find herself cocooned in her mother's arms. She lay as still as the dead, knowing that the slightest movement would break the spell of this sweetest of all embraces. She strained to remain relaxed, to keep herself in that slippery interval between half-formed dreams and disappointing reality as she revelled in the phantom arms that lovingly encompassed her. These moments when she woke to feel someone's arms wrapped around her from behind, spooning against her back, were very, very rare.

The first time it had happened, she had started up in horror, dispelling the sensation inadvertently as she looked over her shoulder in alarm. The next time she had not been so careless. She knew that the person hugging her so gently was her Amma as certainly as Sathi knew there was life in her body. She believed it was a way her mother communicated with her from her place in the world of the dead.

'Chicchikchic.' The sudden flutter of a bird's wings against her newly-purchased tent fractured what little Sathi had left of her mother, and the arms dissolved without a single murmured endearment or parting squeeze.

Sathi sat up on her sleeping bag and glared at the crow that had settled itself in the opening of the tent, pecking at a remnant of a late-night meal.

Filled with rage at the stupid bird, she snatched up the first thing her hands touched and hurled it at the pest. 'I hate you!' Sathi yelled at the departing form of the unhurt bird, and watched as it vanished across the part of the azure horizon she could see out of the tent opening. Then her eyes fell on the broken mess that had recently been her alarm clock. Staring at it, the absurdity of her situation hit her; here she was, in scruffy shorts and a T-shirt, bed-headed, her legs tangled up in a sheet she had thrown over herself in the night, talking to a bird after throwing an alarm clock at it.

She started laughing, laughing so hard that at first she thought the pain in her thorax was a stitch building. Then the sobs started, each one threatening to wrench her heart from her body, and sending electric shocks through her that hurt almost too much for her to bear. She coiled up on herself on the floor of the tent, arms and knees folded over her chest to add futile protection from an unhealed wound within.

Once she had ejected enough aqueous sodium chloride to take care of UK's deficiency of grit to spread on the snow that paid surprise spring-time visits, she wrenched her body towards the stream and stooped to splash her face with the sweet, clean water. Its exuberant music soothed her. She imagined that this was what her mother sounded like; a bubbly voice for a bubbly personality. Even though Sathi seemed to resemble Amma so much physically, from what Mr Yes (aka mad maths prof, as Zakiy called him) had told them it seemed like they were as different inside as a stagnant lake is from a vivacious stream like this one. Maybe even as different as a sewer.

She released her hair from its sleep-loosened knot on top of her head before disappearing into her tent and re-emerging a few seconds later with her backpack slung across her right shoulder. She ducked inside the neatly zipped-up opening of Zakiy's tent and snagged the dongle on the floor next to his laptop. It was a small black stick resembling a USB, but with a more expensive function: it gave wireless internet connection.

As she tucked it into a small outer pocket of her bag, she caught sight of the dark green hoodie that Zakiy had let her borrow the night they met. She squatted next to it, fingering the soft fabric. It had been so warm and comfy. It was a chilly morning today, with the sun yet to show its lazy face, and although she had changed from her shorts into warmer trousers, she had nothing more than a T-shirt on top.

Decisively, she unfolded the sweater (whoever heard of boys folding up their clothes, anyway?) and slipped it over her head, inhaling its warmth and sighing in satisfaction. It was as effective as walking around wrapped in a quilt. She truly loved a good hoodie.

She had been planning on going back to her room at the resort and taking a shower, but decided at the last moment to get her dose of caffeine first and visit Manish, whom she had neglected for the last couple of days.

She set off at a leisurely stroll, passing the resort and dropping off her laptop-burdened bag at her room before beginning the walk through the sprawling tea estate. She pulled up the hood over her head to guard against the pitter-patter of rain that shimmered onto descending beds of tea-plants, its gleam barely visible against the back-drop of the distant mountains.

The steep hill brought a smile to her lips as it reminded her of the threat she'd made the night before, when Zakiy announced his plan to set off to Trivandrum in the early hours of the morning. He'd dropped her off at their clearing after they arrived back from Nemmara, and driven off after promising to be back within an hour. He returned in a quarter of that time, pinching the hell out of his lip as he worried over something.

After twenty minutes of alternative cajoling and bullying, he had given in and told her, 'I couldn't find my assessor. We'll have to postpone the journey by a few hours so I can go talk to him in the morning.'

Sathi had stared at him rather blankly. 'What journey?'

It had all come out then, how the mastermind had been planning on getting an extension on his project so they could leave Nelliampathi in the morning, how he had been thinking about missing one of the most important days in his final year so he could escort her to her mother's old college, how he'd been planning on driving for six, seven hours there and back and waste three days of his life for absolutely no good reason. She'd been speechless for at least another five minutes as she tried to absorb these unflinching facts.

'Okay,' she'd begun once she recovered sufficiently, showing him a closed fist. 'One,' she said, holding up her thumb, 'I wasn't even dreaming of leaving for Triv... Trivan... that place tomorrow. Two, there is no way you're coming with me on such a long trip and missing college for days. Three,' she continued as she held up yet another finger to emphasise her growing list, 'You are not driving me anywhere when I do go. When I go, I will take the train, alone.'

When he started to open his mouth to protest, she glared and talked over him, 'And four, you are going to take your butt to college tomorrow and get maximum credit for that frighteningly amazing contraption you've made and show them all how insanely clever you are. Capisce?'

'You knew?' he asked in wonder, as though she was some sort of magician. Jeez, boys are so stupid. 'Of course I knew, you idiot. You've been tinkering with it for ages,' she retorted. 'If you're not at your college by 9 am tomorrow I will literally throw you down the hill, and then you can do your presentation via Skype in the hospital!'

He was silent for a few moments. Then he'd said a few words that had her looking around for something heavy enough to throw before he ducked swiftly into his tent:

'I don't have to be in till 10 o'clock.'

Manish was on his mobile phone when Sathi finally sauntered up to his teashop; it seemed everyone had a cellphone in Kerala, even if they didn't have a proper home. She'd even seen fisherwomen squatting in the market in front of baskets of fresh fish, clutching dirt-smeared phones to their ears while they dealt with bargaining customers. As to who they were calling so urgently, Sathi couldn't begin to guess. Even Manish, who lived in a tiny thatched house behind his shop, had a colour TV and computer furnishing the single room.

As he caught sight of her approaching, Manish hurriedly spoke into his phone, 'I'll call you back later.' Then after a pause, 'Yes. That's why. Yes. I will.' He took the mobile away from his ear and searched the keys with his eyes before punching at a button and slipping it back into his shirt pocket.

'Sathi!' he called out to her. 'I thought you were working this morning. The usual, right?'

She watched him reach for the pan of hot milk. 'Yes, please. It's my day off today.' Filled with curiosity, she continued, 'Who was that?'

Seeming to be incredibly absorbed in what he was doing, he barely glanced up at her as he replied. 'Who was what?'

'Who were you talking to on the phone?'

'Oh that,' he answered dismissively, almost pulling it off. 'Just a friend.'

'Mmmhmm...' she responded disbelievingly. 'Come on, just spill,' she urged. Getting sudden inspiration, she threatened, 'If you don't tell me the truth, I'll stay here all day and tell everyone who comes that you have a new girlfriend.'

At that he looked up and gave her his usual good-humoured smile. 'Girlfriend? At my age?'

'You wouldn't be the first. Anyway, why else would you be acting so shady?' she defended with a not-so-rhetorical question. Zakiy was definitely rubbing off on her. Manish grinned wryly at her to show that he was on to her tricks and wouldn't fall for it.

Sathi sighed, giving up temporarily as she indulged in the amazing concoction that he had just handed her. 'Yum! You make the best tea ever – just promise me that even if you have a girlfriend you won't close up this shop and leave Nelliampathi for her.'

Something serious glinted in his eyes as he replied, 'I can certainly promise you that, Sathi *molé*.'

Despite the endearment in his words, Sathi had to stop a shudder in its inception as his tone sent a skittering of unease through her. Before she could gather the courage to question him further, his first paying customers of the day arrived, effectively ending their conversation.

She returned to her own thoughts for company as Manish served the new arrivals. Had she imagined what she heard in his voice? She had simply been teasing Manish, but was there something he wasn't telling her? Or was she being paranoid because of the awful morning she'd just had? Annoyed at the lack of answers to the questions that seemed to perpetually fill her mind, Sathi resolved to consult her cards when she got back to her room and distracted herself by studying the others who had stopped by for their mid-morning tea.

There was a youngish man in smart office clothes, his face mostly obscured by the newspaper he held out in front of him as he sipped at his strong *chaya*. Next to him sat a sari-clad woman who was painstakingly blowing at each spoonful from her cup until it was cool enough to give to her son, whose school uniform was already stained as he slurped it all down.

Sathi found herself staring at the mother, who only took a hurried sip every few minutes, and felt her eyes fill.

Oh, for God's sake. How much can a person cry in one day? Sathi bent over her own glass of tea and covertly wiped at her eyes with the sleeve of the hoodie, shifting her attention to the remaining two people at the shop to fore-stall further flooding.

The two men had chosen to sit as far away from the others as possible, and were discussing something with quiet animation, their full glasses sitting ignored on the bench in front of them. Their foreheads were smeared with saffron and a white powder, *bhasma*, indicating that they had either visited a temple that morning or that they were such pious devotees that they kept both sacred powders at home.

Snatches of their conversation drifted across to Sathi and the English words captured her interest as she unconsciously eavesdropped. 'I'm telling you... not natural... why would...? So what... proof... dead overnight...'

She stiffened. Dead overnight. Were they - could they possibly be talking about her mother? She looked away quickly to make sure they did not catch her staring. She had to know who they were talking about. She had to get closer to them. She sat there for a second, staring in front of her like a zombie as she thought quickly. Then she looked down at the chaya still in her hands. She drained it in one long pull, barely noticing that she had burned her tongue, and stood up under the pretence of returning her hastily-emptied glass to Manish. Ignoring the suspicious look the old tea-maker was giving her, she wandered aimlessly for a few moments, pretending to be admiring the roses that bloomed near Manish's shop, and then finally returned to her bench and sat back down, much nearer the arguing men than she had been before.

'Shut your eyes and ears to what's happening if you want, and we'll see how far it gets you,' the middle-aged man badly in need of a hair-cut was saying, throwing up his arms in defeat. 'But I warn you, there'll come a time when you'll regret letting this go on,' he threatened. 'There'll come a time when you'll wonder at the lack of justice in the world.'

The stocky guy sitting next to him put on an expression that made it clear he was just humouring the other man. 'There *is* justice in the world, only it has to be accompanied by something called proof. Do you have any proof?' He paused pointedly. 'I did not think so.'

The other man glared. 'They have ways of destroying proof. They have ways of killing that don't need guns or knives.' Sathi felt her heart-rate quicken in response to the renewed flow of adrenaline in her bloodstream.

Understanding dawned on the younger man's face. 'Is that what this is about? You and your conspiracy theories! I must say I expected more from you, my friend. Especially when considering your education.' He sighed, his tone showing that he was saddened by the conversation.

'Pah! If education means close-mindedness, then I want no part of it. What good did Vijay's education do him? He's still dead, isn't he?'

Sathi allowed relief to course through her, parasympathetic activity superseding the sympathetic one. They were not talking about her Amma after all. She missed part of the man's next words as she let out the long breath she had been holding. Her attention was seized back as the longer-maned man insisted, 'Shankar, I'm telling you, they killed him. I don't know why, but they killed him.'

Jayaram turned away from his stubborn, disbelieving friend and reached for his cooled tea with shaking hands, draining the glass of flavoured milk in an attempt to calm himself down. His rage and grief combined had formed a monster that he was failing abysmally to control.

He set his glass down again, wiping the back of his hand across his mouth, and froze as he noticed an inquisitive pair of eyes watching him closely. The girl's head drooped in embarrassment at being found out, but she did not look away. She was young, with dark hair that tumbled down to her waist and brushed against the seat of the wooden bench in light waves, her petite features pulling together with dark brown eyes to display an intensity that was beyond her years.

'What're you staring at?' Jayaram snapped, knowing that his guttural voice accentuated the harsh tone he wished to project. What business did this puny thing have, to gaze at him as though he were some animal in a zoo?

She recoiled at his aggression, but her dark eyes continued to taunt him. Shankar spoke quickly to him. 'Shut up, Jay.'

'Do *not* call me that!' he snarled, the girl forgotten in an instant. Only two people called him by that nickname. One was dead and the other... the other was as good as. She was lost to him forever.

'I'm sorry,' the girl's low voice said into the silence that his words had conjured. Shankar went back to playing the gentleman. 'Excuse him, dear; he is in a bad mood today.'

'Bad mood?' Jayaram spluttered, feeling the strange desire to laugh for a fleeting moment. The unfamiliar sensation was gone as quickly as it came as he turned on his so-called friend. 'Is that what you call it, Shankar?'

He shot Jayaram a warning look. 'Do not make things worse. Do not take your anger out on innocent bystanders - they will not stand for it as I do.'

That stung more than he cared to show. 'If you feel so sorry for yourself, you can take yourself out of my company. I don't need your help.'

Shankar gave him a weary smile. 'I am not the one feeling sorry for myself, my friend.' Jayaram had opened his mouth to tell him what to do with his condescension when the girl pulled his attention away.

'Look, I didn't mean to cause problems between you two. I was just... never mind.' She shook her head, as though disgusted, as though she knew something he didn't, as though she thought she was better than him. Rage reared in him like a sickening serpent, and Jayaram lunged to his feet, crossing the distance to the bench where she sat in two powerful strides.

Before she could even begin to react, he was leaning over her. 'You thought you would just sit there and listen in to our conversation like a regular nosy-parker, did you?' Jayaram sneered. Fear spiked through the girl's eyes like ink across old parchment as she cringed back, her fingers blanching where they clenched the edge of the bench.

'Enough!'

His attention switched to the old tea-maker, who had inserted his slim frame in front of the girl, blocking her from him. He glared at Jayaram. 'You touch her, and I will have the police on you before you can utter your mother's name.'

By that time, Shankar had arrived at his shoulder and begun tugging on his arm with his considerable strength. Jayaram allowed himself to be pulled backwards, horrified at how close to violence he had become. Towards a girl, no less. But he was on the boil too much still to resist a parting blow.

'Well, *dear*,' he spat, 'since you're so interested in things that are none of your concern, maybe you should think about the fact that pain and death are not things to be gawked at.'

He read the change in her expressive eyes as she stood and pushed her way around the old man, who had continued to maintain a protective stance before her. 'Do not teach *me* about death,' she said to him, her voice level and utterly devoid of her earlier fear as she stared unflinchingly into his eyes.

That's when he knew; he realised that the reason behind her old eyes and composed intensity was the same as the one responsible for his own fury.

Jayaram turned, and jerking off his friend's hand on his arm, stalked off, not aware of where he was going, content with the knowledge that it was away from another soul intimately acquainted with the pain of losing a loved one.

Chapter Fifteen

Vestige of Truth

Sathi gazed after the departing man, her anger at his insinuation cooling into confusion. The younger man, Shankar, sighed and turned to them. He said in Malayalam, 'I can only apologise for my friend. Jayaram's grief has changed him. Please forgive his behaviour.'

Manish snorted. 'He should know better than to take his grief out on little girls.' His words were simmering with indignation, so Sathi let the "little girl" comment slide and laid her hand on his bony wrist, both to show her gratitude and to prevent further outbursts.

She directed her question to Shankar. 'What happened to him?'

He stared after the minuscule retreating form of his friend as he answered. 'Fate took his best friend from him much earlier than was justified, and instead of accepting his death, Jayaram embarked on a quest for vengeance. Though from whom, I believe even he does not know. He keeps insisting that Vijay, his friend, was murdered, despite the fact that the police could not find a single mark on his body to confirm Jay's theory.'

Sathi shivered. His story was uncannily like her own. She blurted out the question she had wanted to ask ever since Jayaram mentioned it: 'What was he saying earlier about being able to kill without weapons?'

Had they simply been a mad man's ravings, or was there some truth in them?

Shankar shifted uncomfortably and averted his eyes, but not before she saw uneasiness slither in them. 'As I said to Jayaram, it is simply a by-product of superstition and old wives' tales.' His words and body language were completely at odds with each other, and she had the distinct feeling that he put a lot more stock in the "superstition" than he was willing to admit.

'What's "it"?' she persisted, making air-quotes. 'What was he talking about?'

He seemed inclined to ignore her as he gazed off into a spot in the distant horizon. After a few moments of pregnant silence he finally muttered a single word: '*Kaivisham.*'

'What?' Sathi didn't understand. She knew the literal translation of what he said when it was split into two words; *kai visham* – hand poison. But that didn't make any sense. If it had been some kind of poison, surely the police wouldn't have ruled it a natural death. She frowned up at the man, her expression demanding answers.

Shankar sighed resignedly as he finally turned back to her. 'In the old days, people used to believe that if someone wanted to do you ill, they would give you kaivisham. It is not actual poison, although most believe that it is something given to you in food. It is much like the evil eye - it is about the negative energy flowing from the putrid resentment in the thoughts of a person, and onto the object of their jealousy and hatred.

'Of course, as prayers to gods have been grounded through material rituals, kaivisham has likewise been substantiated by physical components, such as the hair or fingernails of their intended victim or in extreme cases, animal blood. Uneducated people claim that such malignant rituals can even result in the death of a person, if that is the intent. It is basically what is construed to be black magic.'

Huh. Black magic. That had definitely been the last thing on her mind. *How am I supposed to fight with negative energy?* she wondered slightly hysterically.

Sathi stopped herself sternly. They were talking about that other guy, Jayaram, and his friend's death, not about her Amma. So what was she panicking about? *Stupid female*, she admonished herself before getting her brain back on track. 'So your friend thinks black magic was involved in the death?'

Shankar's shoulders sagged. 'Without any other ideas, that is what he has convinced himself with. He will not listen to reason.'

Manish's grim voice drew her attention back to him. 'This is all utter nonsense. There's no such thing as black magic, and there's no such thing as kaivisham. These are all follies born out of ignorance.' He turned to her. 'You shouldn't waste any more time thinking about this.'

'I agree with you,' Shankar conceded. 'Jayaram has gone past reason, but that does not mean we all have to follow his path. Once again, I beg forgiveness on his behalf.' And with the final clink of his tea glass against the wooden bench, he was gone.

*   *   *

Sathi stood staring up at her great-aunt and uncle's house, unnaturally still in her pre-occupation. It was still empty and locked up, just as it had been every time she had come to check on it in the last month. Usually the knowledge allowed the grief and longing to take themselves up to a higher, more dangerous, level. Today, however, it did not shatter her as it had the last time she had found herself back at Amma's ancestral home.

Maybe it was the fact that she had at last managed to find out *something* about her mother. She at last had proof that her Amma had existed, that she was not simply a figment of her imagination, that there were people who knew her, who really knew her, like that maths teacher, for example. Of course, the fact that her relatives had yet not returned to Nelliampathi after attending the marriage in Kollam still caused a barbed pang of disappointment to go through her, yet it was not a blow that disarmed her like before. She had just enough sustenance to persevere until the cavalry arrived.

She turned her back on the house and glimpsed the Devi temple again. It appeared as dilapidated as ever, and White-beard, the man with the startling blue-green eyes, who had lectured her about fate and the Hindu gods, and disappeared after taking her to the astrologer, was nowhere in sight. She shrugged to herself, and headed back towards the winding path that led down the hill and back to her room at the resort.

More than an hour later, she sat cross-legged on the wide parapet hugging the veranda of her section of the staff cottage, a towel wrapped securely around her wet hair and Zakiy's oversized hoodie pulled effortlessly over her cold toes. She snapped closed the lid of the laptop that was balanced on her knees, causing the dongle to stick out of one side piteously, and sat rapping her fingernails on the metal as her gaze turned to what had rapidly become her favourite view; the distant mountains soaked in the mist that was slowly taking over the surrounding trees and giving the forest an otherworldly feel.

She was now marginally less clueless concerning a number of things that had been puzzling her since the visit to her Amma's school, having spent the best part of an hour piling up Zakiy's internet bill. However, the first word she typed in to Google hadn't been anything related to her mother: it had been "kaivisham". She hadn't found much more information than what Shankar told her, and most of the results had been advice on how offering prayers at certain temples would cure the effects of kaivisham, as opposed to a more detailed explanation of what it actually was.

Someone's incredulous post in a Yahoo Answers thread, marvelling at the fact that modern, twenty-first century people still believed in black magic, had given Sathi pause; surely she ought to have had the same reaction? Even Shankar had delivered his explanation with an air that inspired disbelief, and Manish had likewise declared that it was silly superstition.

Maybe it was simply contrariness, but Sathi actually thought, after the initial confusion had cleared, that it made a weird kind of sense. Perhaps it was a result of the fact that she was already open to the idea of Tarot cards and astrologers because of her own experiences, so the possibility of black magic did not require such a stretch of the imagination.

Whatever it was, she soon reached a dead end with the kaivisham search. After that, she went onto to research her Amma's college, Mar Ivanios, and finally got a grasp of how the college system worked in India; courses in medicine, engineering, law, nursing and dentistry had whole colleges that were devoted to teaching them. For those who were less interested in following a professional degree program, there were ample colleges like Mar Ivanios which, as far as Sathi could discern, ran in much the same as colleges in London, offering bachelor's degrees in Literature, Politics, Commerce, Mathematics, Journalism and the sciences, although in place of Biology were subjects such as Botany and Zoology.

Another key difference was that each student was required to choose three areas of study if they were going for a bachelor's degree, with one main subject that they spent much more time and effort on during the duration of the course; this explained how her Amma had been able to study Chemistry, Physics and Maths at the same time without undertaking three separate degrees.

The next item on her mental list had been to get up a map of Kerala and try to get the geography sorted in her head; Trivandrum was the capital district as well as being at the southern-most end of Kerala, and the college was fairly close to the city centre so there shouldn't be too many problems in reaching it, travel-wise.

The knowledge that it was necessary to pass through Kollam in order to get to Trivandrum had side-tracked her research somewhat; what if she could bring an end to this incessant wait for her great-aunt and uncle to return to Nelliampathi by going to meet them in Kollam? She was no longer constrained by the reasons for not making the trip that she had been when she first arrived here, and in any case, she had already decided to travel south to her mother's college.

Only one problem still remained; how was she supposed to find them in such a large district? After some thought, she had gotten the idea of searching for marriage halls in Kollam. However, seeing that Google yielded up 470,000 search results to this simple request had dampened her resolve significantly. She had, out of sheer stubbornness, half-heartedly clicked onto the first couple of links, but then she realised that each result actually contained links to many different marriage halls. That was the point at which she gave the idea up as a lost cause and shut down her laptop.

She leaned down and snagged her backpack from where it had been resident on the floor beside her, and returned her laptop to it after taking out the sheaf of papers that weighed more than the computer as far as she was concerned; they were the photocopied newspaper articles that she had not yet had the luxury of reading through properly.

There were just three sheets; the oldest one was an article about the horrific car crash that had taken the life of her Amma's parents – an accident in which the bawling toddler had been the sole survivor. Amma's escape was a miracle they had not solved to this day, because the car that the happy family had been travelling in had lost control whilst navigating the ghat road up to Nelliampathi and had taken a leaping dive off the edge of the cliff with little time for escape strategies. The journalist speculated that the parents' last act must have been to somehow safely eject their daughter from the car an instant before they plunged to their deaths.

Comforting words concluded the article, explaining that the sister of the man who died had not allowed her young niece to be handed off to be cared for by strangers, and had instead insisted on becoming her legal guardian and looking after her as her own daughter. Sathi smiled through her melancholy and hoped against hope that her grandfather's sister would view her surrogate daughter's child as much a part of her family as her own grandchildren.

The next photocopy was mostly dominated by irrelevant text, and Sathi's only interest was the short article announcing the impending marriage between Miss Madhubhala Kumar and Mr Nakul Varma.

It was a weird feeling to know that her parents' life together had begun at this moment, in the year 1990, and that they had been joined by Sathi in 1995, and now the small family was fragmented across the globe, and across worlds. She stared at the dry sentences before putting it aside, the love for her mother becoming contaminated by her resentment towards her father at the sight of the intimately intertwined names.

She had saved the longest, and the best, for last; it was an article describing the inauguration of a charitable organisation founded by her great-uncle, and run with the help of his sons, her mother's cousins. The charity carried out arranged marriages for girls in poor families every year in the auspicious Malayalam month that spanned August and September, wedding off a hundred-and-one couples in one fell sweep. The aim was to abolish the still-prevalent issue that was dowry, the bridal money that had to be agreed upon and paid to the groom by the bride's family before a wedding could take place.

The organisation profiled young men who were dependable and of good character and paired them off with poor girls with their mutual agreement in a communal marriage, at full cost to the charity, funded mostly by donations and sponsorships. It also provided financial support for the couple in the form of employment in the many businesses that the family already ran, and gave accommodation at cheap rates for the next six months, giving the newly-weds sufficient time to become financially stable.

It was simple, effective, perfect. The pride Sathi felt threatened to overflow as she tried to comprehend what an enormous kindness her mother's adoptive family were doing for their fellow Keralites.

As she wiped off a few happy tears, her eyes caught on the large bold letters proclaiming "heart attack" on the small section of the neighbouring article that had been photocopied along with the piece about the charity.

She scanned what little text had been copied across, and realised that it was one she had already read in the library. A man had had a heart attack while in the shower and had collapsed due to both his heart and because of asphyxiation. He had been rushed to hospital, but had died shortly afterwards.

What an awful way to die. As usual, the mention of death in any form made her mind turn to imagining her mother's death. Before she had found out that her Amma had been murdered, she had envisioned Amma gasping her last breath precipitated with sweat from a pain-filled birth. Simply for the purposes of torturing herself further, Sathi had looked up all the grisly details of maternal death during childbirth so she could add them to the movie in her mind's eye. The cry of the firstborn drowned in the flood of blood that gushed relentless from her mother's body, and a last vague outline of Amma's lifeless face, sorely lacking in details since Sathi hadn't known what her mother looked like up until a few weeks ago.

Suddenly her phone, which she had put in the only corner of the building that had signal, let out a lukewarm beep that told her she had a new text message.

Grateful for the distraction, and empathising fully with the phone's apathy, she removed the papers from her lap and was glad that she'd had the presence of mind to do so when her deadened feet nearly sent her crashing into one of many sharp corners of the cottage in retribution for the unforgivable crime of trying to stand up.

Cursing herself for being so stupid as to sit on her feet until they lost all sensation, she limped towards her phone like an old woman, clutching the wide mahogany pillars for support and wincing as the electrical activity in her feet started up again with what was, in her opinion, unnecessary exuberance.

Her irritation disappeared as soon as she read the message that was making her phone hyperventilate: *Finished presentation – I outshone the rest so much I reckon there's a fairly good chance of getting lynched on the way back. If you have any decent mafia connections, make sure to put in a good word for me.*

142

Sathi smiled widely, and barely caring about the unpleasant sensation that was making itself known in her gluteus maximus as it eagerly welcomed back the much-awaited flow of blood, she texted back: *Yes, I'll put it a good word to the KKK – especially about your endless modesty. Happy lynching! :p*

Still grinning, she returned to the parapet and froze after one look at the hard surface that was still sending waves of remembered agony through her.

Nuh uh. I have a much better idea. She smiled in satisfaction.

Chapter Sixteen

Babies in the Rain

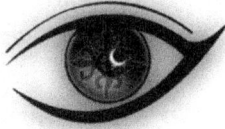

'lms for the potentially lynched,' Sathi announced as soon as Zakiy became visible through the thick cover of teak trees encircling their secluded clearing. The late afternoon sunlight feasted on the scene in front of Zakiy, and fed the information back into his eyes to form an appropriately amazed output; a small round chocolate cake graced the plate on the plastic bucket on top of which it had been set, safe from undeserving ants, while two tender coconuts, still cosy in their mud-green coats and inhabited by straws, kept it company.

The best of the lot, however, was a loaf of freshly baked garlic bread, still steaming as the vapours of heat dissipated into the surrounding air, emitting the spicy fragrance that had been decorating his mouth since the last time Zakiy tasted his favourite European food.

Tearing his eyes away from the delicacies displayed before him, he directed Sathi a sharp look. 'This is for me?' he asked suspiciously.

There was a mischievous sparkle in her eyes as she glanced around at the food. 'Well, I thought you would at least give me a sip of the coconut water, and maybe some left-over crumbs from the cake, but I guess if you want to gobble all of it yourself, you can.' She blinked at him innocently.

Zakiy, in turn, heaved a massive sigh, and eyed the food with mock wistfulness. 'So, I can't eat any of it then.'

She raised an eyebrow. 'And why might that be?'

He struck a pose of deep anguish and heartache, and instead of answering, exclaimed, 'Sathi! I didn't know you had it in you!' For effect, he added a sob, beating his chest with a fist slightly too enthusiastically. Swallowing an 'Oww!' and rubbing his chest, he interrupted his own performance to sneak a peek at her reaction. He was gratified to observe her sufficiently befuddled frown.

'Er, what exactly was I not supposed to have in me, again?' She sounded quite curious to learn the answer.

He grabbed the tree nearest to him, and turned his face away to cradle it against a rough branch as though he could no longer bear to look at her. Generously punctuated by sniffs, his muffled voice at last formed the accusation: 'You're trying to fatten me up so you can feed me to the Wicked Witch of the West!'

There was an explosion of noise, and then he heard Sathi stage-whisper to herself, 'Damn! Foiled in one.' Then something seemed to occur to her, and she turned to him with her brow furrowed. 'Doesn't the WW of the W eat children? Aren't you getting your fairy tales mixed up?'

He looked up, his face strangely devoid of the tears that had appeared to threaten. 'Of course! I believe you're quite right.' With a penitent air that flirted with the fantastical, he gravely went down on one knee on the forest floor, head bowed and hands folded in front as though clenching an imaginary sword. 'M'lady, forgive me for doubting your integrity,' he intoned respectfully.

He watched as Sathi's feet approached steadily, finally resting in front of him. Laying a magnanimous palm on his brown curls, she said graciously, 'I accept your apology, sire. Please rise.'

He hopped back onto his feet, brushing off his dirt-ridden slacks, and grinned at his lady. Giving the treats another appreciative glance, he asked, 'Seriously, what's all the food for?'

Sathi leaned down to snag a paper plate and handed it to him along with a hunk of the garlic bread. 'To celebrate your successful presentation of that energy efficient engine you made, even though to be honest the thing still baffles me beyond belief.'

He gaped at her, almost neglecting his beloved food in his astonishment. Sathi, looking up, smiled. 'Well, it's nice to know that the almighty Zakiy can be rendered speechless once in a while.'

Snapping himself out of it, he corrected her with unaccustomed gentleness, 'Almighty Sir Galliant.' He added, with trademark indignation and a mouth full of flavoured bread, 'And who says I'm speechless? I was simply giving my tongue some time off – the poor thing got exhausted after the hour-long report I had to deliver this morning.'

He didn't quite receive the sympathy he'd been angling for: 'Pity you didn't give it an extended holiday.'

Zakiy resignedly devoted himself to the food, sharing far more than a mere sip of the tender coconut water and crumbs of the chocolate cake with his cantankerously generous hostess. As he was wiping up the last drops of buttery garlic, he said to her, 'I've been thinking...'

'You *think*?'

Zakiy fielded the interruption excellently, in his opinion: 'Yes, I've been known to engage in that strenuous activity now and then, although I don't really like it very much.'

Ignoring her mutters that she bet he didn't, he persisted commendably. 'I've been thinking about this trip to your mum's college.'

She was instantly suspicious, regarding him disapprovingly with her eyes narrowed to slits. He hurried on before she could shock him into acquiescence as she had the day before. 'You know, I don't have to be in to college tomorrow 'cos it's the presentations of the second batch of final-years and Monday's a holiday so I have a three-and-a-half day weekend, so if we head to Trivandrum tonight, we can be there in time to visit Mar Ivanios tomorrow,' he babbled, all in one breath, afraid that he would get shouted at the moment he stopped to refill his lungs.

Naturally he had to stop to indulge, much against his will, in a few seconds of breathing in oxygen before he could look up and face the consequences of his articulate speech. Upon raising his eyes he reflected unusually philosophically that simple changes in the positioning of facial features, such as a certain downward shift of the mouth and a shortening of the distance between eyebrows and forehead could create an expression of extreme displeasure, and could lead to an incredibly eloquent argument such as the one that followed:

'No.'

'Why not?'

'Because I said so.'

'Well, I say yes.'

'And I say no.'

'Yes.'

'No.'

'Yes.'

'No.'

Zakiy kept his expression neutral. 'No.'

'Yes,' she replied automatically.

'What?' Sathi frowned at him in confusion. 'No. I meant no.'

'Yes! You agreed,' he taunted her, beaming.

'You cheated!'

He took a leaf out of her book and stuck his tongue out, which earned him another glare. 'We'll pack quickly and leave on Toothless tonight,' he said.

'We will not... wait - Toothless?' Sathi's baffled tone was that of one successfully side-tracked. Zakiy silently congratulated himself as he replied shortly, 'That's what I call my Jeep.' Purposefully, he did not offer further explanation.

Like an exceptionally altruistic fish, she bit onto the bait instead of going after the morsel of plankton she had been following before he dangled the juicy worm under her nose. 'Why? Does it have the bumper missing or something?'

Zakiy grinned. 'I named him after that black dragon in *How to Train your Dragon*. I thought the little guy was too cute for words, so when I got my black Jeep, I christened him Toothless.'

Despite herself, a spark of amusement crept into her eyes, and the plankton disappeared out of view. 'I thought all cars were girls,' she challenged.

'Oh, Toothless wanted to undergo a gender change. Who was I to stop him/her?' He sighed heavily. 'There's only so much you can do with cars these days. You can only drive them to the petrol pump – you can't make them drink the oil.'

She snorted. 'Yes, indeed. You've really invested a lot of thought in the concept, haven't you?'

As he proudly nodded, he noticed the sudden, disoriented change in her expression which meant he was about to be in trouble again. Sure enough, Sathi glowered at him: 'You changed the subject!'

Zakiy shook his head sagely. 'Actually, *you* did.' That was truly the cherry on the cake. She threw a dirty look at him along with the scrunched-up ball of tissue she had been holding. Both bounced off. 'You're not coming with me to Triv... Trivan... that stupidly named place!' she insisted.

'Oh, that plankton's long left the water,' he responded. Not giving her time to puzzle over his analogy, he continued, 'I suggested, you agreed. End of story. You're not the type to go back on your word, are you? I'm coming with you.'

'No,' she said vehemently.

'Yes.'

'No.'

'Yes.'

She quenched the sudden sly curl of her lips a moment too late. 'Yes.'

'Yes!' he repeated, unable to prevent his burst of delighted laughter. She was truly someone after his own heart. He advised her, 'Always remember the poker face.'

Crushed by her failure, she scowled at him. 'Next time,' she replied scathingly.

'Sure,' he said graciously. 'Will you go pack now? Overnight stuff will do.'

'Fine,' she conceded resignedly. At least the girl knew when she was beaten. 'But,' she went on determinedly, 'can we at least go by train? Maybe that will be faster.'

'Ha! The operative word in that sentence is "maybe". Nah, if we go by car we can mould the traveling to our schedule, rather than having to adjust to the train's. I like long-distance driving, and besides, Toothless has always wanted to go to Trivandrum,' Zakiy concluded, as though that settled the matter.

'Oh, and by the way, did you know that's not the proper name of the place?' he asked. 'It's really called Thiruvananthapuram, after Vishnu the Sustainer in Hindu mythology. Thiru Anantha puram. The Lord's city. Actually...' he trailed off as a thought occurred to him. 'Some people say it's named after Ananthashesha, the mighty thousand-headed serpent on whom Lord Vishnu reclines. Just to make things confusing, other people argue Thiruvananthapuram's called that 'cos one of Vishnu's epithets is Ananthashayana – the one who lies on Anantha the snake. So it's never clear who they're talking about.'

He shrugged. 'I guess since they're both the best of buddies, and don't go anywhere without each other, it doesn't really matter.'

'Thi-ru-van-an-tha-pu-ram,' Sathi tested out slowly. 'Thiru-vanantha-puram.' She shot him a triumphant look. 'I can actually say that! Why do they call it that other abysmal name when there's such a meaningful one already?'

Oh, the irony. 'The British thought Trivandrum would be easier to say, so they changed it when they came to colonise India. Apparently they were wrong, since you can pronounce the old version, but not the new.' Zakiy laughed outright at her dumbstruck expression. 'Now will you go and get packed? We'll have to leave quite soon.' He paused to shoot her an eye-brow raised look. 'Unless, of course, you want me to kidnap you?'

Sathi stepped forward so that she was in his personal space, even though this meant that her nose was somewhere in the vicinity of his chin. 'You just try.' Having delivered the menacing message, she made that little about-turn she seemed to like to make and stalked off through the opening in the clearing, ploughing through the trees like a fiery little bulldozer.

Yup, he thought as he slipped inside his tent to change out of his college clothes and throw some of his own things together for the upcoming journey, *I've definitely mastered the art of pushing her buttons.*

The crescent moon against the black velvet horizon appeared as though someone had taken a scythe and cleaved it clean down the middle, the silky slate-coloured cloud floating like a layer of creamy skin among the inky milk of the sky.

Like an anxious mother hen, the moon followed the little black Jeep that blended in with the night so seamlessly, devotedly hanging in each window by turn until, as though suddenly conscious of the possibility of rebuke for her proximity, she withdrew to continue her tireless vigil from a distance. On this clear young night, the moon peered in first at the driver-seat window at the owner of the Jeep that was interestingly named Toothless; the tall boy folded into the seat had a goofy smile on his face that never really gave his lips a rest, and though his sharp eyes were fixed on the dimly lit road ahead as he navigated his Jeep through the night traffic, one or the other of his arms were perpetually in the air, whether to fly through the air in order to gesture in support to one of his speeches, or simply to use a fingernail to scratch the tip of his nose.

Satisfied with her observations, the moon stole around the front of the Jeep, spying the bags on the back seat as she did so, and her benevolent luminance sparkled on the wistful expression of the small upturned face that leaned out of the open passenger-window.

Not taking her eyes from the brilliant silver precipitation of the moon, partially obscured among the scarred sky, Sathi asked, 'What's your mum like?'

She could hear the smile in his voice as Zakiy answered. 'Well, the first thing to say about her is that she's the best mother in the whole wide world.' Sathi felt her own lips tug up at the obvious adoration in his voice. But the moon was the sole witness to the fact that the sadness in her eyes only intensified.

Zakiy was still talking. 'She's like the perfect stereotype of the perfect mother, but at the same time she's incredibly unconventional. Like, she's unbelievably sweet and thoughtful and amazing, but at the same time she's strong and powerful and as fierce as a... a sabre-toothed tiger.' He paused, unhappy with his simile. 'Actually, the only sabre-toothed tiger I know personally is Diego from the *Ice Age* films, and let's face it, he's not all that fierce is he? I mean, he has those cool teeth, but he was playing peek-a-boo with the baby. I should say, my Amma is as fierce as a real sabre-toothed tiger, as opposed to an animated, Disney version.

'Hey, do you remember that awesome quote from *Ice Age*?' he asked excitedly. '"Sid isn't my kid. He's not even my dog. If my dog had a kid, and the kid had a pet, that would be Sid." Classic, I tell you, classic,' Zakiy said in between bursts of laughter.

Sathi shook her head at the moon. 'Could we possibly move on?' she asked.

He complied. Eventually. 'You know, sometimes it's like Amma can read my mind – I mean, that can be good, like, if there was something you've been wanting for ages, you're guaranteed to find it gifted on your next birthday or Christmas or whatever. If there isn't a reason for celebration near enough in the future, then she'll just invent one!' There was a pause. When he spoke again there was an odd note in his voice. 'You know, you reminded me of her, the way you turned that presentation into a cause for celebration. And garlic bread... Mmmm!

I've been craving your spicy garlic bread since you first made it... and I first scoffed it down!

Sathi smiled uncertainly. She didn't know how to react. It wasn't as if she could take any credit for making his favourite food. She'd just made something quick and easy without getting in the way of the head cook, who'd been rushing about busily as she prepared dishes for lunchtime customers at the resort. She'd felt safe making garlic bread since he hadn't gagged on it the first time she'd made it – although considering the way the boys back at school shovelled in disgusting canteen food as if it was ambrosia, she couldn't be sure he'd actually enjoyed the taste. Well, at least that was cleared up now.

'Anyway,' Zakiy continued into the quiet of the Jeep, 'Amma's psychic powers can work the other way too. Of course, I was a very obedient child, and never gave her any reason to scold me, or punish me for anything.' At this point he turned his head slightly to give her a sidelong look.

'Yeah, right,' she said disbelievingly. 'I bet you were a perfect brat.' Sathi paused as though she was reconsidering. 'Hold on, I forgot. You still are.' She turned away from the window at last to roll her eyes at him.

His eyes sparkled mischief at her. 'Theoretically, if someone did do something he – er, I mean, this person – shouldn't have, then Amma would know by some kind of sixth sense. She doesn't even need to ground you or send you to your room. One glare and five minutes of scolding is enough to make you wish to be suffering in the deep depths of hell rather than literally being liquefied by her disapproval. She should've joined the army – I suggested it to her once, and got an earful for my trouble.'

Zakiy's cowed expression brightened: 'It's fun to watch her get angry at other people though. Like at incompetent sales assistants who try to charm her – they're the best. You just let her loose on them, and then sit back and enjoy the fireworks.' His half-smile blossomed out into a fully-fledged grin as he recalled the sparks that appeared to shoot out from his mother's eyes when she was enraged.

'But,' Zakiy back-tracked, 'she's incredibly fair as well. And she does forgive you if you're really sorry. And she doesn't mention it again after the deed is done, and all is forgiven and forgotten. She's incredibly patient as well – although from the sound of it, Zoya's costing Amma her money's worth.' He laughed.

'Zoya?' Sathi clutched onto the name as a falling woman seizes onto a rope that suddenly appears over the edge of a precipice. She just couldn't listen any more. She couldn't listen anything more about this woman whom Zakiy obviously idolised. She couldn't bear to hear any more about this perfect mother, not when she had no means to compare and contrast with her own mother, a woman she didn't even know.

'Oh my God!' Zakiy's exclamation thankfully absorbed her attention as his hand once again left the steering wheel to smack against his own forehead. 'Haven't I told you about her yet?'

She tried to make herself smile at the dramatics, shoving all her conflicting emotions to one side at the same time. She was tired of thinking the same thoughts and agonising over same what-ifs like a load of clothes that had been left in the washing cycle for too long.

'Zoya,' Zakiy began importantly, 'is the holy terror in our household, the one who's had everyone wrapped around her tiny little finger ever since she decided to invade our family. She'd adopted, by the way. Yeah, my parents adopted her three years ago. Or, well, more accurately, she adopted us!' Zakiy applied a thoughtful hand to his day-old stubble. 'Actually, it's interesting that we were talking about Vishnu - you know, that Hindu god – earlier because my family's always thought Zoya's arrival in our life was a lot like Krishna's in Yashoda's.'

She raised a quizzical eyebrow at him, completely lost. 'Huh?

'You know Krishna was an avatar of Vishnu?' he asked.

Instead of answering, Sathi concentrated, trying to remember which one of the endless rows of framed deities at her old babysitters' house was Krishna. She shook her head in defeat. There were just too many male gods to keep track of all of them.

'The blue-skinned dude with the flute and an insolent kind of smile?' Zakiy prompted. He then broke off guiltily to direct a semi-contrite glance heavenwards. 'No offence. You know I love you, right?'

Sathi left him to his heavenly conversation as she continued the suspended search of her memory, this time armed with more details. A picture floated into her mind's eye: at the centre of it stood a man whose skin was coated with the grey-blue hue of an awakening sky, and around his throat were draped garlands of brightly-coloured petals lovingly woven together. Sathi's forehead cleared as more details came knocking at the opening doors of her memory; peacock feathers sticking out of a lazily-tied headband; a golden flute - artlessly scattered with flowers - held with both hands to luscious lips which curled with a mischief that would instantaneously ignite any teacher's trouble-maker receptors. Coal-black eyes, an exact match for his lush, curly mane, sparkled with that same playfulness and made him look like a naughty little boy.

She switched her attention back to Zakiy. 'I remember Krishna now, but what does he have to do with your sister?'

He shot her an amused look. He took his hand from the wheel yet again to point an accusatory finger at her. 'Don't climb inside the gun and shoot.'

'Huh?' she said (again). What on earth was he on about now?

'Don't jump the gun.'

Sathi followed the usual procedure, which was so ingrained now that she barely had to concentrate. She glared, stuck her tongue out, and motioned impatiently for him to continue.

Zakiy obliged in full lecture mode. 'So, Kamsan, this evil dude who's Krishna's uncle – well, future uncle – got this divine prophecy that he'd be killed by his sister's eighth baby. Because this guy wasn't exactly the fuzzy type, he decided to kill his newly-wed sister on the spot just to be on the safe side. But then his new brother-in-law begged Kamsan to spare her, and he promised to hand over all their children to Kamsan. Although,' Zakiy speculated, 'in retrospect, they could have just agreed to stop at seven.' He shrugged to himself. 'I really shouldn't judge. I'd want more than seven kids, myself. Ah, kids... how I love tormenting them.' His cheeks stretched in a dreamy grin.

'Are you going to get to the point any time soon?' Sathi interrupted.

He wrinkled his over-large nose at her. 'Jeez, you're so impatient. Patience is a virtue, ya know?'

Sathi's eyes narrowed. She opened her mouth to flip out at him and then suddenly shut it again as a thought struck her. She smiled pleasantly at him. 'Did you know I'm a karate black-belt?'

Zakiy blanched. 'Really?'

Her smile widened. 'Yup. I even invented this cool move where I karate-chop someone's nose while sitting down.' She looked down at herself. 'In fact, this position is perfect for that move. Would you like me to demonstrate?' she asked sweetly.

He gulped. 'Maybe some other time. So where were we in the story?' he continued hurriedly.

Sathi grinned. 'Kamsan's brother-in-law promised to hand over their babies.'

'Ah yes. So then Kamsan decided to imprison the couple and needless to say, he killed all his new-born nephews. As you can imagine, Devaki and her husband Vasudeva weren't very happy bunnies by this point.

'Then one day Lord Vishnu himself appeared in the prison and told them that he was gonna take a birth on Earth to save them. He appointed Vasudeva to take their eighth baby boy to Gokula as soon as he was born.' Zakiy paused. 'I don't know if you've seen the major flaw in this plan. If they could have left the prison, they wouldn't have had to offer up their kids like some kind of perverse peace-offering in the first place. But I guess they don't say God is omnipotent for nothing. When Vasudeva prepared to depart to Gokula with a baby Krishna in his arms, his chains fell off, the prison doors opened by themselves, and all the guards he met on his way were snoring obliviously.

'So Vasudeva set out. When he had travelled for some while, he came to a river that he had to cross to reach Gokula. It wasn't that deep or wide, and would have been a piece of cake to wade through if it had been a nice summer day with the sun smiling and wind rustling and all that. But it was midnight, with not even the moon to light their way, and the wind had better things to do than merely *rustle*; it was lashing about the place and pollinating the world with rain, courtesy of the massive storm that was going on. Hey!' Zakiy exclaimed suddenly. 'That was quite literary wasn't it – pollinating the world with rain? Hmm... maybe I should copyright it. What do you think?' he asked Sathi.

'I think that if you don't carry on with the story you're not gonna be able to copyright anything – ever.'

Zakiy pouted. 'You're no fun.'

'I know. It's part of the job description.'

He shot her a puzzled look. 'What job?'

'The exhausting job of being your friend. Now,' Sathi continued without giving him a chance to retort, 'carry on with the story – you left off in an interesting bit.'

'Fine. But I want it noted that I'm only doing it to prove you wrong – being my friend isn't all that exhausting.'

'Duly noted.'

Zakiy appeared satisfied. 'So, Vasudeva had to cross this river in the middle of the storm, getting attacked from both above and below. Now this is the interesting part; Vasudeva carried Krishna on a woven basket that he held above his head to protect the baby from the waves that were crashing around his waist, but he couldn't do anything about the rain thundering down on both of them. And so the myth goes that Adishesha the serpent rose out of the thrashing waters to spread his thousand hoods over baby Krishna.'

Zakiy sighed romantically. 'Could a friendship get any better?'

Sathi agreed with the sentiment, but she *really* wanted to hear the rest of the story: 'What happened then?'

'Well, once he reached Gokula, Vasudeva switched Krishna with the baby girl Yashoda had just given birth to and returned to his wife in the prison in Kamsan's palace.'

156

'What?' Sathi exploded, outraged. 'But Kamsan will kill that baby girl! How could Vishnu let another baby die?'

'Sathi, chill,' Zakiy replied placatingly. 'Of course Vishnu's not gonna let Kamsan slaughter another child. The reason Vishnu wanted Vasudeva to switch Krishna with a baby girl was because the prophecy said their eighth *son* would be the one to kill Kamsan... not daughter. So they all thought the girl would be safe. As it turned out, though, Kamsan didn't really care about gender issues, he just wanted to kill off every threat. You never know, maybe he was worried about a future gender change as well. A progressive villain... how refreshing. Anyway, so Vasudeva got back to Mathura and waited for Kamsan.'

Sathi opened her mouth, about to interrupt indignantly again, but Zakiy took preventative action: 'But this is where girl power kicks in.' He grinned at her. 'Yashoda's baby was actually an incarnation of Durga Devi – the warrior goddess. When Kamsan came into the prison, having been informed that his sister had given birth to his prophesied destroyer, he tried to seize the newborn, who immediately rose into the air and transformed into her heavenly form. She laughed at Kamsan and told him that his nemesis had already been born elsewhere. Then she disappeared in a puff of divine dust, and then it was Kamsan's turn to be the unhappy bunny of the family.' He paused, reconsidering. 'Only for a little while, though. Just until Krishna killed him and freed his parents and the people of Mathura from his tyranny.'

'Hmm,' Sathi said. 'Yes, I'm sure that made Kamsan a happy bunny again.' She shook her head at his logic, and then remembered what Zakiy had said about Krishna's birth being similar to his little sister's. 'So what does this have to do with Zoya? And before you say I have no patience, just remember that karate move I was telling you about earlier,' she warned.

He didn't take the hint. 'I'll tell you, but you have to admit that you are kind of impa... what are you doing?' he asked in an entirely different tone.

Sathi had her right arm pushed out in front of her, fist down, with her left one held bent back so her up-turned fist was in line with her hip. In swift motions, she reversed the positions of her right and left fists, repeating the gesture rapidly, left, right, then left again, so that her arms shot back and forth with enough force to punch through solid metal. Or, say, someone's nose.

'What are you doing?' Zakiy repeated, an unmistakeable note of trepidation in his voice.

She didn't pause in her practised movements. 'Just stretching my muscles.'

'Oh, erm, that's great, that's lovely,' he replied, his eyes struggling to focus on the road instead of on her arms. 'So the reason Krishna's story is relevant to Zoya is because...' Zakiy waited expectantly. 'Drumroll, please!'

She cracked her knuckles and increased the pace of her punches.

'Okay, okay, so basically, the night we "acquired" Zoya, there was this amazing thunderstorm going on. Almost exactly at midnight, we heard a - ' Zakiy broke off, and frowned. 'No, that's not right. Actually, Aman heard it first, and we thought it was just a part of his... well, you know, his hallucinations. Then we heard it as well – the cry of a newborn piercing the night. When we went outside to investigate, we couldn't see anything at first, the rain was pouring down so hard. The moon was so well-hidden behind bruised-looking, grey-blue clouds that it might as well not have been there at all.

'Finally, in one lucky flash of lightning, we saw her; she was the most exquisite baby I'd ever seen, with a face so uniquely lovely you just couldn't look away. It's like you became her prisoner after first glance.'

He laughed fondly, and when he spoke again, there was an undercurrent of wonder and awe in his voice. 'That would have been enough to label her the most special baby in the world, but Zoya had more surprises in store for us. When we finally reached her, we couldn't believe our eyes; she was floating on an upturned umbrella in the middle of a storm, unhurt, and apart from some dampness on the fringes of her baby clothes, she was bone dry.'

Chapter Seventeen

Linguistics

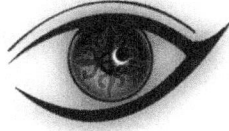

There was silence as Sathi digested everything. Her arms had stilled long ago, and her gaze was fixed on the night flying past behind her window. Finally, she saw Zakiy peeking at her worriedly. A shadow fell over most of her face, and she knew all he would be able to see of her was the edge of her jaw and the sheen of hair that fell over her shoulders.

Zakiy apparently couldn't stand the quiet any more. 'I know it sounds unbelievable,' he offered. 'I wouldn't have believed it if I hadn't been there myself. You'll just have to take my word for it.' He paused. 'Of course, my word isn't really worth all that much.'

There was another moment of pregnant silence, and then Sathi said, 'You're right. It *is* unbelievable.'

She tried not to smile at the sudden grim set of her companion's mouth that had been the effect of her words. 'But,' she continued, 'it's not nearly as unbelievable as finding a best friend who reads Tarot cards, will go to the ends of the earth and back to help me, has the most hilariously goofy sense of humour, and, despite being a complete and utter nutcase, is someone I can trust implicitly.'

She had been watching him, so she saw the way his face, well-lit by the moon, deepened in colour as he flushed. Sathi couldn't help grinning outright at the sweet idiot, who continued to gaze doggedly out of the windscreen as if the line of traffic queuing in front of them was the most fascinating thing in the world.

'So,' she began, trying to tease his attention away. 'Your parents took Zoya in after you guys found her?'

'Yeah.' Zakiy coughed. 'They first asked around everywhere to try and find her real parents, and reported her to the police and everything, but no one seemed to know anything about the little midget. So then my mother decided that she wanted to try a hand at raising a girl, seeing as she'd already had the pleasure of bringing up two boys.'

Sathi snorted. 'Bringing you up must have been a real pleasure.'

He turned to grin at her, and she was relieved to note that the earlier embarrassment was gone from his eyes, although traces of the pleasure remained. That was okay.

'Hey, I was an awesome son. I still am,' he defended.

Sathi raised an eyebrow. 'No comment.'

'Anyway, that's how Zoya joined our family. We've all kind of spoiled her, but she's still an adorable little thing.' Zakiy gave her a pointed look. 'As you'll find out.'

She smiled at the prospect of meeting this much-loved little sister, although apprehension crowded in uninvited as well. She'd never been great with children. She always felt... kind of awkward with them. She never knew what to say, and even when she did manage to say something semi-appropriate, it always sounded pretentious and false. She was sure they detected that falsity as well, the way they looked at her with large, unblinking eyes. Would she get on any better with Zakiy's sister?

Stop it, Sathi berated herself, feeling absurd for her anxiety. What a stupid thing to be worried about. Anyway, she might not even meet the kid until she was a teenager, considering the vast sea of hopelessness that stretched out between them and her mother's killer. 'That's only if we find that beslubbering milk-livered pignut any time in the foreseeable future,' she said to Zakiy.

Which reminded her. 'Don't you want to know what happened today?' she asked rhetorically before launching into an abbreviated version of the Teashop Scene, including what that guy Shankar had said about kaivisham.

Like Manish, Zakiy's first reaction was protective indignation. 'Did that deranged guy hurt you?'

'Huh? Oh, Jayaram. No, no, like I said, he was just kind of in my personal space, that's all.' It occurred to her that Zakiy might know more about kaivisham. After all, he knew so much about Hindu mythology and—

Hold on. Wasn't he supposed to be Muslim?

'Zakiy, how do you know so much about the Hindu gods and their legends? Isn't your God Allah?'

'Well, for one thing, my dad's a Hindu. I've grown up hearing these stories. And about my God being Allah... well, the thing is, I personally like to think about God as being Allah. But I think there's only just one God.' Upon observing Sathi's confused expression at his inarticulate explanation, Zakiy tried to think of a good analogy.

'Okay, think about it this way,' he said after a moment. 'Language is a way of communication, right, it's just something formed of a series of sounds. But every society, every ethnic group, has different sounds to communicate mostly the same ideas. And what language you use is a matter of preference, of familiarity. For example, a Malayali with very limited knowledge of English would prefer to say *"njan oru patti aanu"* instead of "I am a dog" - should he ever feel a necessity to announce to society that he happens to be a dog - simply because he is more comfortable with Malayalam, because it's the language he has grown up hearing and the language that he has been using all his life. In the same way, my dad has been a Hindu all his life, and he grew up in a Hindu community and believes in the Hindu deities as opposed to the single God in Islam or Christianity. And ditto with my mum. She grew up believing in Allah, and still believes in him, even though she's been shunned by her family because she fell in love with a Hindu, aka my dad, and eloped with him.'

He glanced at Sathi. She was frowning, but it was more of a contemplative frown, as opposed to a "what the hell is he talking about" frown. Finally, she spoke. 'So what you're saying is, God, or your faith, is like meaning and the religion you believe in is the language you speak?'

'A clear and concise summary, although not as eloquent as my pretty speech, of course.'

She narrowed her eyes at him, but otherwise ignored the quip. 'So, where do you figure into all this?' She smiled. 'Are you a bilingual?'

'Exactly!' he exclaimed, delighted. 'I had a taste of both religions, and as I grew up I realised that Allah was the one I felt closest to. I'm not sure why. Whenever - '

Zakiy cut himself off automatically, and then forced himself to move past the ingrained reluctance. He took a deep breath. 'Whenever Aman became violent and uncontrollable, I always felt so afraid and so... alone. My parents felt the same, but they sort of leaned on their faith whenever things became too unbearable, and they always seemed to be re-energised afterwards. They tried to help me do that too, they tried to get me to talk to them, but it was just too much, you know? It was bad enough to live marinated in that day after day, I couldn't *talk* about it on top of everything else. I always felt separate from my parents, removed, like they were the mainland and I was a little island floating out into the sea by itself.

'The Tarot cards let me get from one day to another, and then gradually I started seeing messages in them and certain cards kept coming up again and again, as if they wanted to get my attention. Then I realised that somehow Allah was with me, and he was showing me that he was with me through the cards.' Zakiy grinned. 'And I think he's the awesomest entity in the universe. Do you believe in God?' he asked abruptly.

Sathi was startled by the sudden question. 'Um... no.' The image of Devi popped into her mind. 'Not really.'

He accepted the vague answer without comment, and she was grateful. She didn't feel like discussing her mother's goddess – especially when she had no idea what to think about any of it. If Zakiy was bilingual, what was she? Mute?

'You know, I've forgotten how we got onto talking about this.' Zakiy scratched his head, looking legitimately puzzled. 'This happens to me all the time – do you remember?'

'Er...' She thought back over their conversation. 'I asked you why you knew so much about Hindu mythology... Oh yeah. I was telling you what Shankar said about kaivisham. What do you know about it?'

'In a word, nothing. I know that it's black magic, but that you already know.' Zakiy's forehead furrowed, and he tapped a thoughtful finger against the steering wheel. 'But, I do know something about other types of black magic – especially among Muslims. Like, there are these things called jinns. Otherwise known as genies. Unfortunately, they're not all cute and cuddly like that jolly blue guy in Aladdin. They're supposed to be supernatural beings who can be good or evil, but a lot of people believe that they're sent into their homes by someone who wishes them ill, to scare them and destroy their peace. So if you mention jinns to a Muslim, be prepared for them to jump right out of their purdah in fright.'

Sathi shot him a shocked look, sure she hadn't heard him right. 'Didn't you just say something incredibly blasphemous?'

He was unconcerned. 'Why? Is it blasphemous to be truthful and pious to be hypocritical? I don't believe in religion being used as an opportunity for self-serving. Spouting all that crap about the purdah allowing a women to be judged by their inner beauty as opposed to their physical beauty doesn't change the fact that it has been used to subjugate women and confine them to cooking and raising kids. I've always thought women wearing those ridiculous black things look like a flock of penguins.'

Despite her shock, she couldn't help the laughter that erupted from the mental image his description created. Zakiy shot her a grin. 'Glad to amuse you, m'lady. So, anyway, rant aside, the jinns are usually bad news.'

'Do *you* believe in them?' she asked sceptically. Now that he'd mentioned it, she couldn't get the Disney Genie out of her head.

Zakiy's expression became introspective. 'I wouldn't say I believe in jinns specifically per se, but it kind of makes sense that there will be that negative counterpart to God. Energy has to be in balance – where there is a good energy, there has to an equal and opposite bad energy to counteract it. Elementary, my dear Watson.'

'Why do you get to be Sherlock Homes?' Sathi asked indignantly, even though secretly she was impressed with the mixed analogy of the scientific and the supernatural.

That earned her a grin. 'When you have profound wisdom to impart to the world, you can be Sherlock.'

'Good.' Then she got back to the topic. 'What else do you know about Muslim black magic?'

'Well, then there are the animal sacrifices.' Zakiy shuddered, an expression of revulsion creasing his face. 'Even people with good intentions do them – my cousin tried to sacrifice a goat so I would pass my finals, but I found out in the nick of time. I threatened to sacrifice him if he did any such thing. Taking away a life, any kind of life, is unacceptable - shoot!'

Zakiy wrenched the steering wheel sharply to the right and punched down on the break. Thankfully, the new Jeep skidded to a stop just inches from where the motorbike had been mere seconds before. Zakiy wound down the window and yelled, 'Artless codpiece!' after the racing idiot who had cut across Toothless on Zakiy's blindside, driving at least 20 kph faster than he should have been.

Zakiy turned to Sathi. 'You ok?'

'Yeah, I'm fine.' She appeared a bit shell-shocked, but otherwise unhurt.

As soon as the Jeep had stopped, a chorus of honking had started up from impatient drivers behind. 'All right, all right, calm down,' he muttered, getting the bite on Toothless and pulling off again. 'You'd think they'd realise it's either this or a dead body in the middle of the road. Stupid two-wheelers. They'd squeeze through the gap between your nostrils if you let 'em.'

'But why was he driving so fast?' Sathi asked. 'Especially while overtaking?'

"Cos he's a nitwit, like all of them. I like going at high speed myself, but not on something that's less stable than a camel with one leg. Did you know, recently they've even started competitions about who can get to a certain place in the city and back the fastest? Cash prize in hand for the winner.'

'That's suicidal!' she exclaimed.

Zakiy shrugged by way of reply. The depressing thing was that the racers were usually no older than him. It was just so stupid. Bikes were the cause of most accidents in India, and yet they were still the most abundant vehicles on the road. His parents had made him swear at a very early age never to accept a lift on a bike, and he'd never been tempted to break the promise.

He was distracted from the familiar fuming when the headlights bleached the huge leaves of a *vazha* in the road. He swerved carefully around it, giving it a wide berth.

'Um, Zakiy?'

'Yeah?' he replied, even though he could guess her question.

Sathi hesitated, as though she couldn't believe she was asking this. 'Why is there a banana tree in the middle of the road?'

'People living locally plant them where there are huge potholes. In the daylight its fine, but at night it's virtually impossible to see the hole until you're practically on top of it. Half your spine disintegrates if you drive over a big one like that without seeing it. A plant is a bit harder to miss.'

'Hmmm... I'm guessing the government won't fix them any time soon?'

He laughed without humour. 'What are you saying, Sathi?' he asked in mock indignation. 'They have better things to do with all that money than maintain the roads.'

Sathi opened her mouth and then shut it again, a look of chagrin on her face. 'What?' he asked.

'I was going to say that the government in UK manages to maintain roads pretty well on top of other "extra-curricular activities". Then I remembered that I've been noticing more and more potholes in London recently,' she explained, shrugging.

Just then, the light drizzle of rain intensified into a proper downpour. Zakiy cursed and reached for the wipers, turning them to full power. 'Great. We're just getting into an area littered with so many potholes that it makes Swiss cheese look dense, and lack of visibility is something I do not need right now.'

Zakiy blew out a breath in frustration. 'Sorry, Sathi, I won't be very good company for a while, not until we get past this town. Why don't you try and get some sleep?' he suggested. 'It's already past 1 am. One of us will need to be semi-conscious in the morning.'

'Okay,' she agreed, though her expression immediately flooded with guilt.

'And don't you dare feel bad,' Zakiy added. 'I know I moan a lot, but this is a challenge for me. The forces of the Universe shall not defeat me... mwahahaha! Just think about how cocky I'm gonna be tomorrow when I'll have successfully navigated my little Toothless to Thiruvananthapuram - unscathed.'

Sathi was still smiling as she reclined the seat back a little and cushioned her head on her hand. Her eyelids grew heavy as she gazed out of the windscreen in apathy.

Zakiy refocused on the road, reflecting that the bright lights that flashed from the oncoming traffic combined with the torrent of precipitation that rained down from the heavens above made it appear as though the Jeep was gliding above a blanket of pure, untouched snow.

The moon continued its vigil.

Chapter Eighteen

Thiru Anantha Puram

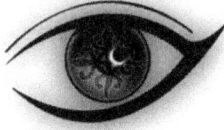

What do you want first – the good news or the bad news?'
Sathi lifted her head from the tourism leaflet she'd been reading in a vain attempt to keep herself awake and blinked up at Zakiy, bleary-eyed. It didn't make any sense that he looked more fresh and alert after a night of driving and only a couple of hours of sleep than she did after sleeping through most of the journey. Then she realised that he'd just asked her... what? Something about good news and bad news?

'Um... the bad news, I guess.'

Zakiy nodded in approval. 'Good choice. That gives you something to look forward to.' He threw a newspaper on the bed in front of her. 'They've declared a *harthal* today.'

Sathi scooted the paper closer to her. It was today's, but when she tried to read it she realised it was in Malayalam. She found it difficult to read her mother-tongue even when she wasn't half asleep - she usually forgot the beginning of the sentence by the time she finally made it to the end.

Time to take the path of least resistance. 'What's a harthal, who're "they" and why is that bad news?' she asked Zakiy.

'The politicians – they've declared a general strike. All the shops, offices, schools and most importantly, colleges, will be closed today.' He gave her a pointed look.

'What?' Sathi shot upright. 'How can they do that?'

Zakiy shrugged. 'Politicians don't really need an actual reason – anything under the sun will suffice. If my memory serves me correctly, the last one was because a minister's third concubine's dog had diarrhoea.'

She shook her heavy head, wishing that she was still asleep. 'Are you telling me that we could have been asleep in bed last night instead of tearing out here and travelling through the whole night and checking into this hotel in the early hours of the morning, just so we'll get here in time to go to the college?' Her voice had risen with each word, and she was near shrieking by the time she finished.

Thankfully, Zakiy seemed to realise that her temper tantrum wasn't directed at him. He held his hands up in an appeasing gesture, and again she wondered how he could be so calm about this, despite having been the one most affected by it.

'I know, I know. This is the problem with coming to Thiruvananthapuram – it *is* the capital of Kerala after all.' He sighed and rubbed at his eyes. She noticed that there were dark circles under them. Zakiy let himself fall backwards onto the other single bed in the room, bouncing a couple of times before lying still with his long limbs falling off on either side. 'Ah well. We'll just have to go tomorrow, and in the meantime we'll get a solid night's sleep.'

'But what about your classes?' Her head was starting to hurt. They had only a limited amount of time to get back to Nelliampathi. 'They start on Tuesday, right? We have to start back the day after tomorrow.'

'Quit worrying, it'll be fine. If push comes to shove, I'll just miss a day.' He opened one eye to grin at her. 'I've always wanted to bunk – and when else am I gonna do it than in my final year?'

Sathi glared at him. 'You'll do not such thing. If that's your plan, I'll make you go back today!'

Zakiy put a hand to his heart. 'You can separate friends, but can you separate a knight from his lady?'

'What's the protocol if the lady wants to, say, kill her knight?'

He sighed dreamily. 'If she did that, she'd die right along with him.'

Sathi groaned, and fell back into her sprawl. 'You know, if I had the energy, I'd throw this pillow at you.'

'Please do.' He plumped up the one under his head. 'This one's a bit hard.'

She groaned again and pulled the pillow down over her head. Then she abruptly sat up, and the pillow fell to the side, forgotten. 'Hold on. Didn't you say there was some good news?' she asked hopefully.

'Oh yeah!' Zakiy replied enthusiastically. 'Guess what there is right outside the hotel?'

'What?'

'An ice cream shop!'

This time she did throw the pillow. It bounced off his stomach and he hugged it to himself happily. 'Hey, ice cream makes everything better,' he argued without even opening his eyes.

She looked at him, lying there with limbs sticking out in every direction, and her heart melted. She got up and kicked at the bed. 'Get up. Come on, up!'

'Wha - ? Oh, come on. Look if you don't want ice cream, I'll have your share. You don't have to kick me out- Ouch!' Zakiy finally became dislodged, and stood off to one side, still clutching the pillow she'd thrown and looking utterly baffled.

Sathi reined in her smile and got to work shoving the two beds together, kneeing them into submission. Straightening up, she surveyed with satisfaction the double bed she'd created. She went over to Zakiy and pulled the pillow away from him. She turned and deposited it on the bed.

'There. If you lie diagonally, you might just manage to fit all of you in.' She pointed a finger at him, and then at the bed. 'Sleep.'

Zakiy didn't move. He kept looking at her as if he'd just been socked over the head. He must be more tired than he looked if he didn't have a witty remark to throw out. 'Don't expect me to read you a bedtime story,' Sathi warned.

That snapped him out of his comatose state, and he shook his head ruefully as he walked over and sat down. 'If you're good, you can have ice-cream for breakfast,' she told him.

'Yay! Hey – wait. Where're you gonna sleep?' Zakiy looked around the room as though expecting another bed to materialise from thin air.

'I'm not going to,' she replied. 'I'll never wake up today if I do. Now *you* quit worrying, and go to sleep.' Some more insistence did the trick, and he was finally stretched across the beds – diagonally. He fell asleep in the middle of a smart-alecky quip.

Sathi stood looking at him fondly for a few moments, and then she yawned and started heading towards the balcony doors she'd spotted earlier. On second thought, she went back and grabbed the leaflet from the bed-side table where she'd dropped it. She had a feeling she would need it.

She stepped out into the full-blown heat of the mid-morning sun. She'd almost forgotten how humid it was outside Nelliampathi – the last time she'd felt this heat had been when she first arrived in Kerala. She knew it would only get worse as the morning progressed into noon.

Sathi strolled up to the iron railings that encased the balcony and leaned her arms on it, looking down at the streets of the capital of Kerala. They were on the second floor of the hotel, but she decided that the view wouldn't have been much better even if they'd had the penthouse. (Not that the hotel had a penthouse, but still). Unlike Nelliampathi, where the greenery and lush vegetation were the ruling factor, in this central town the coconut trees and the scattered mango and banana trees were overrun by huge, oblong buildings and a plethora of apartment blocks that were identically boring and predictable. Electrical wires stretched back and forth above scurrying people like a massive web woven by uncoordinated spiders.

Sathi couldn't imagine how her mother had managed to relocate here after growing up in Nelliampathi.

The grass is always greener on someone else's lawn, an errant thought whispered in her mind. She frowned, thinking that the saying was probably apt (although she did prefer Sebastian the Lobster's version: the seaweed is always greener on somebody else's lake!)

Sathi had lived in London most of her life, alone amidst a hub of constant activity, taking things like easy transport and internet access for granted. Nelliampathi didn't offer up those technical comforts, and for someone who'd been living there for eighteen years, the idea of living in the city must have been alluring, an adventure.

Looking back at the view, Sathi tried and failed to feel that same attraction. She was tired of being a city girl. And that was absolutely fine.

She sank down onto the floor of the balcony, leaning against the side wall with her knees drawn up to her chest. She closed her eyes, trying to cut down on the thoughts and questions swirling around her tired mind. She felt both excitement and dread at the thought of visiting her mother's old college. She might find something that would give her more information about her Amma, but she was scared of what else she'd find, especially after the bad experiences at her mother's school.

Cut it out, she chastised herself. *We didn't travel all the way to Thiruvananthapuram so you could act like a wuss.* She forced herself to stop thinking, to simply enjoy the way the warm sunlight was soaking into her skin like butter into toasted bread, lighting up the backs of her eyelids with a deep red. Sathi never noticed the dull colour gradually flame into a brilliant scarlet.

Her dream involved a talking crow telling her that she would never live up to her mother, and that Sathi was too weak to avenge her. She was trying her best to ignore it, and then she caught sight of a cloudy patch of deep, misty violet, highlighted with gold, floating on the sky above her. It stayed tantalisingly out of her reach as she desperately followed it on her own manoeuvrable cloud...

Sathi jolted awake and blinked against the harsh sun. She looked around her in disorientation. She was still on the balcony, and the tourism leaflet was precariously balanced on her knees, obviously not having done its job in keeping her awake.

She had just rescued the thing from falling off when she heard movement. She looked up. Zakiy was leaning casually against the doorway to the balcony, his arms crossed. His hair was a complete mess, and his clothes were scuffed and crinkled beyond hope of recovery, but his trademark grin was there nevertheless. When he caught her eye, his smile widened. 'Next time, you're sharing the bed,' he told her.

Sathi made a face at him. 'If you want to do something useful, come and give me a hand up,' she ordered.

'Your wish is my command.' Zakiy barely had to take a step forward to reach her with his long arm, but she forgave him his abnormality once she was up on her feet and stretching herself in satisfaction.

'Are your bones supposed to creak like that at your age?' he enquired curiously.

'It's your influence,' she replied. 'I wouldn't be surprised if I had some premature greys already.' She flipped the mass of hundred per cent black hair back over her shoulder, using the opportunity to study him. The long sleep seemed to have done him a world of good, and he was back to the Zakiy she knew and loved. Sigh.

He shot her an injured look. 'You're blaming everything on me lately. Grey hair, osteoporosis, bad mood... Now if I go grey -'

'If?' she interrupted. 'Don't you mean when?'

Zakiy grinned. 'No. You see, I have a theory...'

'No!' Sathi held up her arms in surrender. 'Not another one. There are only so many of your crazy theories I can listen to.'

'They're not crazy!'

'Oh really?' she asked incredulously. 'What about the one where you said you can cut down the carbon footprint of a person by forcing them to spend a couple of hours in an unventilated place with all the carbon dioxide they produced in that week?'

'Hey, it would work! And it was going to be all the CO_2 from the month, so this is actually going easy on them.'

Sathi shook her head, wondering why she was even having this discussion. She just needed to accept that her best friend was also the craziest person on the universe.

'I don't want to know your theory on going grey,' she told him firmly.

Zakiy pouted. 'Fine. But you shouldn't have interrupted me in the first place if that was the case. You should learn from me, I never interrupt myself.' He frowned. 'Wait. That doesn't make any sense.'

Sathi rolled her eyes. 'Er, newsflash. *Nothing* you say makes sense.'

'You have to listen to what I'm gonna do if I go grey,' he insisted stubbornly.

She sighed. 'What are going to do if you go grey?'

'I'm gonna change my name to Silverfox!'

Sathi stared at him. 'Fascinating.' Then she turned on her heel and headed inside to have a shower, firmly shutting the door on Zakiy offering that she could be Silvervixen.

'See?' Zakiy said around a mouthful of cone. 'Ice-cream is perfect for breakfast.'

'Yes,' she agreed, choosing not to point out that it was early evening. She licked at the butterscotch and watched the lonely-looking road, emptied of its usual commuters. Their hotel stood on-looking the main road, but the shop they'd bought their ice-creams from was built in a small cache that shielded them from the vapid sun and the dry, upswept dust of the city.

It had taken a bit of persuasion of Zakiy's part to get the ice-creams; the shop wasn't so much as an ice-cream shop as a shop that sold ice-creams, along with packets of milk, snacks, magazines and newspapers. So it was basically a convenience store of sorts. But, like all the other shops that huddled together at the heart of the city, it had been shuttered up due to the strike.

However, the physical reminder of the harthal had not fazed Zakiy. He'd simply stalked up to the shutter, rapped sharply on it with his knuckles, grinned at the grumpy shop-keeper who poked his head from under a gap in the shutter, and retreated with the goods.

'You see,' he'd explained as he handed her a Cornetto, 'for a college student like me, a strike is good news. It means I get a day off! Same with people who have government jobs – they get to put their feet up, have a holiday and they still get paid. But for people like him,' he continued, gesturing back at the shuttered shop, 'it means a lost day of business. They own their own shops, so what they sell in a day – or don't sell – is what they get. So some of them stay in their shops behind the shutter and do some business on the side. It's mutually beneficial.'

Mulling over the idea, Sathi had to admit that it sounded reasonable. And from what Zakiy said, these strikes seemed to be a frequent occurrence; living in Thiruvananthapuram must be a massive pain in the podex.

'So,' Zakiy began, wiping his hands, 'you ready for a tour of the Lord's own city?'

They had been walking for about ten minutes when it suddenly struck her that their tour would have to be on foot due to the strike. Sathi thought back to her hasty internet search on the capital of Kerala, and remembered with a sinking heart that Thiruvananthapuram district was about twice the size of Palakkad, the district within which Nelliampathi was just a tiny dot. Thiruvananthapuram city itself covered more than a hundred square kilometres. The distance would have been a piece of cake with Toothless the Jeep, or even an auto-rickshaw. But on foot?

She gave Zakiy a sidelong glance. He was ambling along, humming, looking around at the closed shops and empty streets as though he'd been given a free pass in Disneyland. He certainly didn't seem to be worrying about the small marathon that stretched in front of them. Now the question was, did he have a plan or was he just being dopey?

Sathi frowned, thinking that the question would have been easier to answer if he didn't act dopey even when he had a plan. She decided to have some faith, and see what he'd do. If they were still walking after fifteen minutes, she would put her foot down (figuratively).

Thankfully, they reached their destination about five minutes later: a bus stand. There was no one else there. She turned to Zakiy, confused. 'Are we taking a bus?'

He looked at her in amusement. 'Did you think we were walking around the whole city?'

Sathi glared, trying to pretend that wasn't exactly what she'd been thinking. 'I thought buses weren't running today,' she argued.

'Well, they don't run to a normal schedule. Four or five buses go by together every hour, escorted by a mobile squad.' He grinned. 'Safety in numbers.'

Despite his casual tone, the first sliver of apprehension needled through her. Safety in numbers? Police escort? Until that moment, she had been thinking of the strike as something trivial, something inconvenient, something that had to simply be endured. It had never occurred to her, even though it should have, that it was also something dangerous.

Zakiy obviously saw the realisation in her eyes because he said gently, 'Sathi, don't worry. It's just a precaution - this harthal is about petrol price hike, or something like that. No one will be pelting stones at anything today. Besides, the strike ends at six o'clock, and that's less than two hours away.'

She was grateful for his effort to comfort her, but she also heard the unspoken message in the words. Had the circumstances been different, she had a feeling that they would have stayed in the hotel until the morning.

Sathi didn't have much time to speculate on that cheerful thought because just then, five KSRTC buses rolled lazily up to the stand. As Zakiy motioned for her to go up the stairs of one of the red-and-yellow buses, she couldn't help but glance at the police Jeep that idled behind the last bus. The bored appearance of the khaki-clad men gave her more comfort than their actual presence did.

Chapter Nineteen

Ananthashayana

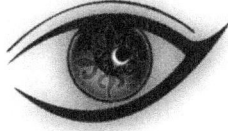

As cities went, Sathi had to admit that Thiruvananthapuram was pretty cool.

Zakiy pointed out the secretariat, a mind-bogglingly majestic white building with gorgeous arching doorways, its centre marked by a protruding post-and-beam structure with a double-triangle roof. A miniature clock tower rose out of the huge building, topped by a long pole that brandished an Indian flag. Then they walked through the busy junction that was simply named the Statue, after the effigy of Madhava Rayar, *Diwan* of King Rama Varma of Travancore.

After that, they moved onto a place that made the secretariat look like a kid's best efforts with Lego; the Kowdiar Palace. It was amazing and *huge* and white with gorgeous red-brick caps that tapered gracefully into sharp points and *huge* and peppered with thousands of amazing arch-windows and *huge*. Did she mention that it was huge?

When Sathi had had her fill gawking, they walked to East Fort and toured the huge run-down shopping complex inside the Fort, as well as visiting the diverse Connemara bazaar behind it, which seemed to be indifferent to the harthal as the lively market maintained a steady buzz of bargaining customers. There was everything in the stalls, from cheap clothes to kitchen utensils to fake jewellery.

They finally left the market as dusk fell, and caught the bus to the coast. They walked along Shanghumugham beach, watching the waves crash against the shore as the sun's fading rays hugged the water goodbye. The giant, thirty-five foot sculpture of Jalakanyaka, or the Mermaid, reclined on her enormous carved sea-shell, her eyes closed as she inclined her huge face up to the heavens.

They were sitting on the beach with the salt water tickling their bare toes with each incoming wave when Zakiy suddenly turned to face her. He regarded her thoughtfully for a few moments and then asked, 'Do you own a skirt? A long one?'

And for a moment there she'd thought he had something important to say. Sathi shook her head and went back to watching the waves. 'Why, are you thinking of cross-dressing?' she asked.

'We can get you one,' he replied, obviously not listening as he continued to stroke his chin in a mastermind-like way.

'Why are you suddenly so interested in the contents of my wardrobe?'

'Well, because you can't go in there wearing jeans, or any kind of trousers,' was the enigmatic response.

'Go in where?' she asked in exasperation, wondering if all the sleepless driving had finally sent him over the edge.

He looked up at her slowly, blinking as though he had only just noticed her. Which didn't even make sense. 'Oh sorry. I just had the best idea ever. You know how you're always raving about architecture?'

Sathi nodded, puzzled.

'Well, while we're in Thiruvananthapuram, I know just the place to show you. It involves meeting an old buddy of mine - if we don't visit him while we're here he's gonna be really mad at me. Come on,' he added, standing up and extending a hand to Sathi.

Still baffled, she put her hand in his and allowed him to pull her to her feet.

'But first,' he continued, brushing sand from his trousers, 'we need to find a skirt.'

Sathi examined herself in the hotel's floor-length mirror, fingering the beads and sequences on the beige skirt that flowed down to swirl around her ankles. She self-consciously pulled her T-shirt down, thinking that it looked very strange when combined with the long skirt.

Zakiy exited the bathroom, where he had been changing, and she called out, 'We should've bought two skirts.'

He stuck his head in beside her so he could check out his hair and make sure that it was sufficiently ridiculous-looking. 'Why's that?'

'Well, you did say that no one could wear jeans or trousers into this place. I've got this skirt, but what are you gonna do?' She paused, pretending to reconsider. 'I suppose you could always wear a towel.'

'Pfft. M'lady, you sorely underestimate me. Behold!' Saying which, he backed away a few steps and spread his arms grandly so that she could get the full effect of what he was wearing. Covering his torso was a midnight blue shirt, its long sleeves pushed up around his elbows. Below that, instead of slacks, was a traditional white Kerala-style *mundu*, a cotton woven wraparound garment that was worn (mostly) by men. This one was starched so that it lay stiffly to the ground, and had a navy blue line running through the edges.

'Very handsome,' Sathi approved, and as he bowed and held the hotel door open for her, she added, 'For a monkey.'

'Sri Padmanabhaswami Temple?' she echoed as she stared up at the temple entrance in disbelief. 'This is where your old buddy lives?'

'I guess you could say that.'

Frowning, she turned to scrutinise his expression. 'How old exactly is this old buddy?' she asked suspiciously.

Zakiy grinned at her. 'Oh, he's not all that old,' he replied casually, beginning to climb the stone steps leading to the entrance. 'He's only as old as time.'

Old as time? Yup, that's what she'd thought. Sathi hurried after him, demanding, 'Since when is Lord Vishnu your buddy?'

'Since he's my dad's favourite Hindu deity. Plus, he's a cool dude. You'll like him,' he promised as he kicked off his sandals and disappeared through the high archway.

Muttering to herself about best friends and Hindu deities, she followed him inside.

'Oh. My. God.' Sathi enunciated each word separately, her mouth gaping open unattractively.

'Told ya you'd like it,' Zakiy said smugly, satisfaction printed across his expression as he watched her reaction to the truly awe-inspiring architecture of the temple. The corridor – or maybe hall was a better word, considering its size – walls were covered in exquisitely carved stone sculptures of various Hindu deities, and the flickering lamps that lit the temple everywhere like a horde of fireflies bathed the stone and bronze in a soft light that made the statues seem to come alive.

They walked slowly through the corridor, Zakiy allowing her to gaze at the gorgeous paintings and murals around her to her heart's content and shielding her from the jostles of the mass of devotees who threatened to carry them off in a tidal wave of their own creation.

When they came up to the eighty feet tall flag post that was made of gold-plated copper sheets, however, Sathi came to an absolute standstill, staring up it in speechless wonder. She slowly turned to him, her eyes shining. 'Best. Friend. Ever,' she breathed, pointing at him.

His smile widened. 'I know,' he assured her.

They toured the *nataka shala* in the ground floor below the main entrance, where Kathakali was performed during festivals, and gushed over the *mandapam* where the Navagrahas, or the nine planets, were represented on the ceiling directly above their heads. After that, they visited the massive hall, where three hundred and sixty five and a quarter massive granite pillars resided, their surfaces carved with beautiful sculptures.

Finally, Zakiy glanced at his watch. 'Come on, let's go and visit the old man before the viewing hours are over. Otherwise he'll sulk until we come again.'

He led Sathi past the smaller shrines to the main *mandapam*, nodding respectfully to Narasimha (the half-man, half-lion incarnation of Vishnu) and grinning and waving at Krishna.

'What on earth are you doing?'

'Just saying hello.' He shook his head sagely. 'In my time, we were taught better manners.'

'Uh, you're only four years older than me,' Sathi pointed out. 'Besides, you look like an idiot, grinning at statues like that. And that priest thought you were waving at him.'

'All the better. I bet I just made his day.' He glanced around covertly and lowered his voice. 'By the way, if anyone wants to know, my name is Hari.'

Sathi started to chuckle, but stopped abruptly when she realised that he was being serious. 'Why?' she asked curiously.

'It's one of my aliases for when I visit temples. Did you know that Hari is another name for Vishnu?'

She shook her head. 'That's not what I was asking. Why do you have to use an alias in the first place?'

Zakiy shrugged. 'They'll throw me out if they find out I'm half-Muslim.'

'*What?*' She had a hard time keeping her voice low, incredulous as she was at the thought of someone being prevented from gaining entrance to this amazing architectural masterpiece simply because they did not share the same faith.

Then something occurred to her. 'But I'm not even a believer,' she hissed. 'So wouldn't I be thrown out as well?'

'Yeah, but at least you're not of another religion. And your name is Hindu, even though you're not.'

She let what he was saying sink into her. 'Unbelievable,' she muttered finally, disgusted. So, if you didn't believe in God, that wasn't as bad as you believing in another God. What a messed up way of thinking.

She was still ruminating over this as they finally got to the head of the queue and onto the platform where the main idol was situated.

She forgot about her disturbed preoccupation as soon as she set eyes on the Vishnu statue; she felt her eyes widening and her mouth dropping. The thing was at least fifteen feet long! And that wasn't even including the various little statues that accompanied the central one. Looking closer, she realised that the statue depicted the blue-skinned god reclining on a bed formed of the coiled and re-coiled tail - wound up like a bit like the coils in a transformer, in fact - of a massive serpent, which had its five hoods bowed protectively over the god's head.

The statue could only be viewed in parts, through the three windows in front of it. Through the first one, the god's head could be glimpsed, as well as an arm languidly reaching in the direction of his devotees. Through the second, his blue navel was visible, and out of it arose a lotus. Another god, Brahma the Creator if she remembered correctly, sat cross-legged on the lotus, his eyes closed in deep meditation. The last window allowed a peek at the god's mighty feet, and there next to the statue were other deities. Sathi squinted, trying to make out which idols they might be.

A shove from a devotee as they pushed their way to the front broke her concentration, and Zakiy and Sathi moved to the back railing so that they could stand without being pushed and jostled. The people lifted their palms high above their heads as they craned their necks to get a good view of the namesake of Thiruvananthapuram, worshipping him with their hearts and minds. They prayed out loud, or through glittering eyes; they fell to their knees, or pressed themselves against the windows, trying to get as close to their god as possible.

Two temple workers stood at either end of the platform, ushering the devotees along if they stopped for too long. 'Move along, move along,' one of them said, pushing an old man who was earnestly speaking to the statue, 'God doesn't want to hear you talking.'

Reluctantly, he allowed himself to be shoved along, glancing back at Vishnu after every step.

Zakiy leaned down to speak in her ear. 'Let's go. When it's closing time, they start to become quite nasty. They don't like loiterers.'

She didn't argue, and as they went down the steps that would get off the platform, she glanced back once at the reclining god. She was certain that, despite her dubious views on religion, if the god was real, then the first people on his blacklist would be the people who claimed to be working for him - the people who abused mistreated his true devotees using the power lent to them by him.

Chapter Twenty

Covert Ops

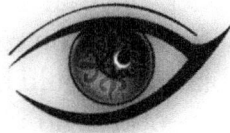

'So, m'lady, what's our plan of action?'

They had been idling in front of the entrance of Mar Ivanios college for over fifteen minutes now. Or rather, Sathi corrected herself, the entrances: the gateway had two driveways sitting side by side and another narrow one for people to walk up without getting run over by cars. The gated archway of the college was in the crook of the main road as it bent around as if it was made of pliable concrete, and cars and motorbikes seemed to be making up for their denied opportunity the day before to whizz around town this morning.

At Zakiy's question, she turned so she could glare at him properly. 'I don't know what your plan of action is, now that you've destroyed mine.'

Okay, she knew that calling her vague idea of finding a yearbook at her mother's old college a "plan of action" was beyond inane. She also knew she should win the Nobel Prize for stupidity for not even thinking about the teeny-tiny possibility that yearbooks might not have been in use in the 1990s. Hell, from what Zakiy said, most colleges still didn't use yearbooks.

Sathi stared at the college again. She was being very unfair. She knew that. It was just that she was so tired of being disappointed, time and time again. She had come to India with high hopes, only to find that her mother's adoptive family was somewhere halfway across the state. Then when she and Zakiy had found the school, she'd thought they would get to talk to someone who had known her mother, and maybe give Sathi some clue about who might have wanted to kill Amma (even though that had been a very long shot). What she'd got instead was an old prom-queen of a headmistress and an absent-minded professor. And no, the cliché wasn't lost on her.

It seemed as if for every step forwards she took, she was being repelled back ten steps. And to top it all off, she had no clue what to do now that they were finally at her mother's college.

'Hey, I said I was sorry,' said Zakiy.

Sathi sighed. Great. While she'd been wallowing in self-pity, he had been feeling guilty about her hateful words. 'No, *I'm* sorry. I know I'm being a bi -'

'Don't,' he warned, cutting her off.

She sighed again. She'd never done anything good enough to deserve his friendship. Her head seemed to sag down onto her hands all on its own. 'I don't know what to do,' she said.

'Well,' Zakiy began reasonably, 'we can always go and protest in front of the college. We'll bribe the student union and get them to boycott with us, since the two of us sitting out there holding plaques might not be so impressive.'

She understood approximately ten percent of what he'd just said, but she couldn't deny that the little she understood had the corners of her lips tilting up involuntarily. 'What would that accomplish, exactly?'

'Er... it would piss off the authorities?'

'And that would be helpful because?'

Zakiy had to think about it. 'It'll make us feel better?'

She lifted her head and grinned at him. 'Okay, I'll give you that one. Have I told you you're insane?'

'Not in the last thirty seconds.'

'You're insane.'

He smiled beatifically. 'Now I can go to sleep a happy man.'

'Don't go to sleep just yet. There *has* to be a way to get some information about my Amma.'

There were a few minutes of silence as they both thought. For her part, Sathi couldn't get past the idea of contacting her mother's old college mates using the yearbook. The non-existent yearbook, that is.

'I don't suppose...' Zakiy hesitated. 'I don't suppose you want to meet the principal?'

She had a flashback of Headmistress Dhayalakshmi Nair, and shuddered. 'No way,' she said emphatically.

Sathi could see that he was trying hard not to look too relieved. 'What's your hang-up with head teachers and principals anyway?'

'I don't know... in my experience they've always been some nasty dudes and dudettes. Anyone with any sense will have, as you say, a 'hang-up' with them.'

'Well, you don't have any sense, so there's no reason for you to worry,' she pointed out.

'Thanks for the reminder.' He sighed sappily. 'What would I do without you?'

'You can start to repay the debt by coming up with a brainwave – preferably before the police decide to arrest us for loitering by the side of a main road.'

'Good point. Okay, so talking to people is out. We have no Principal, and no classmates. We'll have to get more creative,' Zakiy reasoned. 'Okay, let's brainstorm around your mum. What kind of a mark would she have left on the college?'

'Um...'

'I know! The mad maths prof said she was a brilliant student, right? Provided he wasn't exaggerating because she was his favourite, she probably won awards and stuff, no? So we can just go to the library and look for certificates and stuff, and from there... well, I guess we can try and find out what she did after the undergrad degree. It's not the greatest plan ever, but then I'm just impressed I have a plan.' Zakiy looked expectantly at her.

'Mr Zakiy Narayan. How does it feel to have had a good idea for the first time in your life?'

He smiled goofily. 'You think it's a good idea?' Then the smile vanished. 'Hey! I've had plenty of good ideas in my life!'

'Uh-huh. Come on, let's go before the scientists show up to confiscate your brain for research.'

Zakiy complied, grumbling, 'First police, then scientists. What next, alien abductions? I have good ideas, I have lots of them! I have at least five good ideas per day. Huh! How dare you? Even my birth was a good idea...'

She ignored him and followed the sloping path up to the main college building, which she could see looming in the distance. A few minutes of walking brought them to the bottom of a set of long, wide steps, which they had to climb if they wanted to get into the college itself. Still, Sathi held back from going up the stairs straightaway, distracted by the sounds of activity in the grounds to their left. College students were hanging out in a large, empty space that seemed to double as a playground. At least, she assumed they were college students, if their age was any indication. It was such a contrast to the atmosphere of the school; there, the bells dominated what each student was doing at any time. No one, no matter how much they might have desired otherwise, was outside their assigned classroom unless they were on break or playing sick. Here, a mixture of guys and girls, ranging from her age to Zakiy's, lounged about as if they had nothing else to do. At the far end of the playground, two boys were playing one-on-one basketball (and getting themselves thoroughly dirty in the process from the dust they were kicking up). A large group milled around the steps, talking, laughing and eating out of crisp packets as they leaned against the bottom few stairs.

Near them, a couple of girls were painstakingly trying to put up an A2-sized poster on a high wall. As Sathi watched, the poster became unstuck at the top and flapped onto the head of the shorter of the two girls. Disgustedly wiping the glue off her hair, she gave up and relinquished the poster to her taller friend. The girl's initial amusement at her friend's misfortune soon became irritation as she found that the feat was too difficult even for her superior height. Persistent, she reached up on her tiptoes, trying to smooth down the top corners of the poster. She even tried jumping up and down a few times, with no luck. Her friend shook her head and started looking around for volunteers among the group on the stairs, who all seemed to be very busy all of a sudden.

Sathi was about to volunteer Zakiy when the shorter of the two girls suddenly shouted out, hailing the attention of a tall guy in low-riding jeans and a khaki T-shirt who had just walked past them.

'Hey! Can you help us?' the girl wheedled. She gestured to herself and then to her friend, who looked supremely irritated that they had to ask for help at all. The guy went over to them and, on the first try, managed to attach the stubborn poster to the wall, earning cheers and thank yous from both girls.

The guy threw up his arms in victory, grinning widely. 'Five seconds!' he exclaimed. 'That's all it took when I did it. Don't ever let a woman do a man's job, I say!'

The two girls' smiles had frozen into identical expressions of disbelief, and Sathi could feel her own face twist in disgust. Was he actually being serious, or was he just kidding around? She couldn't tell, and she sincerely prayed that it was the latter.

Before she could ruminate further, her attention was caught by the sudden arrival of a gleaming silver car. She didn't know what make it was – she wasn't yet skilled at recognising Indian car models. A girl got out of it. It was Hollywood style all the way; dark, long (and very bare) legs appeared first, while the edges of a short, clingy skirt climbed dangerously up the thighs. Then an athletically-built torso emerged, topped by a head covered in long, sleek black hair. If this was America, the girl would've fitted right into the Shiny clique.

She tossed back her hair so it shimmered down to mid-back and slammed the car door shut. She started walking towards the group on the steps, seemingly unaware that every pair of eyes in the playground was trained on her.

Sathi glanced around. Every male pair of eyes, anyway. They were all unabashedly checking out the new arrival from head to toe. Even the basketball dudes had stopped to stare, dirt smeared across their faces. She shook her head and glanced up to share a look of exasperation with Zakiy.

Her jaw dropped when she saw his face. He was ogling just as much as every other Y-chromosomed person present.

Sathi snapped her mouth shut and sighed. To misquote Stein, "A boy is a boy is a boy is a boy". She watched him watch the girl, her mind spinning with a mischievous thought that had just occurred to her. When he finally dragged his eyes from the girl's insanely long legs to glance at Sathi, he flinched back to see her looking right back at him. She smiled, purposefully sliding her eyes across to the girl and then back to him again.

Yup, his expression was definitely taking on that of one caught red-handed in the cookie-jar. Her smile widened, and without giving him a chance to say anything, she marched purposefully towards the Shiny girl. She was standing in a small group with a few friends, but she turned when Sathi tapped her on the shoulder.

'Hi,' she said. The girl's eyebrows rose as she gave Sathi a puzzled look.

Sathi forged ahead. 'Sorry to disturb you, but my friend,' she jerked a thumb over her shoulder to indicate Zakiy, 'would like to, uh, ask you out.' She wasn't quite sure how the English phrase would translate, but the girl seemed to get the message.

The Shiny girl's confusion faded as she regarded Zakiy with new-found interest. She peered around Sathi, taking in his height (he was tall for an Indian guy), longish hair and obviously designer clothes.

Sathi pushed her advantage. 'He's incredibly shy, so he asked me to talk to you.' The girl tossed her hair back again and floated past Sathi before she'd even finished speaking.

Sathi convulsed into giggles at the horror-struck expression on Zakiy's face as the Shiny girl latched herself onto him. He shot Sathi the international SOS look, but she pretended to wave them off. 'You kids have fun.'

The Shiny girl impatiently reclaimed his attention, smiling coquettishly, and Sathi clapped a hand over her mouth to muffle her laughter. Maybe she should match-make more often. She'd never realised that it was such a hilarious process. Zakiy's expression came back to her, and she bent over as another giggling fit hit her.

When Sathi regained control, with only the odd snort, she glanced at the stairs that led up to the college. She was debating whether to wait for Zakiy or to make her way to the library (and deciding with a giggle not to put a damper on their "date" – after all, he knew where she'd be) when she heard someone clear their throat behind her. She turned.

It was Mr Don't-Let-A-Woman-Do-A-Man's-Work. Sathi resented him for killing her good mood. Unfortunately, she couldn't exactly ignore him, seeing as he was looking at her expectantly. 'Yes?'

'Um, hello.' Was that nervousness underneath all that arrogance? 'I haven't seen you around here before. Can I help?'

'Oh.' Her annoyance deflated. 'Thanks. I just, um, wanted to look around the library.'

He brightened. 'Ah, a research student. We've had a few around this semester – after all, Mar Ivanios does have the best library. I'll show you where it is.' He stuck his hand out. 'I'm Manuel,' he leaned forward and winked conspiratorially, 'but you can call me Manu.'

Sathi didn't really have any choice but to give his hand a brief shake and then, after a last glance at a very pre-occupied Zakiy, follow him up the stairs. Having a guide would make this quicker, at least. Manuel seemed more than happy to talk, so she just made appropriate "aah" and "hmm" noises while she gawked around at her mother's college.

Her first thought was that it was enormous. As if the overwhelming height wasn't enough, the building seemed to stretch on endlessly on both sides, putting on display more of that amazing architecture. For a supposedly poor country, India – or at least this part of it - was turning out to be surprisingly affluent. Every building she'd seen so far had been huge and yet unique at the same time, unlike the skyscrapers back home.

Manuel ushered her through the main door, and then led the way assertively through crowded corridors teeming with people who were all busily on their way somewhere to do something. He wasn't afraid to employ his elbow where needed to knead his way through, and Sathi tried to keep close to his back so she could follow without getting trapped in the crowd.

When they emerged out into a little courtyard area, she used the increased space to push her way to his side. 'Are there yearbooks in the library?' she asked, slightly out of breath after their efforts.

His answer was mysterious: 'Not yet, but there will be.' Then, looking at her quizzically, 'Why are you asking about yearbooks? I thought you were here for research.'

'Oh, I am,' she lied. It was a convenient cover story. 'It's a, erm, special project. For media,' she added.

Manuel seemed to swallow that, so she pushed her luck. 'So, what were you saying about yearbooks?'

'Well, you see, this is my last year here and we've been bugging the principal to let us have a yearbook for months. He's finally given in, so our year will be the first to have one,' he concluded proudly.

It looked as if Zakiy had been right. Sathi let go of the last tiny flutter of hope she'd been harbouring. She lost interest in the conversation and tuned out again, going back to making non-committal noises as Manuel led her inside another, smaller, building.

'It was hard work persuading that old man to let us have a yearbook. Old-fashioned bore. We should all follow western culture – they obviously know what's good. Anyway -'

They had just walked into the library, and whatever else Manuel may have said was drowned out by Sathi's gasp. When they'd talked about the college library, she'd been imagining something very much like the local library in Nelliampathi: dark, dusty and populated by nondescript steel bookshelves stacked against the walls like sardines in a can.

Au contraire, walking into the Mar Ivanios library was like walking into heaven. Or more specifically, Sathi's personal version of heaven. It was a Victorian-style room with massive proportions, constructed entirely of what she was beginning to recognise as teak wood structures. Sunlight spilled copiously into the room through the arched mullioned windows that lined the far wall, and on the opposite side were tables and chairs for students to sit and study. It was the first floor that held the most gorgeous feature of the library, however; held up by pillars, it consisted of a veranda of bookshelves placed back to back, with a small square of space between each section. All the shelves were made of wood, setting a lovely backdrop to the thousands of books filling them.

Sathi walked deeper into the room, still staring around and generally acting like a person whose brain had lost control of their gaping mouth. The railing lining the veranda upstairs had intricate patterns etched into the wood, forming swirling lines, and heavy chandeliers hung from the ceiling like luminous jellyfish.

'Wow,' she breathed.

Manuel had followed her. 'Not bad, is it?' he asked proudly. 'It was rebuilt after a tree fell on this building in a storm years ago, and destroyed a lot of it. There's a plaque here somewhere naming the student who designed all this – some kind of architectural genius, if what my uncle says is right. He was at college at the same time as when the library was rebuilt, you know...'

Sathi only half-heard this, still caught up as she was in the beauty surrounding her. She wouldn't have minded spending the whole day there and looking over every inch of the room.

Unfortunately, she had a job to do. She turned to Manuel and offered him a smile. 'Thanks for showing me the way. I'll manage now, you can go back to your classes.'

He looked crestfallen. 'But I've only just met you,' he protested. 'I'll stay and help you find the books you need.'

'No!' Sathi exclaimed, and then quickly back-tracked. 'I mean, it's okay, don't worry about it. You don't know how I get with books,' she said sheepishly, shrugging. 'I get completely immersed in them and don't pay any attention to anything else. You'll be bored.'

Manuel gave her a slow once-over. 'I'm quite sure I will be able to keep myself occupied,' he said slowly, a weird smile on his face. Before she could argue (and demand what that smirk had been about), he was insisting that she follow him to the media section of the library.

She stood frozen as he went off to the far right corner of the room, and to the partially concealed stairway beyond. Shoot. What was she supposed to do now? She hadn't been banking on an audience! She would have to pretend to be looking at books when all she wanted to do was hunt for certificates.

'Hey!' Manuel called in a whisper, impatient at being made to wait at the bottom of the stairs.

Shoot, she thought again. Well, she couldn't just leave him standing there. But first she had to know if there were any certificates on the ground floor. Sathi scanned the room again carefully. Apart from some posters about newly-released books, however, there was nothing on the walls.

'The books for media are upstairs,' Manuel hissed.

Sathi made an 'I'm coming' motion, and quickly went to him. 'Sorry.'

Manuel appeared not to have heard, and began to climb the stairs to the veranda above. When they reached the top, Sathi kept her eyes peeled for anything breaking up the light cream walls, and was finally rewarded. The very first mini-room – the Literature section – had a frame hanging on the wall behind the little table.

Ignoring Manuel's protests that they weren't at the right section yet, she rushed in and peered at the writing eagerly. She read that the Indiaplaza Golden Quill Book Award had been awarded to... Sathi's eyes skipped ahead to the next line, bracing to see her mother's name... Bindhu Menon.

Her hopes came crashing down, and she glared at the foreign name with prickly eyes. Urgh. Stupid English prize.

Amma would've gotten something for science or maths, Sathi consoled herself.

She wiped the back of her hand across her eyes, and went back out to the veranda. She ignored Manuel's puzzled expression and forged past the back-to-back bookshelves, and into the section for Biology.

Chapter Twenty-One

Veritas Vos Liberabit

A pattern emerged. Each section of the library had an identical frame on the wall behind the table, holding the certificate for some kind of prize in that subject. Each time Sathi rushed to read it. Each time the name on the certificate wasn't her mother's. Even when they went to the Maths section, the story was the same.

Sathi couldn't understand it. Was it because her mother had been here more than twenty years ago, and they'd replaced the prizes with more recent students' achievements? She wanted to believe that was it, but the Chemistry section showed a certificate won even before the time Amma had been at Mar Ivanios. There was only one explanation that she could think of, and it was one she wished hadn't occurred to her. Perhaps Amma had not been quite such a brilliant student as Mr Yes had boasted.

Sathi didn't care that her mother wasn't as clever as she'd believed. What made her heart sink in despair was the realisation that if Amma hadn't been an award-winning student, there would be nothing that tied her to the college. And the trail Sathi had been following, the trail she had found after nearly two painstaking months, would go cold.

No! That couldn't happen. She would hunt down every certificate in this college if she had to in order to make sure that didn't happen.

A thought flitted through her mind, and she seized on it. 'Manuel!' she cried. 'Are there any certificates or trophies in the principal's office?'

Maybe her mother's achievements had been too important to be left to gather dust in the library like these others. Maybe they'd been hung proudly in the office of the head teacher as at her Amma's old school. Sathi wouldn't think twice about paying a visit to the principal if that was the case.

Alight with excitement, she looked up to see why Manual hadn't answered her. It took some time for his expression to sink in. He was looking at her warily, and she realised that the way she had been flitting in and out of each of the little rooms and gawking at the certificates must have seemed very odd behaviour to him, especially coming from a supposed research student.

'It's...' she began, but her excuse gave up on itself as her mind failed to come up with anything good. Resigned, Sathi fell to grovelling. 'It's important. Please?'

She had the gratification of seeing him go back to his usual, slightly arrogant self in response to her plea.

'No, the old man doesn't care about that sort of thing,' he replied. 'He keeps all his weights in there so he can build up some muscle in his free time.' Manuel broke off, suddenly looking panicked. 'Don't tell him I said that!'

Sathi hurriedly reassured him that of course she wouldn't, struggling to hide her disappointment. *Serves you right, Sathi. Next time, don't be so big-headed.*

She sighed. All she wanted to do was to get out of here and go and mope. For a week. Even the gorgeous architecture didn't hold enough charm to make her want to stay any longer, and just the thought of certificates made her feel slightly sick now. She began to turn around.

'Hey, you're going the wrong way!'

She glanced back at Manuel and her heart sank. He'd volunteered to take her to the library. He'd given her valuable information in much less time than it would have taken her to find out on her own. The fact that the information had just reinforced the fear that she wouldn't find any leads to her mother didn't matter. She would have to stay in this blasted library and pretend to research some books for his sake.

Sathi straightened her shoulders and gave him as convincing a smile as possible without bursting into tears. 'Lead on.'

They passed a couple more mini-rooms, and finally arrived at the one at the end of the veranda. Manuel strode into the last section, leaving her to duck in after getting a brief glimpse of a guy with spectacles and a severe case of acne sitting at the table in the penultimate section.

'There you go,' Manuel said, gesturing grandly.

'Thanks,' she replied, mustering up the last drops of enthusiasm she had left in her. She walked to the shelf and pulled out a huge, dusty volume at random. She started leafing through it half-heartedly, all the while waiting for Manuel to get bored and slink off. A few minutes passed, and she grew impatient. Would he never go?

Sathi studied him out of the corner of her eye and saw that he was just standing there with his head inclined in her direction. She made a great show of reading a passage intensely, following the lines with her finger and completely blanking him out. Surely, he'd get bored eventually.

She had another peek, and he was still in the exact same position. What the - ?

Sathi jerked her head around quickly, trying to figure out what he was doing, and caught him staring right at her. Manuel glanced away at once and went to the shelf opposite, hurriedly saying, 'Look, this is where our yearbook will go.' He pointed down at a free shelf at the bottom.

'Really?' she felt obliged to say.

He was hyped now. 'Yeah. I cleared it out when old Princi gave the nod to yearbooks. I even hammered on a label. Come have a proper look,' he insisted.

Sathi rolled her eyes heavenwards and resisted the temptation to hit him over the head with the heavy book in her hands. Instead, she put it down on the table and walked over to join him.

'See?' he said, pointing again, this time to a shiny label. He'd crouched down in front of it, so she did the same. Maybe if she played along, he would go away more quickly.

'Very nice,' she remarked, and used the edge of the table to lever herself back to her feet. It had been incredibly uncomfortable in the tight space, and they had very much been in each other's personal space. She brushed her hands together to get rid of the dust they had harvested.

And that was when she saw it.

There was something plastered to the wall by the low shelf, by their feet. Something that was rectangular and inscribed with curly writing and shiny like the metal label Manuel had just shown her. She stood stock still, her eyes fixed immovably on the metal plate.

Manuel noticed her interest. 'Oh yeah. That's the plaque I was talking about. You know, about that chick who designed this library.'

Sathi bent slowly, reeling inside with the sudden premonition she felt. She knew what she was going to see. She didn't know how she knew, but she knew. She traced the words lightly with her fingertips: "Designed by, and constructed under the supervision of, Madhubhala Kumar, 1992".

Her mother hadn't just won a labelled award that went up as a piece of paper on a frame. She had designed the library where everyone's awards were displayed. She was... she was... Manuel's earlier words came back to Sathi. Amma was an architectural genius! And she had been given the task of redesigning this beautiful, enormous room in this prestigious college.

Sathi had inherited her love of architecture from her mother!

If she could have burst from happiness and satisfaction, she would have in that moment. Sathi's eyes closed and her head tilted up. *Thank you*, she thought as a few tears slipped down her cheeks. She didn't care that she didn't know who she was thanking.

Then she remembered something else Manuel had said earlier. She shot to her feet and whirled to face him. 'Didn't you say something about your uncle knowing her?' she demanded, pointing down at the plaque.

Manuel shrugged. 'He was at college with her.'

She stepped forward. 'I need to meet him!' she said frantically.

He looked shocked. 'Wow, you're fast.'

'What?' she exclaimed, thoroughly confused. She didn't wait for him to answer, though. She grabbed his arm unthinkingly. 'Please, you have to let me talk to your uncle,' she pleaded.

Manuel appeared startled, but he didn't protest or pull his arm away. 'Well, he's been in Dubai for years now, but he'll visit this Christmas.'

Christmas? She couldn't wait that long! Sathi took a deep breath and tried to think past her frenzy. 'Okay, then can you give me his phone number? Or his email address?'

Manuel did something that stunned her. He moved closer to her and put a heavy arm around her shoulders. He squeezed the top of her arm. 'How about we exchange phone numbers first, hmm?'

For one moment she couldn't move. She froze in complete and utter shock, her nose assaulted by the smell of sweat and cheap cologne.

Then other emotions took over; she pushed her elbows out in a bucking motion, throwing off his leaden arm. Sathi projected herself backwards with more force than she'd known she was capable of and stood with her back against her mother's plaque, arms held protectively in front of her.

'What the hell do you think you're doing?' she demanded angrily.

Manuel appeared more puzzled than anything else. 'What's wrong? You can't meet my uncle until December, but I'll take you to meet my family today if you like.' He smiled hopefully, as though this was supposed to reassure her.

Sathi stared in horror. 'Meet - your - *family?*'

'Hey, don't worry, *yaar*. They'll love you.' Confident, he took a step towards her.

'No!' she screeched. Sathi jumped back again, and this time her back hit the unyielding wall. Crap. She scanned the empty area, hoping that someone would magically appear. She wished she hadn't let Manuel lead her so far away from other people. She didn't think he would actually assault her, but this still wasn't a situation she wanted to be in.

Sathi's panicked gaze returned to Manuel, who thankfully hadn't moved any closer to her, and then went back to desperately scanning the mini-room. Her eyes passed over the doorway that led to the long veranda outside in agitation and did a double-take.

Zakiy was in the doorway.

All the tension and panic drained out of her, and she nearly sagged in relief. She had never been so glad to see someone in her life.

Then Sathi blinked and realised that he didn't look nearly as pleased to see her. In fact, he was giving her a look that said, *I'm going to chop you into little pieces, and then I'm going to kill you.*

Oopsie. Apparently, he wasn't impressed with that little dating stunt she'd pulled in the playground earlier.

Well, they did say offence was the best defence. Time to find out whether that strategy would save or damn her.

'Zakiy!' she exclaimed as she skipped past a bemused Manuel. She threaded her arm through Zakiy's. 'Darling!'

Zakiy stiffened and leaned away to look at her in shock. She could practically see a massive thought bubble with a huge bold question mark sticking out of the side of his head.

Sathi turned sideways and grinned widely, and the movement coincidentally hid the movement as one sharp elbow shot out to jab the side of Zakiy's ribs.

'Oww! I mean, yes, hello, Sathi... er, darling.'

She groaned internally and notched up the wattage of her smile. 'What took you so long, darling? We got bored waiting for you.'

Zakiy was to gritting his teeth. 'Sorry, darling, I got a bit,' he paused for effect, '*delayed.*'

Sathi ignored the menacing tone and beamed at Manuel, tightening her grip on Zakiy's arm. 'Darling, meet Manuel. He's been showing me around. Manuel, this is Zakiy. My boyfriend,' she added, just in case all the "darlings" hadn't sunk in.

She barely heard Zakiy mutter, 'Really? I never would have guessed,' before he slung his arm possessively around her and stuck out his other hand for Manuel to shake. 'Hi, how're you doing?' he said in a condescending tone, nodding at Manuel and looking away dismissively.

Manuel bristled immediately, but Sathi was distracted by the arm around her shoulders, and how different it was from Manuel's. Zakiy's arm was the perfect weight and didn't force her to push upwards in order to keep herself upright, as she had with Manuel's.

'Have you asked Man-well here about the yearbook, darling?' Zakiy asked, interrupting whatever Manuel had been about to say.

Sathi nearly sniggered. She had to hand it to Zakiy. He didn't even know the reason for this façade, yet he was rolling with it effortlessly. 'Yes, darling, but the college has only just started using them.'

Zakiy deigned to look at Manuel. 'I figured a college like this would've been faster on the uptake.'

Manuel puffed up indignantly. 'We are! That's why, after months and months of persistence, we finally have permission to get yearbooks printed. It would have happened more quickly if not for the girls.'

'What do you mean?' Sathi asked, intrigued. Was this more of his ridiculous prejudice?

Manuel managed to tear his attention away from trying to stare Zakiy down long enough to answer her. 'The girls' parents didn't want their addresses and contact details printed – scared that it would somehow damage their future marriage proposals, I reckon. And with more than half the year being girls, it'd be a complete waste to print it if their details can't be put in.'

There were so many things wrong with what he'd just said that Sathi didn't know where to start. First of all: arranged marriage? Of course, she'd known it was practised in India. She'd just assumed that it had been some time shortly after dinosaurs had been wiped out. And what was this about only *girls'* parents being worried? What about the boys' marriage proposals?

Some random part of her brain started wondering whether phrases like "sexual double standards" and "angel/whore dichotomy" were frequently tossed around in conversation here.

Thankfully, Zakiy cut off the blabbering inside her mind. 'Really?' he said, managing to make the single word drip with the utmost contempt. He was quite the actor, although Sathi wasn't entirely sure why he was working so hard to keep the testosterone flowing. 'I thought a guy like you would have figured out how to get over obstacles like that in your first year,' Zakiy continued, still sounding incredibly snooty.

Manuel apparently couldn't find a response for that. His dark skin took on a tinge of deep red with suppressed irritation, and then, shooting Sathi a look of betrayal, he said, 'I have to get to class now. Bye.'

Then he hightailed it out of there before Sathi could ask anything about his uncle.

There went her link to her mother.

She slipped out from under Zakiy's arm and went to sit in front of Amma's plaque, trying to commit it to memory. After a moment, he joined her on the floor. 'Wow. Your mum designed this whole library?'

Sathi nodded woodenly. 'Yes, and Manuel's uncle knew her. But he's in Dubai, and Manuel was too busy hitting on me to give me his uncle's contact details,' she concluded sarcastically.

'He was hitting on you, huh?' She could hear the smugness in his voice. She glared at him. 'Hey, don't take it out on me,' he sniggered.

Zakiy exploded with laughter. 'We're quits now,' he said between guffaws.

She huffed in annoyance and shoved him hard. He was too busy laughing to push back and just sat there shaking with mirth.

'Irritating person,' she muttered under her breath.

'Anyway,' she continued loudly, 'the point is, we don't have a lead. Because we don't have a yearbook. And we don't have Manuel. Or his uncle. And now I really need to stop talking,' she sighed, turning back to the plaque and ignoring Zakiy's renewed snorts of laughter.

A spectacled eye was peering at her from the gap between the wall and the edge of the bookcase. 'Hey!'

'Argh!' she yelled, falling backwards in shock.

Thankfully, her fall was cushioned, and she didn't hurt herself. Unfortunately, her cushion had been Zakiy. 'Mmmphh! Get. Off. Can't. Breathe.'

Sathi rolled off him and looked back apprehensively at the crevice by the bookshelf. There was nothing there. She crept right up to it on hands and knees and peered through the gap. She couldn't see anything except the wooden planks of the floor of the adjoining section. Had she imagined the whole thing?

'Hey!'

It was the same voice again, this time coming from the doorway. Sathi's head whipped around, and she saw a short guy with glasses standing by the railing, his shoulders hunched over so that he looked even shorter than he was. Then suddenly she realised why he looked familiar. She'd seen him earlier in the mini-room next to theirs, bent over a book. He'd been right there when Manuel started being creepy, and she had completely forgotten about him in her panic. *Idiot*, she reproached herself.

Zakiy had gotten to his feet, and looked almost as startled by the guy's appearance as she did. 'Er, hi,' he said uncertainly.

The guy walked forward like he was on a sugar high, and his gait had a weird quality: his every step looked like his body was fighting to move backwards instead of forwards. He stopped after a few steps, leaving a wide space between them.

There was an awkward silence as each party waited for the other to make the next move.

'Look, sorry,' the guy blurted out suddenly, his head swinging between Zakiy and Sathi, but never actually meeting either of their eyes. 'I couldn't help overhearing that you were looking for a yearbook?' He made it sound like a question.

Zakiy and Sathi looked at each other, a bit stunned. Sathi recovered first. 'Yes, that's right. Why?' she asked curiously.

He looked as if he wished he'd misheard. 'Well,' he began reluctantly, shuffling his feet, 'I may be able to help you.' His gaze flitted around the room. 'You see,' he whispered so softly that they had to lean forward to catch the rest of his words, 'I'm in the same year as Manuel and we got the inspiration to push for a yearbook from an actual yearbook made by a batch of students years ago. The thing is, they did it in secret. The principal at the time forbade this kind of thing, but the students in that batch ignored him and made handmade copies of a yearbook, one for everyone in the group. They left one copy here in this library as a kind of rebellion. That part was her idea,' he finished, pointing down at the plaque.

Sathi felt herself go cold and then hot, and she felt a rush of goose-bumps dance down her arms. She saw Zakiy looking at her, but she couldn't take her eyes from the guy in front of them, the guy who had just revealed the missing link in the chain that led to her Amma.

'A group of us discovered the yearbook in our first year here, and we decided we wanted to rebel too. That's when we started the campaign to have yearbooks, even though only a handful of us know about the original one. We wanted to keep it a secret, but I thought there was no harm in telling you two.' He looked at her properly then and shrugged his shoulders slightly.

'Thank you,' she said, her voice a bit choked. 'Can you... can you show us the yearbook?'

He nodded and glanced away, embarrassed with the thanks, and moved to the bookshelves. Sathi watched as he scanned the rows of books, full of nervous energy.

Then something went wrong. His examination became frantic, and he started dragging his fingers over the same collection of spines again and again. He was obviously searching for something that should be there but wasn't.

Sathi tried to ignore the cold steel ball in her stomach as the guy shook his head, back and forth, back and forth. 'No, no, this can't be possible, no, no,' he wailed, sounding like he was trying to convince himself.

Zakiy spoke what she had been afraid to voice. 'Wait. You hid it inside a *book*?' he asked incredulously. 'But, then it could have been taken out by anyone!'

'No, no!' the guy exclaimed. 'It's here somewhere, it has to be.' He swung around and started moving towards the bookshelves on the opposite side, no reluctance in his gait this time. Then he suddenly halted and cried out, 'There it is!' He exhaled in relief and approached the table. He picked up the massive volume Sathi had pulled out at random to fool Manuel, the book she had put on the table and forgotten all about when she saw her mother's plaque.

She had to force herself not to shake her own head in denial. It had been right there in her hands!

The guy expertly found the section he was looking for and lifted the heavy pages over to a page that was past the middle mark. Or, rather, what used to be a page. Sathi moved closer to get a better look, amazed by what she saw. A rectangular hole had been cut into the dense pages of the book, smaller than the dimensions of the volume so the raised edges of uncut pages hid all evidence of the hole. Into the crater had been sunk a much thinner booklet, obviously hand-bound, but neat and a perfect fit for the hole. The guy lifted it out reverently. 'Here it is.'

Sathi snatched it from him, unable to fight the suspense anymore. The once-white pages were yellowed with age, but otherwise undamaged. The cover said, "MIC: 3rd Batch of Year 1993" in beautiful hand-calligraphy, and underneath in smaller letters were the words "Veritas vos liberabit: The truth shall liberate you".

The irony of the college motto twisting her lips, Sathi turned the page. At the front was an introduction (handwritten, of course), and as she scanned it she found words similar to what the bespectacled guy had told them earlier, about the year-group's "rebellion". She flipped through and found that the booklet was laid out quite like modern yearbooks, with one spread devoted to each person, containing an address and phone number. There were very few email addresses listed, but most had addresses.

Sathi quickly skipped ahead to the Ms, and there she was, her mother smiling up at her. The picture was identical to the one Sathi had found in her father's house in UK.

That made her pause, and she frowned down at it, puzzled. How could that be? This must have been put together when Amma had been much younger. Sathi kept looking at Amma's serene gaze, and then something suddenly clicked in her mind. She closed the yearbook so she could see the cover page again. This time, she focused on the date on it: 1993.

Huh?

Even though the dates were imprinted in her mind, Sathi reached into the little purse she had slung over shoulders to compensate for the lack of pockets (she was wearing the skirt she'd worn to the temple the previous day) and pulled out a crumpled scrap of paper. On it she had written down the year of her mother's birth, the year she would have started school, the year she finished school (and started college) and the year she finished college. And of course, the date of her death.

For once, though, the year 1995 didn't immediately capture her attention. Instead, her eyes went to where she'd scribbled "1990/1 - end of college (depends on whether 3/4 yr. course)". Amma would have finished way before 1993, even if she'd done a four-year course. Was it possible that the person who'd done the cover page had made a mistake? They'd had to do a copy each for the whole year, after all. It would have been simple to slip up.

Sathi couldn't let the mistake go, however, and the dates puzzled her. Something nagged at her and it took a while for her to realise why. When she did, she strode past the two utterly baffled males in the room and crouched down in front of Amma's plaque for what seemed like the hundredth time. She read the writing again carefully: "Designed by, and constructed under the supervision of, Madhubhala Kumar, 1992".

1992. So Amma *had* been at this college for longer than usual – at least two years longer. She absently tapped the yearbook against her knee, trying to think of the reason behind it. The booklet suddenly slipped from her fingers and fell open to her mother's designated page. When she leaned to pick it up, she noticed the smaller text underneath Amma's photograph: "MSc (Chemistry)".

Of course! Post-graduation. Now that she'd seen the inscription, she remembered looking up the Mar Ivanios's webpage and reading that two-year Master's courses were offered there. Her mother had decided to do her postgrad in the same college as her BSc, and their post-graduation group had been the ones to make this yearbook.

She smiled. There was nothing like clearing up a mystery to make her feel cheerful. Actually, she felt quite giddy with the thought of the treasure in her hands. Her mother had, as usual, helped her out at the exact point when she felt she would burst from frustration. She looked up and beamed at the aforementioned baffled males.

'Amma did her post-graduation here as well,' she told Zakiy before turning her attention to the guy who'd led her to the yearbook. 'Thank you so, so much,' she said, filled with gratitude. 'I will never forget this.'

The guy fidgeted and looked away. 'Um, yeah, sure. Er, I'm going now.' As soon as the words were out, he rushed away from the media section.

Sathi looked at Zakiy. 'Do I smell, or something?'

Amusement glinted in the depths of his eyes, but he obediently leaned forward and sniffed in her direction. 'Nope. Why?'

'Well, that's the second person I've just driven away.'

Zakiy chuckled. 'Nah, I think it's my overwhelming personality. It's a difficult thing to stand against.'

She grinned and muttered, 'Don't I know it.' They looked at each other and snorted with laughter, both on a high of achievement.

Zakiy finally pointed at the yearbook. 'We should probably find a photocopier and then put that back in the book. Wouldn't want to expose their little secret.' He snorted again.

She didn't say anything, just looked steadily back at him with her face expressionless.

His brow furrowed, and then his confusion metamorphosed into comprehension. 'No,' he told her sternly, as though he was disciplining a naughty puppy.

Sathi kept on staring at him expectantly.

After a few minutes, his expression faltered. 'We can't,' he wailed, and his voice held the promise of her victory.

They walked down the concrete stairs outside the college building. There was a strange bulge in Zakiy's shirt that he tried to hide with a hand placed over it, and he kept looking around furtively.

'A clean record, and then she comes along and makes me into a criminal. If the police catch me, I'm ratting her out for sure,' he grumbled to himself under his breath.

'Aww, come on,' Sathi said at a normal volume. 'You won't testify against me, will you? I'm just a poor, defenceless girl, after all.'

'Hah!' he exploded. 'Defenceless, my foot! You are too dangerous for my own good.'

She smiled angelically. 'Who, little old me?'

Zakiy regarded her suspiciously. 'Yes, you.'

'Come on, though, you have to admit that keeping that book in the library was a pretty dim-witted idea. You said so yourself, anyone can take it out and easily lose the yearbook.'

208

'Yeah, yeah, I know. I just wish you hadn't made me an accomplice to theft.' He sighed in a world-weary way. 'I blame myself. It's my own fault for being too good at everything.'

Sathi narrowed her eyes. 'Actually, you're not an accomplice,' she said conversationally.

'Oh?' Zakiy brightened.

'You're the perpetrator.

Chapter Twenty-Two

Red Herring

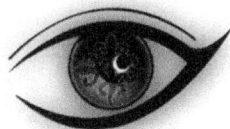

Sathi! Are you okay? Have you eaten? Did you get lost anywhere?'
She shook her head and smiled as she balanced the phone to
her ear with her shoulder, freeing her hands to turn over the
pages of the yearbook. This was the second time Zakiy had called
today, and it was only two o'clock in the afternoon. 'Yes, yes and no,'
she said into the phone. 'Stop being such a worry-wart.'

She could almost see him pouting. 'If you'd let me stay there, I
wouldn't have had to worry so much,' he complained.

Her voice became stern. 'We've been over this.' She had managed to
send Zakiy back to Nelliampathi yesterday, after spending a whole
afternoon arguing back and forth with the stubborn idiot. She'd finally
had to guilt-trip him by talking about *her* guilt over him missing
classes. Which made her head hurt to think about, and she still didn't
know how it had worked, just that it did.

'Yeah, yeah, yeah,' he replied, sounding exactly like a spoilt brat. 'So,
have you found any more peeps with Trivandrum addresses?'

Sathi's hand paused in the process of scribbling in the little
notebook she'd bought from a local store. 'No. That was the lot.'

When they'd gone through the yearbook properly, they'd found that several of Amma's classmates had addresses that were based in Thiruvananthapuram – not surprising, seeing as they'd all attended college there, but it still wasn't something she'd thought of. Twelve out of the forty-three people in her mother's batch had at one point had permanent Thiruvananthapuram addresses, and, if she was lucky, at least a few of those twelve still did. She had no choice but to rely on phone numbers - and occasionally email addresses - for the other thirty-one people, but at least for these twelve she would get immediate results. That was the reason for Sathi's prolonged stay in the capital of Kerala.

Sathi had spent the morning sorting the people in the yearbook into four categories; those with Thiruvananthapuram addresses; those with non-TVPM (the shorthand was a real godsend) addresses who had the Kerala area code in front of the phone number – or rather, didn't have any extra code in front of the number (Zakiy had pointed that out before he left, along with a hundred other random, but useful, pieces of advice); those with email addresses and then the left-over people, who either didn't have an address or number written down, or had addresses in a foreign country like Dubai or another Gulf country. She was keeping that category as a last resort.

'Well, that's just as well,' Zakiy was saying, his familiar voice slightly tinny through the phone. 'Imagine if you had to visit forty different houses – you'd burst from all that food.'

Sathi, distracted, said, 'Eh?'

'Well, you'd have to take a separate stomach along if you're gonna survive tea and snacks from forty different households. If you'd had me along, of course, it wouldn't have been a problem.'

'Are you referring to the fact that you can eat enough in one sitting to feed a hundred people?'

His voice was smug. 'On a good day, I can do one-fifty.'

She shook her head, this time in exasperation. 'Nitwit,' she muttered under her breath.

'Hey, I heard that!'

She started smiling despite herself. 'Don't you have anything productive to do?'

'Annoying you is pretty high on my productivity scale. It's right under sleeping.'

Sathi rolled her eyes. 'I'm not sure if that's a compliment or not, but right now why don't you put down the phone and go do something useful?' She paused for effect before playing her trump card. 'Or I'll call back.'

There was a hurried, 'OK, bye,' and then a click as the phone went dead. She was grinning as she returned it to the desk: Zakiy was even more conscientious about her spending money than she was. He'd even offered to pay for the Indian sim-card she'd bought and probably would have done so if she hadn't adamantly refused. In a very grateful way.

Her grin faded as she focused back on task. She'd already sent around an email to all those who had an address listed, and there wasn't much she could do but wait for the replies. She double-checked that her email was still open on her laptop, and then picked up the list of phone numbers of people who lived in Kerala. Sathi eyed it wearily.

Thirty-four perfect strangers to ring up and wrangle answers out of. Not exactly her idea of fun. Still, she told herself, it's better than having to show up on the doorstep of perfect strangers. That joy would come later.

She picked up her phone again and dialled the first number on the list, almost hoping that it would go to voicemail. It rang, and rang, and rang. Sathi was already looking at the next number when suddenly it stopped ringing, and a woman's voice said, 'Hello?' right in her ear.

Sathi dropped the list in surprise, but she managed to keep enough wits about her to stammer, 'Um, Aranya Ganapathy?'

'No, I'm her mother. Who is this?'

She fought back a wave of hope. 'I'm sorry for disturbing you, ma'am,' she croaked. 'I'm the daughter of Ms Aranya's old college classmate. Would it be possible for you to give the phone to your daughter?'

'Oh no, Aranya is married now and settled in her own house. But,' the woman's voice hesitated, 'I can give you her new number. I have it written down here somewhere, just a moment.' There was a soft thud, as though a handset had been laid down, and when Sathi strained her ears she heard scuffling and the rustle of clothing. Finally the woman returned to the phone. 'Do you have something to write with?'

'Um, yeah,' Sathi said quickly, scrambling for her notebook and pen. She wrote down the number the woman recited, and then read it back to her to double-check. Thanking the woman profusely, she hung up and quickly dialled the new number. This time, she didn't have long to wait before the call went to voicemail.

She grimaced as the usual deadpan voice told her to leave a message after the bleep, and ended the call. She drew the list towards her, scribbled out the old number and copied down the new one to try later. Then she sat staring at the list for another minute.

One down, thirty-three to go.

She got eight more voicemails (after she eliminated two from their personalised voicemail messages), eleven wrong numbers (one particular person resented having to answer the phone so much that he screamed a couple of obscenities and then slammed the receiver down. Another tried to get her to take a life insurance policy), and seven of the numbers no longer existed.

That left only five people who actually picked up the phone, and had some sort of connection with the assigned classmate. Out of those, one had an address that was outside Kerala. She had a brief conversation with the man on the phone, but he had not been inclined to cast his mind back more than twenty years on the whim of a girl claiming to be the daughter of an old college classmate. He had to be reminded of Amma's name, and even then his responses had been vague and unsatisfying.

Sathi had already crossed him off her mental list – there was no point visiting him (even if she could) if he didn't even remember her mother. No, it was the other four that held her interest: one had a non-

Thiruvananthapuram address, but the other three were still living here. What's more, they had all – barring one – given her permission to visit their homes that evening in order to talk about her mother. The classmate she couldn't visit this evening had told her she could pop in the following day – they had guests around this evening.

All in all, getting permission beforehand made the prospect of knocking on the doors of strangers all that much less painful. Sathi grabbed her phone, her purse and her notebook, and left the hotel room, locking the door behind her.

She finally bit the bullet, and pressed firmly down on the doorbell. A faint ring sounded inside the middle-class Indian house, but there was no answering noise. Sathi waited. And waited. And waited.

She was about to give up when she finally heard movement behind the closed door. A middle-aged man opened it, saying impatiently in Malayalam, 'Look, I don't have time for whatever you're selling'.

'But -'

'I said no, didn't I?' he said, about to shut the door when he finally glanced at her. He took a double take and the door halted mid-swing. 'Sathi? Is that you?'

Five minutes later she was sitting on a sofa with an uncomfortable back, blowing at the cup of tea the man's wife, a sweet-smelling, round-faced woman who spoke little, had handed her. The man who'd opened the door had sat Sathi down and then excused himself for a couple of minutes, disappearing into the bedroom.

It had taken her nearly a week of procrastination to build up to this moment.

Of course, she had convinced herself that she was too busy visiting classmates and calling back those who she hadn't managed to talk to on that first day. Then she'd had a wonderful piece of luck the previous night that had unexpectedly drawn her sojourn in Thiruvananthapuram to a halt. She'd suddenly ran out of days to procrastinate.

The man who'd opened the door came back into the living room, buttoning up the cotton shirt he'd just put on over the vest he had been wearing before. He offered her a slightly nervous smile. 'Welcome, welcome,' he said, sitting down opposite her. 'You've grown,' he observed.

Sathi smiled back equally awkwardly, the dialogues she'd mentally rehearsed cowardly fleeing her memory.

He glanced at his wife uncertainly, and then back at Sathi. 'Well, dear. Is this your first visit to India? Has Nakul come, too?'

The question rattled her, even though she should have expected it. Of course her father's old friend would ask after him. Of course he would. She couldn't quite meet the kindly man's eyes as she replied. 'No. He's in UK. I'm here on a gap year.'

'That's wonderful! Exploring your roots, yes?' He laughed conspiratorially. 'So, has your dad told you how he and I used to be joined at the hip?'

Sathi smiled as genuinely as she could manage and shook her head. As if she knew anything about her father.

'Oh yes, we were good friends at college. Well, we still are, I suppose, although, after what happened -' He broke off abruptly and looked down. His hands clenched on the sofa arms.

She felt her heart starting its usual uncomfortable constriction/dilation process. She leaned forward, wanting to reach out to this man who was so obviously hurting. 'You mean with my Amma?' she asked softly.

He looked back up at her, his eyes sad. 'Your Amma was a remarkable woman. Truly remarkable. When Nakul met her and fell in love with her, I saw him change before my eyes. All his good points... it was as if she amplified them. She made him into an even better man than he already was.'

His gaze was faraway, so he didn't notice the way Sathi was leaning away now, her back stiff.

'They were so happy. Then you came along.' His gaze returned to her, and he beamed. 'I've never seen Nakul so delighted. He was rushing around like a headless chicken in the hospital while he waited for the news – I think the hospital staff were this close to throwing him out altogether.' He chuckled. Then his face fell, as if he had just remembered that this story didn't have a happy ending.

'Anyway,' he said, his voice teeming with false brightness. 'What brings you here, Sathi, dear?'

She looked at him, trying to make up her mind. On the one hand, she risked upsetting this man even more than she already had. On the other hand, she had a chance of getting more information about her mother.

She sighed resignedly. That decision had been made as soon as she had rung the doorbell.

'I came to find out more about Amma,' she said slowly, examining the man's expression carefully as she spoke. His face didn't show anything expect polite puzzlement. 'I want to know who killed her.'

Shock crossed his face. 'What?' he exclaimed, horrified. 'Madhu? Killed?' He sat stunned for a moment, and then compassion filled his voice as he leaned towards her. 'Sathi, your mother died in childbirth. No one killed her.'

She was silent, thinking of what she would have said to that a few months ago. Someone had killed her mother. *Sathi* had killed her.

She shook her head, shaking off the unwelcome thought. She didn't have anything to do with her mother's death. It wasn't her fault.

'No, Uncle. Amma didn't die in childbirth. She was...' Sathi drew in a deep breath. 'She was murdered.'

'Murdered?' he repeated, bewildered.

'Yes. Uncle, you knew her. Can you think of anyone, anyone at all, who would have wanted to harm her?' she pleaded, her desperation leaking into her voice.

He shook his head, still looking dazed. 'No. No, everyone loved Madhu.' He said 'Murdered' again, unable to digest it. 'I can't believe this,' he muttered. 'I can't believe Nakul didn't -'

Sathi looked at him knowingly as he broke off and glanced furtively at her. They didn't say anything, although both were thinking about the things her father left unsaid.

Finally she broke eye contact. She put the teacup on the table in front of her and stood up, saying, 'Thanks for everything, Uncle. I should be going now.' There was no point in hanging around any more.

'Your father,' he said suddenly, his tone entirely different.

Sathi turned. 'Yes?'

He gazed at her earnestly. 'He's not a bad man. He...' He sighed and clasped his hands together. 'When Madhu died, it broke him. Don't judge him too harshly,' he begged.

Her only answer was a sad smile.

'You're kidding me!' Zakiy exclaimed.

Sathi winced, and held the phone further away from her ear. 'Could you possibly try not to destroy my eardrums? I might have some use for them in the future.'

For once, he refused to be distracted. 'Are you telling me that one of your mum's classmates lives in Nemmara?' He'd decreased his volume, but she could still hear at least ten question marks behind the one question.

She smiled, enjoying his reaction. 'Unbelievable, isn't it?'

'That's an understatement. So, wait: was this woman's address in the yearbook this whole time?' he demanded.

'No, that's the most amazing thing. She was actually in Kuwait for fifteen years, ever since she got married, but she relocated to Palakkad with her family a few years ago. When I dialled the Kuwait number, the call got redirected to Kerala.'

When Sathi had finished re-trying each of the eight numbers that had gone to voicemail that first day, and got nowhere with them, she had resigned herself to dialling the out-of-Kerala group of numbers. The few people she managed to get in touch with had been as unhelpful as their Kerala classmates. All expect for one.

One woman had remembered her old college classmate more than the others – they'd had a long conversation on the phone, the woman reminiscing about her college days, and Sathi had wished out loud that they could meet in person. Amma's classmate had replied, surprised, that of course she could visit. Of course, it might be difficult to travel all the way to Palakkad but if Sathi could manage that, then she was welcome to come to her house. She would be home all day on Thursday, how did that sound?

For a few seconds Sathi hadn't been able to reply. Then she had laughed until tears came to her eyes, her laughter full of relief and joy and yes, a touch of hysteria as well. She'd had to reassure the bewildered woman on the other end of the phone that she hadn't suddenly inhaled laughing gas (or gone mad). Sathi got the woman's address, arranged a time for the visit and finally put the phone down.

'I can't believe it,' Zakiy said, echoing her own incredulity.

There was a minute of silence, and then he asked, 'So, you're coming back tomorrow?'

'Yup,' she replied. She held her breath, praying that he wouldn't ask why she hadn't started the journey back to Nelliampathi today.

'Do you know which train to catch, and where you need to go and everything?' he asked instead.

'Mmmhmm.'

'Okay,' he conceded reluctantly. 'Call me as soon as your train gets to the station.'

'Aye, aye, sir!' she joked through her guilt at lying to him. Lying by omission, but that didn't excuse it.

She remembered how she had come across the address on an old letter pushed to the bottom of her bag; it was the letter that she had used to deduce that her mother's hometown had been in Nelliampathi, back when she'd initially been setting out to India. She had idly glanced at the return address, and done a double take. The address was in Thiruvananthapuram.

And so she had psyched herself up to visit her father's old friend. Fat lot of good *that* had done her.

'Aye, aye, Captain, you mean,' Zakiy corrected, his voice disapproving.

Even though she knew that he was just kidding around, she wondered whether there was something more meaningful behind his mocking tone. She tried to shake off her paranoia, reminding herself angrily that not everyone had an ulterior motive for their every action like she did.

'Hellooo? Mike testing, mike testing... Delta-4 has been abducted by aliens. I repeat, Delta-4 had been abducted by aliens. Arrest aliens immediately. Over.'

She managed to keep her amusement out of her voice. 'Aliens have been arrested. Their leader is called Zakiy Narayan. Vaporisation of leader has commenced. Over and out.'

'No, no, no! Cease vaporisation! I repeat, cease vaporisation! False alarm! Red herring! Get back here, damn it!'

Chapter Twenty-Three

Reminiscences

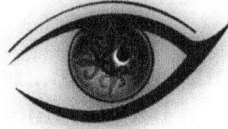

'This woman isn't a serial killer or anything, is she?' Zakiy asked as he turned off the ignition. 'I mean, you've only talked to her on the phone.'

'You're right,' Sathi replied solemnly as she waited for a break in the stream of traffic so she could get out of the Jeep. 'As my knight, you should go in first – alone – and make sure that my mother's classmate isn't harmful.'

'Oh, ah, I'm sure that won't be necessary,' he backtracked quickly. 'Wait, I'll help you get out.' Zakiy jumped out and came around to her side, his hand on the door handle. 'After the red car,' he muttered.

The scarlet *maruthi* thrummed past, and Zakiy threw open the door. Sathi hopped out, and he hurried to close the door.

'Oww!' Sathi yelled, and her hand shot to her head.

'Crap! I'm sorry!' Zakiy opened the door again quickly and freed her hair. 'I'm so sorry!'

'Chill, its fine.' She massaged her head tenderly, scoping out the damage. 'It was just the initial pain,' she reassured him.

'Sorry,' he mumbled again anyway.

'Shush. Besides, this means I get to do lots of physical damage to you as retribution,' she told him as they crossed the road.

Zakiy had only just lost his repentant look when a voice suddenly rang out: 'You should be more careful!' Startled, Sathi looked up to see an Indian man with a scraggly beard standing in front of them. He was staring accusingly at Zakiy, and continued, 'She could've been really hurt.'

Shocked, she looked at Zakiy just in time to see his face fall.

Rage filled her. Before she knew it, furious words were out of her mouth. 'If you were that concerned about my welfare, why didn't you come and help?' she spat before grabbing Zakiy's arm and stalking off down the street. She was fuming inside. How dare that old man criticise Zakiy? Interfering prat!

They were nearly at the classmate's house when Zakiy finally spoke. 'You've got quite a temper, haven't you?'

'I don't like hypocrites,' she replied shortly. No one was allowed to criticise the people she loved. No one.

'Hello! Come in, come in.' The young woman who had opened the door smiled at her. 'You must be Sathi.'

Sathi nodded, smiling back and trying to hide her confusion. This woman couldn't be her mother's classmate! She appeared to be in her late twenties, or at most, early thirties. The voice was wrong too.

She watched the woman's eyes travel to Zakiy questioningly, and hurried to introduce him. 'This is Zakiy. We came to meet Mrs Nirmala?'

The woman smiled at Zakiy, and beckoned them into the large, airy living room. 'Yes, I know! She is just coming. Sit, sit,' she insisted, making shooing motions to the sofa.

'I'll just see if Aunty is ready,' she said, beaming again before leaving the room.

'Mystery solved,' Sathi whispered. 'She must be Nirmala's niece.'

'Could be,' Zakiy conceded. 'Or, she's just a random person who is calling her Aunty out of respect.' He smirked at her.

'Oh. I forgot about that. How are you supposed to keep track of everyone when they all greet each other like family members?' she muttered, disgruntled.

'Stop trying to keep track,' was his very helpful advice.

She was cheated of her opportunity to make a scathing reply when the woman who'd answered the door came back into the room with a tray of snacks in her hands, and a small child hanging from her sari edge.

'Now, Paru, you stay here and talk to this nice *chechi* and *chetan* while Mummy helps *Ammumma*,' she said, gesturing to Sathi and Zakiy as set the tray down in front of them and disengaging the kid's hands from her clothes.

Sathi shot Zakiy a confused look as the woman left again. 'Ammumma?' she mouthed, repeating the Malayalam word for "grandmother". He shrugged absently, his attention centred on the little girl. She was now standing in the middle of the room, playing with her frilly skirt and glancing up shyly every few minutes.

'Hello Paru,' Zakiy said brightly, dropping to the floor on his knees and moving closer to the child.

She looked at him fleetingly, her gorgeous dark eyes huge in her small, round face, and then her eyes returned to the floor just as quickly.

'That's a lovely skirt,' Zakiy complimented, still kneeling. 'May I see it?' he cajoled.

Her gaze flashed back up at him again, and she inched closer to him. He smiled encouragement, and moved forward slightly on his knees. She moved a few steps closer as well, her eyes bright. Zakiy grinned and shuffled forward another couple of steps. The kid giggled, a high, pealing sound, and dimples bloomed on her face as she copied him, enjoying this new game.

Sathi smiled, watching them. He was so good with children. The little girl was completely enamoured with Zakiy now; she reached out hesitantly and squidged his unresisting nose, appearing fascinated by the way his nose returned to original shape when she took her tiny hand away. The bell-like giggles were more frequent now as she repeated the motion again and again. Zakiy just sat there grinning widely, and occasionally pretended to sneeze. That always brought on fresh rounds of laughter from both of them.

Zakiy looked up and caught her eye, his expression full of mirth, and she shook her head indulgently, secretly wishing that she could be so comfortable with children.

'I see you have met Paru.' Sathi glanced up to find the source of the deep, amused voice. A middle-aged woman was standing in the doorway, her face lined with age but her eyes clear and gentle.

Zakiy rose to his feet in respect to the older woman, and Sathi hurried to do the same, still not having got the hang of traditional Indian customs. She knew you had to stand up if someone older than you entered a room, but what if they left the room and came back again? Were you supposed to stand up every time they came into the room? And did you have to stand up if the person was just a few years older than you, just a teenager?

Thankfully, the older woman interrupted the endless list of unanswered questions. 'I am Nirmala. I know you are Sathi,' she confirmed, and glanced at Zakiy. 'And you are...?'

Before Sathi could introduce him, a different person did the job for her. 'This is my new friend,' the little girl announced, her high, clear voice confident.

Everyone laughed, and Nirmala said jokily, 'Then I welcome you, Paru's new friend.'

Zakiy grinned and gave a mock bow from the waist. 'Let's shorten my name to Zakiy,' he stage-whispered to the girl, jerking a thumb back at Sathi and Nirmala. 'They won't be able to remember that long name.'

'Okay,' she agreed, delighted that she was more capable than the grownups in this aspect.

Nirmala laughed again, and Sathi noticed that she had a nice laugh, rich and filled with genuine warmth. 'Please, sit down,' Nirmala said. She waited while Sathi sat (Zakiy chose to remain on the floor with the child), and then fixed her with a smile. 'So, my dear, you are Madhu's daughter?'

'That's right. I hope I'm not disturbing you, barging in like this?' she asked anxiously.

The woman waved this away: 'No, of course not. Now, what would you like to know?'

Sathi had prepared her questions. 'I was wondering if you know anything about Amma's family?'

Nirmala surprised her by grinning, which made her look like a mischievous girl. 'Know them? I practically lived with them at times.'

Sathi's brow furrowed. 'But... I thought you and Amma only knew each other from college.'

'Oh no. We were friends even before that. We were at school together, and sometimes she would come and stay here with me.'

'Here? But... this house... Kuwait...' Her words and her thoughts were equally incoherent now. She tried to re-order her thoughts. 'I thought you only just moved in here.'

Nirmala shook her head. 'This is my family home. I got married straight after post-graduation and went to Kuwait with my husband.'

'Oh.' Sathi bit her lip, digesting this. This was good news: it meant Nirmala knew her mother very well, maybe even better than Vidhya had.

Vidhya! Maybe Nirmala knows about her. Then her excitement faded; Vidhya hadn't been in the yearbook, so she probably hadn't gone to the same college. It was unlikely that Nirmala would know the whereabouts of Vidhya if they had separated after high school. Better to keep to the original questions.

She smiled at the older woman. 'Well, if you knew Amma that well, would you tell me more about her family?'

'Certainly. They were − are − lovely people. Her aunt and uncle treated Madhu like their own child, and she was always very happy with them. You know, they just had three boys, so by taking in Madhu, they got a daughter, too. Madhu absolutely adored them, and she loved her cousins like her own brothers.' The older woman smiled, her gaze unfocused although she was still technically looking at Sathi.

'What about her aunt and uncle themselves?' Sathi prompted gently. 'What kind of role did they have within the community?'

Nirmala frowned thoughtfully. 'From what I can remember, they have always held a position of high esteem in society. Madhu's uncle is a man of honour, a noble man, and his wife and family have always been a role model for other families in Nelliampathi because of the strong bonds of love and trust they've built between them. I remember being quite intimidated by the uncle because he always seemed larger than life to me. Everyone saw him as a *maanyan*.'

'Maanyan?' Sathi had been following along on the fluent Malayalam pretty well, but she had never come across this word before.

Nirmala struggled to define it: 'A maanyan is someone... someone who holds a lot of respect. Yes, a respectable person,' she clarified in English

Sathi nodded slowly. All she had heard confirmed what she already knew through Manish, Ravi and those newspapers articles about the charity organisations Amma's family ran.

It was time now to move onto the more difficult questions, but she was daunted by the child in the room. To ask that the girl be taken out of the room would make the conversation more strained and would raise unnecessary questions.

Her eyes slid over to the little girl; she and Zakiy were now employed in playing an extensive game of peek-a-boo. Sathi decided that the kid looked distracted enough, so she turned back to Nirmala.

'Can you think of any reason why... why anyone might have had reason to dislike my mother's family?' Sathi formed the question gradually, thinking about each word carefully before speaking.

Nirmala was taken aback; her eyes were full of curiosity, but finally she answered Sathi. 'No, not really. I can't remember anyone speaking of them in any terms but that of respect.'

Sathi nodded, oddly relieved. This idea had been brewing in her mind for the past couple of weeks; everyone she had talked to said her mother was someone whom everyone loved, who didn't have any enemies at all. Until recently, Sathi had been working under the assumption that whoever killed Amma did so for personal reasons. But what if her mother had been targeted to hurt her family?

It appeared now that her speculations had been wrong. And yet she couldn't bring herself to feel disappointed at the revelation.

'But,' Nirmala continued slowly, oblivious to Sathi's thoughts, 'I would imagine that a high-profile person such as your great-uncle would be bound to have ruffled some feathers, politically, at least.'

She stared back at this too-intelligent woman, feeling her optimism falter. There was just one more question she wanted to ask, even though it would reveal too much. She didn't feel that there was much point in tiptoeing around, though: Nirmala obviously knew something was wrong.

She stared at the floor as she spoke. 'Do you think that he might have ruffled enough feathers to incite someone to... take revenge?'

There was a low gasp, followed by a long silence. Sathi refused to look up. She could hear Zakiy and the little girl having a conversation; she was acting as a waiter, taking orders for a massive meal for Zakiy. He was being a difficult customer, asking for unreasonable things like an ice-cream samosa and chocolate dosa.

'Sathi...'

She stood up so quickly that the blood swirling in her brain made it impossible to concentrate for a moment. 'Bathroom,' she blurted once the dizziness had settled.

Sathi stared at her reflection in the mirror, desperately trying to find her mother in it. But mostly she saw a scared, clueless little girl.

This was hopeless. She was never going to find her mother's killer. Not if the reasons were political. She leaned her forehead against the cool glass to try and cool the ruthless fire of her pounding headache. Her mother's image floated behind her closed eyelids like a watercolour painting.

She didn't dare to stay here in the sanctuary of the bathroom for too long; the last thing she wanted was for someone to come looking for her and witness her coming apart at the seams.

Resolutely, she fixed her reflection with a grim look. 'You can do this,' she told it determinedly, and opened the bathroom door before her reflection could start mocking her pathetic attempt to lie to herself.

As she passed the hallway on the way to the sitting room, the sunlight glinting brightly off the glass of a photograph caught her eye. Sathi moved closer to the frame that stood next to other photos showing a younger Nirmala and an Asian man, and another showing the little girl and her beaming mother.

She picked up the rectangular frame that had first caught her eye; it was by one of those professional photographers, like the ones her school hired to take group photos of each class. Her interest caught, Sathi scrutinised the rows of miniature-sized people. A few seconds later, she found her: a young Amma, looking exactly as Sathi did now, stood towards the end of the last row, smiling widely. She was pulling a face at the girl standing directly in front of her. Sathi's breath caught; Amma looked so happy and carefree.

Then she looked more closely at the girl in front of Amma in the photo. She couldn't see her face, because she had turned around to face Amma just as the photographer clicked the camera. But there was something familiar about the girl, something about her slender features, her swinging pigtails-

That was it! It was Vidhya! An older Vidhya, sure, around eighteen or nineteen, but she had the same hair, tied back neatly into plaits that swung around her like pendulums.

Sathi stalked back into the sitting room, clutching the photo tightly in her hands. She felt more than one pair of worried eyes on her, but she focused only on Nirmala.

'When was this photo taken?' she demanded without preamble.

The older woman regarded her silently for a moment. Her eyes were full of questions, but she did not give voice to any of them. Instead, she turned her attention to the photo, and Sathi felt a sudden rush of affection for her, got a glimpse of why her mother had chosen her as a close friend.

'Oh yes. I remember this,' Nirmala said, taking the frame from Sathi to get a closer look. 'It was when we were at college; I think... yes, I think it was our first year at Mar Ivanios. Look, there's Madhu.' Nirmala tapped a finger against the glass of the photo, smiling slightly.

'And this?' Sathi asked quietly, pointing at the girl with the pigtails. Her hand was trembling slightly.

'Vidhya Raman. She and Madhu were always inseparable, even back at school. They even lived right next to each other. They sat together, ate together, played together.' Nirmala laughed. 'You know, we all thought they were hilarious as best friends because they had such opposite characters; Vidhya called Madhu Maggi because she said her hair was like black noodles, and Madhu always referred to Vidhya as Buji, because she was a bit of a brainbox. Look, even when they were posing for the photo, Madhu just couldn't stand still. She was playing with Vidhya's hair the whole time and finally Vidhya got exasperated and turned around to tell her off. That's why she has her back to the camera.'

'Hold on. Vidhya was at Mar Ivanios too? Vidhya Raman?' Zakiy had appeared at Nirmala's shoulder. He looked across at Sathi, but she didn't meet his eyes.

'Yes,' Nirmala replied, surprised. 'Why? Do you know her?'

'But she wasn't in the yearbook.' Zakiy's voice was uncertain, the statement a question.

'Yearbook?' Nirmala repeated, bewildered. Then her expression cleared. 'Oh, you mean that little booklet we made. Well, no, Vidhya wouldn't have been in it. She had to cut her post-graduation short after her first year. She didn't finish the whole two years.'

'Why?' Two pairs of eyes shot to Sathi. 'Why didn't she finish the degree?'

Nirmala shrugged. 'I think there was a bereavement in the family. She had younger siblings, and had to start work straightaway to fend for them. They even had to move out of their house in Nelliampathi.

228

We were all upset, but Madhu... she changed after Vidhya left. She didn't have the same sparkle in her eyes, she didn't make jokes, she just wasn't her usual fun-loving self anymore. She retreated into herself.' Nirmala sighed heavily. 'And as far as I know, Vidhya never returned to Palakkad.

Chapter Twenty-Four

Loss & Gain

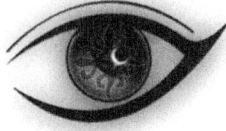

Twilight crept upon the trees, obscuring the subtle shades of colour until the greens and the browns blended together seamlessly to make unfamiliar shapes in the dark. Branches reached into the night as though trying to snatch back those last moments of sunshine, and the looming mountains in the distance looked on, their exile hitherto incomplete.

Sathi and Zakiy walked side by side into their clearing, arms full of freshly-laundered clothes. Zakiy dumped his armful on the tarpaulin spread on the floor in front of their tents, and started to make a fire.

Sathi put her own load down and sat in front of it. She started rolling her stiff shoulders, trying to alleviate the soreness of the long train journey that had only just begun to make itself felt. She shivered; the temperature was dropping rapidly, and she was glad that Zakiy's little campfire had started making merry popping sounds. The embers shone with a cosy light.

Yawning, she began to sort the clothes into two piles; one for Zakiy, and one for herself. Once the fire became self-sufficient, Zakiy joined her on the floor and started helping.

'So' he began. 'What do you think we should do next?'

Stifling another great big yawn, she suggested, 'Go to bed?'

Zakiy turned to flash her a tired grin. 'You're starting to sound like me,' he warned. 'I meant, what are we going to do about finding out about your Amma?'

'Oh,' she said apathetically. She went on sorting, folding each article of clothing with infinite care. 'I don't know,' she admitted finally.

For a moment there was only the sound of clothes rusting. Then: 'It seems to me that our best bet is to try and find this Vidhya person. If she doesn't know more about your mother, I doubt anyone else will.' Zakiy paused. 'Except for her family, of course,' he added.

She sighed. 'You're right. But, come on, be honest; what hope do we have of finding Vidhya?'

He shrugged. 'We just need to ask around. Find out where she used to live, where she went when she left college...'

'You've just said it,' Sathi argued. 'Vidhya *left*. And presumably lost all contact with Amma. It's possible than she doesn't even know that Amma died. No one else does,' she muttered bitterly.

Zakiy leaned his warm shoulder into her. 'Hey, don't lose hope. We'll get to the bottom of this eventually.'

Sathi shook her head quickly. 'No, Zakiy. This is just wasting everyone's time. You have college to think about, you have *Aman* to think about. Those things are much more important than this wild goose chase.'

'Wait a minute, wait a minute. I thought we've been over this before. My time is mine to waste, and not even you, m'lady, have a right to tell me not to waste my own time.'

She smiled weakly. 'Fine. But I've decided not to waste any more of my time.' Her shoulders slumped. 'I've had enough, Zakiy,' she whispered, staring into the fire with moisture blurring her vision.

His arm tightened around her. 'Look, let's compromise. I think there's a chance of finding this Vidhya, and I think there is also quite a good chance that we'll get some information from her. We can't give up until your Amma's parents return to Nelliampathi, anyway. So we might as well fill the time by trying to find Vidhya. We're closer than we were – we didn't know for sure that Vidhya was Amma's best friend before and now we do.'

Sathi thought about it, and finally nodded. After all, he was completely logical. *Then why do I feel like I'm just being sucked further and further into a black hole?* she wondered.

'Great!' Zakiy gave her a final squeeze, and reached for another article of clothing from the pile. 'We'll start the hunt tomorrow. We should ask that ancient guy you're friends with, that Manish...' Deep in thought, he reached for a bra and began to fold it. Then suddenly he realised what he was doing, jumped, and hastily threw the offending item into Sathi's lap.

She broke out in hoots of tired laughter as he sat there blushing furiously and trying to look dignified. The utter failure of this attempt sent her into further giggling fits. 'As I was saying,' he began again with great composure, 'we should ask Manish tomorrow if he knows about Vidhya.'

She nodded her head emphatically, biting the inside of her cheeks.

Looking away from the source of her amusement, she turned and picked up the last of the laundry – a green hoodie – and began folding it up.

'Oh, that's mine,' Zakiy said, reaching for it.

'I know,' she replied, calmly ignoring his hand and putting the sweater on top of her pile of clothes. Then she stood up with it and walked sedately into her tent.

Zakiy stared after her for a minute. Then, shaking his head ruefully, he lowered his arm and took out his Tarot cards.

They had made it a habit now to look at the cards every night when they could: it was just a nice way to end the day, he thought. He shuffled the silky, well-used cards, not hurrying the process, just carrying on until he felt inclined to stop. Then he held them between his palms, closed his eyes and concentrated on Allah, and on His infinite wisdom and benevolence.

Please guide us, Zakiy thought as he drew out a card at random. It showed a depressed-looking man clutching his chest and staring off into the distance, a hot glow over his heart that spiralled out into a huge conch-shell. Emotional Loss.

Zakiy frowned as he gazed at the card. It was one that was common enough for him, one which he used to get quite frequently, in fact. But recently, he'd been getting a lot more positive cards. After a moment, he shrugged; maybe it was just an indication of the past, and of how much things had changed.

He returned to the deck and pulled another card for Sathi: Shadow. It was an interesting card, but one he wasn't very familiar with. The artwork was, as usual, uniquely gorgeous; two men facing each other this time, both identical except for the fact that while one was alight in the innocent luminance of sunlight, the other was shrouded in rays of moonlight. They each held a bejewelled staff, and wore cloaks that were decorated with the sun and the moon respectively. The moon dude was much less substantial than the other one.

It was indisputably beautiful artwork, but Zakiy knew almost nothing about this particular card. If he remembered correctly, it was supposed to be the Moon in traditional tarot. As to what that signified... That was another matter altogether.

Giving up, Zakiy reached for the little guidebook that accompanied the cards and flipped it open to the correct page. He scanned the text, snippets of phrases streaming through: *nothing in life is at a standstill... calling you to action... face your worst fears... confront what you've avoided... cleansing process to wash away and clear out what was once avoided, ignored or pushed aside...*

Zakiy shook his head dubiously. There was a lot in here about facing problems head on, but Sathi was one of the most straightforward people he knew. Just look at the way she handled the news about her mother; she left her life in UK and came out to a completely foreign country without even knowing how long she'd be staying for. You couldn't get much more heads on than that.

He considered for a moment, and then picked up the deck again. Shuffling, he concentrated, asking for an explanation. Two cards were flicked out as he shuffled, and they fell to the floor.

Why, aren't we chatty tonight? Zakiy thought wryly.

He picked up the cards; Authority and Financial & Material Changes. The Authority card was pretty self-explanatory – it showed a buff man standing with his arms crossed across his substantial-looking chest, biceps and triceps and all other visible ceps bulging. He had a rectangular face, with little bits of leaves sticking out from behind his ears; Zakiy supposed that people had been too intimidated by his physique to point that out to him. Two pillars stood behind him, and there was a glowing golden circle encircling his head like a halo. He was authority personified.

Financial & Material Changes was a little more ambiguous. The card was dominated by a human hand, which was overlaid by the design on the card itself. It was divided into four unequal sections, with each segment a different colour: green, red, purple, blue. The colours that were symbolic for the emotional, physical (or material), spiritual and mental spheres. The fingers of the solitary hand were splayed so that there was at least one in each of the coloured blocks.

It could be saying that Sathi had a finger in every pie, but somehow Zakiy didn't think that was it. No, this card was about change, about choices. There was some kind of change looming in her future. Zakiy sincerely hoped that it was a positive change.

Sathi finally emerged from her tent. 'I've taken the cards,' he called out to her.

Covering her mouth to muffle a yawn, she went to stand behind Zakiy so she could look over his shoulder.

'I got this melodramatic dude here,' he began, holding up the Emotional Loss card. 'I think it's indicative of all the emotional bruises you've given me by not giving me due respect as your knight in shining armour.'

'Or, it's indicative of heart-break,' she remarked. 'Is there something you need to tell me, Zakiy? Is there a girlfriend you've hidden away somewhere? As you found out from experience, I'm pretty good at match-making.'

'And this one,' he continued as if she hadn't spoken and picked up the Shadow card, 'is yours.'

Sathi leaned closer to the card, abruptly serious. Something about the dark, misty colours, the smoke-like appearance of the man on the left, made her uneasy.

'I wasn't sure what it meant, so I drew a couple more,' Zakiy was saying. 'I got this,' holding up the Authority card, 'and this.' He held up Financial & Material Changes. 'Well, first of all, Financial & Material Changes seems to be saying that there's some sort of change happening, or about to happen. It'll be difficult, but in the end it'll be for the better. As for this one...' he trailed off, picking up the Authority card. He frowned, engrossed. He picked up the booklet again and leafed through it.

Sathi waited with pseudo-patience, her stomach in knots for some reason.

'Hmmm. You know what, this card is supposed to indicate a person of authority, someone with masculine qualities. Someone who uses logic and reason in their approach to life. Much as I'd like to think that the card is referring to me, I actually think... Yes, I think it's talking about a father figure.'

Sathi froze.

Zakiy carried on, oblivious, as he stared into the forest, his brows furrowed in deep thought. 'And I think these cards are connected, somehow. I think your father has something to do with this change that's about to occur. I wonder what the Shadow card has to do with the rest though... Your dad's still in the UK, right?'

She was silent for so long that Zakiy turned around to face her. When he looked at her inquiringly, she stiffly moved her head up and down, once.

'That's always surprised me, actually. I would have thought he'd come with you,' he said absently, slowly gathering the cards back into a pile. He didn't see Sathi flinch. 'I guess he must be very busy with his job. Unless... does he know your mother was murdered?'

She wanted so badly to say no, that her father didn't know, he didn't know why Sathi had come to India, he didn't know and that's why he hadn't come after her, that's why he hadn't even called her to make sure she was safe, that she was still alive. Everything in her told her to say no.

'Yes.' Sathi didn't recognise her own voice. It sounded dead.

'Oh,' he replied, fiddling with the cards. His voice had a touch of disappointment in it. She wanted to demand why he sounded disappointed, wanted to force him to tell her what he was thinking, but she was too scared of his answer. 'Has he known for a long time?' he asked.

'I don't know.' Again, that same dead tone.

'Mm.' There was a pause, and then: 'Did he come to India at all, after your mum died?' he hedged.

Her every muscle was tense. 'What are you trying to ask, Zakiy?'

He finally glanced up, looking at her a bit guiltily. 'Well... I was just wondering why your father didn't have the same reaction to your mother's death as you did. I mean, you came out here to try and find her murderer and bring him to justice. It must have taken a lot of courage to do that, especially alone.'

'Are you calling my father a coward?' Her voice was low, dangerous.

Zakiy's head whipped up. 'No! That not what I -'

'My father is not a coward, do you understand me?'

'Sathi, I -'

'Do you understand me?' she screeched.

He fell silent, shocked.

She took a step forward, so that she loomed over him. 'What my father does or doesn't do is none of your business. You have no right to question his actions, and you bloody well don't have any right to judge him.' She paused, her chest heaving. 'And from this moment on, you and I have nothing to do with each other.'

She stood there, her coal black eyes reflecting the tumultuous flames and daring him to defy her. Then she turned and without another word stalked off into the forest, where the reaching darkness waited to swallow her up.

The loud, steady sloshing had become background noise as her feet stomped through the omnipresent puddles of rainwater. The torrents of rain had soaked her through in less than a minute once she cleared the heavy protection of the forest, and her clothes were dripping wet and clung to her skin, clammy. Ice-cold water trickled steadily down her neck.

Sathi didn't notice. She felt so angry that she didn't know what to do with the anger; she felt as if the rage was a fever taking over her body, growing and growing until it took over everything. Until it had nothing left to take over.

Walking was helping to keep the anger at bay; if she stopped it would make her implode. Despite that, she still had to work diligently to keep her mind carefully blank. She had to keep the anger from taking over her mind. And she had to avoid the other emotions too.

However much she tried, the anger still seeped through, as persistent as the rain. She couldn't fully quench her furious thoughts. *How dare he? How dare he call Dad a coward? Who the hell does he think he is, anyway? What gives him the right to judge* my *father?*

Then when she wasn't careful enough, different thoughts invaded her reluctant mind: *I'm sure Dad would've come. He couldn't leave me there alone in UK to avenge Amma, he had to look after me. And I'm sure he would've come with me when I left... I left so quickly, he didn't have time... he would have come by now if there wasn't that big project going on at work...*

Wasn't that why she'd been checking her email so judiciously, hoping for a message from him saying that he was coming, that he was sorry, that he loved her? Wasn't that why she'd been looking up flights to India so frequently, wondering if her father was on one of them?

Sathi increased her speed, lengthening her stride and feeling her calf muscles burn, almost relishing that pain. She didn't pay attention to where she was going until her feet trod the well-worn path to Amma's old house. Disoriented, she gazed up at the familiar house; it was as cold and shut up as ever.

The rain had intensified, slashing heavily across the saturated sky; it looked as if it was building up into a proper storm.

Vaguely, Sathi noticed that she couldn't feel her fingertips or toes any more because of the cold. Almost without forming the conscious thought to move, she turned her back to the house and walked the short distance to the Devi temple, stepping under the crumbling archway to get out of the lashing rain. She looked around the dark place, half-expecting White-beard to materialise from a shady corner. He didn't.

Sathi moved closer to the outer wall, and slid down until she was in a sitting position at the foot of the life-sized Devi idol that had drawn her to this temple for the first time. She drew her knees to her chin and wrapped her arms around her legs.

After a moment, her phone started buzzing insistently, and not for the first time. She turned it off.

About half an hour or so later, the sky started to thunder and flash up in brilliant displays of lightening. The sky seemed very close here, the lightning blinding in its brightness.

That was about the time when she started to hear someone call her name. Not just someone - she knew exactly who it was. She stayed in her dark corner, and after a while the voice grew faint, and then finally disappeared altogether.

The shivers started another hour later. They seemed to originate from her core, hitting, bruising, from the inside out. She huddled against the wall and wrapped her arms around herself more tightly. Overpowering her control, her teeth started chattering. She tried to clamp her mouth shut, but it didn't work. The noise was horrible, chilling.

Maybe it was her body shutting down to prevent more damage, or maybe it was just that she was tired from concentrating so fiercely on not allowing herself to think, but she eventually fell into a hazy, fitful daze where she was only half-aware of her surroundings. The previously ear-splitting chaos of the thunder seemed suddenly very dull and far away, and she didn't feel the cold any more. Actually, she didn't feel much of anything any more.

Time passed, but she was no longer aware of its passing. Her stupor was disturbed by flashing images: she saw her father's haunted face when she told him she was coming to India; she saw White-beard, looking piercingly at her with his disconcerting blue-green eyes; she saw this temple, the same but oh so different, bright and lit and filled with the sweet scent of incense; she saw Zakiy, his tortured expression when he talked about his brother; she saw her mother shaking her head sadly, her liquid eyes brimming over with disappointment...

Sathi jerked, and her eyes opened. Her head swam, feeling like it was made of jelly as it pitched and revolted. It took a long time for her eyes to focus, and when they finally did, she thought she was still hallucinating.

She rose unsteadily to her feet, nearly falling over again as her body protested. She hobbled to the archway, shielding her eyes as she squinted, trying to clear her vision and see past the rain and into the night. Trying to convince herself that the light she had seen in her mother's house was not her imagination.

Suddenly, without warning, she was running. She fell twice on the cold, muddy ground, but she picked herself up again only to continue her weird, lurching sprint towards her mother's house, her only wish to reach there before she passed out.

Breathless, she collapsed against the door panel. She was coughing painfully, but she somehow managed to raise a leaden arm to knock weakly against the plywood. She didn't manage more than a couple of knocks before the combined effects of the shivering and the coughing forced her to bend over, feeling like she was hacking up her lungs.

The door opened, and Sathi painfully straightened up. Artificial light streamed in from behind the person who had opened the door, illuminating Sathi, but leaving whoever it was in the dark an unsatisfying silhouette. There was a gasp, and a female voice cried out, calling out to someone behind her. Sathi tried to hold in the coughs just for a moment, just until she could see for herself...

A second figure appeared next to the first; this one was taller, stockier, with broader shoulders than the woman.

'Sathi,' the first voice breathed, sounding as if she was close to tears. 'Oh, Sathi *molé*, you've come! Oh, you've come home at last!.'

Home: no word had ever sounded more beautiful to Sathi. She'd finally found her home.

As she stumbled across the doorway, arms reaching, a chill passed down her spine and she sank blissfully into the strong, maternal arms that caught her, giving up willingly her burdensome consciousness.

Chapter Twenty-Five

Cloud Nine

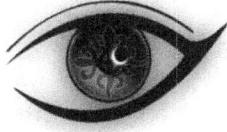

She slept on and off for four whole days, they told her later, fighting off the horrible fever that had weakened her to the point of exhaustion, and recovering from her night of exposure in the storm. Her great-uncle and aunt – they told her to call them Granddad and Grandma! – had called a doctor when she fainted and he'd been paying daily visits to check on her since. On the fifth day, she woke to find she was aware of every muscle in her body more vividly than she'd ever wanted to. Her whole body ached, and she felt weak, shivery and parched. She had to be bundled up all day in the room her great-aunt and uncle put her in.

It had been bliss.

Her great-uncle and aunt (it took her a while to get used to calling them grandparents – it just seemed too good to be true that they'd accepted her as their own grandchild) had never left her side, even when she was completely out of it. They had nursed her back to health, patiently, tenderly, lovingly. They'd taken care of her as if they had nothing else to do, and fed her hot chicken soup and held the glass to her mouth as she sipped coffee spiced with black pepper and dried ginger.

When the cheerful doctor declared, on the twelfth day, that she was completely healed, she and her great-uncle and great-aunt had sat in their spacious sitting room and spent the whole night talking. They had bombarded her with questions, saying they wanted to know everything about her. When did she come to India? How long had she been in Nelliampathi?

Sathi, in replying, had started from the very beginning, about how she had been thinking about her mother on her eighteenth birthday, how she'd been so desperate at least to find a photo of Amma that she ransacked her father's study, how she'd stumbled across some of Amma's things, like her wedding chain and ring.

At this point, she had carefully edited her story, saying that she'd had a massive fight with her father when he refused to open up about Amma. Her great-aunt and great-uncle had somehow managed to sympathise with her without criticising her father, and she had confided in them how her father had always acted as if he hated her. She had cried into her great-aunt's *sari* until it was drenched, while they both comforted her, saying of course Nakul didn't hate her, he loved her. It was just that he had taken Madhu's death so hard...

Tears in her eyes, she told them how she had decided to come to India and then how, upon arrival, she learned that they were in Kollam for the wedding. Her great-uncle and great-aunt had clutched her close and lamented that they'd been so unlucky as to be separated from their little Sathi for such a long time.

Her head resting on her great-aunt's shoulder, Sathi told them how she had got a job and then met Zakiy. She skated quickly over him, suppressing the anger that boiled within her at his memory. She told them about going to Amma's school in Nemmara, about going to Thiruvananthapuram to her college and then finally how she had gotten into contact with Nirmala, her mother's old classmate. Then, much as it caused her pain, she told of Zakiy and his accusations against her father, and their ensuing fight.

Her great-aunt and great-uncle had comforted her, saying that he probably didn't know any better, he just couldn't understand her relationship with her father. They told her not to worry about Zakiy, that she would find better friends who were more understanding.

Then, emotionally exhausted, the three of them had slept, Sathi feeling as if a great weight had finally been lifted from her chest. Her heart felt as light a bird now, thrumming happily to be with people who loved her. To be with her family.

Her great-aunt and great-uncle were more amazing than she could have ever imagined them to be. They doted on her, and frequently remarked that having her at home was like having their dear Madhu back again. They were perfect.

Sathi felt no inclination to step outside the ecstasy of her new-found family, but she realised with chagrin that she had left all her belongings at the campsite (she refused to think of it as "their" campsite). She would have gone without her clothes and carried on using hand-me-downs of her uncles that her great-aunt had found for her, but her backpack contained precious things that she could not leave behind; her mother's photo, her letter, the newspaper articles.

When she hesitantly broached the topic – for her great-aunt and great-uncle were as reluctant to let her out of their sight as she was them – they finally agreed to let her retrieve her things, provided that a close family friend of theirs accompanied her.

This family friend turned out to be an auto-rickshaw driver by the name of Ajit, a remote man who nevertheless drove her in his rickshaw to the resort. She popped in for a few minutes to see Ravi, guilty at the way she had suddenly disappeared (she had spent a whole day furiously texting after her arrival at her grandparents' house before she managed to convince Ravi that she was alive and well and hadn't been abducted). He admitted to her in a panic that his wife's due date was close, and fretted that he had no idea how to be a father.

Sathi at last managed to reassure him that he would be a great father, and then went to see her boss at the restaurant to explain about her illness. Her boss was very understanding, and said that they had taken on a temp, but that Sathi could return to her old job when she felt up to it. Thanking her, Sathi made her way to the campsite.

The short walk made her perspire heavily into her clothes. The monsoon seemed to have dried up a bit after that massive storm the other night; the clouds hung heavy with the rainwater that stubbornly refused to give up on its fight with gravity, and the air was humid, oppressive.

When she entered the campsite, she found her things exactly as she had left them. She had purposely chosen a time when she knew Zakiy would be at college. Forcing herself to move briskly, Sathi went into her tent and packed her clothes and other bits and bobs into her large suitcase. She decided just to leave the tent there – there was no point in taking it down and bringing it to her great-aunt and uncle's house.

Picking up a pile of her clothes from the floor of the tent, she noticed Zakiy's dark green sweater. The sight of it made her abruptly furious; she zipped up her suitcase, grabbed her backpack and, sweater in hand, strode out of the tent. Opening his tent a minuscule amount, she flung the hoodie inside. Then she dragged her suitcase back towards where Ajit was waiting without a single backward glance.

The days passed by, and her anger at Zakiy began to cool. She found that once she had lost the resentful edge that her anger put into her thoughts, her mind wandered to him at every opportunity. His absence was something she was vividly aware of, much as she didn't want to be. Sometimes she would think of a joke that Zakiy would appreciate and turn halfway as if to tell him. Then she would catch herself as she realised he wasn't standing next to her. Or she would make a remark, one which she knew would elicit a humorous response from him, half-expecting him to appear, a ready quip on his tongue.

The logical part of her mind attempted to reason with her: *If you miss him, why don't you go and talk to him and say sorry?*

Her defensive self would always revolt at this idea. *I'm not sorry! He shouldn't have said those things about my dad.*

He only said things that you've thought of yourself. It's hypocritical to blame him for that, her logic reminded her sternly.

I have the right! she snarled back. *He doesn't.*

A mental conversation like this always made her angry again, erasing, for a brief time at least, the sense of loss she felt. She tried to avoid consciously thinking of Zakiy, but he was like a jack-in-the-box, inevitably popping into her thoughts unannounced.

Another thing that niggled at her was the fact that she still hadn't found a way to tell her new family about her suspicions that her mother had been murdered. How could she? They had obviously adored her mother, and though they still grieved over Amma's untimely death, their memories of her were as yet untinged with horror.

And yet, as time went by, she began to question herself. What proof, really, was there that her mother had been murdered? A few sentences in a letter and a bunch of assumptions hardly added up to evidence. Besides, everyone, even Amma's family, thought she had died in childbirth.

Maybe there was no grand conspiracy. Maybe the simple truth was just that: simple. Maybe her mother had just died in childbirth.

Maybe, maybe not.

Whatever it was, she was not about to unnecessarily hurt her mother's aunt and uncle with wild assumptions. She learned to exclude this topic from her thoughts as well.

Life was good. Sathi spent every waking moment with her great-aunt and uncle, and they were delighted to have her. They had given her Amma's old room, and she loved the fact that she was living her mother's life, living in her home with her aunt and uncle, in her room. She sat in her chair, she gazed out of her window, she slept in her bed. It gave her a sense of deep satisfaction that she had never experienced before.

Most mornings, she went with Great-uncle to visit the various charity organisations he had founded, and to make sure they were all running smoothly. It was a humbling experience to see all those workshops he ran, especially the art workshops that got children from a local orphanage involved in expressing their creativity. She had spoken to many of the kids, and they adored her great-uncle and constantly vied for his attention so they could show off the paintings they'd created.

In just under a month, Sathi became so seamlessly woven into her mother's family that no outsider would be able to tell that she hadn't always lived with them.

There was, however, something that put an edge to the undiluted happiness that was her present life.

One day, she had been surprised to find her great-aunt and uncle ingesting a fistful of tablets each – ones of all shapes, sizes and colours. They informed her that they suffered from diabetes, hypertension, osteoarthritis, heart disease... you name it, they had it.

Her great-aunt smiled at Sathi's astounded expression. 'This is ordinary for old people like us, molé. We're just thankful that we got to see you before we die. We can go in peace now.'

'You're not going anywhere,' Sathi replied fiercely. 'You're going to stay here and look after me forever.' Even as she said it she was aware of how childish she sounded. She didn't care.

Great-uncle changed the subject. 'Your uncle used to make sure we took all these tablets on time. But now he's got married as well, and he has a family of his own. There are so many I can never keep track of them all,' he added.

Sathi pulled the huge box of medicines towards her. 'Well, meet your new nurse. I am Nurse Sathi, and I will be the new bully in the family.'

Her great-aunt and great-uncle laughed, and she joined in. But the real fear underlying the joke was never far from her thoughts.

Another month passed by, and towards the end of October, the newly-married couple returned to Nelliampathi after their marriage in Kollam. Sathi met her Uncle Girish for the first time, her Amma's youngest cousin-brother. He was utterly shocked when he first saw her, but once he got over his initial surprise he seemed pleased to see her. In fact, Sathi was sure his eyes teared up a bit. He quickly introduced her to his new bride, a beautiful Malayali woman who smiled shyly back at her.

At that moment, Great-aunt emerged from inside the house with a lit oil lamp in her hands. She handed it to her new daughter-in-law, saying, 'Come in with your right foot forward, dear, and bring blessings to this household.'

The couple smiled at each other and did as she asked, stopping just inside the doorway to stoop and touch Great-aunt and Great-uncle's feet for their blessings. Then they were ushered into the living room, where they sat and had a cup of tea as Great-aunt and Great-uncle regaled their new daughter-in-law with fond tales about Uncle Girish's childhood.

As noon approached, there began to be talk of preparing a *sadhya*, an Indian banquet, in honour of the newly-wed couple. It meant preparing about fifteen different vegetarian curries, including *sambar, parippu, rasam, pulisseri, avial, thoran, pachadi* and *poppadum*, all served together with boiled rice on plantain leaves. Great-aunt also ordered a whole chicken to be fried, Kerala style, because it was a favourite of her son's.

Even though the brunt of the work was done by the two servants who cooked and cleaned at the house, everyone chipped in and helped, as was the norm when preparing a sadhya. Great-aunt and Great-uncle, Sathi, even her uncle and her new aunt, joined in with various jobs like grating the white flakes of coconut from the dark shell, peeling and chopping vegetables, cutting down and washing plantain leaves and frying poppadums.

Great-aunt made a great fuss of her daughter-in-law, as it was her first time cooking in the kitchen that now belonged to her. She gave her the job of peeling and chopping ginger for special ginger curry, which Sathi had never tried before but had been told was delicious.

The group effort made the whole thing an enjoyable experience, and Sathi imagined that it would have been even more fun had her other uncles and aunts had been there as well. She wondered what it would be like, to live together in one house with all your aunts, uncles, cousins, grandparents. It must be bliss.

When the dishes were about done, Sathi was sent out into the dining room with her uncle to set the table. They spread the leaves over the table, wiping down droplets of water as they did so. The curries were arranged in a very specific way, Uncle Girish told her. The pickles had to be in the top left corner, and the poppadum went next to it. The order of the curries had to be the same on every leaf as well. At the end of the meal, he continued, you fold the top half of the leaf towards you to signify that the meal was satisfying, whereas closing it away from you is a message to the chef that it could do with some improvement.

Uncle Girish suddenly reached across the table, and rotated around the leaf she had just laid down. 'The curve of the leaf always points to the left, Madhu.' Then, when he realised the mistake, he glanced at her furtively and blurted, 'Sorry.'

Sathi smiled at him. 'Mistaking me for my mother is the best compliment you could give me, Uncle.'

He looked at her intently then, and looked as if he was on the verge of speaking when Great-aunt came into the dining room, followed by Great-uncle, Aunt Maya and the two servant women, each carrying a dish, like a procession. The moment lost, Sathi and Uncle moved out of the way as Great-aunt began to fire instructions about serving. She shouted orders like a general in battle, and everyone tried to stay out of each other's way as they rushed to obey. Finally, everything had been served according to proper sadhya etiquette, and everyone settled down to eat.

Great-uncle sat at the head of the table, while Great-aunt presided opposite him. She pulled Uncle down next to her, and when Aunt Maya moved to sit next to him, she stopped her.

Great-aunt smiled apologetically at Aunt Maya. 'Molé, you sit there today,' she said, pointing to the seat next to Great-uncle. 'It's bad luck for the wife to sit on the left of the husband during their first sadhya. Sathi, you sit near Girish.'

248

Sathi hesitantly did as she asked, leaving Aunt Maya to sit in the chair across from them, looking slightly puzzled. Great-aunt passed around the rice, and then kept a tight guard over the chicken, making sure that Uncle Girish's leaf was never bereft of a fleshy piece.

They were tucking in enthusiastically when suddenly Great-uncle laid a hand on his daughter-in-law's shoulder, and asked in concern, 'Aren't you eating, Maya molé?'

Sathi looked up, and noticed that her aunt was clenching and unclenching her hand as if it hurt her. When everyone looked up at her, however, she quickly hid her hands under the table and forced a smile on her face, assuring everyone that she was fine.

'Poor thing, she must be tired after the long journey. Eat what you want, molé,' Great-aunt said kindly.

When everyone had looked away and resumed eating, Sathi caught her aunt's eye and gave her an enquiring look. Aunt Maya just smiled back tightly and broke eye-contact. She went back to moving her food around the plantain leaf.

'You sit, Aunty. I'll bring the *payasam*,' Sathi called, walking out of the dining room to retrieve the best part of any meal: dessert. This particular dessert could be made with many combinations of ingredients, including jaggery, rice, banana, broken wheat or gram. Today, they'd decided to make *semiya payasam*, strands of vermicelli boiled and drenched in milk and white sugar. The sweet pudding was flavoured with cardamom and accessorised with fried sultanas and cashew nuts.

Thinking happily of the milky treat in store, she did not immediately pay much attention to the whispers emanating from the kitchen.

'What a thing to make her new daughter-in-law do!'

The indignant, almost angry, exclamation froze Sathi where she stood, unnoticed, in the shadow of the doorway. As she watched, the other servant woman nodded in agreement and said, 'Did you see her hands, the poor thing. All that ginger must be burning her skin so badly, but she never said a word.'

'She's a good girl.' The first woman paused to give her companion a meaningful look. 'It's always the good ones -'

She didn't get to finish because the second servant had just seen Sathi standing there, and nudged her friend.

Her eyes bored into theirs coldly for a long moment. Then, moving woodenly, she went to the stove and picked up the payasam dish. Sathi could feel their disapproving gaze on her back as she, ignoring them, silently left the kitchen.

Chapter Twenty-Six

Heartache

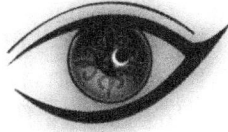

'Who was that on the phone, molé?' Great-aunt asked as soon as Sathi returned to the living room.

'That was Ravi, my friend from the resort where we both worked. His wife's given birth to a baby boy! He's a father now!' She beamed at her great-aunt. 'He wants me to visit them.'

'When?' Great-aunt's voice was a bit sharp, and she didn't return her smile.

'Today, if possible,' Sathi replied, worriedly scanning her great-aunt's expression. 'I'd like to go this afternoon.'

'Where is his house?'

'It's outside Nelliampathi, but he said he would meet me at the resort so we can take the bus to his house together.' She had tried to dissuade him of this plan, seeing as it involved him leaving his wife and baby alone, but Ravi had been deaf to her objections.

'Is that a good idea?'

Sathi frowned, puzzled. 'What do you mean?'

Great-aunt didn't elaborate. Instead, she said, 'Well, if you must go, take Ajit with you.'

She exhaled in relief. Her great-aunt was just worried about her. 'There's no need for that, Ammumma. I'll be perfectly safe, and I'll be back by eight,' she promised.

Great-aunt still did not appear convinced. 'All right, molé,' she sighed.

As it happened, her great-aunt need not have worried. An hour before Sathi was supposed to meet Ravi something happened that made all thoughts of visiting his family flee her mind. In fact, what happened was so horrible that everything in her mind that could have comforted her abandoned her to the abject terror that filled it.

Sathi had been lounging on the sofa and wondering idly whether or not to get a snack for herself before leaving the house. She had then started thinking about Ravi's baby, and then before she could stop them, her errant thoughts had turned to wishing that Zakiy could see the baby too. She caught herself smiling as she imagined what his reaction would be to a tiny, cute, flailing little baby - he would probably turn into a fully-fledged baby himself...

This moment of bitter-sweet visualisations gifted her with a split second of blessed ignorance because, the next thing she knew her great-uncle was shouting wordlessly, supporting her great-aunt, who had somehow fallen down, her hand fisted on her chest, pressing against it weakly, her face crumpled with pain.

'Amma!' The cry jolted Sathi out of her horrified state, and her uncle rushed to help prop up his mother in a sitting position on the floor. One of his hands went to her wrist, while the other held up his watch. Her uncle's lips moved silently as he counted to himself.

'Call Ajit!' Great-uncle shouted at her, holding his wife close and trying to arouse her from the unconscious stupor she had fallen into.

Somehow, Sathi forced her legs to move to obey him, feeling sharp, piercing lances of icy fear creep through her and wind its way around her chest in a cold vice, squeezing it.

The next half-an-hour was a blur to Sathi; it seemed to be simultaneously minutes and hours until Ajit showed up and helped carry Great-aunt into the car. Sathi couldn't have said how long the ride to the hospital took. The only thing she was aware of was that her great-aunt's feet were on her lap, and her head was cradled on Uncle Girish's shoulder. Diluted light of the setting sun blended through the car window and touched the pale, tight skin of her uncle's face, set in worried lines. He looked like a man who would never feel happiness again.

Unable to bear his tortured expression any longer, she glanced away and gazed out of the window instead. The small town was in a flux of activity as the car sped too fast through its narrow roads, but she couldn't take any of it in. All she knew was that she couldn't lose her great-aunt. Not now.

When they finally reached the accident and emergency section of the hospital where her uncle worked (or "Casualty" as the red letters outside declared), Great-aunt woke a little and was able to stagger inside, leaning heavily on Uncle. The waiting room was filled with people, people who coughed and moaned in pain or bled silently, people talking in loud, complaining voices or sitting abnormally still, the quiet fear in their expressions louder than the voices of those talking.

Uncle Girish briefly relinquished Great-aunt to Ajit and hurried to the nurse's station. He waved his ID at the woman who was staffing it, and said something to her. She nodded and led him off to a side door. They emerged a few moments later, this time accompanied by a thin, harried-looking middle-aged man in a smeared white knee-length coat with wide square pockets. A stethoscope was partially visible, hanging out of one of the pockets.

As he approached, Sathi realised absently that she recognised the man; he was the doctor who had paid house visits when she had been ill.

'What do we have here?' he said, keeping his tone cheerful as he went over to Great-aunt and put the earpieces of the stethoscope to his ears, and the round end to her chest.

'I'm fine, really,' Great-aunt protested weakly, wheezing with the effort. 'It's just a little pain.'

'I know it is, and that's why I'm just checking you out to prove that you're a hundred percent fine,' the doctor assured her. 'Now, I want you to get an ECG and a blood test to make sure that your heart is healthy, and then we'll have nothing to worry about.'

He lifted his head and directed his next words to Uncle. 'Girish, you know where the ECG room is. Get the report and bring it back to me, okay? I'll be right here.'

Uncle nodded mechanically as the doctor gave Great-aunt a final pat on her shoulder and winked at Sathi before leaving them. He seemed to take with him some of the optimism Sathi had begun to feel at his words.

Then Uncle Girish seemed to shake himself. 'I'll find a wheelchair,' he said, attempting a smile that turned into a grimace mid-way through its conception. 'Meet me by the lifts.'

'You can't all come in here!' the nurse exclaimed in exasperation.

Great-uncle, Uncle Girish, Ajay and Sathi looked at each other, and then back at the nurse. She shook her head in annoyance and focused her gaze on Sathi. 'You! Come in with the patient.'

Uncle Girish stepped forward. 'But, look I'm a doctor. I should come in -'

The nurse cut him off with a sharp look. 'Look, Doctor, there is no point in all of you rushing in. I only need one person to help me, and they don't need a medical degree. Come on,' she added, motioning impatiently to Sathi.

Sathi stepped forward and gripped the handlebars of Great-aunt's wheelchair. She sent her uncle a quick apologetic look before pushing the chair forwards into the ECG room. The nurse held open the basic half-glass door for her and then let it click shut behind them.

The nurse muttered orders to Sathi as they helped Great-aunt onto the bed and got her to lie down. Sathi noticed that while the nurse's words sounded rough and caustic, the way she dealt with Great-aunt was very gentle. She covered her with a blanket and fussed with the pillow until it was arranged comfortably beneath her head.

The nurse began to remove tubes from the machine sitting near the hospital bed, and attached them to Great-aunt's arms, legs and chest. Sathi helped her without being aware of her own movements.

She felt like one of those puppets; her limbs were being lifted and pulled by someone else, and as soon as the puppet-master let go of the strings at the end of the show, receiving applause that was his due, she would fall to the ground.

When the nurse shooed her off before starting the ECG machine, Sathi backed out of the way. The lack of space in the small room meant that she ended up standing near the door as she waited. She could still see the others through the glass, milling around the doors, forbidden from going further, but unwilling to move away without receiving some sort of reassurance.

The comparative silence was suddenly interrupted by Great-uncle's voice. 'Girish? Where are you going?' His voice was clearly audible through the door, and Sathi pressed closer to it, wondering what was going on.

'Maya,' her uncle groaned. 'We didn't tell her.' Absently, Sathi remembered that her aunt had been out buying milk when Great-aunt collapsed.

'So, call her.' Great-uncle's tone implied that this conversation was unnecessary.

Uncle shook his head. 'She'll be so scared. Besides, she'll want to be here. I'll go and get her,' he said decisively.

'You can't leave now,' Great-uncle said, sounding exasperated. 'We don't even know what's going on with your mother.'

'I'll be back before you know I'm gone. You can call me if there's any news in the meantime.'

Great-uncle's voice was very low when he next spoke. It was also much harsher. 'You don't care that your mother might be dying in there, do you?' Sathi cringed.

Uncle's answering words were filled with horror. 'You know that's not true! How can I live if she... she...' He paused, as though he was taking a deep breath. 'That's not what I meant,' he said, his voice sounding more composed than before. 'I just thought Maya should be told -'

'Maya, Maya, Maya! You can't think beyond her, can you? Fine, go. Just go. If your new wife is more important to you than your parents, then go. Get out of my sight.'

There was silence.

Sathi peeked through the door to see her uncle standing staring defiantly at the floor. Then his shoulders sagged, and he reached into his pocket. He muttered something in a low voice and moved away a few paces from the group, his phone held to his ear.

The sight of the phone reminded Sathi with a jolt of Ravi. She had completely forgotten about him. Covertly, she drew out her own phone and sent a quick text to him explaining the situation and promising that she would make it up to him. Hoping guiltily that he hadn't already reached Nelliampathi to pick her up, she slipped the phone back into her pocket.

'Hey, you!' the nurse barked. 'Come here.'

Sathi looked up. The nurse ripped off a long strip of paper from the ECG and handed it to her. Then they helped Great-aunt off the bed and into the wheelchair, and Sathi wheeled her out of the room.

Uncle, returned from his phone call, all but snatched the report from Sathi's hands. He scanned it as the group made their way to the elevators.

Great-aunt suddenly made a weak sound and waved her arm at Uncle. He immediately knelt by her. 'What's wrong, Amma?' he asked, touching her forehead gently.

He had to lean forward to catch her rasped words. 'You... wheel me.'

Uncle Girish looked up at Sathi and shrugged lightly. She moved out of the way as he took her place behind Great-aunt's chair.

The doctor told them there was nothing to worry about. The ECG was normal, and the initial troponin level was negative (whatever that meant). Great-aunt looked better, though still weak. Considering the various other medical conditions she had, however, he said it would be better for her to stay in the hospital overnight – just so they could monitor her and make sure she was completely fine before sending her home. He found her a room, and with a final smile, left them to it.

Once Great-aunt was settled in her bed and dozing off, Great-uncle, Uncle Girish, Ajit and Sathi moved out into the corridor outside to give her some space and so as not to disturb her sleep.

Sathi couldn't stop thinking, *Thank you thank you thank you thank you!* Her great-aunt was going to be fine! She felt almost weak with relief and gratitude.

'Girish!'

Uncle looked around at the familiar voice and stared as Aunt Maya hurried towards them, carrying a large thermos flask and a worried smile.

'I got your message. I caught an auto here,' she explained a bit breathlessly. 'Is Amma ok?'

Instead of answering, Uncle strode over and burrowed his head in her shoulder.

Great-uncle smiled. 'She's fine, Maya molé. She's resting,' he assured her. He patted his son's back and then pulled him away from Aunt Maya so that he could embrace him. Uncle began to sob.

'Shhh, it's okay,' Great-uncle murmured, as though soothing a small child filled with guilty repentance. Sathi felt her own eyes tearing up a bit, watching them.

When Uncle finally got himself under control, and they had all had a cup of steaming coffee from the flask Aunt Maya had brought, there began to be talk of what to do for the night. Ajit had taken Great-uncle back home so he could eat something and take his medicines.

'I don't want Amma to be alone here,' Uncle said, glancing at his wife.

'I'll stay,' Sathi offered. She wanted to make sure that her great-aunt was fine, and she didn't want her to wake up alone in the night.

'Are you sure, Sathi?' Uncle asked. 'You can go home with Maya.'

'No, Uncle, I want to stay. Why don't you go home as well? I can manage here.'

He looked dubious. 'I don't know...'

'Honestly, its fine,' Sathi insisted. 'You and Aunty go. I'll call when Great-aunt wakes up tomorrow.'

'No, no, we'll be back long before that. All right. Sathi, you have my mobile number don't you? And the house number as well?'

She assured him that she had both, and he and Aunt Maya finally left, glancing back uncertainly until they were out of sight.

Sathi stretched and went back into Great-aunt's room. She went to stand next to her great-aunt's bed, and studied her. She was deeply asleep, but she looked unbearable frail and insubstantial against the coarse hospital linens. Carefully, with only the very tips of her fingers, Sathi reached out and lightly stroked her great-aunt's cheek. Her skin was flaky and powdery, fragile, under her fingertips.

A tear rolled down Sathi's cheek as she realised how close she had come to losing her great-aunt, her mother's aunt, her grandfather's sister...her grandmother. She wasn't sure of much in her life, but Sathi was absolutely certain of one fact: she couldn't live in a world without her grandparents.

What would she do when they died? Because, much as she wanted to deny the truth, much as she wanted to pretend that it wouldn't happen, one day their lives would be claimed, just as her mother's life had been claimed. What would she do when that day came? Could she go back to living, if you could call it that, the way she had been before she came to India and met her mother's adoptive parents? Back to living in an empty house that did not change depending on whether her father was there or not? Back to being surrounded only by cold furniture, with only her own thoughts for company?

Her head was shaking fiercely even as her mind continued to whir. So what else could she do? She could stay in India... her uncle might even let her stay in the house... But could she bear to stay in India, let alone in their house, when her grandparents were gone, gone to a place that her Amma had already left to, gone to a place that Sathi couldn't enter for many years?

Her breath caught in her throat. Why couldn't she enter?

I won't live in a world without them.

Her thoughts began to spiral down a wholly different track, and a part of her was amazed at how calmly, how logically, she reacted to these new thoughts.

Of course she could enter this new place – why not? It would be easy. There was no one to miss her. Her father had made it clear long before that he didn't care whether she lived or died. Who else was there?

Zakiy...

The name whispered through her like a ribbon rippling in a light breeze, but it was quickly swatted aside. *I told him to mind his own business. Once he goes back to Mysore he'll be too busy to think about me.*

A reluctant part of herself uneasily pointed out that it wasn't true, that he had come looking for her even after she told him to mind his own business, that he would miss her if she...

How would she do it? By rope? Or maybe a sharp knife? A gun would be difficult to get hold of. Poison? The roof of a tall building? Fire?

Despite the feverish intensity of her thoughts, she couldn't help the shudder that passed through her at the last suggestion.

Painlessly. That's how she would do it. Maybe a cyanide pill – it would be over before she knew it.

And then she would get to see her mother. She would get to stay with her grandparents forever.

She stared unseeingly at the pale wall of the hospital room, planning it out. She wondered how she would get the pill... was it available in Kerala? Of course it must be. If not, she could always get some rat poison instead. A small bottle of the stuff would be easy enough to obtain at a pharmacy...

The door suddenly swung open, startling her. She whirled guiltily, and saw the nurse from ECG standing equally frozen in the doorway. They stared at each other for a moment. Sathi had to focus on slowing her racing pulse, and unobtrusively took deep breaths to calm her rapid breathing.

The nurse came in and headed over to the IV drip by Great-aunt's bed, adjusting the bag and checking the level of liquid inside. Then she appeared to fiddle with the machinery, not actually changing anything, just brushing her hands over it as if she didn't know what to do. Then she turned to the bed and flicked off non-existent dust from the pillow. After that, she started to straighten the already straight sheets.

Whether because she ran out of things to do, or because she sensed Sathi's gaze on her, she looked up and sniffed. 'What?' she snapped, her eyes suspiciously bright.

Something clicked in Sathi's mind. 'You know her, don't you?' she asked, nodding towards Great-aunt.

'Yes I know her. So?' she asked defensively, wiping at her damp eyes.

Great-aunt stirred restlessly in her sleep.

'Now look what you've done!' the nurse hissed at Sathi, her hands fluttering helplessly over Great-aunt. After a moment, she fell back into deep sleep, and the nurse relaxed. Without another word, she moved to the door.

'Wait!' Sathi whispered, taking a step forward. The nurse turned and jerked her head at Sathi to follow her out. Sathi spared Great-aunt another glance before quietly leaving the room and shutting the door after her.

The nurse was waiting for her in the corridor. 'Well? What is it?' she asked impatiently.

'I...,' Sathi floundered, at a loss when faced with the woman's rapidly changing moods. 'I was just wondering how you know Great-aunt.'

'Well, her son works here, doesn't he? They've been coming to this hospital for years. Use your brains, girl!'

Sathi flushed, but she persisted. 'If that's all, then why did you cry just now?' she countered.

The nurse puffed up indignantly. 'Cry? Me! Oh, girl, you should get your eyes tested.'

'Why did you come into the room then? A different nurse was looking after my great-aunt, and she said there was nothing she needed but rest. You wanted to see Great-aunt, didn't you? You wanted to make sure she was okay.'

The nurse stared stonily back, but if Sathi didn't know better she would have said there was a glimmer of newfound respect in her eyes.

'You're wrong,' she said.

'Fine,' Sathi said in exasperation, giving up with the stubborn woman. She put her hand on the doorknob.

'What did the doctor say?'

Sathi looked back at the older woman, and felt herself soften. 'He said there was nothing to worry about. He wanted her to stay overnight because of her diabetes and everything else.'

The nurse sniffed again. 'Poor soul. There isn't a known disease those two don't have.'

'Have you treated her before?' Sathi asked tentatively.

'Yes, haven't I already said that?' she snapped.

Sathi was sorely tempted to reply 'Not really' but she let it go.

'It's because *she* died this happened,' the nurse said abruptly. 'They were fine and healthy before that.'

Sathi stared at the woman. 'Because who died?'

The nurse glared at her. 'That girl, of course. Madhubhala. They loved her more than they loved their own sons. A part of them went with her when she died after her pregnancy.'

'You mean when she died giving birth,' Sathi corrected absently, old pains making themselves known at the unexpected mention of her mother.

'Don't tell me what I mean!' the woman retorted, shattering Sathi's daze. 'I mean what I said, that girl died after her pregnancy. She went back to the UK and died there and broke her parents' heart.'

'What?' The question left her lips like the crack of a whip.

The nurse studied Sathi's face for a moment and answered more slowly. 'Madhubhala died from an infection. It's something that happens sometimes, unfortunately. Mothers give birth normally, and then they get post-partum sepsis. With that girl it was undiagnosed and she died from septicaemic shock.'

'Whoa, whoa, whoa,' Sathi interrupted, holding up her arms. 'Wait a minute. What do you mean, she died from an infection? She died in childbirth – in *this* hospital. That's what everyone has been saying all along! And what is that post-part-whatever-it-was?'

'Post-partum sepsis,' the nurse clarified, looking annoyed, but right then Sathi didn't care. 'It's when small parts of the placenta and membranes are retained within the womb after pregnancy. If it's not discovered, it stays in the body and causes an infection that can lead to death.'

Sathi was speechless. Was this the simple answer to everything? Was this how her Amma had really died? The plane tickets had shown Amma's return to UK months after Sathi's birth because she had in fact returned. She hadn't been murdered. Had Sathi had spent the last few months chasing a non-existent killer?

The nurse was still speaking. 'Septicaemic shock can happen in women who have given birth within six weeks. Their blood pressure drops to very low levels because the infection spreads through the body and damages the organs. It's fatal if -'

'Six weeks?' Sathi echoed, interrupting again. 'Can it happen after a few months?'

The nurse gave her an irritated look. 'Of course not, don't be ridiculous. If a woman has infectious material in her womb it will create symptoms long before that. As I was saying, septic shock is fatal if it's left untreated.'

Sathi had had it with this woman. Not only were the confusing snippets of information about her mother's death doing her head in, on top of that this nurse thought it was okay to judge her mother and talk down to Sathi. Enough was enough.

'And exactly *why* was it left untreated?' she demanded scathingly. 'Was everyone here just too damn busy to make sure that a woman who had just given birth didn't have bits of her baby still stuck inside her?'

The nurse drew herself up coldly. 'We would have been able to do that if the silly girl hadn't been so desperate to leave the hospital. She was in here for so long she couldn't wait to leave.'

Sathi frowned. 'Why was she here that long?'

'She had pre-eclampsia.'

At Sathi's blank expression, the nurse sighed and began to explain. 'It's a condition that can affect women in their third trimester of pregnancy. If it's not treated immediately it's very dangerous and can cause complications for both the mother and the child. Madhubhala recognised the signs of pre-eclampsia and managed to get herself here to the hospital. It was severe, so we had to monitor her until she gave birth. She was nearly eight months pregnant at the time, and she hated having to stay in hospital.'

Eight months... Sathi felt like she was waking up from a long sleep as the whole conversation began to make sense to her. Hadn't her mother's letter been written when she was eight months pregnant, and hadn't she mentioned how the hospital had made her stay against her will, messing up her plans to... well, Sathi didn't know what Amma had been planning to do, but she knew that Amma had returned to India in March to sort out whatever it was. And hadn't Amma mentioned those night-time visitors who had left her so uneasy, visitors who had come while she was in hospital?

Sathi met the nurse's eyes. 'Did anyone come to see her here?'

The nurse looked surprised. 'Well, yes. She had visitors almost all the time. Her parents didn't want her to feel lonely here so they made sure one of them was always with her. Their sons came to visit Madhubhala too.'

It was just like her great-aunt and great-uncle to ensure that her mother didn't feel lonely while she was in hospital. They were just that lovely. But if they had been with Amma most of the time then it would have been difficult for someone else (more than one someone else in fact, seeing as the letter referred to 'they') to come in and threaten her without her family noticing.

'Did anyone else visit her?' she asked. 'Apart from her family, I mean.'

'For God's sake, girl, I don't remember! This was all twenty-odd years ago!'

Sathi's fingers twitched from wanting to wrap them around the woman's neck. She inhaled, counted to five and exhaled. 'Can you please try to think back and remember?' she asked through gritted teeth. 'It's really important.'

The nurse scowled and opened her mouth, but then her expression suddenly went blank. 'Wait. There was that one day,' she said slowly. 'It was just a week or so before the girl gave birth. One of her brothers was the only one here, but he left for a couple of hours in the evening. I'm not sure why, I think there was some reason why he had to leave. Anyway, the point is, a couple of people came to see Madhubhala when her brother wasn't there.'

Excitement flickering through her, Sathi looked expectantly at the nurse. 'And?'

'And nothing. They talked to her for about ten minutes and then they left. Although... Madhubhala looked like she was doing most of the talking.'

'Do you remember anything at all about them? Age, gender, anything?'

The nurse's brow furrowed in thought. 'They were both definitely women. And one of them was much older than the other, so much that they could have been mother and daughter.'

Sathi chewed her lip, trying to figure this out. Mother and daughter? That seemed an unlikely killer pairing. She was also more shocked than she wanted to admit by the revelation that her Amma's killers had been female. Frowning, she supposed it had been quite sexist on her part to assume that the murderer was a man.

'Oh, and the younger girl – she was about the same age as Madhubhala, in fact – was wearing a purdah.'

Startled, Sathi snapped out of her reverie. 'She was Muslim?'

'Well, that was what puzzled me. She was wearing the purdah, but she had a *pottu* on her forehead,' – the nurse pointed to her own forehead, where a small black round sticker decorated the skin just above the bridge of her nose – 'and you know Muslim women aren't allowed to wear those. And she seemed on edge as well – the crone stood in the doorway the whole time they talked. It was almost like she was acting as a look-out for the other one.' The nurse shook her head, clearly baffled.

For Sathi, it was all too clear. The younger woman must have been wearing a purdah so that she wouldn't be recognised, and the mother had been looking out in case someone came by and heard the veiled threats they must have been making.

This was huge. They wouldn't have had to make all this effort if they hadn't expected to be recognised by Amma's family. Which, of course, meant her mother's family knew Amma's killers.

Or, at least, they knew the younger woman. And it was most likely that the younger one was the killer, seeing as she had been the one to be wearing a disguise, the one who was by the bed with Amma while the older woman kept a lookout.

Sathi needed to speak to her great-uncle straightaway. If he knew this woman, she would at least have a name to go on. Her attention shifted back to the nurse, considering. Maybe first she should try and find out as much as possible from her.

'Do you happen to remember the name of the younger woman?' she asked.

'Well, as I already said, it was twenty years ago,' the nurse replied tetchily. Sathi's eyes narrowed, but the nurse carried on speaking, oblivious. 'But, again, I thought there was something odd because she was dressed like a Muslim and yet she had a Hindu name.'

'A Hindu name?' Sathi repeated, her irritation forgotten.

'It was a distinct one. Like... like a Hindu god's name.' The nurse screwed her eyes shut, trying to think of it. Sathi waited silently, her heart pounding. She was this close, this close, to finding out the identity of her mother's killer.

'Krishna, maybe? It might be that, but I'm not really sure.'

Krishna? Well, it was a unisex name, so she supposed it was possible. How ironic that a murderess was named after a deity, Sathi thought wryly.

'No, not Krishna!' the nurse exclaimed suddenly. 'I don't know why I thought that... well, I do know why, because the girl's name was the name of another of Lord Vishnu's avatars.' She paused, and Sathi could have killed her with her bare hands.

'Well?' she demanded impatiently.

'Raman. Her name was Raman.'

There was a moment of complete emptiness before realisation slammed into her. 'Raman?' she gasped. '*Vidhya* Raman?'

The nurse stared at her and then nodded peevishly. 'If you already knew her name why did you ask me, you silly girl?'

266

Chapter Twenty-Seven

Purdah

I declare you officially perfect now! The second blood test came back negative as well – which means you are fit to go home whenever you want to.' The doctor beamed at Great-aunt and left the room, leaving Sathi and her great-aunt alone.

Sathi rushed to her side and gave Great-aunt as enthusiastic a hug as she dared. 'I'm so glad you're okay,' she sobbed into her silver hair.

Great-aunt patted her back. 'Don't worry, molé, it was nothing.'

When Sathi finally pulled away, Great-aunt glanced around the empty room. 'Are the others getting coffee, or something?' she enquired, a mild frown on her face.

Sathi's hand clapped to her forehead. 'Oh no, I promised to call them as soon as you woke up!' Shaking her head at her forgetfulness, she quickly dialled the house number on her phone as she answered Great-aunt. 'They went home last night.'

'What? Even Girish?'

'Yeah. He looked so tired that I insisted he and Aunt Maya go home as well.' No one picked up the house phone, so Sathi cut the call and pulled up her uncle's mobile number on her phone screen. But just before she pressed the call button, the door opened and her uncle, aunt and great-uncle walked into the room.

'Amma, you're awake,' Uncle said joyfully, moving to embrace Great-aunt.

'Well, yes,' she replied stiffly. 'Although it would have been nice to see you as soon as I woke up,' she added as she pushed him away.

Uncle looked a bit like a spanked puppy, but before anyone could speak Great-uncle laughed. He moved to his wife's side and rested his hand on her shoulder. 'My dear, you're just tired after the excitement of last night. Now, are you allowed to come back home?'

Great-aunt pursed her lips. 'Yes. I was just waiting for everyone to come back.'

'Okay, then let's get you home. Where's that wheelchair?'

Aunt Maya wheeled it to the bed and reached out to help Great-aunt into it. Sathi stepped forward to help.

'No,' Great-aunt protested, waving them away. 'Girish, you do it.'

Aunt Maya and Sathi moved out of the way, but not before hurt registered on their expressions. Great-uncle was quick to notice it. 'Don't take it personally,' he told them both in a low tone as Uncle situated Great-aunt in the wheelchair. 'She's just used to Girish doing these things for her. She's exhausted – indulge her in her old age.'

Sathi smiled sleepily at him. 'You'll both never be old,' she replied, grinning and pulling back when he reached out and pretended to cuff her ear.

Aunt Maya's full lips tilted up at their antics, but Sathi noticed that the smile never actually made it into her eyes.

'*Appuppa...*'

'Yes?' Great-uncle replied from behind his newspaper.

Sathi changed her mind again. 'Nothing.'

He lowered the newspaper and peered at her over his reading glasses. 'What is it, Sathi molé?'

She looked at him earnestly, but then shook her head. 'It's nothing.'

268

The armchair creaked as Great-uncle got up and joined her on the sofa. 'Tell me what the matter is,' he coaxed.

She reluctantly met his eyes, and saw nothing but kindness there. She glanced around to make sure that they were, indeed, alone. 'It's about my Amma,' she whispered to him.

'What about her?' he asked gently, stroking her hair.

She couldn't blurt the truth out immediately. She just couldn't. 'Do you remember Vidhya Raman?' she asked instead, the name filling her mouth with the bitter taste of betrayal.

Great-uncle's hand stopped in their movement. 'She was one of Madhu's good friends,' he replied finally. 'Why do you ask?'

'Good friends.' She gave a derisive laugh. 'Yeah, that's what I thought, too.'

He put a hand on her chin and twisted her face around to face him. 'What are you saying? How do you know Vidhya?'

She shook her head cynically. 'I don't know her, Appuppa. The truth is, I don't think anyone knows her. Not the real her.'

'The real her?' Great-uncle echoed, his deep voice filled with confusion.

Sathi took a deep breath. She couldn't put it off anymore. 'Appuppa, there's something I haven't told you.'

He was really still. 'What is it?'

She couldn't hold his gaze, so she stared at her hands instead. 'Do you remember when I told you that on the day of my eighteenth birthday I rummaged around in my dad's study and found some of Amma's things, like her ring and wedding chain?' She didn't wait for an answer – now that she had started explaining she couldn't stop. 'I found something else as well. I found a letter that she sent to Dad a few months before she died. In the letter she wrote some things that suggested that she didn't die in childbirth. The letter made it sound like... it made it sound like she was murdered,' Sathi finished in a rush, afraid to look at her great-uncle.

Great-uncle shot to his feet. 'What?' he asked, horrified. 'No. No,' he repeated more forcefully. 'Madhu died in childbirth.'

'I know, I thought that too,' she said hastily, reaching out to touch his arm. 'But, please, hear me out,' she pleaded.

She pulled at his arm, and he stiffly sank back onto the sofa, sitting staring straight ahead as she poured out everything from the very beginning, telling him how she had become suspicious with the letter after reading about the visitors who had unsettled Amma. She told him how she had found the plane tickets and how they showed that Amma had come back to India in March, months after she was supposed to have died.

Tears trudging silently down her cheeks, she told her great-uncle about how she had tested her father by mentioning Kerala, and how he had reacted violently to the idea of her coming here to Nelliampathi.

She was about to tell him how she had consulted her cards to glean the truth when suddenly he unfroze and lifted his hand, brushing it against her cheek in a loving caress. 'I know that wherever my daughter is, she is as proud of you as I am right now,' he said to her, eyes glimmering with unshed tears. 'You're such a brave girl.'

Her heart felt so full in that moment. She clutched his hand to her and bowed over it, fighting back sobs.

Great-uncle stroked her hair again until she quietened. Then he said, 'Whatever happened, Madhu is at peace now, molé. Should you pursue this?'

Sathi pulled back, wiping her cheeks with her hands. 'I have to,' she whispered brokenly. 'Otherwise I'm a failure as a daughter.'

'Nothing will make you a failure, Sathi, do you understand me?'

'I have to do this,' she repeated.

Great-uncle sighed. 'OK.' He paused, and asked almost tentatively, 'Do you have anyone you suspect?'

She nodded. 'That's why I was asking you about Vidhya.' She told him everything the nurse at the hospital had told her.

He was speechless. 'To think that the one time we weren't there with Madhu, that worm managed to sneak in,' he muttered in disbelief, speaking more to himself than to her.

'So you think Vidhya could have done it, then?' Sathi asked.

He hesitated. 'To tell the truth, your Ammumma and I never really approved of their friendship. Vidhya was always a plain, sullen child, and she was jealous of your mother because Madhu was beautiful and vivacious and just so full of life. She had everything Vidhya wanted. But Vidhya could never express her envy because her brother worked for me. He was the family's sole breadwinner, and she knew if she did anything to upset Madhu he could lose his job.' He scowled. 'I think in college Vidhya was interested in Nakul as well, so you can imagine how she felt when he married Madhu instead. We wanted to warn Madhu, but, like you, she was fiercely loyal. We didn't want to upset her, so we didn't say anything. Now I wish to God that we had! Maybe we would still have our Madhu with us now.'

Sathi digested this, feeling more and more disgusted with Vidhya by the minute. All those beautiful stories of friendship... had all those been a lie as hatred masqueraded as love?

'I want to find her,' she growled, 'and rip her into pieces.'

Great-uncle's voice was panicked now. 'No, molé, don't set your heart on vengeance from that excuse of a woman. She's slyer than a fox, and if she finds out you're onto her there's no telling what she might do.'

When she didn't respond, he pulled her to him. 'Please, Sathi,' he begged. 'I can't lose another daughter.'

Sathi sighed and laid her heavy head on her great-uncle's shoulder.

'Promise me you won't go after Vidhya,' he insisted.

Her eyes closed of their own accord, and she saw her mother's sweet image in her mind's eye, willing her to make the right decision.

'I promise,' she said to both of them.

Chapter Twenty-Eight

Cracks & Fissures

Sathi was almost ninety-nine percent sure that Great-uncle had told Great-aunt everything about Amma and her death and the fact that Vidhya might have been the one to cause it. She hadn't said anything to her, but Sathi noticed her great-aunt's eyes on her more often than usual over the next few days.

Her great-aunt and great-uncle also paid extra attention to her in the days following that fateful conversation. Their smiles and embraces contained an extra warmth when they talked to her, and Great-aunt, especially, was so solicitous about her that Sathi felt almost weepy with it all. At mealtimes (and lots of other times in between), she would sit Sathi down next to her and feed her choice titbits with her own hand until Sathi felt she would burst with all the food and attention.

Sathi would never admit this out loud, not even under intense torture involving bamboo shoots shoved under her nails, but she was feeling a bit... hemmed in. She loved her family, but sometimes she felt like there was no real privacy in the house. And she really wanted some after the things she had found out – she wanted some space to just think about Vidhya and let everything she had learned about her mother's death sink in.

Even though she had promised not to go after Vidhya, the thought of her mother's fake friend often filled her with so much rage that she was several times tempted to break her word. Maybe that was why her great-aunt and great-uncle were keeping such a close eye on her.

Besides, it was hypocritical of her to complain, even in her mind. All her life she had bitterly blamed her father for never being there. Why was she moaning now that she had received her dearest wish?

She snorted in self-disgust. Human nature. How fickle it was.

Dusk had fallen outside, and the reflection of streetlamps winked at them all through the glass of the living room window.

'So, Girish,' Great-uncle began, 'when are you going back to the hospital?'

Looking up from the laptop balanced on his lap, Uncle blinked at his father. 'Hospital? Oh, you mean work.' He glanced at Aunt Maya, who had just sat down next to him on the sofa. 'Oh, well, erm, well we actually... that is, Maya and I actually wanted to maybe go away somewhere for a couple of weeks first.'

Aunt Maya's expression was more animated than Sathi had ever seen it. 'Yes, we were thinking of going to Ooty, or maybe Munnar.'

Great-uncle's brow creased, but before he could answer Great-aunt came into the room, saying, 'Maya molé, can you fetch that pain ointment for me? Your arms were hurting earlier, didn't you say?' she said, looking expectantly at Great-uncle.

He nodded and rubbed his elbow. 'That's right. It's been painful all day.'

'I'll get it, Ammumma,' Sathi offered, not wanting her aunt to have to get up so soon after only just sitting down.

'No, no,' Great-aunt replied. 'Maya knows where it is. Can you get it now, molé?' she added, smiling apologetically.

'Yes, of course,' Aunt Maya said, shrugging off Uncle's arm from where it was draped around her shoulders and standing up.

Great-uncle picked up the conversation from where it had been left off. 'So, you want to have a honeymoon? I thought that was why you and Maya stayed in Kollam for so long after the wedding.'

Uncle Girish shifted on the sofa, looking uncomfortable. 'You know what it's like after a marriage, visiting houses and staying with relatives. We never really had a moment alone together. And Maya likes Ooty.'

'What's to like?' Great-aunt asked, unimpressed. She moved further into the room and sat next to her son. 'It's just another hill-station, a crowded hill-station at that. Nelliampathi is much better, and you don't have to take even more leave from work.'

'And you know how expensive holidays are,' Great-uncle added. 'What with all the travel and checking into hotels. I think you should work for as long as you can, and you can still come home in the evenings and spend time with Maya.'

He exchanged a glance with Great-aunt. 'Girish, we don't even own our own house,' he said earnestly. 'We have to think practically.'

Uncle Girish didn't say anything in reply. Aunt Maya appeared in the doorway, clutching the ointment and looking puzzled at the sudden tense atmosphere in the room.

'Come, Maya, sit here,' Great-uncle said, patting the seat next to him. 'We were just talking about this honeymoon trip. Molé, I think it might be best to postpone your holiday,' he said gently. 'You see, Girish has already taken a lot of time off work for the wedding, and for the preparations that went on beforehand. I don't think it's wise to take any more leave.'

Aunt Maya's face fell, even though she tried to hide her disappointment. 'I see.'

Uncle anxiously scrutinised her expression. 'We can go to Ooty in December. It'll be nicer at that time.' His eyes pleaded with her.

Aunt smiled a sweet smile at him. 'Of course.'

'Maya, I'm leaving!' Uncle called as he got up from the breakfast table and started washing his hands. 'I'll be back at six!'

Great-aunt frowned up at him from the table. 'Don't you have duty until eight today?'

'Yes, but a couple of Maya's friends are in town and they wanted to meet me and say congratulations. Maya and I are going to dinner with them this evening,' he replied, mopping his mouth with a towel. 'One of the other doctors is covering for me.'

He glanced impatiently at his watch, and then at the doorway to the kitchen. 'I'm late, I have to go,' he said resignedly. 'Tell Maya I said bye and that I'll be here in time to pick her up.' He leant down to kiss Great-aunt's cheek and waved at Sathi before leaving.

Aunt Maya rushed into the dining room just as the front door banged shut, breathless and with her arms covered in soapy water. She stood motionless for a breath of time, and then slowly swivelled to face the two at the table.

Great-aunt smiled. 'Girish said bye.'

After lunch, Sathi was surprised to find her great-aunt and great-uncle preparing to go out somewhere. She had already accompanied Great-uncle to the charity site that morning, so she had no idea what the unusual outing meant. Nevertheless, she offered to go with them.

They exchanged glances. 'No, molé, you stay home. You'll be bored if you come with us.'

Sathi shrugged. 'I don't mind. I'd like to come anyway.'

Smiling and patting her cheek, Great-aunt answered, 'You stay and keep Aunt Maya company. We don't want her to feel lonely.'

So Sathi, puzzled, stayed at home. They didn't return until early evening, and even though she watched them closely when they came back, she didn't get any insight into their strange behaviour. She shrugged and put the little mystery out of her mind. After all, people were allowed to have secrets.

Great-aunt didn't let Aunt Maya wash up after they had tea and a mid-evening snack. 'Let the servants do it. You go and get ready before Girish comes, molé,' she told Aunt Maya, patting her cheek. Aunt Maya blushed in pleasure at the obvious affection in Great-aunt's voice.

They were in the living room when Aunt Maya emerged from her room about an hour later. Sathi whooped in admiration. Her aunt looked absolutely gorgeous in a sparkling chiffon sari the colour of autumn leaves, the graceful folds shimmering and billowing like a real hearth as the gold embroidery caught the light and returned it more beautiful than it had arrived. Her long hair was swept up into a loose bun, with short strands curling and yielding to the pull of gravity to frame her face elegantly. Dangly earrings snuggled up to her neck on either side, and the slim golden bangle she always wore danced its way up and down her wrist as they kept tempo with the movement of her arms. Her golden thali was the perfect finishing touch: it hung proudly around her neck, nestled against the front of her sari.

'Can someone teach me how to wolf-whistle?' Sathi asked the room in general. 'So I can express my appreciation in the most appropriate manner?'

Aunt Maya laughed, her eyes sparkling like black pearls.

'Absolutely ravishing,' Great-uncle complimented, smiling at her.

'Beautiful,' Great-aunt agreed.

She flushed in response to all the praise and attention, the hint of pink setting off her dark, flawless skin perfectly.

Great-aunt walked up to her daughter-in-law and handed her a tall glass of warm milk. 'Here, drink this molé. It's a cold night, we don't want you catching a chill.'

Aunt Maya, looking pleasantly surprised, obediently lifted the glass to her lips. Great-aunt put a hand under the glass and tipped it up so that Aunt Maya drained the last drop. 'There, that should keep you nice and warm,' she said, taking the glass back from her and beaming.

After about half-an-hour later Uncle Girish came back from work, and after spending a few slack-jawed minutes admiring his wife's beauty, he was hurried off to take a quick shower and get changed before their dinner date.

Aunt Maya was telling Sathi about the friend they were meeting tonight, who she knew from college, when suddenly she broke off in the middle of a sentence, her complexion alarmingly pale. There was no visible reason for the sudden change, and Sathi touched her arm, asking what was wrong, but she received no reply.

Uncle Girish, alerted by their exclamations, rushed back into the room with his hair dripping wet. His expression etched with worry, he put his arm around his wife and tried to find out what was wrong, but like Sathi, he had no success. Aunt Maya seemed to be in too much pain to speak.

'Ungh!' Aunt Maya groaned, her eyes squeezed shut as she pressed her arms into her stomach and bent over, her torso almost flattened against her knees. A sheen of sweat covered her skin, spoiling what little make-up she had on.

Sathi, feeling useless, wiped her hands across her aunt's forehead, and was shocked by how hot her skin was. 'She's feverish!'

Uncle Girish looked up, saying anxiously, 'We should take her to the hospital.'

'Nonsense,' Great-aunt said briskly. 'She's just got stomach cramps. A good night's sleep will do her more good than anything else. Come, molé,' she added to her daughter-in-law, pulling her up by the arm. Great-aunt staggered under her weight as she realised that Aunt Maya had gone completely limp.

'She's fainted,' Uncle whispered hoarsely as he held up his unconscious wife, looking down at her in horror.

'Now, don't be silly, Girish,' his mother told him. 'Lay her down on your bed and then come straight back. Maya needs complete rest, and she'll recover better on her own. You can sleep in the guest bedroom tonight.'

Uncle appeared not to have heard. He didn't move, seeming to be frozen in shock.

'Now, Girish,' Great-aunt said sharply.

Uncle Girish obeyed her.

Chapter Twenty-Nine

Rose Tint

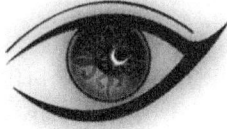

J ust as Great-aunt had predicted, Aunt Maya woke up the next morning feeling a hundred percent better and with barely any memory of the previous evening. No one could think why such a sudden bout of cramp and fever had come on so quickly, nor could anyone puzzle out why there was no trace of it the next morning.

Of course, their planned evening out had been spoilt, and they could not reschedule as Aunt Maya's friends were leaving Nelliampathi the next day. Aunt Maya had been disappointed by that, but as everyone was just thankful that her strange illness had passed without more severe repercussions, no one deemed it a topic worth much discussion.

Life returned more or less to normal. A few weeks passed. Sathi was not exactly sure of the exact count and to be perfectly honest, she did not really care. What did time matter when life was filled with joy?

The next excitement for the household was when Sathi's Uncle Karan came for a visit, along with his wife, Aunt Anika, and their six-year-old son, Arjun. Sathi was, of course, delighted to meet more of her newly expanded family, and they had a great time getting to know each other. Uncle Karan was very different from his younger brother; he had a loud, funny voice that boomed all over the house and he dominated whatever conversation he happened to be involved in. He also kept the women in the family busy preparing snacks and such that he craved to satisfy his seemingly never-ending appetite.

Aunt Maya and Sathi quickly warmed to Aunt Anika, a dynamic, lively woman who didn't seem to believe in the act of sitting down. She was constantly on the move, and her mouth was as busy as her hands, working non-stop relating mindless information that was nonetheless fun to listen to because of the entertaining manner in which it was delivered.

Sathi imagined with amusement that the couple, when they were in their own house, probably just talked at each other without either listening to what the other was saying. It was an interesting relationship to observe.

Having another set of uncle and aunt livened up the atmosphere of the house a bit, and for the first week or so of their stay, the days took on a festive feel. However, as the weeks passed by, some things happened that made Sathi uneasy, even though she did not want to admit, even to herself, just how much.

The first thing happened on a Saturday afternoon, when Uncle Karan and Aunt Anika's son, Arjun, was not at school. The child had been enjoying the days in the company of his grandparents, and this afternoon in particular the three of them had been watching some kind of cartoon together.

After about an hour of letting him watch TV, Aunt Anika called him to come outside and ride his bike for a while. Arjun pretended not to have heard his mother and carried on sitting in between his grandparents.

'Arjun!' she called again sharply, standing in the doorway with her hand on her hip.

'I want to watch some more,' he whined, not taking his eyes off the television screen.

Aunt Anika walked into the door and frowned down at her son from one side of the sofa. 'You've watched enough for today, Arjun,' she said firmly. 'Now come outside before the sun goes in.'

Not one of the three looked up. Not one of them even acknowledged her presence. Sathi had been watching Aunt Anika's face, and so she saw the precise instant when her previously expectant, maybe a little annoyed, expression was taken over by sudden fury.

She reached over and closer her fist over her son's arm. 'Arjun, come outside this instant!' She pulled, trying to force him to stand up off the sofa.

'No, I won't!' he resisted, complaining loudly and leaning into his grandmother for support.

'Let him stay,' Great-aunt said, putting an arm around her grandson.

Aunt Anika shook her head fiercely. 'No, he has to learn to listen to me. If I say that's enough TV, that's enough TV.' She again pulled at her son, but Great-aunt's words stopped her.

'Are you sure that's what your problem is, Anika? Or is it that you don't want him spending time with us?'

Aunt Anika dropped Arjun's hand as if it burned her. She stared at her mother-in-law in shock. 'No... No, of course not,' she spluttered. 'That's not what I - the sunshine is good for him...' she trailed off.

Great-aunt looked out of the window pointedly and then back at Aunt in triumph. 'Well, the sun's gone in now so there's not much point, is there?'

Aunt Anika didn't have an answer for that.

'Arjun?' she tried one last time to appeal to her son, but when his head turned reluctantly in her direction, his eyes were so cold that Aunt Anika actually flinched.

That night when she got up to go to the bathroom, Sathi heard arguing voices coming from the guestroom, which was next to her mother's old room. Even though they were talking quietly, she could still hear Uncle Karan and Aunt Anika's voices clearly.

'I can't deal with this any more, Karan,' Aunt Anika hissed. 'Every time we bring Arjun here, the same thing happens.'

'What are you talking about?' Uncle Karan's usually mild voice was infiltrated with exasperation. 'Arjun just likes to spend time with his grandparents. You don't have a problem when we visit *your* parents.'

'That's not the point!' came the heated reply. 'I don't mind him spending time with them, what I object to is them trying to come between me and my son. He turns into a stranger when we come here.'

'Oh really! They're not trying to come between you and Arjun. For God's sake, they barely see him, Anika! What's the big problem if he prefers to stay and do something with them than be with you all the time?'

Aunt Anika obviously didn't find that a remark worth answering. She just made a derisive noise in her throat and then there was a creak of bed springs as if someone had flounced down onto the bed. After that there was nothing more to be heard.

Sathi couldn't deny the truth of Uncle Karan's words. Great-aunt and Great-uncle barely got to see their only grandson, except on visits such as these. Of course they'd like for him to spend what little time they had together. That was completely understandable. After all, the kid had only sat with his grandparents for less than an hour.

And yet, despite all that, she still couldn't shake the memory of the coldness with which a small child had regarded his own mother.

There was some friction between Great-aunt and Aunt Anika in the ensuing days. Aunt seemed to be determined to keep a polite front, however. She didn't like it, but on Sunday she let Arjun stay in front of the TV for as long as his grandparents did. She didn't interfere any more in what he was doing when he was with Great-aunt and Great-uncle.

But when school came round again, victory was in Aunt Anika's hands. Every morning she took smug satisfaction in sending her son off for most of the day, away from the hated TV. Peace gradually returned to the household.

Then one day Sathi came into the living room unexpectedly to see Great-aunt showing Arjun something and telling him, '*Moné*, when you're in Daddy and Mummy's room look around and see if there's something like this in there, okay? Open all the drawers and have a good look around.'

Her grandson obediently took the rectangular object in his two small hands and nodded solemnly. When she moved slightly further into the room, puzzled, Sathi saw that it was a sheet of tablets, much like the ones Great-aunt and Great-uncle had to consume every day.

She stopped in her advance suddenly, horrified. There was one crucial difference between this sheet and the rest in the medical box. The tablets were placed, not in rows as usual, but in an almost complete circle with a clear beginning and end.

They were contraceptive pills.

She staggered back, and must have made some kind of noise, because Great-aunt suddenly looked up and saw her.

Sathi cringed away from Great-aunt's expression, but before she could say or do anything to erase it Great-aunt had shooed Arjun out of the room and approached her. She took hold of Sathi's arm, but Sathi yanked it away. 'How could you show a child those...?' Sathi gasped, unable to finish.

Great-aunt grabbed onto her shoulders, looking at Sathi pleadingly. 'Molé, wait, no, you're misunderstanding this.'

Sathi screwed her eyes shut and shook her head tightly. 'I know what I saw,' she said through clenched teeth.

'I'm not arguing with that,' her great-aunt replied. Sathi made to pull away again, but Great-aunt only tightened her hold. 'But you need to understand the whole story first. You need to understand why I'm forced to take such awful measures.' She paused and took in a deep breath, closing her eyes momentarily to collect her thoughts. 'Before Anika became pregnant with Arjun, she'd already had an abortion. We didn't know about it until much later, but Anika didn't want children and when she became pregnant unexpectedly she decided to kill her child. My first grandchild.' Great-aunt couldn't help the little sob that escaped.

Her shock beginning to be smothered by pity and compassion, Sathi put her arm around her great-aunt. Tears in her eyes, Great-aunt looked up at her. 'I don't trust her not to destroy another child like she did her first. I... I couldn't bear it if she did something like that again.' She started crying in earnest then, sobbing into Sathi's clothes while Sathi absently patted her back, her thoughts tumultuous.

She could sympathise with her great-aunt's pain, and hated the fact that someone could so callously make and then destroy a child, simply for selfish reasons. But did that initial wrongdoing and fear of further pain excuse a grandmother asking her grandson to snoop for contraceptive pills in her son and daughter-in-law's bedroom?

Sathi honestly didn't know the answer. Right and wrong seemed to be so muddled and entangled in this household, and worse, in her mind. She didn't know what to think, not about any of it. Who was she to decide who was wrong and who was right? And more importantly, was anyone ever completely wrong or completely right?

She didn't know.

The day before Uncle Karan, Aunt Anika and Arjun were scheduled to leave, Sathi noticed that Aunt Anika took Aunt Maya aside and had an earnest conversation with her. There was no one else at home, and it was obvious to Sathi that Aunt Anika had chosen the moment for that precise reason. She couldn't hear the conversation, but whatever Aunt Anika was saying to her sister-in-law was having an upsetting effect on Aunt Maya. She kept shaking her head vehemently, and her eyes welled with tears a couple of times. Aunt Anika took no notice, leaning forward and keeping a firm hold on Aunt Maya's hand as though scared that she would fly away.

Then as the conversation lengthened, Aunt Maya stopped trying to pull away and really listened to her sister-in-law. She nodded a couple of times, albeit reluctantly, and she began to take a stronger part in the exchange, beginning to talk as well. She said things that filled Aunt Anika's expression with first anger, then sadness, then pity. Finally, they embraced and kissed each other's cheeks affectionately before parting. They never gave any intimation of their sudden closeness when in the presence of the others.

Sathi was burning with curiosity about the content of their conversation. She was equally terrified of satisfying that curiosity.

*   *   *

'Girish!' Aunt Maya yelled, stopping Uncle in the process of getting into his car as he left for work. 'My dad just called,' she said, clutching his shirt with her eyes wide with fear. 'My mum's had a stroke. I... I don't know what to do,' she said incoherently, tears spilling over from her eyes. 'I need to go to them...'

Uncle comforted his wife, leading her back inside the house and sitting her down on the sofa.

'What's wrong? Why haven't you left for work?' Great-uncle asked, looking from Uncle Girish to Aunt Maya.

Uncle pressed his lips to Aunt Maya's forehead. 'Maya's mum has had a stroke. She -'

'Girish, I need to go to them,' Aunt Maya said again urgently, interrupting him.

'Of course, yes, come, get ready, we'll both go now.' He stood up and gently pulled her up with him. Walking as if in a daze, Aunt Maya stumbled her way up the stairs so she could change out of the nightdress she was wearing.

They all stood around in the living room, waiting for Aunt Maya to return. After a couple of minutes, she appeared back at the top of the stairs.

'Arrgh...'

The sudden groan gave only a split-second warning before Great-aunt fell to the floor in a dead-faint.

'Amma?' Panicked, Uncle dropped to his knees next to her and lightly slapped his hands against her cheeks to try and bring her back to consciousness.

As both Uncle and Great-uncle hovered over Great-aunt in an anxious frenzy, Sathi marvelled distractedly at the fact that she felt not one ounce of the worry she had been afflicted with the first time her great-aunt collapsed.

A few moments later, Great-aunt regained consciousness. She seemed too weak to get up, however, and lay on the floor moaning softly, her hand covering most of her face.

'What's wrong?' Aunt Maya asked, appearing next to Sathi. She didn't move any closer to her mother-in-law.

Uncle Girish was distraught as he answered her. 'I don't know! She just collapsed. I don't know what to... I don't know how... Amma? Amma, please tell me what's wrong, please. Please, Amma.' Sathi's heart broke hearing the anguish, the terror in his voice.

Aunt Maya laid a protective hand on his shoulder as she crouched down next to him. Then addressing her mother-in-law, she asked coldly, 'Isn't it time you stopped torturing your son with these dramas?'

There was a gasp. Sathi didn't know who uttered it. It may even have been her.

Great-aunt slowly moved her hand, uncovering her face. Her expression was filled with genuine shock and hurt, but in her dark eyes glittered a kernel of triumph.

'Dramas, molé?' she repeated, her voice the perfect match for her expression.

'If you wanted to prevent me and Girish from leaving the house, you could have just told us not to go,' Aunt Maya said in a tone that was devoid of any inflection. She could have been discussing the weather.

'Maya!' Uncle Girish uttered her name reproachfully. 'What are you saying?'

She looked at him, and her calm mask cracked. Earnestly, she took his hand. 'Please, Girish, let's get out of here. Let's live anywhere but here,' she entreated passionately.

He frowned down at her. 'What are you talking about? What's wrong with you all of a sudden?'

She shook her head. 'It's not me who has a problem. Don't you see, every time we plan to do something together, they do something to stop us. And now, when I want to see my mum because she's had a stroke, suddenly *she* has a fainting fit!' Aunt Maya pointed a finger at Great-aunt, her hands trembling with rage.

Uncle shook off her hand angrily. 'She is a heart patient! She can't control when she has an attack!'

Aunt laughed humourlessly. 'Trust me, Girish, there isn't a healthier person on the planet than her.'

'I see. So, your parents and their illnesses are far more important than those of my parents.'

'No,' Aunt replied. 'That's not the point. If only you could see how much they're manipulating you-'

'Enough.' Uncle Girish held up a hand, cutting her off. 'I didn't realise that the woman I'd loved and married was so cold-hearted.'

'Girish, I -' Aunt Maya began, but she was interrupted again.

'As you have so little concern for the welfare of my parents, I don't feel any inclination to have any for yours. If you want to visit your mum, that's fine with me, but rest assured, once you leave this house, the next time we meet will be in a family court as we file for a divorce.'

Aunt Maya stared at her husband in speechless shock. 'Please don't do this,' she finally pleaded in a choked whisper. 'Please don't make me choose between you.'

Uncle stared back at her, unmoved. 'And what about what you did? Weren't you just five minutes ago asking me to leave my parents to live with you? The same standards apply to both of us, Maya. It's your choice.'

With that, he turned his back on Aunt Maya and extended his hand to help his mother up off the floor. With his arm around her supporting her, and with his father walking by his side, he strode out of the room.

Aunt Maya was left to remain standing motionless in the middle of the living room, staring after them numbly.

Sathi was hesitating, trying to decide whether to go to her, when without warning her aunt sank onto the floor, buried her head in her knees and began to utter a low, wordless keening that was so rich with pain that it raised goose-bumps along Sathi's arms.

Chapter Thirty

In the Shadows

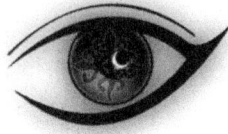

unt Maya stayed in her in-law's house. However, considering the way she and Uncle Girish acted around each other, she might as well have gone home. They acted like two strangers who had been forced to live under the same roof. No, if they had been strangers, they might have at least talked to each other, or smiled out of polite courtesy when they met on the stairs or when they were both in the same room. Instead, they both acted, quite simply, as though the other didn't exist.

Sathi tried a couple of times to approach her aunt and uncle separately and talk them into seeing sense. She could see both their points of view. Uncle was upset because, in his eyes, Aunt didn't care about his parents. Aunt was angry with him for making her choose between him and her parents, and for putting his parents over her. She had talked on the phone to her father, and her mother was fine – her stroke had been of the mildest type, and she was on the mend. But the fact that Aunt Maya hadn't been allowed to go to her mother in her hour of need had the consequence of completely freezing over her attitude towards Uncle Girish.

In short, it was something that could be worked out if they would both just get off their high horses and talk to each other.

When Sathi tried to persuade her uncle to do just that, he listened stonily for a few minutes and then told her, in very controlled, polite terms, to mind her own business.

Aunt Maya, though not so directly offensive, nevertheless refused point-blank to talk to Sathi about the situation, and wouldn't listen to her either. She did, however, stop Sathi when she, resigned, was about to leave, and give her a hug. 'Thank you for trying,' Aunt Maya said. 'You're showing a lot more concern about this than some other people,' she added pointedly.

It didn't take Sathi long to guess who her aunt was referring to.

Her great-aunt and great-uncle went on about life without seeming to be the least bit affected by the tension and discord between their newly-married son and daughter-in-law. The day after their fight, Great-aunt and Great-uncle even went out again together. This time Sathi didn't bother to ask to go with them, and they were gone for most of the day. However, when they came back, Great-aunt rushed into the house in a panic, screeched, 'Girish, come quickly!' and then hurried out again. Uncle immediately jumped to his feet and followed her. Aunt Maya and Sathi exchanged puzzled glances, and they too headed outside to the car.

The driver's door was open, and Uncle Girish leaned into it as he tried to help Great-uncle get out of the seat.

'My knees are locked,' Great-uncle snapped as his son tried to make him swing his legs out. Great-aunt hovered anxiously, her face twisted with what may have been real fear.

'What happened?' Uncle Girish asked in frustration as he tried and failed to extract his father from the car.

'I don't know! He was driving as normal without any problems and then we parked and he suddenly couldn't move,' Great-aunt replied, her voice still frenzied. 'He's never had a problem with his knees before, I can't see how this could have happened.' Then her expression froze. 'Unless...' she breathed, her shocked eyes flickering over to her husband.

'Shut up!' Great-uncle barked sharply, glaring coldly at her. When he had made sure that his wife wouldn't blurt out whatever thought had just occurred to her, he shifted his attention down to his knees. Frowning in concentration, he tensed his leg muscles and gradually, inch by inch, he swung his right leg out of the car. Breathing hard and clutching the top of the headrest for support, he did the same with his other leg and managed to heave himself to his feet. He wobbled unsteadily, and immediately Uncle Girish moved to hold him up. Great-uncle shook him off with what sounded almost like a growl. He straightened his spine and walked stiffly to the doorway of the house, leaving everyone else to stand rooted to their spot as they watched him leave.

*   *   *

She stretched her arms above her head and felt around for the bolt to the door in the dark. Finding it, she slotted the lock back and pushed up. The door fell back over itself with a thud.

Cautiously, she stopped and listened. Good. Nothing stirred.

Expertly, she found the little iron foothold built into the stone and used it to haul herself up into the room. Kneeling on the dusty floor, she adjusted the black cloak-like material that was draped around her to make sure that it fully covered her face. She reached over and lifted the door off the floor. She closed it over the hole and carefully slid the bolt across it with her gnarled fingers just for extra measure. It wouldn't do to let anyone intrude upon the ritual.

Then, with a strength that belied her age, she pushed up off the floor and strode to one of the many shelves that stacked the room. With practised movements, she moved aside the bottles that filled it, impatiently reaching for the small vial she had placed there at the back not so long ago.

She moved aside a particularly large – and vile-looking – flask, and there it was.

An almost maternal feeling welled up in her as she slowly pulled the vial towards her. The heavy liquid slopping defiantly against the sides of the glass bottle was music to her ears.

She lifted it up and held it up in front of her eyes. Such a lovely colour, she thought, a rich burgundy that was the perfect match for the bloodlust in a savage wolf's eye just before it lunged, a colour that called awake forbidden desires and wasted dreams, the colour that marks an innocent girl's ascension into the vengeful world of womanhood.

A ripple of laughter burst its way through her lips. What an exquisite thought.

She carried the viscid liquid of her loins over to the *mandapam*. A smile crossed her lips at her nickname for the brick fireplace. *Very appropriate*, she congratulated herself.

Ritualistically, she fed the fire and stoked it. It spluttered and sparks shot out, only just missing her clothes. 'Shhh, my darling, you'll receive your treat very soon,' she crooned to the fire, and the flames seemed to ripple and billow with extra vigour, as though there was something at the heart of it that reacted in excitement to the promise in her words.

She crouched down in front of her beloved flames and concentrated, bowing her head and reciting those powerful words which she had uttered so many times that it seemed like they were a part of her. She allowed her voice to rise with each chant so that by the time she reached the conclusion of the mantra, the last sacred word was expelled as a shout.

Satisfied, she reached into her voluminous cloak and drew out a small wooden box. She quickly pried the lock open and shook the contents onto her hand. She looked benevolently down at the lock of hair where it lay in her palm, curled in an almost perfect C.

She's always had such lovely curls. A shame, a shame.

She picked it up with her old digits, her expression becoming gleeful as she studied it.

She thought she could defy us, did she? The little brat. She dropped the hair into the flames, watching her pet devour it greedily. *Well, this will take care of her, as well as the vermin growing inside her.*

She reached for the phial of blood, and a spark of flame spat out and singed her sleeve. The flame growled. 'Patience,' she said to it. 'All will go as planned. The brat's goddess can do nothing.'

The fire calmed in response to her soothing tone, and she emptied the vial into the flames, smiling as it hissed and stretched in pleasure.

Now for her favourite part. Her breath sped in anticipation as she held her finger in front of her and studied it. The pale bulb of flesh was appealingly smooth and unmarred. She turned her finger away from her and approached the flames.

Illuminated as well as sustained by the inferno, her pet's scales gleamed and its seven heads blazed. Those dark eyes followed her every movement as she brought her finger closer and closer. Finally, impatient with waiting, the dragon reared, lunging forward and claiming its due sacrifice as she threw back her head and laughed in exultation and victory and madness.

Sathi wrenched upright, her breathing ragged and her clothes soaked through with her own sweat. She tried to draw in a calming breath, but the dream – or was it a vision? – refused to relinquish her. Against her will, her eyes closed and she saw again the burning flames in her mind's eye, and the grotesque, sickening seven-headed creature within. She felt her index finger tingle with remembered pain, and had to fight against a sudden wave of nausea.

The scene suddenly shifted away from the dark, murky room with the fire, and she saw the clearly distinguishable arm of the woman in the dream, who now clutched a glass filled with viscous black liquid. As Sathi watched, she held it out and another hand closed over it, a younger hand with a single gold bangle on her wrist, and as the glass changed hands the murky shadows of the gurgling liquid transformed into a clear, light, wine colour, the colour of summer. Then, finally, the vision faded into blackness.

Sathi shuddered out a breath and opened her eyes. Her heart pounding, she tried to tell herself that it was just a dream... just a dream... just a dream. Yet, even as she repeated the litany in her mind, she couldn't help shuddering again as she thought of the awful woman and the disgusting things she'd been thinking and doing in the dream. The fire, the lock of hair... the menstrual blood. Urgh!

And the memory of that creature in the fire filled her with sheer terror. There had been pure evil looking out through those seven pairs of eyes...

Sathi gasped in shock as she realised that she had seen the creature once before in a dream. It had been a long time ago. She concentrated, thinking back.

Yes, that first night she'd spent in Nelliampathi she had dreamed of the dark room and then caught a glimpse of the dragon-like creature within the fire.

She couldn't get the image of the dragon out of her head. Every time she closed her eyes to try and go back to sleep, the creature mocked her from behind her eyelids.

Sathi finally threw her covers off and stood up. She'd walk around for a bit. Actually, she'd go and get herself a glass of that watermelon juice kept chilled in the fridge. The dream had left her absolutely parched, and the sweet juice of the summer fruit would be perfect to cool the dry fire in her throat.

Resolved, she quietly opened the door of her mother's bedroom and slipped out into the corridor outside. As she turned to shut the door after her, she heard movement up ahead and looked around to see Aunt Maya letting herself out of the guest bedroom where she'd been sleeping since her fight with Uncle Girish.

Her aunt must also be on her way to get something to drink. Sathi hurried after her, and had opened her mouth to alert her aunt to her presence when suddenly Aunt Maya stepped into a shaft of moonlight that was spilling over from one of the high windows lining the corridor, illuminating her face.

Sathi's words froze in her throat and her mouth went dry. Her aunt's eyes were wide open, but as unfocused as those of a marionette's. Her gait was unnatural as she walked mechanically forwards, and while Sathi watched, helpless with shock, she stopped in front of her father-in-law's bedroom. As her hand lifted to push down the door handle, a slim gold bangle slid down the length of her dark forearm.

Sathi couldn't breathe. She clamped her lips together tightly to hold in the bile that had risen in her mouth.

She could feel her individual body parts and their reactions. Her heart was racing, and her mouth was set in disgusted lines. Her hands were clenched into fists at her side. Her whole body was poised and ready for action, whether to break down the door, or to run screaming out of the house, she didn't know.

Yet she couldn't make her mind work. Her mind refused to think about what she had just seen, and she still stood in exactly the same position as she had when her aunt had slipped inside her great-uncle's room. In the small amount of time that the door had been left open, Sathi had seen the tips of hairy toes disappear off the edge of the bed as Great-uncle stood up to welcome his daughter-in-law into his bedroom...

It was the thought of the owner of those disgusting, hairy toes touching her aunt that finally jolted Sathi out of her shock. Desperately, her eyes roamed all over the corridor as she tried to think what to do. Should she pound on the door and demand that the bastard be castrated? Should she wake up Uncle Girish and tell him to rescue his wife from his father's bed? Should she try and find Great-aunt? Where was she, anyway? Horrified, her breath huffed out of her. Was she in there with them, too? Sathi's eyes closed in revulsion.

Devi, help me!

The unexpected prayer burst forth from her mind, and much as a mute person finds herself able to cry out in a moment of intense emotion, Sathi realised that her mother's goddess had always been there at the root of her every thought and action, waiting for her to pierce the wall her conscious mind had thrown up.

When she opened her eyes again they focused on an aerosol can of insect repellent sitting on the window ledge.

Just like that, she got an idea.

Trying to stay calm, she took a couple of steps away from Great-uncle's bedroom door and turned so that she was no longer facing it head on. Then, taking a deep breath and thinking of all the disgust and repulsion and fear she was feeling, she opened her mouth and let loose the most piercing, ear-splitting scream she could muster. She kept it going until her throat felt as if it had been rubbed raw, and all the lights in the bedrooms switched on.

Doors began to open, but the one that was opened the fastest was that of the sickening monster that masqueraded as her great-uncle. Out of the corner of her eye, Sathi watched as he hurriedly shoved a dishevelled-looking Aunt Maya out into corridor, and slammed the door again.

Sathi examined her aunt closely; her hair was messed up, and her expression was of one waking up from a long, confusing sleep, but otherwise she looked fine. Her clothes were all in place, and she had been in there for too little time for anything to have happened.

Thank you, she breathed to her goddess before all hell broke loose.

'What is it? What's happened?' Uncle Girish and Great-aunt appeared in next to them, asking the same questions worriedly.

Sathi told her face to look scared, which wasn't too hard to do, and pointed a trembling finger at the doorway to the kitchen. 'I... I saw a cockroach.'

While Uncle chuckled weakly in response and Great-aunt glared balefully, a deep voice rang out. 'What's going on here?'

Sathi forced herself not to shiver as she slowly swivelled to face him, but she couldn't make herself meet his eyes.

'Nothing,' Great-aunt replied, her tone caustic. 'Sathi just saw a cockroach.'

Meanwhile, Uncle Girish was peering at Aunt Maya. 'Maya? What's wrong with you? Why are you so pale?'

'I...'

'Aunt Maya was feeling thirsty and so was I, so we were going to the kitchen to get something to drink,' Sathi interrupted, and then wanted to kick herself as Great-uncle's sharp gaze shot to scrutinise her face. Quadruple crap! He knew she was lying now. She tried to keep a neutral expression. 'I'm really sorry for waking everyone up. I just really hate cockroaches and seeing one scuttling around in there freaked me out. I think it's gone now anyway, so goodnight!' she blabbered, just wanting to get out of there. She turned, but Great-uncle's voice stopped her.

'Wait. Didn't you say you were thirsty?'

She looked back, and read in his cold, reptilian eyes a challenge. He opened the fridge door and reached for the jug of watermelon juice, which was a clear, light-wine colour...

'No!' The word burst out through her lips as she stared at the jug in horror. Then, realising that everyone was staring at her, she drew in a deep breath. 'No,' she repeated in a more normal tone. She attempted a smile as she strode over to the kitchen sink and quickly filled two glasses with water. 'I think water will be more refreshing.'

Holding the glasses in her hands, she scurried away from him and put one glass in Aunt Maya's unresisting hand. Then she pushed her towards Uncle Girish, saying, 'You should stay with him tonight, Aunty, in case you feel ill again in the night.'

Addressing everyone, she repeated, 'Sorry again for waking you all up. Goodnight.'

Then she turned and tried not to sprint to her room. She felt a pair of eyes following her every move until she reached the sanctuary of her mother's bedroom and for the first time, she locked the door behind her.

Chapter Thirty-One

Wolves Within

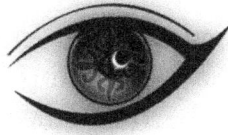

Sitting in the middle of her mother's old bed, Sathi allowed the full repercussions of the night's events to sink into her.

Her mother's adoptive parents were not the loving, philanthropic couple she'd believed them to be. Instead, they were a pair of cunning, manipulative old people who played with the emotions of those who put their trust in them. Her great-uncle was a repulsive monster whose lust was slaked by putting his son's bride in some sort of hypnotic trance that made her willingly come to his room so he could rape her.

Sathi shuddered. How sick would you have to be to in order to trick your daughter-in-law into bed with you?

Repulsed by the thought, Sathi thought back over all those other incidents she had seen but pretended not to. Alienation of a child from its mother. Manipulation using pretence of illness. Causing strife in a marriage. Mistreatment of a daughter-in-law because of jealousy and hatred. The list could go on. And every step of the way, Sathi had made excuses for her grandparents.

She mentally reviewed her life with her great-aunt and great-uncle through new - or rather old - eyes and became truly disgusted with herself. How could she have closed her eyes to the injustices they had committed from day one? Always quick to judge before, how had she so easily lost her sense of judgement when it came to her grandparents?

She felt so utterly alone, and felt she deserved it for the way she had behaved for the last few months. But what if this happened again? Aunt Maya had escaped from her father-in-law's clutches for this one night, but what was to say that he wouldn't try again tomorrow?

She shuddered again as she remembered the jug of watermelon juice, the exact shade of the liquid that the woman in the dream had offered to Aunt Maya. What if, in addition to emotional power, these people also had supernatural power that they could call on to bend the will of others in order to satisfy their own needs and desires?

Close to drowning in despair at the thought of that awful possibility, Sathi abruptly remembered her one ally, the one being who had never, ever, left her. Possessed with sudden violent energy, she lunged out of bed and grabbed her backpack, which had been growing dust in a corner of the room.

She turned it upside down, and the photo of her goddess, her Devi, fluttered down to the floor. Sathi bent and gently gathered it in her hands, her eyes hungrily seeking the unlimited kindness in Devi's face, the face that had gifted her with courage and comfort when her world had turned a hundred and eighty degrees on its already unsteady axis. Holding the picture to her chest, she collapsed back onto the bed, exhausted.

Her dream began in a lovely meadow. A meadow that was so different to the dark, cramped room that had set the stage for her most recent nightmares that her dream consciousness skittered delicately away from the memory of the darkness associated with that room.

Looking around, she decided that the best thing about the place was the light infused into it. Sunlight filtered through the amazing circle of teak trees surrounding her, and even the ground below her seemed to glow softly. Awed, she leaned down to gently brush her hands over the damp earth, and when she took her hands away, her eyes widened. Her palms had begun to glow subtly as well. Experimentally, she rubbed the back of her hand across the dirt and then turned it over and examined it. Sure enough, the skin there began to shine as well.

What a cool dream!

Enjoying herself, she straightened up so that she could gawk around more at the meadow, and staggered back a step in surprise.

A mirror had materialised in front of her. At least, she was pretty sure it had only just appeared. Somehow she thought she would have noticed if there had been a huge, gilt-framed mirror right in front of her face.

Speaking of her face... she moved closer to the mirror so that she could see her reflection. There was nothing extraordinary about it – there were ginormous circles under her eyes from lack of sleep, but other than that -

She gasped. Her reflection was changing. Right before her eyes, her body had blurred until it was reduced to a simple anatomical outline, almost a line drawing. Then, ugly black liquid began appearing here and there in her body; it encased her heart and her mind, it was there in her every limb and joint, rippling with malevolent energy.

Sathi's horror-struck eyes lifted to where her reflection's eyes ought to be, and a large, single eye suddenly opened in the middle of her forehead; it was brilliant, formed of exquisite gold and electric blue lines and incandescent with righteous fury. Sathi would have cringed at its wrath had she not sensed that it was not directed at herself, but at the pools of viscid liquid that had been allowed to pollute her body, mind and soul.

As Sathi watched, Devi's eye shot out pure golden light inwards and outwards, encasing both her reflection and her physical body. The gold light attacked the black, which, stubborn, had got a good hold.

No amount of evil can withstand such unrefined good, however. Inch by inch, resisted fiercely all the way, the golden light slowly overpowered the black sludge.

As her body was cleansed from the inside out, a thick, well-thumbed book appeared at her feet. She bent to pick it up, and felt a jolt of shock as she recognised it as one of her all-time favourite bedtime storybooks.

Opening it, she realised that it was not just any copy of the book, but her own. She found the pen mark she had accidentally made on Robin Hood as she had waved her arms about a bit too enthusiastically in excitement while reading it.

Smiling softly, she made to turn the page, but a sudden wind rose out of nowhere and flicked back the pages to the title page of a Cherokee story she'd hardly ever read. Frowning, she tried to move past it, but it was as if the pages had suddenly become stuck together. She couldn't go back or move forward.

Giving up, she resigned herself to reading the story. It was entitled "Wolves Within".

An old Cherokee told his grandson, 'My son, there is a fierce battle between two great wolves within us all. One is Evil; he is anger, greed, pride, gluttony, lust, envy and laziness. The other wolf is Good; he is forgiveness, generosity, humility, love, empathy and truth.'

The boy thought about what his grandfather had said for a moment, and then asked innocently, 'Grandfather, which wolf wins?'

The old man smiled and replied quietly, 'The one you nurture.'

Numbly, Sathi looked up from the book and fixed her eyes unseeingly on her reflection. She realised that she had been feeding the Evil wolf for quite some time; hurting her father through anger, losing Zakiy through pride and lies, and then the ultimate evil: lying to herself. She had forgotten Devi and the goodness that was her mother, starving the Good wolf. Now, piteous, it was giving her a second chance.

Sathi woke feeling more like herself than she had felt in months. She got up, showered quickly and changed her clothes. Then she packed her suitcase and backpack, lovingly tucking the picture of Devi in the outermost pocket.

She quietly made her way through the still-sleeping house, and the fact that the moon had not yet yielded its spotlight to its daytime twin meant that Sathi did not have to confront the house's occupants. She felt no self-disgust at leaving in this way; Evil could not be destroyed, only overcome. Overcoming it was a series of long battles – she had won this one, but only barely, and only with the help of her precious goddess.

As she walked past the kitchen, the jug of watermelon juice that had been left outside earlier turned black in the changing colours of the night.

*   *   *

The first thing she did was to return to their clearing. Even though she should have expected it, the absence of Zakiy's familiar tent and hamper was still a sharp blow. Her tent was still standing, though, looking terribly lonely and out-of-place in their paradise.

Bad-temperedly chucking her suitcase and backpack down, Sathi stalked over to disassemble the tent, and that's when she saw it.

In the middle of her tent, neatly folded, sat Zakiy's green sweater, the one she had stolen from him and then in her anger, haphazardly flung back inside his tent.

Tears trailing from her eyes, Sathi picked up the sweater and pressed it to her nose, inhaling Zakiy's warm scent. Then, wiping her eyes impatiently, she pulled the hoodie over her head and, abandoning her tent where it was, she strode purposefully through the forest to the west side of the resort, following a path which she had travelled only once before, accompanied by a mad boy who had wanted to pit his masculinity against a magpie's.

'Madam, I am sorry?'
Turban-guy blinked at her, looking disconcertingly like a little bird.

Sathi sighed. 'Where is Zakiy?' she asked again slowly, enunciating each word clearly in Malayalam. He carried on with his bird impression. Then, struck with inspiration, she said, 'Your little master - Chota maalik. Where is he?' she asked, struggling to get the words right.

Comprehension dawned on his face. 'Chota maalik!' Then he went into a long stream of Hindi that she couldn't make head nor tail of. From his expression, it sounded like a love-fest. Maybe her initial impression had been correct. Maybe Zakiy's servant *was* gay.

'Wait, wait,' she interrupted him, wishing that multilingualism wasn't such a necessity in India. Time to draw on her rudimentary Hindi lessons from Ravi. Frowning in concentration, she said, 'Where... little master...'

Crap. She didn't know how to say 'gone' in Hindi. Instead, she pantomimed packing a bag, pointing to her own suitcase, and then gave a rather elaborate impression of getting into a car, closing the door, fastening the seat-belt and turning a key in the ignition. She was just putting it in gear when a politely curious voice behind her asked, 'Is there a problem, madam? I am the gatekeeper here.'

'Oh, for God's sake!' she growled as she made scrap metal of her imaginary car and turned around to face this fluent Malayalam speaker.

'Madam?'

'If you call me madam one more time, I will happily chew both your ears off,' she threatened in English while smiling widely at the gatekeeper.

He smiled back uncertainly. Ha! For once the language barrier was on her side.

Sathi shook her head and came to the point. 'Can you tell me where Zakiy is?'

'Ah, madam, Mr Zakiy has returned to Mysore. He has finished his Engineering course, so he has gone back to his family there.'

She sat, dejected, on one of the hard wooden benches on the platform. She wasn't sure why she was even here. It wasn't as if she could randomly get a train to Mysore and wander around blindly until she found him. Hell, she didn't even have his address. He wasn't answering his phone, either, so she might as well give up on finding him.

She glanced around until she found a clock. 11:40. She leaned back against the seat and daydreamed for a while. Then she leaned forward to look at the clock again. 11:40.

Unbelievable.

Muttering unintelligibly to herself, Sathi got up and walked to the little shop and bought a bottle of water. She stood at the counter chatting to the person there for a while. Then she meticulously counted out the right amount of change and gave it to him, and made him count it again as well.

She returned to her bench and screwed off the top of the bottle carefully, took a few measured sips, put the lid back on, sat down, set the bottle on the floor beside her and then squinted at the clock. 11:42.

'You've got to be kidding me!' she exclaimed to no one in particular.

She started counting seconds, and this made sure that she only looked at the clock every fifteen minutes. She made a game of getting her counting exactly synchronised with the clock's, down to the last second. This got her up to 2 pm, at which point she decided to get some lunch. She spent exactly an hour eating it. After that she had to go back to counting seconds.

The monotony of the same sixty numbers over and over again meant that at first she didn't recognise the significance of the shadow that was falling over her. Then something clicked in her drowsy mind, and she looked up.

And there he was, the idiot.

'I thought you might be here.' He smiled his crinkly-eyed smile, his eyes shifting to the sweater she was wearing. 'I see you got my present.'

In the split second between sitting and standing she deliberated whether a hug or a punch would be more satisfying. She decided on the former and launched herself at him, throwing both arms around the nitwit, letting relief and happiness wash through her. After all, there would be lots of time for punching later.

Pulling back, she didn't let go of him, scared that he would disappear as soon as she looked away. 'How? You... Mysore...,' she spluttered. 'You're supposed to be on your way to Mysore by now!'

Zakiy looked at her quizzically. 'Who told you that?'

'That Indian butler guy!' she exclaimed. 'Your gatekeeper.'

He snorted. 'Indian butler? Yeah, that describes Abdullah's personality perfectly. I just told him that to get him off my case. He was nagging me to go back every day. You should've asked Dattu, my little Andhra buddy with the turban. He was in on it.'

'I tried! But he couldn't understand a word I was saying, and I couldn't understand a word he was saying. By the way, I think he has a crush on you,' she added. Then she shook her head, amazed by how easily they had fallen back into their comfortable bantering.

She met his eyes. 'Zakiy, I'm so sorry. I was such an idiot, I -'

He clamped his hand over her mouth, making it difficult for her to carry on speaking.

'I'm sorry, too. I didn't mean to cause you pain,' he said, looking uncharacteristically serious and subdued.

She hated being the cause of the change. 'You have nothing to be sorry about,' she said. Trying to lighten his expression, she added, 'I was the one acting like an unmuzzled sheep-biting dewberry.'

He lifted one eyebrow, impressed.

Sathi grinned mischievously at him. 'I've been doing my homework.'

She was delighted to observe her favourite cheek-stretching grin on his face. 'Well, consider yourself valedictorian material, m'lady. I particularly like the way you gave a fruit carnivorous qualities – delightful. Shakespeare would be proud.'

She curtsied, and then straightened up with one hand on her hip. 'So, have you got the tickets?'

Understandably, Zakiy looked baffled. 'Eh?'

'The tickets to Mysore?' Sathi purposefully said the words as though he was being dim, hiding her smile.

'We're going to Mysore?' Then his expression became ecstatic. 'You're coming with me?'

'Well, duh!' she replied.

They looked at each other, both beaming, and burst into laughter.

Within the murky mask of fire, the reptilian creature stretched impatiently, its distorted scales gleaming and feeding the flames as it watched the doves hungrily. It waited, those seven pairs of rusted eyes flickering restlessly, raring for its next opportunity.

To be continued in the next book in the Prism of Truth trilogy,
Doves in Flight.

306

Glossary

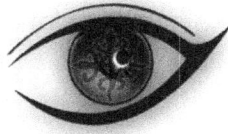

Malayalam terms:
Malayalam is the native language spoken in Kerala, south-west India.

Malayali/Keralite – someone from Kerala/someone who speaks Malayalam.

Amma – mother
Ammumma – grandmother (also used to address those in your grandmother's generation)
Appuppa/n – grandfather (also used to address those in your grandfather's generation)
Asura – mythological demons that inhabit the Underworld, usually depicted as being evil
Bhasma – sacred ashes believed to be blessed by Hindu gods
Chakra – literal meaning: circle, but in Hindu mythology a weapon of goodness – rotating discus with serrated edges, used to decapitate demons/enemies of the gods
Chaya – tea
Chechi – elder sister
Chetan – elder brother
Churidar – Indian clothing consisting of long flowing top, with matching leggings and shawl
Dharma – "essential function of a living thing". The duty that a living thing has to fulfil in the birth it has taken on Earth
Dhaya – mercy

Diwan – Persian word adopted by the Malayalam language to denote rank of high nobility in South Asia

Dosa – Indian pancake

Jeera – cumin

Kaivisham – literally hand-poison, a form of black magic

Karimeen pollichathu – a Kerala dish in which fish is fried and served inside a plantain leaf

Kishney – an uneducated man's version of "kidney", used instead of "brain" in a standing joke nowadays to tease the old belief that intelligence originated from the kidneys

Mandapam – altar/shrine

Masala – mixture of chilli powder, curry powder, turmeric powder, garam masala and other Indian spices

Molé – term of endearment, like "dear" (female)

Moné – term of endearment (male)

Mundu – cotton wraparound garment worn tied around the waist

Mutton varval – Indian dish consisting of fried lamb pieces with onion and black pepper

Nataka shala – dancing room/area

Navagrahas – the nine planets in our solar system (these have religious significance in mythology)

Njan oru patti aanu – I am a dog

Pottu – small sticker placed on forehead as decoration

Purdah – religious clothing for Muslim women

Roti – Indian bread

Sadhya – Indian banquet

Samosa – Indian snack

Sari – traditional Indian attire for women, composed of six metres of cloth wrapped artistically around the body

Thali – the ceremonial necklace placed around the bride's neck by the groom during a Hindu wedding

Vazha – banana tree

Veena – a traditional musical instrument played in accompaniment to Karnatic music

Veno – do you want? In context, 'frying pan veno?' means 'do you want a frying pan?'

Yaar – a (Hindi) slang for friend, widely used by Malayalis, especially by teenagers

Hindi terms:
Hindi is the official language of India.

Aman – literally peace, also understood as world peace
Bhabhi – sister-in-law
Chota maalik – little master
Chota maalik, aap kal raath kidhar gaye the? – Little master, where did you go last night?
Dhoti – cotton wraparound garment worn tied around the waist
Gora – white. It is used as slang for white people
Ulukka patta – slang for idiot

Indian National Anthem:

Jana-gana-mana adhināyaka jaya hé
Bhārata bhāgya vidhātā
Pañjāba Sindh Gujarāṭa Marāṭhā
Drāviḍa Utkala Baṅga
Vindhya Himācala Yamunā Gaṅgā
Ucchala jaladhi taraṅga
Tava śubha nāme jāge
Tava śubha āśiṣa māge
Gāhe tava jaya gāthā
Jana gaṇa maṅgala dāyaka jaya hé
Bhārata bhāgya vidhāta
Jaya he, jaya he, jaya hé
Jaya jaya jaya, jaya hé

- Rabindranath Tagore

Acknowledgements

My loving thanks to everyone who supported me through this journey.

Thank you to my parents, who constantly believed in me through all the hurdles we've faced together.

Iqbal Uncle – thank you for your undying support.

Unnikrishnan Uncle – your words were often our lifeline.

Mummy's Daddy, Mummy's Mummy, Suresh Uncle and Salim Uncle – thank you for looking out for us.

More by Shivon Mirza Sudesh

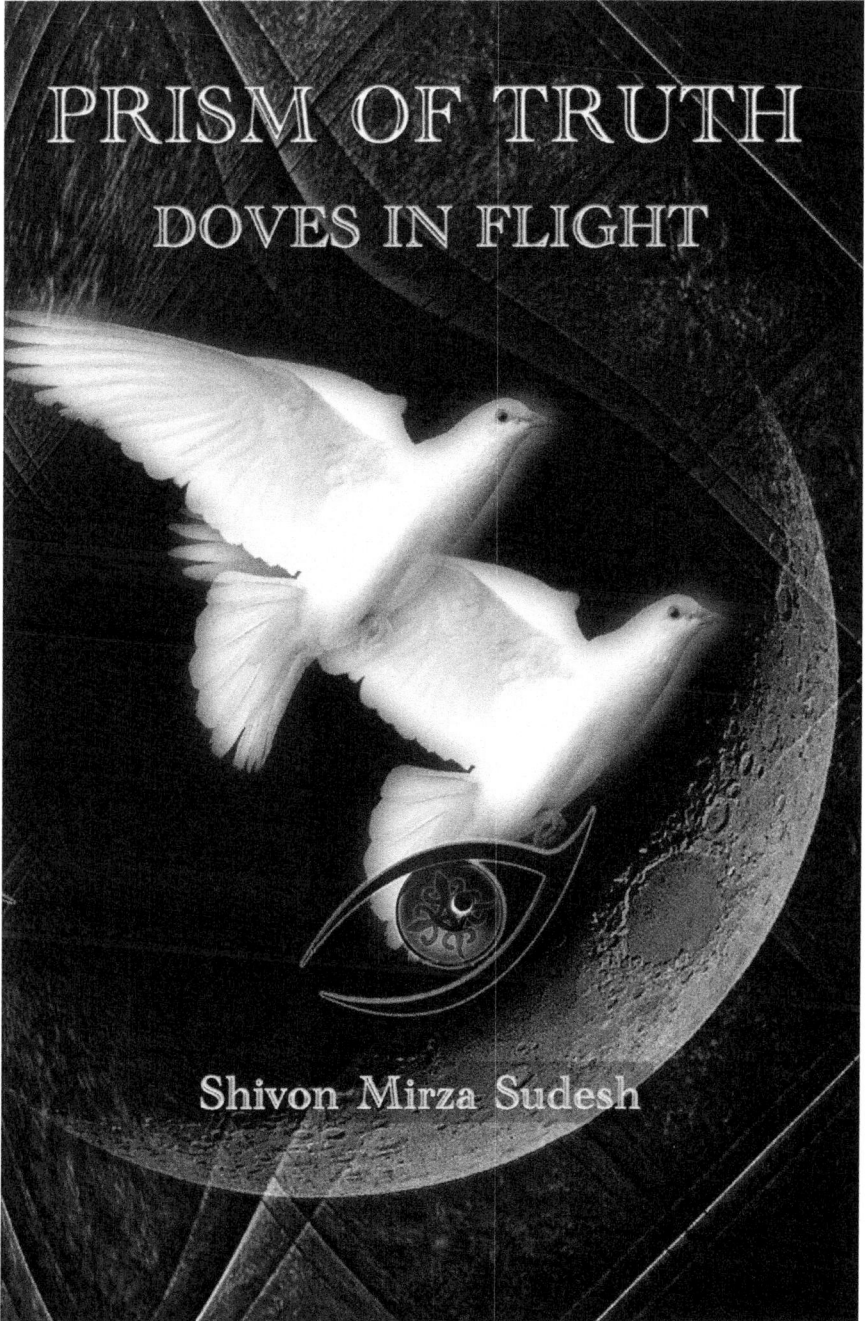

More by Shivon Mirza Sudesh

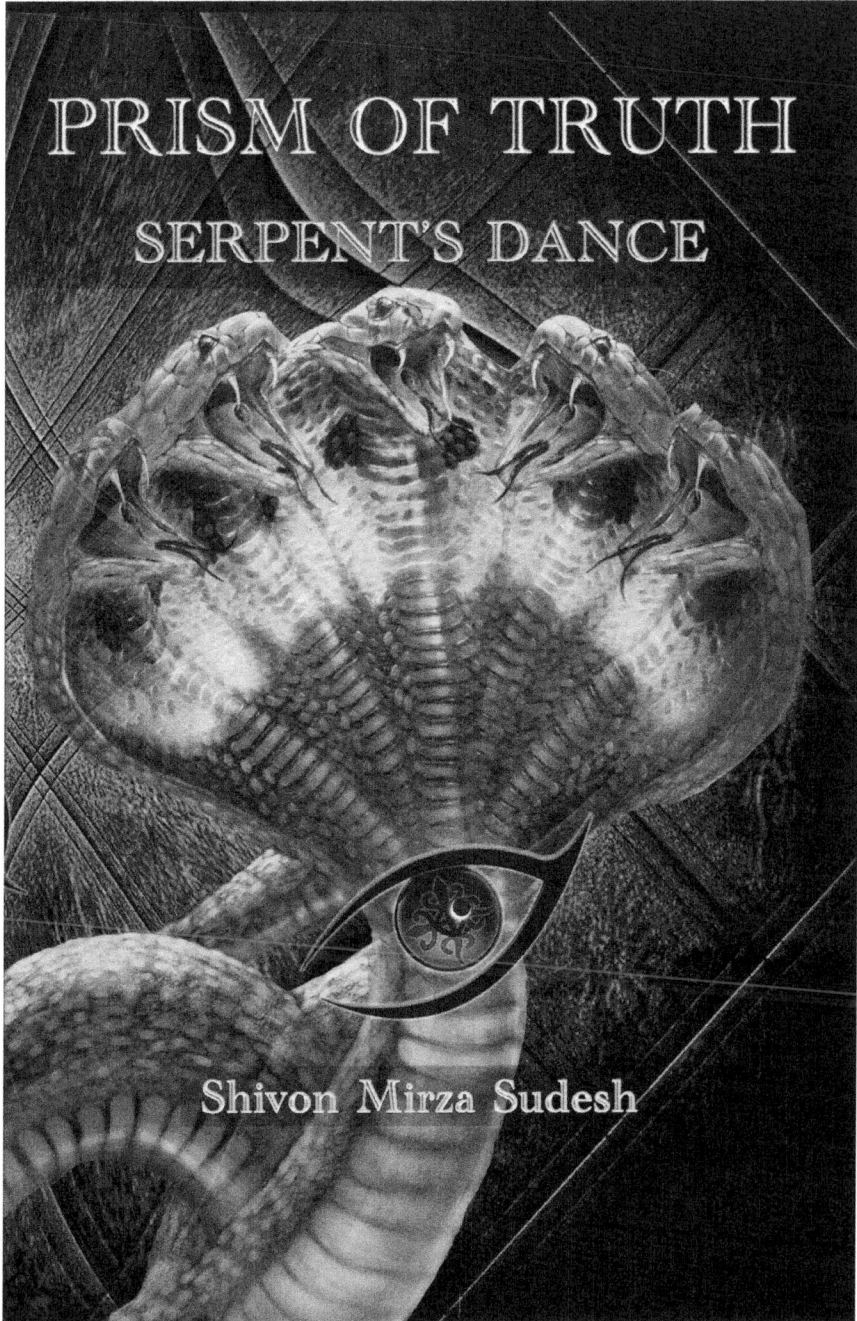

Printed in Dunstable, United Kingdom